Book 1

John Meagher

Tales of the Left Hand: Book One

ISBN-10: 1517643058
ISBN-13: 978-1517643058
Library of Congress Control Number: 2015917490

CreateSpace Independent Publishing Platform, Charleston, SC

For Sarah.

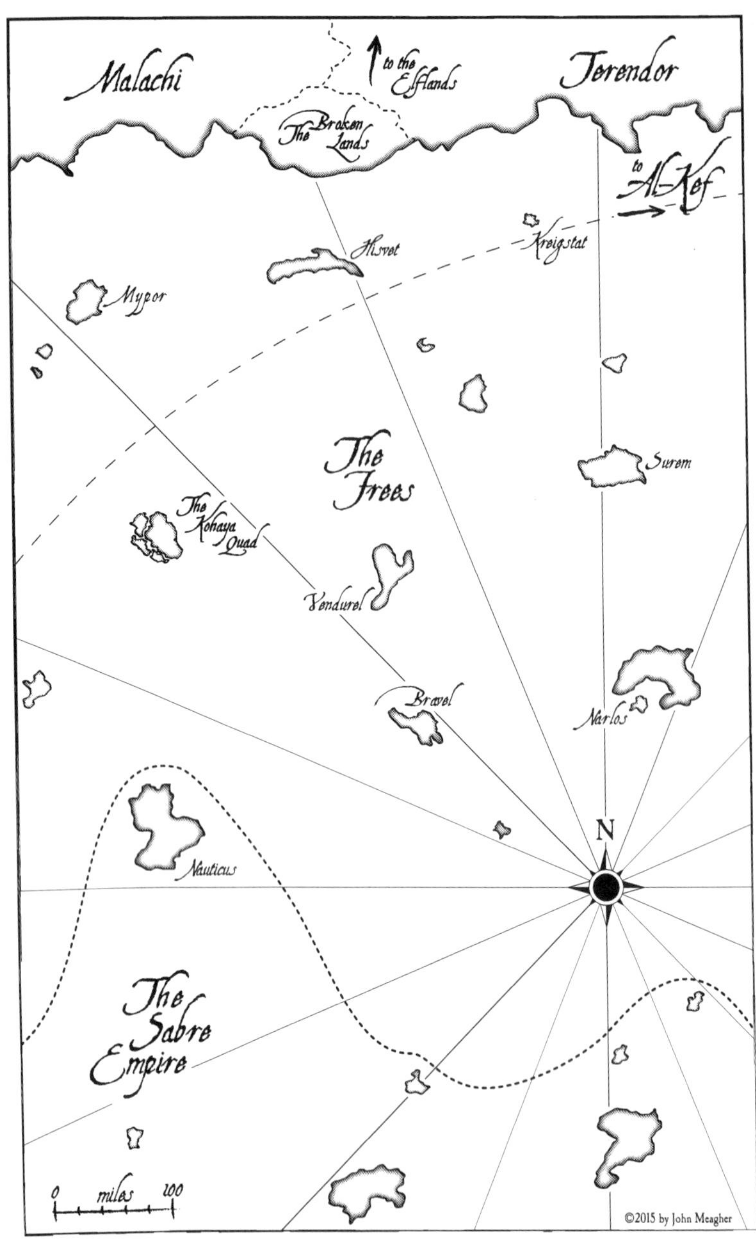
Malachi
to the Elflands
Terendor
The Broken Lands
to Al-Kef
Hisvet
Kreigstat
Mypor
The Frees
Surem
The Kohaya Quad
Vendurel
Bravel
Narlos
N
Nauticus
The Sabre Empire
0 miles 100
©2015 by John Meagher

Chapter One

Across the black waves, the lights of Kohayne twinkled a welcome golden glow to the approaching merchant ship. Faint strains of music and revelry rolled over the surface of the water, telling everyone on the ship that the city was done with honest business for the day, and that the night's business had begun.

The captain hummed along to the music as he sighted the harbor beacons through his spyglass. Then he snapped it shut and tucked it back into the leather sheath at his belt. His first mate stood at his side waiting for orders. "Bring us in, Shaddeck. Drop the sails to half and prepare to thread the beacons."

"Aye, sir," the mate replied. "Shall I signal the harbor of our approach?"

"Do that, though like as not they're aware of us out here already."

"Aye, sir." The mate turned and began relaying his orders to the crew. The captain turned to the other man standing in the bow with him. He was clad in black and bore the same grim expression as when he'd come aboard the ship at Narlos. In the week's voyage from there, the captain had never seen his expression change.

"We'll get you to dock in a few hours at most, sirrah," the captain said, using a polite honorific that did not indicate any rank or title, for he did not know what to make of his passenger. The man had paid his passage in full and looked to have more gold than that in his purse, but he didn't bear himself as a nobleman. He had no retainers and gave no orders. A large leather travel bag, always slung over his shoulder, appeared to be all the luggage he had. He visited the cook for his meals rather than send a crewman to fetch it for him, but he always took his food back to his small quarters rather than join anyone else.

When asked his name, the man had simply replied, "Tesca." The captain spoke a smattering of Sabrian, enough to recognize the name's origin. Sabrian was becoming a more commonly spoken tongue these days, as traders from the empire sailed north into the Frees bringing and seeking goods. But with those traders had come the warships to protect them, and the borders of the Sabre Empire were now closer than they had ever been before. The southernmost island of the Frees, once called Valmor, was now the Sabrians' newest province. The Sabrians had renamed the isle Nauticus, and quickly filled its city with their folk and its harbor with their fast and deadly frigates. Men of the Frees still traded with the Sabrians, despite the recent conquest, and the profit was good, but all seemed to understand they were swimming with a shark, and it was only a matter of time before that shark got hungry again.

But this stranger, though his given name was Sabrian, was clearly not of that race. The Sabrians were tall men, lean and strong, with ebon skin. Their hair was black and grew in tight, thick curls, though it was the current fashion for most Sabrians to keep their heads shaved. This man was lean, but no taller than the captain. His skin was deeply tanned, but it had been pale once, pale as a northman's. His hair, though black, was straight, pulled into a short tail at the nape of his neck.

However, his two blades, the long and the short, were of Sabrian make and he wore them in the style commonly used by Sabrian officers and nobility, save that they hung on the opposite sides. The captain figured him to be left-handed. The other oddity the captain noted was that a Sabrian noble's weapons were an intrinsic part of his honor, and always bore unique marks and etchings telling the history of the bearer and his lineage. The stranger's blades, while looking well-made and well-maintained, were unadorned, bearing no insignia whatsoever.

The captain's passenger nodded in response. "I thought we would be arriving before dark."

"If we could have managed it, sirrah, we'd have done so," the captain replied. "The wind cheated us of some time today. But we'll thread the beacons well enough and get to the shallows of the harbor soon. In any case, it's not wise to stay idle out here in the deeps. Things'll come up for a look, and maybe a bite."

The man nodded again. He and the captain were using the Freespeak, a trade language based on the northern tongues brought by exiles from Malachi and Terendor, with some phrases and terms thrown in from Al-Kef tradesmen. Each of the Frees had its own dialect of Freespeak, often colored with bits of language from the native peoples who'd lived on the various islands before the exiles had arrived. Though most residents of the Frees could understand each other well enough, a sharp-eared man could determine which of the islands the speaker hailed from. The captain was a sharp-eared man, but a week of short, clipped conversations with his passenger hadn't narrowed down the man's origins. It was only now, at the end of their voyage, that the captain had begun to suspect his passenger was even more well-traveled than he was, and hadn't lingered anywhere long enough to develop a regional accent.

"I doubt we'd have any trouble within sight of Kohayne," the man replied, inclining his head slightly to look down at the dark water. "Your crew is trained to handle any attacks?"

"Aye, sirrah," the captain assured him, "though all men would agree the best way to avoid trouble in the deeps is to keep moving, so my boys are most trained to keep the ship going and steer her out of trouble if it comes. But we've had to deal with some eels before; not the shocking kind, there's a blessing. A school of armorbacks gave us a chase once, but those few that managed to leap up to the deck were dealt with handily, I'll be glad to say."

"I doubt you'll have to worry about armorbacks around here," the man replied. We're too far south and the waters around the Quad are too deep for their nests."

"Mayhap, sirrah," said the captain, "though they've been spotted as far south as Hisvet, and the Quad's not much farther from the mainland as that. I like to be cautious with my ship and her passengers."

The man nodded once more, but gave no further response. The captain had come to recognize this as a silent dismissal, but did not take offense. His passenger had paid in full, and the captain was willing to restrain his pride when paid in advance.

The ship passed out of the deep water with no incident, rapidly approaching the glow of the small city ahead of them. Kohayne was the capital of the four close-set islands that were referred to as the Kohaya Quad. The channels between the islands were narrow, twisting and brackish, a mixture of ocean water and the fresh spring waters that flowed down from the heights. Only one channel was deep enough for ocean-going vessels to enter it, and beyond the slender entrance to that channel, the water widened into a bowl before pinching tight again at the other end and quickly growing shallow. Kohayne was built around that natural harbor, straddling both sides of the bowl and rising up the ever-steeper slopes towards the peaks.

Aside from the channels between them, the islands of the Quad were steep and rocky, thrusting out of the sea like the tips of four stone fingers. The cliff faces were sheer, ascending into jungled mist above the waterline and descending into the dark abyss below. But the waters were warm, especially on the western side of the Quad. The skies were filled with seabirds that nested on the high peaks and the seas around the underwater cliffs teemed with life.

A single light, blinking in a quick sequence, appeared from the starboard tower. "He's hailing us, sir," the first mate called out. The captain nodded, though he could read the code as well as anyone.

"Give him our name and the height of the mast, Shaddeck," he replied. As the first mate instructed a crewman to send the message using their own signal light, he turned to his passenger again. "It's good we're not such a tall ship and the tide is ebbing. I do not think the harbormaster would want to raise the Eisenteeth this late."

The man nodded, looking up at the ship's mast. "I think you're correct, captain; your mast is short enough to pass under the bridge."

"And it's well enough that we're coming in late," the captain continued, "else we might have to wait for other ships to enter the harbor. We'll be berthed soon, I warrant."

A brief smile crossed the man's face. "Thank you, captain," he said, with a gleam in his eyes the captain had not seen before.

"This is your home, I make my guess," the captain ventured. "You're of the Quad."

"Of the Quad, no," the man replied. "But I am FOR the Quad, if you take my meaning."

The captain wasn't sure he did, but he puzzled over it as the ship sailed under the Eisenteeth Bridge and entered the harbor. Aside from numerous ferries and rowboats darting back and forth from one side to the other, the two halves of Kohayne were linked by three bridges. The first bridge arced over the entrance to the harbor, a wide wooden span set between two tall stone towers. From the tops of the towers, Kohayne's harbor beacons shone out over the water, and from ports below, the muzzles of large cannon bristled. A great chain linked both towers, resting upon the bottom of the channel. In times of emergency, this chain was hauled taught at the waterline, physically sealing off the harbor. This structure of towers and bridge had once been called "the eyes and teeth of Kohayne," and now was known simply as the Eisenteeth. Its wooden span was high enough for most ships to pass under with ease, but it was also split in the middle and could be raised to make room for taller-masted ships.

Though the Eisenteeth was open to pedestrian traffic; it was rarely used by anyone but the soldiers stationed there. Further west, the Channel Bridge, known more commonly as the Duke's Bridge, was the primary conduit between the city's two halves. It marked the end of the deeper portion of the channel and the region of the city known as Harborside. At almost any time of day or night, it was bustling with traffic, both horse-drawn carts and pedestrians.

Beyond the Duke's Bridge, smaller boats could travel further up the channel for close to a mile before the channel narrowed to a broad, shallow stream. Once, the bridge had been the western boundary of the city, but as more people arrived, they continued to settle further and further west along the channel until the Duke's Bridge was more or less in the very center of the city. Traffic and crowding around the bridge had become so great that five years ago the Duke permitted construction of a third bridge over the channel, several hundred yards further west. Once the New Bridge, as it became known, was completed, the newer-settled portions of Kohayne flourished. This new area was referred to as Channelside, little sister to the rough-and-tumble world of Harborside, and was generally devoted to business and trade that didn't leave the Quad itself. Local tradesmen and craftsmen plied their wares and lived their lives away from the harbor and the ocean-going businesses.

The captain's passenger stood patiently by as the ship was brought in to one of the southern docks. As the ship was being tied off, he stepped to the rail and looked back at the captain.

"Sir, I take my leave of you," he said. "My compliments to you and your crew; it was a smooth voyage." And with that, before the captain could reply, he leapt from the rail, landing nimbly on the dock and striding away. A deputy harbormaster, flanked by two guards, looked dubiously at him until he drew close to them. After a few short words of discussion between them, the harbormaster gave him a brisk nod and the man moved on in the direction of the Duke's Bridge, slipping into the crowd and vanishing from sight.

Some time later, after the deputy harbormaster had concluded his inspection of the ship and collected the harbor fees, the captain asked him about that man he'd brought to Kohayne.

"Ah, him," the official commented with a shake of his head. "I'd suggest you forget about him."

"Indeed?" the captain asked, now more curious than ever.

The harbormaster looked at him. "I'm sure you know that there are many different avenues within the realm of diplomacy?"

"Aye," the captain replied.

"Well, that man tends to travel the back alleys, if you take my meaning," the harbormaster said with a nervous smile. "If all you got for your time with him was some coin and a peaceful voyage, I'd count yourself lucky and leave it at that."

Chapter Two

"Harborside's the best port in th' Frees, lass," Clegg shouted over the clamor as he and Kayrla carefully made their way along the street. "Best in th' Frees."

"Certainly is the loudest!" Kayrla called back to him.

"Wha's that?"

"THE LOUDEST!" she shouted.

"Aye, aye! Tis that! When the revels start, some nights I think they'll crack th' heavens."

"At least we're on the posh side," Kayrla muttered, wincing at the dull roar swirling around her. Although revels and merrymaking were commonplace on both sides of the harbor, the northern side of the city held the ducal estate and the port's administrative offices. It was generally considered the more distinguished and safer side of the city. Even so, when revels were at their height, celebrants surged to and fro over the Duke's Bridge and the north side could get as rowdy as the south.

"It's the damn mountains around us," she said, trying to get Clegg's attention. "It's like we're stuck in a box...the sound just keeps bouncing back and forth in here."

"Aye!" Clegg yelled back eagerly, but she wasn't sure her drunken companion had heard a word she'd said. She sighed and gave up. They made an odd pair; the older man with a stained blue overcoat stretching over his wide belly, rolling along with a seaman's gait next to a short, stick-thin girl in man's clothes, a rapier at her bony hip.

She wore a bright green kerchief about her brow. Straight brown hair spilled out from under it and fell like long meadow grass down around her face and shoulders.

"So, lass... why'd ye drag us over t'the posh side anyway?" Clegg asked. "Best parties are all on the south side, and the captain's standin' all th' crew a round at The Bloated Eel."

Kayrla shook her head. "I'm not getting within arm's reach of the captain once his belly's full of rum."

Clegg looked surprised. "I'm not followin' yer course, lass."

"Jolly's a good captain," Kayrla said with regret, "but I've seen how his eyes follow me when I'm in the rigging." She shivered. "I've seen that look before. I know what it means." She sighed. "Why does this always happen?"

"What d'ye mean?"

She stopped, fuming. "This always happens, Clegg. I join a crew, posing as a boy. Then eventually someone either finds out I'm not a boy, or they find out...the other thing. But I don't bolt and run, I stay on the ship; I earn the crew's trust. Eventually it gets to the point I can stand out on the deck without even this," she gestured towards her hair, "and no one on the crew cares anymore. I'm one of them."

Clegg nodded fiercely. "That ye are, lass. Ye're the best spotter we've had in th' *Cutlass's* crow's nest since I've been cookin' the meals, and that's some 10 years now. Ye're not a bad hand with a blade and ye can..." he made a slight wiggling motion with his fingers, "...help out a bit here and there."

"I'd be able to do more of...that," she said with a shrug, mimicking his gesture, "if we were further north. But I hear Jolly's of a mind to take the *Cutlass* further south towards the Sabrian trade routes."

"Better plunder," Clegg offered, but his expression was somber. "The cannon'll be more reliable as well, which is near as good a reason as the chance for better plunder. I'll say though, there's some in the crew who wonder if it's worth the risk. I've seen what those black-skinned bastards do to pirates." He shivered in the warm air. "Dreadful, lass."

"The Empire doesn't worry me so much as Jolly," Kayrla admitted. She stamped her foot in frustration. "I just wanted to be one of the crew!"

"And ye are that, Kayrla," Clegg agreed. "I must confess I don't see the problem, but I'm near pickled as a pig's foot about now. Ye get a full share of the swag, there's not a man on the crew who'd object to standin' next to ye in a scrap, so what's wrong?"

Kayrla sighed. "Jolly's the problem. He doesn't see me as a member of the crew anymore; he sees me as a woman; someone to take to his bed. That's not what I signed on for. And there's no talking him out of it either, you know how he gets."

Clegg nodded in glum agreement. "No, I see yer point, lass. Sad as it makes me, ye're probably right. When are ye leavin'?"

Kayrla smiled sadly at her friend. "Oh, Clegg…I already have." She patted the two large leather pouches hanging from her belt, both bulging with hidden contents. "Everything I need, I'm already carrying. I've even taken my fair share of the swag from the hold."

Clegg gave a low whistle, impressed, but he also looked alarmed. "How'd ye manage that?" he asked in a whisper. "Did ye filch Jolly's key to the hold?"

"I didn't need to," she said with a laugh, trying to look innocent as she wiggled her fingers in front of her. The old man and the girl laughed together in the street.

"Oh, you do play it close, girl…" Clegg wheezed, "but when Jolly learns what ye've done, like as not he'll come after ye, and not to put kisses on yer cheeks."

"He brought it on himself," Kayrla said stubbornly. "According to the contract, it's another three months before the swag's divided and we go our separate ways. Jolly won't wait that long before he tries something. And there's nowhere to go on a ship at sea if the captain's after you. I either leave now or someone's blood is getting spilled." She looked angry. "But I've earned my share and I'm not leaving without it. You'll explain it to him, won't you, Clegg? That I only took what was mine, and not a silver more?"

Clegg sighed. "I'll try, lass. Maybe after we're a week at sea and his temper's settled some." He chuckled, smiling fondly at her. "So, that's why ye brought ol' Clegg out here, wasn't it? It wasn't so much to stay clear of Jolly, it was t'say goodbye."

"Yes," she said, throwing her slender arms around his neck and planting a kiss on his weathered cheek. "Take care of yourself, Clegg."

"What's this?!?!" came a booming voice, slurred with drink. The two jumped in surprise and turned to see Jolly Red himself with several of his crew in tow. All had full tankards in one hand and not a few of them had one of Harborside's lady companions in the other. "The Bloated Eel's kegs run dry, so off we go in search of somewhere else, and what do we find here on the north side? Fair Kayrla, giving out kisses?" He roared with laughter and the crew joined him. "That suits me fine! The line starts behind me, lads…"

Clegg joined in the laughter, but Kayrla knew he was trying to defuse the situation. "Ah, Jolly," Clegg began, "It's not like that at all–"

"Step aside, Clegg," said Jolly, a glint in his eyes that Kayrla had seen before. That glint had told her it was time to leave the *Cutlass*. But that glint had never been so bright as it was now. "What's good enough for the cook should be good enough for the captain," Jolly added with a drunken leer.

Clegg held up his hands in a placating gesture. "Now Cap'n…she's a member of the crew and entitled t'fair–"

Still laughing, Jolly ambled up and shoved Clegg to one side. "Ah, c'mon Clegg. There's naught wrong with a kiss or two, is there?"

Kayrla realized she should have jumped ship at the last port, before Jolly could have worked himself up to this point. She laughed, a light and merry sound, to keep him off his guard. "A kiss from you, redbeard?" she bantered, "I'd as soon kiss a Sabrian." Jolly smiled and threw his head back to laugh. In that moment, when his eye was off her, she turned on her heel and dashed into the crowd. Before she'd taken two steps, she crashed into someone who was also trying to weave his way through the crowd in some haste. She saw only a mass of black clothes and two blades hanging from his belt before she collided with him. Then both of them went down.

She heard several things at once: a grunt of surprise from the man she'd run into and the muffled thud as they both fell to the street. She heard Jolly's yell and knew he was stumbling towards her, still laughing. And then she heard a sound that made everyone on the street go silent: the musical jingle of coins tumbling over the paving stones as one of her belt pouches burst open.

Things seemed to slow down as she and the stranger struggled to get free of each other. She saw faces, frozen in surprise, stare at the money spilling from her waist. She saw Jolly's face, the laugh on his lips twisting into shock. He was fuzzy with drink, but he was no fool, and Kayrla knew he had guessed where the money had come from. "Thieving minx!" he bellowed. "I'll have your hide for this!"

But the crowd surged forward first, hands diving and grasping for the coins as they bounced along the street. Kayrla felt hands upon her, tugging and grasping, plucking at her clothes in hopes of dislodging more money. The hands also grappled with the man she was still entangled with, tugging at his clothes and the bag he'd inadvertently dropped in the collision.

The flash of naked steel in the lamplight made the crowd leap back as the man stormed to his feet, rapier and dagger in his hands. Taking one step, he stood over his bag and eyed the crowd with a cold gaze. "The first man to touch this bag dies," he said in a clear voice. There was no bravado in his tone, no boasting. He spoke as matter-of-factly as if he was commenting on the weather.

Jolly Red was too angry to hear him. With a roar, he rushed forward to seize Kayrla, but she rolled along the ground to put the man in black between her and her former captain. He swung his tankard to smash the smaller man out of the way.

With a single smooth motion, the man ducked under Jolly's thick arm and flicked the point of his rapier out, drawing a line of red across Jolly's leg. The captain howled and stumbled on past, falling to the street after a few paces. Clamping his hands over his bleeding leg, Jolly's eyes flashed with rage as he glared at Kayrla and her unexpected rescuer. He saw the bag the man was guarding and came to a quick conclusion.

"So, got a partner, do ye?" he yelled at Kayrla. "Trying to take more than yer share?"

"What?" the man asked, glancing down at the girl. "I've never seen her, or you, in my life." In an instant, he'd scooped up the bag, tossing it securely over his head and one shoulder. "This isn't my fight," he said to Jolly in that same calm voice. "If you don't want more trouble, redbeard, you'll let me pass."

Jolly sneered at that and the crewmates he'd been carousing with drew their blades. Kayrla got to her feet and drew her own sword.

"Well, girl…you've certainly put me in it," the man snapped. "Watch where you're going next time."

"Sorry," Kayrla said, standing back to back with him as the *Cutlass's* crew began to spread out, encircling the pair. Beyond them, Clegg was trying to calm some of them down, but it was too late. Now that they'd seen both gold and blood spilled, their minds were made up.

The man frowned, glancing behind him to see how Kayrla was holding her blade. "Are you any good with that?"

"I wouldn't carry it if I wasn't," she snapped back at him.

"We'll soon see."

Jolly lurched to his feet. The pain in his leg appeared to have sobered him up in a hurry. "At 'em, lads!" he snarled through clenched teeth. "Show 'em nobody steals from Jolly Red and the *Cutlass*!"

"By the way," Kayrla said over her shoulder as the crewmen charged forward, "I'm Kayrla."

The man nodded, bracing for the attack. "Tesca."

Chapter Three

The circle of pirates closed in with a rush, trying to catch Tesca and Kayrla in their midst. Behind her, Kayrla heard Tesca's feet shift on the stones as he dashed forward to meet them. Using both his blades, he parried two of the pirates' attacks and slipped between them, getting outside the circle. Kayrla thought that was a good idea and tried it in her own fashion, running straight at one of the pirates, then dropping low and tumbling right between his legs, springing up behind him. She jabbed out with her rapier as he turned, skewering his calf, and the man sank down onto one knee, cursing.

As another man bore down on her, the others turned to pursue Tesca. He wasn't going to let them surround him again, and struck quickly, parrying one man's clumsy attack and stabbing up with his dagger. The man gave a gurgling yell as he sagged to the street. The others, glaring at him with hate, came on.

They were more wary now, seeing that they were up against a trained swordsman who didn't hesitate to kill. The crowd, watching the spectacle, spread further back to avoid the flashing blades, all the while yelling encouragement to both sides and quickly making wagers on the outcome. The pirates closed in, again trying to surround him, but he kept slipping free, backing up and circling away, never letting more than two of them within arm's reach of him. As he parried their blows, he looked for an opening, a chance to cut down another man and improve his odds further.

He wasn't finding one. The pirates were sobering up fast now that one of them was dead. Tesca leapt back from a savage blow but couldn't step in for a counterattack without exposing himself to one of the other attackers. He continued to backpedal, flicking his head left and right to avoid tripping over anything.

Kayrla was having her own troubles. She was dueling one-on-one with the first mate, a hairy cur named Parkin. As she'd told Tesca, she wasn't a bad hand with a blade, but Parkin was at least a foot taller than her and twice her weight. Even parrying one of his heavy swings rattled her teeth and sent a jangle of pain up her arm. She dodged and darted away from his attacks, then spotted a glint of light on the spreading pool of blood from the man Tesca had just killed. She started to fall back, slowly circling around towards the body. Parkin stepped in close, reaching for her hair. She stabbed up at him but missed, and he struck her in the face with the handguard of his cutlass. Stars bursting behind her eyes, she sailed through the air and landed in a sprawl some feet away.

Parkin darted forward to finish her off, but he ran through the puddle of blood and his boot skidded on the slick paving stones. He wavered, precariously balanced on one leg for a frozen moment. It was enough for Kayrla. Blood streaming from a split lip, she sprang up, hurling all her weight behind the point of her sword. It drove into Parkin's chest and he fell back to the street with Kayrla on top of him.

Kayrla stared blearily around her, her vision still swimming. Tesca was getting forced back towards a wall by his assailants. Three of them were pressing him close; soon he'd have nowhere to run. Clegg was tying off the wound of the man she'd stabbed at the start of the fight, and Red Jolly, still down on one knee, was yelling for his men to finish Tesca off.

Her first instinct was to run, now, before anyone noticed she was gone, and she was already getting to her feet before she stopped. *No,* she thought. *I can't just leave him to die.* She didn't know anything about him; if he hadn't gotten in her way, she'd have escaped into the crowd and this fight would never have happened. But he hadn't stepped aside or just handed her over to Jolly; he'd stood back to back with her in a fight. In the Frees, that was a rare thing.

She saw that a few feet away from Tesca there was a wooden wagon parked against the wall. There were several barrels of rum in the wagon and two men guarding them. They were eagerly watching the spectacle unfold a few feet away, and made no move to get involved at all. *That'll have to do,* she thought, concentrating and raising her arms in front of her.

Magic took a good deal more effort than just wiggling one's fingers, no matter what Clegg might have thought. It was hard to gather up enough power to accomplish very much, this far south, and Kayrla didn't know many spells. But those she did know, she'd had a lot of practice with. There were three spells she knew best. One of them was the power to make small repairs to objects. This had made her incredibly valuable on board the *Cutlass* once the crew got over their initial mistrust of magic. She could repair leaky barrels, reattach cut ropes and mend small holes in the sails without a needle and thread. The second spell was the opposite of the first. Nails would rust and break, sails would become threadbare and split in a strong breeze, and wood would turn to dryrot in a heartbeat.

She focused her spell on the rear axle of the wagon, which suddenly groaned, sagged and split in a puff of dust, tipping the wagon over. The barrels and the men sitting on them tumbled off the wagon into the street, rolling straight into the three men pressing Tesca to the wall. The barrels bent, bounced and burst open as they rolled, and an avalanche of men, wood and rum cascaded past Tesca. He stared in disbelief for only a moment before glancing around to see Kayrla sagging back to the ground, panting in exhaustion.

He charged forward into the pirates who hadn't been swept away, killing another man as he cut his way through. As they fell back, he ran to Kayrla. Sheathing his dagger, he threw her over his shoulder and ran for the shadows. All the while Jolly Red's voice called after them: "Stay on 'em, lads! They're thieves! They've robbed us blind!"

The crowd gave way before Tesca's bloody sword and grim face. He pounded up an alley that sloped gently upwards, the start of the long incline that led towards the upper portions of the city. The pirates took off after him. Tesca was sober, and he knew the city well, dodging left and right down narrow alleys with practiced skill. But he was weighed down by the girl over his shoulder, and he couldn't extend his lead.

He knew this couldn't last much longer. Behind him he could hear the pirates yelling to each other to start spreading out, to cut him off. Before long, he knew he'd turn down another alley and find it blocked. Then they would have him.

An idea came to him: *Strike back while they're scattered. Even the odds.*

He came to another T-intersection, and instead of heading up towards the higher parts of the city, he turned back down towards the harbor. "Where…are you going?" he heard Kayrla mutter as she stirred over his shoulder.

"No time to explain," he panted. "Can you run?"

"I was…just winded," she said, the air bouncing out of her lungs with each step he took. "I'm okay, but I left my sword back there."

"Okay," he said, making a quick right turn and skidding to a halt. "I'll get you a sword." He rolled her off his shoulder and turned to face the first pirate approaching them. As he had hoped, they'd spread out themselves over a few blocks and now he was facing only two of them.

As the first pirate stepped in, sabre flashing, the one behind started to circle around behind Tesca, calling out "Here! They're here!"

But Tesca wasn't being attacked by a mob now. Blades flashing, he pressed the attack against the first pirate. In a quick flurry of attacks, he'd disarmed the man and sent his blade clattering along the ground towards Kayrla. The man scrambled back as Tesca turned to the other man, whom he slew in short order.

Kayrla scooped up the sabre. It was a little heavier than she'd have liked, but she was glad to have any means of keeping her enemies a few feet further off. She looked down the alley they were in. They appeared to be behind a large warehouse or other building that opened onto the main street of Harborside, but they were some distance from the light and noise of the revelry. She guessed that they were getting close to Channelside; that portion of the city more or less shut down at night. It was near pitch dark here; there were no torches or lamps lit and she wondered at that. But her night vision was very sharp, and she could see Tesca kicking the remaining pirate in the head. The man fell and did not rise.

"You didn't kill him?" she asked.

"I don't kill unarmed men if I can help it," he said, coming over to her

She could hear footsteps echoing around them, coming closer. "More are coming!" she said in a low voice.

"I know, I know," he replied, squinting into the darkness. "We need to keep moving." He could make out her shadowy form as she leapt onto some crates stacked up against the building. Nimbly, she climbed the stack until she was at a second-story window. "No!" he hissed. "They'll hear the glass break!"

"I know what I'm doing!" she snapped back. Stifling a growl of frustration, he clambered up onto the crates after her. He thought he could hear her mumbling something as he approached, then he blinked in surprise as she pulled the window open and slipped inside.

Tesca was just putting one leg through the open window when he heard the footsteps enter the alley below him. He didn't bother looking, but as he pulled himself through the window he heard "Up there!" and knew his silhouette had been seen against the black form of the warehouse.

He started to close the window, but Kayrla touched his arm. "Lock's broken, don't bother."

"How do you know the lock's broken?"

"Because I had to break it to get us in here," she replied. She glanced at the open window, her face colorless in the starlight. She cocked her head, listening to the sounds of men talking in quick, urgent whispers below. "Well, they're not stupid enough to clamber up here after us; they know we'll kill anyone trying to get through the window."

"You can hear what they're saying?" Tesca asked. He could hear the men speaking, but not clearly enough to understand them.

She nodded. "But they won't let us get out that way either. They're trying to find another way in."

"It's what I'd do," Tesca said grimly. "Let's see if we can find a way out before they get in here."

Chapter Four

"What kind of place is this?" Kayrla asked. The air inside the warehouse was warm and thick, with a dry organic scent.

Tesca took a deep breath, recognizing the smell. "We're in a flour mill. That's why it's so dark outside; no streetlamps are allowed around here."

"Why?"

"That smell in here is flour dust. If there's enough of it in the air, bringing open flame in here would be like tossing a lit fuse into a powder magazine."

"Oh," Kayrla replied, a chill of fear running through her.

Tesca peered around him in the darkness. They appeared to be on a catwalk overlooking a wide deep space. He could make out vague outlines of large gears and an open round space in the center. "There have to be more windows in here," he said in a low voice. "During the day they would want to keep this place aired out so the dust doesn't accumulate." He looked up. "If there's a way onto the roof, we might be able to escape that way. There's at least one building close enough for us to try jumping."

Kayrla nodded and stepped up to the railing. There were large wooden crossbeams extending out from under the catwalk into the darkness. "Well, if there's a way to the roof, it's closed. But if they need to keep this place ventilated, then there's got to be something out there. We just can't see it." She leaned her blade against the banister and stepped over it out onto one of the crossbeams. "I'll take a closer look."

"No, wait–" Tesca began, but she was already moving off along the beam. He lost sight of her quickly. The sounds outside were growing louder; more pirates had arrived. Tesca moved up to the window to listen more closely. Kayrla was right; her former crewmates were not climbing up towards the window, at least not yet. But they were splitting up; some of them were circling around. Tesca looked down towards the front of the building. He thought he'd walked by it once or twice in the past; he was sure there was a large set of double doors in the front. *Like as not they'll try to force them open and pin us in here. The roof's our only chance.*

"Found it!" Kayrla's voice came out of the darkness, quiet and tense. She didn't sound very far away. "I think it's a small door, with a rope attached to the latch." He heard some scuffling noises from her direction, or was that from the front door? Then there came a loud bang from below and the voices of angry men.

"They're forcing their way in," Tesca called. "Can you get it open?"

"Trying," she said, grunting. "It's a little out of my reach…I think it leads down to the floor."

Makes sense, Tesca thought. *No one would want to clamber out on those beams every morning.*

Another bang from downstairs, louder this time.

"Damnation!" she swore. "I can't reach it!"

Tesca was already moving along the outside wall, looking for stairs down to the ground floor. He found them and was halfway down when there came another bang. For a second, he saw movement in the blackness below and realized the front door was buckling, opening for an instant and letting in quick bursts of starlight. The banging continued, faster now with a regular rhythm of grunting shouts. They were hurling themselves against the door in unison. But that gave Tesca just enough light to see the basic layout of the room.

The mill was in the center, dominating the space. There was a smooth circular trail in the wood around it; presumably from a horse or a mule harnessed to turn the wheel. There were more than a few ropes hanging from above; the glimpses Tesca had of them in the brief bursts of light made him think of snakes descending from trees to the jungle floor.

"Which one?" he called up. The door was groaning now, light was beginning to spill in from one corner of it as a hinge weakened and it began to sag on its frame.

"You're too far over…go to your left! One more, no wait…yes, that one, that one!" He grasped one of the ropes. It hung from ceiling, but trailed off towards one wall, anchored there. "Pull it!" Kayrla urged. "Pull it!"

Tesca pulled it. Several things happened at once. He felt the rope resist him at first, then something came loose above him. He heard a quick creak of wood and a square of starry sky appeared directly over his head. The front door to the mill burst open, spilling several pirates to the floor. And there were more noises up by the window; it sounded like at least one pirate had decided to climb through the second-story window after all.

Kayrla's night vision was much sharper than Tesca's, and when the front doors burst open she could see the room's layout very clearly. There were six doors in the roof, each with a rope attached to the latch and another rope on a pulley. Almost immediately, she understood that the first set of ropes were used to open the doors in the morning, and the second set would pull the doors closed again. This arrangement would allow the mill operator to keep the place well ventilated while staying on the ground floor.

To her right she could see one of the pirates was pulling himself through the window. He didn't look happy about it; she guessed he'd drawn the short straw to be the first one through. It was often how they'd arranged who would be the first to cross to the other ship during boarding actions. As he scrambled through the window and started getting to his feet, Kayrla stretched out and grabbed the rope attached to the pulley. Now that the roof door was open, it was within her reach. She pulled a good deal of the rope to her, drew her knife and started cutting. The pirate got to his feet, his expression brightening as he realized there was no one on the catwalk with him. Kayrla pressed herself against one of the beams coming down from the roof into the crossbeam, staying out of his sight. She let one end of the rope fall to the floor and began tying the other end swiftly into a wide noose.

Below her, Tesca had wasted no time once the door was broken. His blades were out and he had leapt among the sprawled pirates at the door, striking quickly before they got to their feet. He managed to slay two of them before another rose and charged him. Backing away, he batted the man's attacks aside and retreated into the shadows of the mill's interior. The pirates surged after him. He led them around the large mill, occasionally darting in for a strike when they were caught between him and one of the mills' great gears. He wounded two more pirates in this fashion before they started to come around the other side of the mill as well, forcing him further back.

His foot skidded on loose grain and he stumbled against a stack of flour sacks. Before the pirates could reach him, he bounded backward to land on top of the stack and slashing down with his rapier, he sliced the topmost sack open. With one hard stomp on the sack, he sent a small burst of flour into their faces. He stomped the sack twice more, fogging the air around him and giving him the chance to retreat out of sight.

Kayrla kept glancing down at the battle below her, but her primary focus was on the pirate standing on the catwalk. "It's clear!" he called out through the window to his mates below. Then he looked down over the catwalk and saw Tesca at bay. With a grin, he started for the stairs.

Kayrla dashed along the crossbeam the instant he had his back to her. In one leap, she bounded to the banister and flung the noose over his head. Then she leaned back, pulling the noose taught. He grunted, choked and staggered back against the banister. He weighed more than she did, but he was off-balance and she was leaning far out from the banister, using all of her weight against him.

As she felt him coming over the banister, his own weight doing the work now, she let go of the rope and tumbled out into space, landing on the crossbeam again. "Tesca! The rope!" she yelled as the man went over, trailing the rope that led to the pulley behind him.

Tesca heard her. It took one glance behind him to see the rope whizzing up towards the ceiling. With practiced skill, he sheathed his dagger and grabbed the rope. The falling man's weight was greater than his own, and he was quickly hauled up out of the pirates' reach. The open door in the roof was looming before him as the pirate on the other end of the rope hit the floor. Tesca dangled precariously on the rope as it went slack for a moment, then snapped taught again. He did not look back and scrambled up the rope, reaching the open door and pulling himself out onto the roof. A moment later Kayrla leapt for the rope herself and scurried up after him.

"I…I didn't think that would work, you know," she panted.

"Neither did I," he admitted, getting his bearings. He pointed east. "That way. The next roof there is the closest. We'll have to jump."

Nodding wearily, she followed after him. The alley yawned below them as they hurled themselves across the empty space between the rooftops, but they cleared it.

Tesca quickly looked about him as they scrambled to the top of the roof. "No way to get down from here," he said, panting slightly. "We'll have to keep going and put some space behind us. Let's move!"

Kayrla's chest was already aching, but she gritted her teeth and ran down the other side of the rooftop after him. They crossed one, two, three more rooftops in quick succession. On the next one, Tesca cleared the space, but he realized with a shock that it was wider than the others had been. The roof here was older, sagging in places and it groaned under his feet as he landed, shingles sliding under his feet. He turned just in time to see Kayrla leaping after him, her eyes going wide in horror as she realized she wasn't going to make it.

Tesca flung himself down on the roof and thrust his arm out to catch her. Her scrabbling fingers touched his and grabbed hold. He braced himself for the shock, but still he nearly slid off the roof himself when she hit the wall below him. For a moment, neither of them moved, then Tesca hauled her up onto the roof with him. She clung to him for several seconds; neither of them moving. At last she stirred, lifting her head up and peering at him through the tangle of her hair.

"Do you think...we can just...stay here for a minute?" she gasped.

"I think so," he replied, his shoulder throbbing in pain. "We'll just...catch our breath here."

For a moment, he thought he was going to pass out; he felt as if he was slowly rolling over. Then he heard the roof groaning again. "Oh, hells..." he muttered before it gave way beneath them.

They tumbled through the roof in a shower of broken shingles, dust and rotted beams. Coughing and spluttering, Tesca stood up, blinking in the bright candlelight around him. He could shouting, screaming, splashing as he staggered forward. Two people were sitting in a large bathtub, frozen with shock as they stared at. The woman was young and shapely, the grapes in her hand forgotten as she gaped at him. The man was old and paunchy, sweat beading on his bald pate.

Tesca raised one weary hand to point at them, then gestured towards the door, resting his other hand on his sword hilt to accentuate his point. In a flurry of water, naked limbs and towels, they fled. Behind him, Tesca heard a groan from Kayrla. She sat up amidst the wreckage and coughed several times.

"You all right?" Tesca asked, crossing to the door, listening to hear if the bathing couple had raised the alarm yet.

"I'll live," she replied, brushing her green hair out of her face. She stood up and walked up to the tub. Cupping her delicate, blue-tinged hands, she filled them with water and splashed it across her face. Spotting a full goblet of wine on a gilded tray next to the tub, she drank it down in one long pull. "Ah, that helps," she sighed.

"Okay, I hear shouting downstairs," Tesca said. "I think we'd better see if we can get out to the street before someone comes up here." He turned to look back at her. "Are you rea–" he began to say, then froze, staring in disbelief.

She looked back at him. "What?" But the look on his face told her all that she needed to know. There were three spells she was very comfortable with casting: repair, entropy and one other. She'd cast two spells since the fight had begun; and at some point during the race through darkened alleys and across moonlit rooftops, she'd stopped focusing on the spell she'd been maintaining all day; the third spell. Her disguise spell.

"You're an elf," Tesca whispered.

Chapter Five

"You're an elf," Tesca whispered.

She raised an eyebrow at him. "Is that a problem?" The disguise spell she used wasn't a very powerful illusion. All it really did was alter the color of her hair and skin. By keeping her hair spilled over much of her face, the most obvious signs of her race were concealed. With the disguise spell gone however, her hair was a bright green, the color of seaweed in shallow water. Her skin was a pale, luminescent blue, like the sky on a hazy day. Her eyes, larger than a human's, were almond-shaped and angled in towards her nose. They were a sparkling emerald green.

The green kerchief around her brow had come loose, uncovering the pointed tips of her ears. She tucked them back under the kerchief and examined herself under the candlelight. She had a few minor cuts and scrapes, and one gash along her left arm that oozed blood. Her blood wasn't the same color as a human's either. It looked like a pale orange translucent ichor, with pinpoint flecks of something floating in suspension sparking in the light.

She looked closely at her arm, carefully probing the cut with a finger. "You didn't answer my question," she said without looking at Tesca.

Tesca seemed to blink out of his paralysis. "I haven't seen an elf up close before, that's all. I've never heard of your folk coming travel this far south."

"That's not surprising," she commented. "Magic's not strong this far south. I cast a lot of spells during that fight; my disguise spell unraveled at some point after we started running."

"Well, we have to move soon, and we can't go downstairs with you looking like that," Tesca said, turning back towards the door to listen again.

"Give me a few moments," she said, closing her eyes. "I'll recast it. Just don't ask me to cast any more spells tonight after this."

"I didn't even know you'd cast any spells at all," Tesca muttered. He glanced back at her, hearing her muttering strange words. She wove her arms before her in delicate patterns, her fingers rigid in an odd twisted manner. After a few moments, Tesca could see dark shadows moving over her body. He thought the candles were burning low for a second. Then he realized it wasn't shadows, it was colors. A deep, rich black was spreading through her green hair, like paint being floored onto a floor. A similar thing was happening to her skin, but this color was a rich brown; a similar hue to the one borne by the native Islanders of the Frees. When she opened her eyes, the emerald color was gone, replaced by a deep brown, almost black. Even the blood trickling from her arm was the color of human blood now.

"How do I look?" she asked him, a wry smile on her lips. He stared in astonishment. The change was astonishing. Now that he knew what to look for, he could still see the signs of her race in the line of her cheekbones, the size and shape of her eyes and the willowy grace as she moved. Her hair was still straight, unlike the thick curls common to the Islanders.

But he was trained to be a careful observer. To most, he knew she would just look like a skinny girl, not yet a woman; a tomboy who'd left home for a life at sea. Many different peoples traveled in the Frees; her straight hair and dark coloring would likely be put down to an odd crossbreeding, perhaps between an Islander and an Al-Kef tradesman.

"How long have you been doing this?" he asked her.

"Longer than most would guess," she replied. She looked him over. "You're what…twenty? Twenty-five at the oldest."

"About that," he confirmed.

"I've probably got a year or two on you," she said. "I'm not sure myself, to be honest. I've been crewing ships for over ten years now."

"And all that time, no one's ever noticed?"

She sighed. "Of course they notice! Eventually. But usually, by the time they do I'm one of the crew and they don't care anymore. Those that would have had trouble with it never find out. I don't stay long crewing a ship that's got elf-haters on it." She shrugged. "This far south, there's not many sea-dogs who've ever seen an elf anyway. Let's see if we can get out of here, all right?"

"All right," Tesca replied, opening the door. They could still hear the shouts of the man and woman driven from the room, but it didn't sound like anyone was coming up the stairs to investigate. Tesca glanced quickly to both sides of the door, then slipped into the hallway. Kayrla followed him.

They were on a long wooden balcony running around all four sides of an open space. Doors were spaced evenly around all four walls. Below them, there was one more floor like the one they were standing on, then the ground floor. Several people, including the two people who'd fled the bath, stood in the middle of the floor, looking up towards them.

"That's them!" the man in the towel shouted. "Burglars!"

"I doubt burglars would have been so unprofessional as to crash through my roof," the innkeeper replied, glaring up at Tesca.

"Indeed," Tesca called down. "My apologies, good sir. We were trying to go over your roof, not through it."

"If he'd bothered to keep it in good repair, we wouldn't have crashed through it at all," Kayrla muttered. Tesca kicked her in the shin.

For several seconds everyone stared back and forth at each other. Then the man in the towel finally spluttered, "Well?"

"Well, what?" the innkeeper asked.

"Well...get them!"

"Get them?" the innkeeper said. "What for? Are you hurt?"

"No, but–"

"Did they take your money or your clothes?"

"They had money back there?" Kayrla asked, half-turning. Tesca grabbed her arm and yanked her back to the banister.

"No," he called down. "We haven't taken anything. We're sorry to have given you a scare. We'd just like to come downstairs and be on our way, if that's all right."

"Well, I'd like to oblige you," the innkeeper replied, "but there's the matter of my roof."

"We'll pay for that," Tesca offered.

"We'll what?!?!" Kayrla hissed.

He turned to Kayrla. "You had two pouches on your belt when you crashed into me back there. One of them burst open and spilled gold everywhere. Does the other one have gold in it as well?"

"Yes, but…" she trailed off, then her eyes bugged open as she realized what he was talking about. "I am NOT paying for that idiot to repair his roof!" she said angrily.

"We have three choices," Tesca said firmly, "one, we pay the innkeeper what we can and walk out of here. Two, we refuse to pay and have to cut our way out through several people who didn't attack us first and three…"

"Yes?" she asked.

"We go back up onto the roof and start trying to find another way down."

Memories of narrowly avoiding a deadly fall rushed back to her. "We split the cost," she muttered. "It was your idea to escape across the roofs in the first place."

"Fine," Tesca replied quietly as he leaned over the railing. "Yes, we'll pay for that. How much would the repairs cost?"

The landlord remained quiet for several seconds, thinking it over. Tesca knew he was deciding how much he could squeeze them for. "Let's start heading down," he whispered to Kayrla. "He knows we want to avoid trouble, but we need to make him understand we'll start trouble if he tries to fleece us."

"Okay," she replied. They walked around the balcony, taking the stairs down to the next level. Numerous patrons of the inn had opened their doors and were watching them, ducking back inside their rooms and locking their doors as they passed. But one patron did not retreat as they drew close to him. He was Sabrian, in his early middle years. Creases furrowed the ebony skin around his eyes and the corners of his mouth. He looked curiously at Tesca, his eyes coming to rest on Tesca's two blades. Staring intently at the unadorned hilts, his face drew into an angry frown as Tesca passed. Then he withdrew into his room and shut the door with a slam.

"Do you know him?" Kayrla asked. "He seemed to recognize you, and he wasn't happy about it."

"No," Tesca sighed, "I don't know him. But I know why he's angry." They had reached the next staircase and began to descend to the ground floor. "Let's just try to get out of here quickly before he decides to act on it." Kayrla wanted to ask more questions, but they were approaching the landlord now, so she put an arrogant grimace on her features and gave the man her best "we're not to be trifled with" look.

"What's the price of repairs?" Tesca asked him.

The landlord looked back and forth between Tesca and Kayrla, thinking carefully. "Twenty-five marks."

"Twenty-five?" Kayrla spluttered. Tesca motioned her to silence and smiled thinly at the landlord.

"We're not paying for a long-overdue replacement of your entire roof, sir," he said. "But the hole we made can be mended for, I'd say, five marks."

"Are you insane?" the landlord snorted. "Five marks for a damaged roof?"

"You haven't even been up there to survey the damage," Tesca said. "It's not that much. One hole, in one section of the roof. Easy to patch up. We haven't stolen anything from the room, and we haven't injured any of your patrons," he added, letting his hand brush against the hilt of his rapier.

The implied message was not lost on the landlord. "Fairly spoken," he said with a nod. "Fifteen marks."

"We'll go as high as ten," Tesca replied, ignoring Kayrla's barely stifled yelp of surprise. He continued to stare at the landlord, his eyes meeting the other man's, his face composed and calm.

The landlord looked away from that clear gaze and sighed. "Ten marks will do just fine, sirrah."

"Thank you," Tesca replied. He turned to Kayrla. "Pay him."

She glared at him. "You said you'd pay half!"

"I don't have half on me right now," he said. "But I can get it as soon as we're done here."

"Promises of money are like milk," Kayrla snapped. "They go sour fast."

"You've trusted me all night when your life was on the line," Tesca said, somewhat amused, "but once money's involved you won't take my word anymore?"

She glared up at him, then with a grumble, tugged her pouch open violently. Gold and silver coins spilled out onto the floor. Coins, and something else: a pendant on a thin chain. It had a large circular red gem set in the center of it.

"I'd take that in lieu of coin," the landlord said, bending over to take a closer look at it.

"You will NOT," Kayrla hissed, snatching up the jewelry and stuffing it back into the pouch. "Ten marks and not a penny more." She began scooping the coins toward her, carefully counting them and assembling the landlord's price. After a minute or two she stood up and put a small pile of coins into the landlord's outstretched hands. "Ten marks worth of coin," she said.

The landlord frowned. "Some of these coins aren't from Kohayne. These here," he said, holding up a few silvers, "are from Hisvet. Everyone knows the Baron shaves his coins down; they're not worth as much."

Kayrla glared at him. "That's ten marks in any port o' call. It's come out of my purse and that's all that's coming out of it. We're done here."

The landlord opened his mouth to speak, but a glance from Tesca made him choose different words then he'd intended. "Fine," he spat, "be on your way, and be glad I don't call the Watch."

"No!" called a new voice. Everyone turned to see the Sabrian, who had come down the stairs to the ground floor without anyone hearing him. He was now wearing a pair of blades at his hips similar to Tesca's, though they were intricately etched with symbols and Sabrian characters. A beautifully made, expensive flintlock pistol was in his hand, and it was pointed at Tesca's chest.

"There is a matter of honor that must be settled," the Sabrian said. His Freespeak was oddly accented, full of sonorous, rounded vowels. "This man bears blades he has no right to." He glared at Tesca. "You will answer for your crime. Now."

Chapter Six

"Draw those weapons," the Sabrian ordered, dipping the pistol down momentarily to point to the blades hanging from Tesca's belt, "and we shall see if you are worthy to bear them."

Tesca groaned inwardly, but didn't let his annoyance show on his face. "Good evening, honored sir," he said in flawless Sabrian. "I understand your anger, but I must assure you there is no violation of honor here."

The Sabrian's eyes went wide with astonishment to hear himself being addressed in his native tongue, but the pistol never wavered. "How did you come to learn the Mother Tongue?"

"I had a good teacher," Tesca replied.

"You are well-spoken," said the Sabrian. "A credit to him." He glanced at Tesca's blades again. "I presume he instructed you in the Argument and the Retort?"

"In all aspects, honored sir."

"Show me."

Tesca's eyes narrowed. "We are outside the Empire, honored sir, and my allegiance is not given to you."

"That may be true," the Sabrian replied, "but I am the one holding the pistol. You speak well and this is why I have not already shot you. But your skin is as white as my teeth and you bear the Argument and Retort, which no one but a peer or officer of the Empire may do. I will learn the reason why." He took a step forward, studying Tesca closely.

"The hilts are unadorned; there are only three reasons why this would be so: you stole these blades before a young nobleman made them his own, you took them from the corpse of an *agentis*, or…" he trailed off, shaking his head in disbelief, "…you are an *agentis* yourself."

"The last reason is the correct one," said Tesca.

The Sabrian grew angry. "You lie! A white man trained as an *agentis*! Preposterous! Impossible!"

Tesca's voice became very crisp and glacially cold. "Regardless, honored sir, it is the truth. I bear these blades because I earned them. I am an *agentis*, with a master whom I serve, and to whose return I have been greatly delayed tonight. You further delay me in that task, and threaten my honor. You call me a liar and insult me when I have done neither to you." He stepped forward himself until the two men were only a few feet apart, the barrel of the pistol less than a foot from Tesca's chest. "And I tell you now what any *agentis* would tell you: Draw your steel, and I will draw your blood."

The Sabrian stared into Tesca's eyes, uncertain. Then he took one step back and lowered the pistol. He made no apologies to Tesca, simply gave a formal nod to him, slipped his weapon into his wide belt, and headed back upstairs to his room. Tesca turned back to the rest of the people around him: the landlord, the half-naked couple who'd fled the bath, assorted other patrons of the inn, and Kayrla, all of whom were staring at him in open-mouthed surprise.

"Are we paid up?" he asked, switching back to Freespeak. "Then let's be off," he added, catching Kayrla's elbow and leading her out the front door of the inn.

"What in the Deeps was all that abou–" she began, but Tesca shook his head and nodded towards an alley to their right.

"We want to get out of Harborside before any of Jolly's men spot us," he said, leading her up the alley. "Your skin's a different color, but am I right in guessing that they know you can do that?"

"Most of them by now," she admitted.

"Well, you're wearing the same clothes, and I look the same as ever," Tesca replied. "Once we're out of Harborside, I have a place to go where they'll never find us."

Kayrla nodded. "We need a bolt-hole," she agreed. They began to head up the long streets that curved towards the higher parts of Kohayne. "Do I get to meet your master, then?"

Tesca whirled around to face her, astonished. "You understood that?"

She grinned at him. "Sabrian's not some secret code language. Maybe a decade or so back nobody around here could speak it, but that's changing. Folk need at least a bit of the tongue to deal with merchants like him."

Tesca shook his head. "He wasn't a merchant. He'd never have challenged me if he was. And he owned his own set of the blades."

"So he's a nobleman?" Kayrla asked. "A Sabrian nobleman, living in a bilgewater inn like that?"

"I don't know," Tesca said. "A Sabrian nobleman traveling without an entourage is rarer than a hen's tooth. And I can't see one of them coming this far outside the Empire for any reason. No, my guess is he's a retired naval officer. They also bear the blades, but I didn't get a chance to look at the hilts to tell for sure; the etchings would be different."

"Could he be one of those things you said you were?" she asked. "An...*agentis*?"

"No," Tesca said flatly. "An *agentis* would never have challenged me either. He probably would never have let us know he was there at all, although he'd want to know why I bore the blades. He would have started following us from the inn, but an open challenge like that..." he trailed off, shaking his head. "That's not our way."

"What is it he called those blades?" she asked. "Something about an argument?"

Tesca smiled. "They refer to the blades, worn in that fashion, as 'the Argument and the Retort'."

"Odd name."

Tesca chuckled. "Not really, if you consider the majority of the time these blades are drawn is during a formal duel. The Sabrians don't see any real difference between using words and blades in a duel; both are valid means of winning the contest."

She snorted in derision. "Sounds no different than two men arguing in a tavern. Eventually one gets so angry he draws steel."

"Oh, no…there are strict rules for dueling in the Empire," Tesca countered. "Blades are drawn, but sometimes the duel is settled without using them. Sometimes they will start with swordplay and turn to wordplay, and sometimes vice versa. It's rather complicated."

Kayrla looked up at him. "You really do know a lot about the Sabrians for a northerner," she said. "That fellow back there was right, I think, to be curious about you. What is an…*agentis*, exactly, and how did you end up becoming one?"

Tesca appraised her for a long time. "It's a long story, and not one I'm prepared to share with someone I've only known for a few hours. Is that a problem?"

She turned serious. "You know, I just asked you that exact same question not long ago," she said. "There's a part of me that's not happy with you knowing my secret and not sharing yours." She looked at him with the same appraising look he'd just given her. "But," she sighed, a grin crossing her sharp features, "it's more of a challenge to figure it out myself, eh? You've got me all curious now, Tesca. And," she added with a grimace, poking him in the chest, "you still owe me money. I'm not going anywhere until that debt is cleared and my money purse is full again, understand?"

Tesca smiled down at her. "Fair enough. Let's get moving."

"Where to?"

He gestured towards the rising street. "Up." They took their time moving through the dark streets; the sounds of Harborside became quiet echoes behind them, muffling the tread of their feet. Tesca would frequently change direction, turning east or west for a block or two, then double back to make sure they weren't being followed.

The streets were nearly deserted here, save for an occasional guard standing watch at various gates to impressive manor houses, sealed up for the night. All of the guards watched them go past with narrowed, wary eyes, but none challenged them.

Kayrla's legs were aching with the effort. She was used to scampering up and down a ship's rigging, but this relentless climb up the hard stone road was wearing her down. She noticed Tesca's breath was coming harder now as well. "How...much further?" she quietly gasped.

"A little further," he panted. "I'm out of shape. Spent too long in Narlos."

"Oh, Narlos. I've been there. The whole city's flat," she said with a weary smile. "Wish...we were there now."

"It'll be easier in a moment," Tesca replied. "We're reaching the terraces."

This high, the angle was now too sharp for the roads to safely ascend the slopes in a straight line. On both the north and south sides of Kohayne, the vertical roads rising up from Harborside ended in a wide street running east-west across the upper portion of the city, which then wound back and forth in switchbacks, cutting into the slopes and continuing up. Each length of the switchback was linked by staircases cutting between them, narrow alleyways with rich manors on both sides. Kayrla found the climb much easier now. She stopped at the top of the first stair and looked back down. Between the dark walls, she could the city twinkling below them. "Must be an impressive view from inside one of these homes," she said, catching her breath. "You've got be pretty rich to live up here, I daresay?"

"Oh, yes," Tesca agreed. "In Kohayne, the rich literally look down on the poor."

"Well, that's good. I guess you really will be able to pay me back, then."

Tesca chuckled and started up again. Kayrla followed, wondering when he was going to stop. The manors built between the switchbacks were becoming grander and grander, their layouts becoming palatial. One manor was so large it took up both sides of the stairs they climbed, the two halves linked by a stone bridge high above them. As they reached the top of each stair, she looked down both sides of the road to guess which manor Tesca was heading for. They all looked impressive to her; each one with two guards at the front gate and a large banner hanging over it. But it was too dark to make out the details of the banners, so she had no idea who lived in them.

But Tesca didn't change direction; each time they reached the top of one of these cut-throughs, he glanced side-to-side, then crossed the street and started up the next set of stairs. Finally they came out of a stair and saw that there was no stair on the opposite side of the street ahead of them, just a wall of thick jungle foliage. Tesca turned to the left and continued walking. The road turned around another switchback and continued up. Now both sides of the road were thick with trees, cutting off most of the light. "Where in the Deeps are we going?" she asked. He pointed further up the slope, and she saw there were lights shining through the trees above them.

"Oh, Hells…" she muttered, realizing where they were headed. The road bent around once more and the lights above them were much brighter. She could see high walls and guards pacing the tops of them. Then, as the road made one last turn, it widened into a courtyard before a large, fortified gate. There were two guards on either side and a large banner hanging over it, swaying in the strong night breeze. The large flaming braziers set outside before the gate gave enough light for her to see the details on the banner. It was the same as the one that flew over the two towers of the Eisenteeth; the emblem of the Duke of Kohaya.

The guards lowered their pikes to face the pair as they came into the courtyard. Tesca stepped forward, raising his head so his features were visible in the firelight. He raised his hand in front of him and made some sort of motion with it, one that Kayrla couldn't see with his back to her. The guards immediately snapped back to guarded attention.

"Master Secarius," one of them said crisply, "welcome back."

"Thank you," Tesca replied. "I have news to report to His Grace."

"Understood, sir." The guard called through the gate to the other side. "'Ware the gate! The Left Hand has returned!"

Chapter Seven

Kayrla stared at Tesca as the gate began to swing open. "You work for the Duke?"

He looked down at her, a slight smile on his face. "Is that a problem?"

She frowned, but said nothing as he walked through the gate. Gauging how hard it would be to get back outside once the gate was closed, she grudgingly followed him.

The inner courtyard was mostly empty at this time of night, but there were several more guards here. One of them, wearing a plumed cap upon his head, stepped up to Tesca and gave a formal nod in greeting.

"A pleasure to see you again, Master Secarius."

Tesca nodded back. "Likewise, Castellan. Is his Grace receiving tonight?"

The officer shook his head. "His Grace has retired for the evening, Master Secarius, but the Right Hand is in the library." His glance dropped to Kayrla, sulking at Tesca's side. "And this?"

"She's with me," Tesca said.

"He owes me money," she interjected. The castellan's eyebrow raised, half-indignant, half-amused.

Tesca chuckled. "She's right, as it happens. Her purse paid the way out of a sticky situation in Harborside after I arrived."

The castellan nodded. "We heard the alarm bells of the city watch some time back, but we've had no messenger from the Watch with a report yet." He shrugged, as if this was not unusual. "Your work?"

"Not of my choosing," Tesca replied. He turned to Kayrla. "You have a choice here." He gestured at the open gate. "Once those gates close, it's not given to me to say that they be opened again until dawn. You can either get your money now and pass back through before they close, or–"

"Or what?" Kayrla interrupted.

"Or you enjoy the hospitality of the manor for the night, sleep in a bed, take a bath and get paid in the morning."

"And I can leave then?"

Tesca paused. "Most likely, but you'll have to present yourself before the Duke's Right Hand first. His Grace allows only a select few to come and go from the manor as they please, and fewer still have the right to allow others that privilege."

"The gate, Master Secarius," the castellan said politely. "It cannot remain open much longer."

Kayrla bit her lip and decided to stall for a little more time. "What will the Right Hand want to know?"

"Who you are, how you came to be here with me, and your intentions upon leaving the manor, at the very least," Tesca said, but there was a warning tone in his voice. His eyes met Kayrla's and she understood the warning: once Tesca had reported in, the Duke would learn she was an elf. If she was in the manor when that secret was revealed, she might not be allowed to leave.

The idea of escaping from one captor to run into the arms of another made her skin crawl, but Tesca's unspoken warning to her made the difference: he was risking his master's wrath by letting her leave, but because of that, she'd take her chances with him. *Besides,* she thought to herself, *I still don't know how he managed to become an* agentis, *whatever that is.*

"I'll stay," she said, looking back at him. "A bed and a bath is too tempting after a night like this."

"Close the gate, lads," the castellan said to the guards with a sharp gesture towards the heavy doors. "Seal it up for the night."

Tesca put his hand on Kayrla's shoulder as the gate drew closed on groaning hinges. "Are you sure about this?"

"Don't make me start second-guessing," she said quietly. "I might change my mind."

"Too late for that," he said with a quiet sigh as the doors shut with a low booming thud.

The castellan turned back to them as the guards settled the heavy beams into their brackets, barring the gate closed. He appeared more relaxed now that the manor was sealed once more. "If you'll follow me, then?" he gestured up toward the long stair that led up into the estate.

More climbing, Kayrla thought glumly, but she stayed silent as she and Tesca followed the castellan up. The grounds of the estate, like the upper parts of Kohayne itself, were built as terraces into the steep sides of the sloping lagoon. The foliage here was thick, dark and lush, with many bright and exotic flowers and equally exotic scents. Long porticos, some of them angled staircases, cut through the vegetation, connecting the various buildings of the estate to each other.

"How many groundskeepers does the Duke have to employ?" Kayrla asked.

Tesca chuckled. "His Grace spends a fortune to keep the porticos clear of foliage." Kayrla could see evidence of this, but it appeared to her that it was a never-ending battle. Despite the constant vigilance of his groundskeepers, vines and fronds appeared to quickly wind their way around the pillars and poke up between the flooring tiles. Her keen night-vision could see into the darkness beyond the porticos. There, the jungle provided a canopy she was sure was thick enough to keep the sun at bay.

As the castellan led them higher and higher through the estate, the foliage became less intrusive. Kayrla realized these higher terraces were for the Duke's personal use, and so received the lion's share of attention from the groundskeepers. It was easier to see the architecture here: stone walls, plastered smooth and painted a pale tan, high arched doorways, generally left open for ventilation but ready to be locked with stout wooden doors at need. The windows were much the same, tall and narrow. She noticed that these, like the doors, were open to the night air. Some of the trees outside were tall enough that she figured she could climb up and slip in through one of those windows with little trouble. *Or,* she reflected, *I could get out of the building the same way, if I had to.*

The Castellan brought them to the largest of the buildings here. "This must be his personal residence, I imagine," she said to Tesca.

"Correct," he replied. Two guards snapped to attention at the doors as they approached, and one opened the door for them. Long rugs ran down the middle of hall, covering smooth-set tiled stone. The interior walls were the same painted plaster as the outside of the buildings. She noted there was little framed artwork on the walls, realizing the Quad's climate would be murderous to paintings and parchment. Those few pieces that did hang on the walls were sealed behind glass-and-wood frames to hold back the humidity as best as possible. The lack of paintings and portraits was compensated by numerous statues and sculptures of stone, precious metals and lacquered wood, all set along the walls, some free-standing and some on pedestals.

Kayrla's mind went slightly numb as her eyes took in the wealth around her. *If I was a thief,* she thought, *the guards would catch me because I wouldn't be able to decide what to steal first.* The rooms they passed were richly furnished with large, heavy chairs, cabinets and tables, sturdy and without excessive adornment, but heavily varnished and polished to a rich glossy sheen.

They reached an intersection of hallways and the castellan paused, turning back to them. "Kayrla," Tesca said, "the castellan will show you to a room that's yours for the night. A servant will attend to you, bring you food and drink, draw you a bath, anything you wish."

"A bath," she said, shivering in anticipation. "A big one?"

He nodded. "All I ask is that you stay in that room for the night. The guards won't recognize you if you go exploring."

She sighed. It was no more than she'd expected. "I'll see you in the morning?"

"Oh, yes. I'll present you to the Right Hand."

"Will I..." she paused, "...will I meet the Duke?"

The castellan frowned at the forwardness of her question, but Tesca smiled. "We'll see. Good night."

The castellan nodded to Tesca, then led Kayrla down the left-hand corridor. Tesca watched them go for a few moments, then turned and continued in the opposite direction. Before long he stopped at a large set of double doors that were closed. A guard stood at attention there, who nodded formally to Tesca, knocked once on the door, then entered. Tesca followed him inside.

The library had two walls covered by shelves that were filled with a multitude of books. The third wall had one cabinet stocked with several decanters and glasses and one large cabinet with a great number of wide, short drawers, which Tesca knew to be the Duke's map archive. Between these two cabinets was a large fireplace that Tesca suspected to have been built out of habit by an architect who'd come from colder climates; he'd never seen it lit. The fourth wall was a set of wide windows that looked out over the harbor twinkling below in the night.

In the middle of the room were several large, comfortable reading chairs set around a small table with a lamp upon it. There was also a large table some feet away with no chairs around it. Tesca knew when the Duke was researching a particular topic, he would pull down all the books that might be of use and set them out on this table, so he could peruse them at leisure.

A thin, older man was standing by the table, peering through a set of thick round spectacles at the book in his hand. His garments were expensive and well-tailored, but very simple and unadorned, a gray-green shirt and black pants. He looked up, squinting as the guard and Tesca entered the room. Tilting his head back to peer at them through his spectacles, he nodded in recognition.

"Master Galen," said the guard, "His Grace's Left Hand has returned."

"So I see," Galen said in a dry, studious tone. For several seconds, no one moved or spoke, then Galen spoke again. "Thank you. You may go." The guard saluted and withdrew. The man put the book down on the table and walked towards Tesca, looking him over carefully. "So… the Left Hand finally returns to the comfort of His Grace's home after gallivanting about the seas in search of adventure."

"While the Right Hand stays at home and runs the estate, keeping His Grace's home tidy," Tesca replied in the same flat tone. "It always pleases me to know that thanks to you, I will have clean sheets to sleep on when I get back."

"Clean sheets," the older man repeated, frowning. Then a wide grin slowly spread across his face at same time it spread across Tesca's. They clasped arms in greeting. "Clean sheets," Galen snorted. "Don't dismiss my task so quickly, lad. One day, the Left becomes the Right. Then YOU get to keep the house clean and watch another do the gallivanting."

"Let's hope that day is many years off," Tesca said. "Do you miss being the Left Hand?"

"By the time you came along, I was more the Right than Left anyway. My eyes were getting weak; I was sending younger men with sharper eyes out to do the knife work." He looked closely at Tesca's clothes. "Speaking of which…you had some trouble getting here, didn't you?"

"Not related to this," Tesca said, nodding over his shoulder at the bag hanging there, "but you should know there's a few dead men in Harborside."

"Your work?"

"Mine and another's," Tesca replied. "I got pulled into a scrap between revelers and their blood was already up. I had some help cutting my way out; I brought her here and she's being given quarters for the night."

Galen looked concerned. "You brought a stranger onto the estate?"

"You'll want to meet her yourself," Tesca promised him. He paused, then said, "She's an elf."

Galen's eyes went wide in surprise, but he recovered very quickly.

"We'll talk about that in a moment. Business first." He held out his hand.

Tesca nodded, taking the bag off his shoulder and handing it to Galen. Galen opened it and took out a leather folio. He unbuckled the clasp and began thumbing through the pages with practiced speed.

"There's a lot of pages here."

"I spent an extra week in Narlos watching the shipyard."

"An extra week?" Galen asked. "Why?"

"I began to suspect the Lord Mayor was using the activity in the shipyard to hide…other activities. The shipyard is a busy place; a lot of coming and going. But I spotted someone I recognized: Philippe Marsienne."

Galen blinked. "The Malachan engineer? Are you sure?"

"Yes. He was somewhat disguised, but that limp is a giveaway. He's working for Narlos now. My notes on it are all in there."

The older man closed the folio and sealed it back up. "His Grace will be delighted to receive this news with his breakfast tomorrow. Well done, Tesca."

"How is he, Galen?"

Galen chuckled. "About the same as before. Doctor Felton says that rattle in his chest can barely be heard now, so it seems he's on the mend. He's not happy with the new diet being forced on him, though."

"I can imagine," Tesca said. "So, about the fight in Harborside," he began.

"Tell me about the elf," Galen replied, stepping over to one of the reading chairs and sitting down. "Just a quick summary, lad. You're exhausted; that's easy to see even with my eyes." He waggled the folio in his hand. "And I will need to review this before I get some sleep myself."

Tesca sank wearily into the chair next to Galen. "She's, well…she's an elf. I don't know much about them, to be honest. What do you know?"

Galen furrowed his brow as he thought. "What I know about them is mostly guesswork and theories coming from the mainland. The general consensus I gather is that the Elflands are far to the north, beyond the frontiers of Malachi and Terendor. They returned some fifty years ago."

"Returned?"

"Well, you know the old tales, the really old tales, all had an elf or two in them," Galen said. "But they were just tales, myths. Then, suddenly, tales began to come south of elves being seen, here, there. And the tales were new ones, told by men who weren't prone to fancies. There have been enough new tales that a few scholars started writing down what they'd heard, and those books became popular, as well as valuable. I've read some of them, and I've met an elf myself once, some twenty years ago. But that was on the mainland," he continued, puzzled. "I've never heard of one coming this far south. "According to the books I've read, their magic only works if they stay close to the Elflands."

"That's not entirely accurate," Tesca replied. "She can do magic. She says it's difficult down here, but I watched her cast a spell, and she said she'd cast others during the fight."

"Really?" asked Galen, his eyes suddenly sharp and bright. "That is...quite a bit of news." He put the folio on the end table next to him. "I'll read this in the morning, lad. Tell me more about her."

Chapter Eight

Kayrla awoke with a start, as she always did when she slept in an unfamiliar setting. Bright sunlight shone through the narrow window in a long shaft, illuminating the room. She could hear a faint bustling roar outside. Casting aside her sheets, she rose from the bed and walked to the window, stretching her arms to loosen them up. She was wearing a white nightdress; her clothes from last night in a loose pile next to her bed. Her hair still felt damp from the hour-long bath she'd taken last night.

The sight outside the window made her dizzy; the entire city of Kohayne was below her. The quiet roar she could hear was the sound of Harborside's morning activity, bouncing back and forth within the bowl of the lagoon. She'd never been so high, so far above the streets of a city. She could see expansive manors on the opposite slope, across the city from her, and she wondered who lived there, in homes that mirrored the wealth and grandeur of the Duke's.

She yawned, stretched again. Glancing back at the bed, she was tempted to slip back under the covers and doze a bit longer. The bed was the largest she'd ever been in, the most comfortable, and the cotton sheets had been luxuriously soft. But she could feel herself coming awake now, her curiosity getting the better of her. Almost on impulse she leaned out of the window and looked directly down. One of the roofed porticoes linking the Duke's residence with the rest of the estate was some thirty feet below her, and none of the trees in the thick canopy on either side of it came anywhere close to her window. Recalling her thoughts last night about gaining access to the buildings here by climbing the trees, she wondered if the castellan had specifically put her here for that very reason. *Perhaps they pay more attention to security here than I thought,* she wondered.

She examined the color of her skin. Her illusion spell hadn't unraveled during the night, which it sometimes did, but she reflected that she had only recast it upon herself last night, so it would probably last for a few hours more before expiring. It was always amusing to watch that; the artificial color began to come apart and swirl around on her body like panicked fish seeking an exit from a water-filled box, all the while the patches of color getting smaller and smaller until they vanished altogether.

She didn't want to risk the spell coming undone while she was in Duke's estate, and decided to recast it again, keeping her skin and hair the same dark colors she'd selected last night. The thought of the look on the castellan's face if he came in and discovered she'd become a fair-skinned blonde overnight made her laugh.

Having the luxury of time, she carefully reinforced the disguise spell, methodically building the patterns of energy that changed the color of her skin and hair. While she could cast her best spells quickly and under duress, as she had last night, she always tried to take her time with any magic, if at all possible. There were several reasons for this. First, it reinforced the discipline of casting spells properly. Miscasting a spell could have unforeseen consequences. She knew a spell to light a candle and had once tried to do it quickly, but the spell backfired, and she had accidentally burned off one of her eyebrows.

"Spells are like birds," her father had said to her time and again when she was younger. He was pointing at a sparrow winging past them overhead. "Birds both breathe and fly through the air. Spells must both breathe and fly as well, through mana."

Magic could not happen if there was no mana to draw upon. Her father had explained to her "Mana is the food of magic. All magic, any spell, is simply using mana to make something happen." *Father always was fond of aphorisms,* she thought, then frowned slightly as she realized she was losing focus; the spell was starting to get away from her. She concentrated and resumed her spellcasting.

The second reason she tried to cast her spells slowly whenever possible was that by taking her time, she didn't tire herself out. Drawing upon mana, pulling it into patterns, making magic, was difficult work. Doing it quickly drew upon the caster's own reserves of energy. Doing this repeatedly could be exhausting, or even fatal if the spell was a complex one or caster was in poor health or injured. By casting the spell slowly, she could create the spell out of the surrounding mana without using any of her own energy in the process.

At last, the spell was completed; locking the mana around her body to keep her hair and skin the colors she had chosen. She had taken ten minutes to do it, and felt as refreshed and awake as she had before casting the spell. She imagined this spell would take far less time to cast further north; there was simply more mana available on the mainland. She wasn't sure why; her father had only said that the closer one got to the Elflands, the more mana there was to draw upon. But he'd moved them further and further south over the years, away from the Elflands, never explaining why.

She wondered how long it would take to cast more complex spells this way. The coloring spell was not a difficult one, as her father had told her. It was one of the easiest; a stepping-stone onto far more powerful illusions. But he hadn't been able to teach her any of those before-

She grimaced, forcing the angry thoughts away. This wasn't the time to brood over old wounds and she knew it. *I've got to stay focused today,* she thought to herself. *Scratching old scars just opens them up again.*

There was a knock at the door; she checked that her hair was covering her ears before replying. "Come in." A maid opened the door, the same one who'd drawn Kayrla's bath the night before. She was carrying a tray with a covered platter.

"Good morning, miss," she bubbled at Kayrla. "Would you be

wantin' breakfast?"

"Oh, yes!" Kayrla replied, hopping back onto the bed and waiting as the maid put the tray down in front of her. She lifted the cover to see a large quantity of fruits, sausage and biscuits and she started eating with relish.

The maid watched her for a moment. "Been some time since you've had a square meal, I daresay, miss."

"Long enough," Kayrla replied between bites. Knocking the weevils out of biscuits on board the *Cutlass* had always lowered her appetite, and they'd tasted like stale bricks. Clegg had been a good enough cook when he had the right ingredients to work with, but he'd never got biscuits right to Kayrla's taste. She wondered if he was all right, if Jolly Red might have taken some of his frustration out on the old man last night. She frowned, doubting she'd ever see him again.

"You'll be meeting with the Right Hand this morning," the maid continued, looking at the pile of Kayrla's clothes on the floor with obvious disapproval. "Let's see if we can find a nice dress for you; make you look nice."

"You can't just wash these?" Kayrla asked, pointing at the clothes.

"Not in time, miss...and well, these are boys' clothes, aren't they?"

Kayrla smiled. "A dress isn't much use if you spend all day climbing the rigging. If you could get some more boys' clothes, that would suit me just fine. No fancy costumes or anything; just a shirt and trousers; maybe a vest with some pockets in it. And if you could get the boots polished too; they're broken in and I won't get rid of them for anything."

The maid scowled. "Now, miss...really," she asked. "Pants on such a pretty girl as yourself. What will the Right Hand think?"

"He should be impressed I'm wearing clean clothes to see him," Kayrla replied. "That's not something I've done for any of the captains I've served with, and there's been more of those than you're like to believe."

"As you say, miss," the maid sighed in defeat. "I'll get these boots polished and I'll see if I can find some lad's clothes for you."

"And a scrap of cloth for my head," Kayrla added. "It keeps the hair out of my face."

"Oh, miss," the maid said with disappointment, "Hiding all that pretty hair." She wiggled her fingers with a smile. "I don't get much practice with doing braids these days, but I don't suppose I've forgotten everything yet. Perhaps I could weave a ribbon or two in there as well?"

Kayrla sighed. It was so tempting. She was good at hiding her true nature from others, but she really hated having to do it. When she was at sea with a crew that had come to accept her, she let her hair fly free and her ears stay uncovered. She'd try all sorts of hairstyles just for fun. But she never did that onshore, and she didn't think the maid would keep her enthusiasm once her hands brushed up against Kayrla's pointed ears. *No matter how comfortable this bed is, no matter how good the food is,* she thought, *you are not in a safe place. Don't drop your guard.*

"I just want something simple to keep it out of my face," she said firmly. The maid sighed again, and Kayrla became curious. "Are there no young ladies resident in the estate? You sound like you don't get a chance to help a maid pretty herself very often."

The maid turned somber. "No, miss. There's been no children here for some time, lad or lass. The Duke took a wife some years back, but she, well... she died in the birthing room. The girl didn't survive long either."

"Oh," Kayrla said, "I'm sorry. I didn't know."

"It's all right, miss," the maid replied. "It was some years back now."

"The Duke hasn't remarried?"

"No, miss, that he has not," the maid replied, picking up Kayrla's clothes, her tone suddenly businesslike. "The Right Hand'll be ready to see you soon, and he's not one to be kept waiting. I'll find you some other clothes for today and see if there's any part of this," she held up Kayrla's old clothes, "that's worth salvaging."

Kayrla picked at her food after the maid had left. *If the Duke dies without an heir, who inherits the throne? Could they even claim the title?* She glanced out the window to the rich estates on the opposite side of the city. *Maybe one of them?* She realized with a guilty start she didn't even know the maid's name, and the woman had made several attempts to be friendly.

Ten minutes later the maid bustled back in with a set of clean clothes; a dark brown pair of pants, a red linen shirt a little too large for her, and a simple black vest with an inside pocket. Kayrla dressed eagerly as the maid cleaned her boots.

"Oh, miss…" she said in surprise, "Is this blood on your boot?"

"Not mine," Kayrla replied, tucking the shirt down into the trousers and wrapping her belt about her waist.

"Well, I can't get that stain out now," she said, "not enough time. There's another stain here I don't recognize. Looks sort of glittery."

That would *be my blood,* Kayrla thought. Her color spell changed her blood's appearance as well, but only if it was still in contact with her body. Once it was spilled, the blood resumed its natural color. "I don't know what that's from."

The maid sighed. "Well, miss, that's the best I can do in short order," she said, standing up and handing the boots to Kayrla. "Brushed the dirt and…other things off, but they'll need to be taken to the cobbler if you want them looking like new."

"This will be fine," Kayrla said as she looked in the mirror above the dresser, checking that the tips of her ears were securely tucked under the silken band around her head. She liked the color of the clothes; they suited the colors she'd picked for her skin. "This looks perfect. Thank you, um, I'm sorry…" she trailed off, embarrassed. "I don't know your name."

The maid smiled genially. "There's no rule saying you're required to ask, miss, but I do thank you for it. I'm Ella."

"Well, Ella, my name's Kayrla."

"Odd name, that. Where's it from?" Ella asked curiously.

"Not sure, really," Kayrla replied truthfully. "My father gave it to me." She took one last look at herself in the mirror. "Well, I guess I'm ready to go." As Kayrla tugged her boots on, Ella opened the door and spoke to the guard standing there.

"He says you're to come with him, miss."

Kayrla sighed. "Okay, then." As she passed by Ella, she stopped and said, "Ella. What's the Right Hand like?"

Ella looked thoughtful for a moment. "Sharper than all the pins in my cushion put together, miss. He can hear a lie on your tongue before you speak it, so be honest with him and he'll most like treat fair with you."

"Thanks," Kayrla replied, a flutter of fear in her stomach. "Hopefully I'll see you later."

Chapter Nine

"How did Marsienne get out of Malachi?" Tesca asked Galen. They were back in the library and the older man was reviewing the notes Tesca had brought him. "That's what puzzles me. He designed the siege defenses for at least three cities up there and the sewer systems for their capital. There's no way the crown would have let him travel abroad; he knew too much."

"I heard he may have made some enemies at court," Galen replied. "Enemies that would have run him through in a duel before the crown could intervene. But I also suspect that he finally realized he was trapped. You've met Marsienne yourself. He always struck me as a man convinced of his own genius; full of pride. He wouldn't allow himself to be kept in a cage, even a gilded one."

Tesca nodded. "But how did he get out if he'd have the Malachans on him in a flash?"

Galen lifted his head and smiled. "Use your head, lad. He's the one who designed the sewers of the capital city; he'd put in a few secret passages and make sure they didn't get marked on the official maps, just in case he had to use them." He turned back to the notes, his eyes quickly dashing over the coded writing like it was his native tongue. "It's what I'd do."

"You're right," Tesca added, shaking his head.

Galen finished reading the notes and closed the folio. "I'll take this to His Grace and see how he wants to proceed. Narlos is working on something big; they wouldn't harbor Marsienne just to design a new ship for them. No, it's something more than that."

"You want me to head back to Narlos?" Tesca asked.

"That'll be decided later," Galen said. "You've done good work here, lad. Very good work. I think we'll put other assets in place there, however...it's time to put Narlos under closer observation, and we have other tasks for you." Tesca nodded. "Something wrong?" Galen asked, watching Tesca. "You're distracted this morning."

"It's...her," Tesca said.

"The elf?"

Tesca didn't reply right away. "I'm just wondering if she's going to be treated like the Malachans treated Marsienne. A gilded cage, as you put it."

Galen chuckled. "It's a valid question, lad. She'd be a valuable asset for the Duke. But from what you've said, she's not one to appreciate being caged either, no matter how pretty the bars are."

"No, I don't think she would."

"You still have that annoying tendency of giving undue loyalty to someone who's helped you out in a fight," Galen commented, waggling a finger at Tesca. "'Scrappers' honor' is a romantic notion, lad, but it's a liability. You don't know where she came from. For all you knew last night, your 'accidental' meeting with her could have been staged; a trick to gain your confidence."

"But we know it wasn't," Tesca said. "The reports from our people in Harborside; everything that captain of hers said after–"

"Yes, I know," Galen interrupted, "but that's not the point, lad. Once blades were drawn, you put a lot of trust in her. She could have been an agent for Hisvet, or even one of the local merchant families, looking for a bit of leverage on His Grace. Or, maybe she's working for the Sabrians."

"Not the Empire," Tesca replied. "They hate elves."

"They hate magic," Galen corrected. "It can't be any comfort to them to know that where magic has become strong, gunpowder is less reliable." He tapped the folio. "The Malachans hired Marsienne to redesign their cities' defenses because their cannon and rifles aren't as useful as they were before the Elflands returned. Don't think the Sabrians aren't aware of that. The reason for their success to date has been that their navy is the strongest afloat; their ships are faster and their cannon are more powerful. But if those wonderful cannon only fire half the time, they lose their edge." He leaned back in his chair. "And now you bring home an elf, an elf you say can cast spells down here, in the Frees. If that's the case, it means the magic is spreading. It's not just confined to the mainland, like everyone thinks. The Sabrians want to expand further north; if they learn magic is going to make their guns useless here in, say, another ten or twenty years, what's to stop them from invading now, before that happens?"

"So if they hate magic that much, what makes you think they'd use an elf as an agent?" Tesca asked.

"No one would ever suspect it," said Galen. "Think, lad. If the Sabrians were able to get an elf or two on their side, maybe they could figure out how to make magic work for them, sow a bit of unrest and confusion in the Frees, soften us up for an invasion." He sighed. "But the news from Harborside this morning doesn't fit that theory."

"I know that fight wasn't staged," Tesca said. "She killed one of the pirates herself, and when we were running across the rooftops and she almost fell, I could see real fear in her eyes when I caught her."

"Your instincts are pretty good," Galen agreed, "despite that blind spot you allow yourself." He watched Tesca for a few moments, then continued. "The castellan told me you offered her the chance to leave the manor last night. You knew I might not let her leave once I knew about her." Tesca shrugged; Galen smiled at him. "You're convinced she's not an agent; I'm leaning that way but I'll meet her first before making my decision. At a guess, though, she's got the same blind spot you do." He sighed. "Scrapper's honor."

Tesca gave a faint smile. "That, and I owe her money."

Galen chuckled. "The guard said the maid's taken her a set of fresh clothes; she should be here before long. We'll lay things out for her and see which direction she goes."

A few minutes later, there was a knock at the door and the guard entered, bringing Kayrla in with him.

"Thank you," Galen said to the guard. "You may go." The guard closed the door. "Do you know who I am?" Galen asked her.

Kayrla looked from Tesca to Galen. "He seems to defer to you, which I haven't seen him do to anyone else. I can't imagine I'd be allowed to meet the Duke alone like this, so you must be the Right Hand."

Galen smiled. "That's correct. You understand the nature of this meeting?"

She nodded. "Tesca's told you about me; you want to see me for yourself before you decide if I'm of use to you." She looked at Tesca again. "And, if I'm not of use to you, you'll decide what's to be done with me."

"Straight talk," Galen said, still smiling. "I appreciate that. What is your name, miss?"

"Kayrla."

"Your full name, please."

She hesitated, frowning. "Kayrla é sa-Kyrloun."

Galen narrowed his eyes, thinking. "Kyrloun means you're of the Water clan, doesn't it?"

Kayrla blinked in surprise. No human had ever known the meaning of her surname before. "Yes," she breathed. "How did you know?"

"Your people have been emigrating into our world for over fifty years," Galen replied. "Some humans have written down what little they've learned of your people, and copies of what they've written down are valuable documents now. I have managed, over the years, to collect a few of them." He leaned forward, curious. "All of the records I've seen say that the elves are unwilling to discuss the Elflands themselves. Are you equally reticent?"

She smiled sadly with a shrug. Telling a lie here could be fatal, so she decided total honesty was the only safe course. "I can't tell you about the Elflands, because I've never been there. I was born in Terendor."

Both men were astonished. "How old are you?" Galen asked.

"Around thirty years," she replied. "I'm not sure of the exact date."

Galen studied her closely, then leaned back in his chair. "Well, Kayrla. Since you know why you're here, I would like to see what you can do."

She nodded and looked at a small lamp on the table next to him. Taking a moment to concentrate, she cast one of her spells. The lamp's wick glowed for a moment, then popped into flame. Galen started at that, but recovered quickly.

"So it's true," he said, half to himself. "You can perform magic, even this far south."

"Not very well," she admitted, "and if we went any further south, I doubt I could do even that."

"I see," Galen replied, fascinated. "And I am told that you can disguise yourself?"

"I'm disguised right now. He's seen me do it," she said with a nod at Tesca.

"Can you turn off your disguise?"

She nodded, thinking now that recasting the spell earlier had been a waste of time. Of course this man would want to see her perform magic. Very likely, he'd never actually seen any magic before in his life.

Turning the spell off was far easier than casting it. With a thought, she tugged loose the patterns of mana about her and the spell unraveled quickly. In a few seconds, she stood before them unglamored, her hair and skin their proper green and blue tones.

Galen stared at her, nodding. "The Water tribe indeed. Do you have an affinity with water?"

She raised an eyebrow at him. "An affinity? I love being on the sea. The wind in my hair, spray on my face; I'm happiest there." She shrugged. "There's many a human sailor who'd say the same. But if I take your real meaning, I don't believe my lineage grants me any magical influence over the water. I don't know any spells to affect water, that's for certain."

"I see," Galen replied. "Well, let's get to the main business, then.

Tesca says he owes you money. Is that why you came here?"

She thought for a moment. "At first," she admitted. "I wasn't going to let him walk off with a promise to pay me. I came with him to make sure I got what I was mine. Once I saw where he was going," she sighed, "I knew I couldn't just let him go into the manor on his own. He'd tell whomever he worked for about me, and then you'd send someone to find me. That meeting might have been less pleasant than this." She watched Galen shrug and knew she was right.

"Well, you will get paid," Galen promised. "By helping Tesca get here safely, you've done His Grace a service, and that shall be rewarded. And yes, if I had learned there was an elf in Kohayne who could cast spells, I'd have dug you out of whatever bolt-hole you'd hidden yourself in. Not to kill you, though," he assured her.

"Unless I was already working for someone else," she said.

Galen shrugged again. "Possibly. I would certainly have made you an offer at the very least."

"Well, I'm not working for anyone at the moment," said Kayrla, "As Tesca no doubt told you, I've parted ways with my latest captain."

"Oh, yes," Galen said. "I've already had word from some of my people in the city below. Your former captain is not happy with you, not happy at all."

Kayrla felt a chill run through her. "What's Jolly Red up to?"

"According to my sources, he spent the remainder of last night after you got away cursing your name and telling everyone who passed by to 'never trust an elf'. He's promised two hundred and fifty gold marks to anyone who brings him your ears, whether they're attached to your head or not. But he's offering five hundred marks to anyone who brings you to him, alive and untouched."

Tesca spoke up. "We only learned it this morning, Kayrla. I'm sorry."

She barely heard him; her knees felt weak. "He's telling everyone about me? He's put a price on my head?"

Galen nodded. "It's not so much the bounty that worries us. It's that other people may start looking for you to keep you for themselves." He smiled sadly at her. "I'm sorry, my dear...but for your own safety, I cannot allow you to leave the manor."

Chapter Ten

Kayrla looked down at herself, trying to gauge the success of her work. "All right, you can turn around now." Tesca turned and looked at her. Kayrla could feel every square inch of her being carefully examined as her friend walked in a slow circle around her. "Well?"

Finally Tesca stopped, a thoughtful frown on his face. "Your ears are still too long."

"Damnation!" Kayrla swore, stepping towards a chair and sitting down. "I thought I'd gotten the ears sorted out."

"You got the ears once yesterday," Tesca offered, "but then your hair went all green."

Kayrla sighed with exhaustion and sipped from a large goblet of wine on the table next to her. She let the new spell she was developing unravel, resuming her normal appearance and color. "Not enough… mana," she panted. "There just isn't enough this far south."

From somewhere outside her window, she heard the music of a small orchestra begin once again, and she ground her teeth in frustration. "And it doesn't make it any easier with that garbage going on!"

Tesca sighed. "Well, the music won't be going on that much longer. The fete's only a few days off now." He tilted his head to listen. "And you have to admit they're getting better."

"That doesn't help," she snapped. "If they just played a song straight through, that would be fine; I could get used to it. But they keep stopping and starting and repeating the same part over and over."

"It's rehearsal; they're doing it until they get it right. That's very much like what you're doing, isn't it?"

She was tempted to hurl the goblet at him, but decided not to waste the wine. She'd been a guest of the Duke for over two weeks now. Kayrla had expected Jolly Red to give up his search for her long before and sail off in frustration. She'd only taken her fair share of the swag, after all. But the *Cutlass* was still anchored in Kohayne harbor, and according to Tesca, Red had paid the harbor fees to remain docked there for some time to come.

Harborside was afire with gossip and news about "the elf." Jolly had been telling any who would listen that Kayrla frequently used magic to change the color of her skin and hair, but he also said that she still looked like an elf under the long hair and kerchiefs bound over the tips of her long ears. Her disguise was ruined.

She glared at a large moneybag on her dresser, a visible reminder of how she'd gotten into this mess. True to his word, Galen had made sure she'd gotten the money Tesca owed her, and had added to it considerably, as a reward for helping Tesca deliver his information. Kayrla had been so pleased with this that she'd given her promise to both of them that she would not try to leave the estate until the furor had died down over her. But as it became clear that her former captain was still fanning the fires in an attempt to find her, she had come to regret making that promise. It was more money than she'd ever had at one time before, but she had nowhere to spend it. She couldn't even open the bag anymore; just the sight of the coins galled her.

Tesca smiled down at her in sympathy. "I'm sure you'll come up with something." He tried to sound encouraging. "I think you're getting closer."

Kayrla flashed him an angry look. "You're just saying that," she grated. "The spell's just too complicated. It's like juggling too many balls at once." At first, the idea of improving her illusion spell had seemed like a good one. Having a human's coloring wasn't enough anymore, thanks to Jolly Red. She knew she had to make her features look human as well if she ever wanted to get out of the estate.

Her progress had been very encouraging at first. She quickly figured out how to make either her ears or her eyes look human, and from there she became capable of altering both at the same time. This did not make her look completely human, however. As she altered her spell to mask her sharper cheekbones, she then realized she also needed to round out her chin. All the little differences between human and elf skulls became glaringly apparent as she made constant modifications to the illusion, all of which added to the spell's complexity. She struggled through these changes, but once she tried adding her color alteration into it, something she thought would be the easiest part, the spell became virtually impossible to maintain. There were simply too many things going on at once, and weaving them all together into one spell drew on more mana than was readily available.

"Well," said Tesca, not sure how to respond, "you could take a break from this while they're practicing outside. I'll have to head down to Harborside before too long, but there's still time for some blade practice if you're interested."

She smiled at him from the chair, too weary to move. "Tempting offer, Tesca. But I've got no strength left this morning. Will you be back this evening? I'd relish it then."

"We'll see," Tesca commented. "I don't know how long I'll be. But I'll stop by when I get back and we'll set a time for pract–"

There was a knock at the door. Tesca turned towards it, blocking Kayrla from view as Kayrla called out, "Who is it?"

"It's Ella, miss!" called the maid from the other side of the door. "I've just been to the laundry and have some clean clothes for you here." Kayrla and Tesca both relaxed.

"Come in, please," called Kayrla. The door opened and Ella bustled in, carrying a large basket of clothes and bumping the door shut with her hip. She looked startled, as she always did, when she saw Kayrla in her natural colors. "Been at your disguise again, miss?" she asked, looking at Kayrla's slumped posture and half-empty goblet.

"Once more," Kayrla said with a nod. Once it had become clear that Kayrla would need to stay longer than a few days, Galen and

Tesca agreed to bring two more members of the estate's staff in on her true nature. The castellan had been the first, to adjust his security arrangements to include the new guest. And for Kayrla's comfort, they explained the situation to Ella, who attended the Duke himself and whose loyalty was unquestioned.

The maid had received quite a shock to discover the young lady she'd been looking after was actually an elf only a few years younger than herself. Getting over her surprise quickly, she seemed delighted that there was at last a female in the manor to look after, and her attempts to put Kayrla in a dress continued unabated. For her part, Kayrla was grateful for Ella's frequent company. It meant that even if she was more or less confined to her room, she didn't have to keep her ears hidden as well. Keeping them bound against the side of her head became painful after a while.

"Well, you rest now," Ella clucked, setting the basket down on a small table at the foot of Kayrla's bed. "I'll put these clothes away and then bring you some lunch." She looked at Tesca. "Will that be lunch for two, Master Secarius?"

Tesca shook his head. "I'm afraid duty draws me away, but only for a short time, I hope." He smiled at Kayrla. "Keep at it, and don't let that music drive you insane, all right? It's only for a few more days."

"I'll try," she said to him as he headed out the door. Sighing, she sipped her wine, listening to the music stop once more. She could hear the conductor yelling at one of his musicians and rolled her eyes. "Just a few more days," she muttered.

"Oh yes, miss!" gushed Ella, folding clothes with a practiced and professional speed, "the entire estate is in an uproar for the Duke's Ascension Day. Twenty-five years he'll have been on the throne. There'll be guests from all over the Frees!"

Kayrla looked glum. "Quite a party, eh? I suppose I'll enjoy the sound of it from here."

Ella looked sympathetic. "Ah, miss…I'm sorry you won't be able to attend."

"It's not like I was going to get an invitation before meeting Tesca, is it?" Kayrla said with a shrug. "Tell me more about the party. If I can't go, I at least want to hear what's being planned."

"As you wish, miss," Ella replied, her eyes twinkling with excitement. "Well, first of all, everyone's got to present themselves before the Duke and offer congratulations to him. Then comes the presents!"

Some thirty minutes later, Kayrla sighed and looked wistful. "Oh, that sounds just delightful…now I really wish I could go."

"Well, miss," the maid replied, "if you could get this disguise of yours working, I daresay the Right Hand might allow you to attend."

"Not a chance," Kayrla replied.

"Well now, you'll not know until you try, will you?"

Kayrla shook her head. "No, it's just…" she trailed off. "It's too hard, Ella. There isn't enough mana."

"What do you mean, there's not enough mana, miss?" Ella asked. "You've told me time and again about this stuff you call mana, but I still don't understand it."

"Well, it's…mana is… mana is like water," Kayrla began. "Water for spells. Plants need water to grow, right?" Ella nodded. "Let's say my disguise spell is like a…potted plant. It needs water, or mana, to stay alive. It's not a big spell, so I don't need that much mana to keep it going. But trying to add a much harder illusion to that spell, like changing my face, that's suddenly a much bigger plant. I can't carry enough water to the pot to keep that plant alive."

Ella seemed lost in thought, furrows appearing on her brow. Then she looked at Kayrla, curious. "Pardon my saying, miss, and this may be a stupid question, mind you, but…"

"No, please. Go on," urged Kayrla.

"Well, miss," said Ella. "I think I understand you, talking about mana as if it were water. There's been plenty of times I've had a job where I had to keep someone's plants watered, and I learned quick that it's far easier to carry two smaller pails of water than one big one. Perhaps you can water these two plants one at a time?"

"I don't think I follow–" Kayrla started to say, but then she froze, astonished, as Ella's words sunk in. "By the Deeps," she whispered, "you're a genius…"

Chapter Eleven

Tesca thought his disguise was rather good, even if he couldn't cast a spell to change his color. Padding under his shirt made his waist seem wider than it was, the false nose and beard would stay in place as long as he didn't walk into anyone, and a few spritzes from a perfume bottle filled with cheap rum completed the illusion of an old sailor down on his luck. But these were all just parts of a costume. It was the attitude that was the most important. He recalled Galen's instructions from a few years ago: *"The most important aspect of any disguise is projecting the attitude that wherever you find yourself, you seem to belong there. Outsiders, nervous visitors and showing hesitation: these things are noticed faster than a false wig."*

So Tesca had created the identity of Jargy Barluf, a likeable but chatty drunk, and someone who'd tell you what he knew for the price of another drink. When Tesca wasn't away from the Quad, he made sure Jargy made the rounds at least once or twice a week. He was an accepted, if often ridiculed, member of Harborside, a familiar face in many of the taverns. Tesca had taken care to get thrown out of several of them as well to further solidify Jargy's reputation.

Tesca tipped back his mug of ale, taking care to let some of it trickle down into his beard while not swallowing any of it. He watched Jolly Red on the other side of the tavern. The beefy freebooter had made the corner booth of the Lark's Song his unofficial office since he'd put a price on Kayrla's head. The layout of the Song was such that the corner booth was on an elevated platform running along one side of the tavern. It was too far from the main floor for conversations to be overheard, and curtains could be drawn across the booth's opening for greater privacy. Jolly also always had at least two of the *Cutlass's* crew with him who stood as sentinels on both sides of the booth.

At the moment, Kayrla's former captain was having a conversation with two men that had come into the tavern ten minutes ago to see him. Tesca noticed that both men had been required to surrender their blades to Jolly's guards before being allowed to sit with him. He found that interesting, and took in as many details as he could about Jolly's two guests. They resembled each other enough that he suspected they were brothers, or at least cousins. They were probably Tesca's height or slightly shorter, with dark tanned skin and bright eyes. Both wore brightly colored, striped sashes instead of belts, knotted on the opposite hips from their now empty scabbards. That was a custom of the men of Mypor, one of the smallest and northernmost of the Frees.

Jolly Red made several gestures towards his own face as he spoke, tugging at the far corners of his eyes and then touching the top of one of his ears. Tesca had seen that before; the captain was describing Kayrla to them as he had to several other guests over the past two weeks. *More bounty hunters,* Tesca thought to himself. He watched Jolly Red shake the Myporeans' hands and bid them farewell.

He calculated the average travel time between here and Mypor, and decided that if these two had come from their home island, then word of Jolly Red's bounty would be all over the Frees by now, and more hunters would be arriving for weeks to come.

Shortly after learning of the bounty on Kayrla's life, Tesca had suggested removing Jolly Red, either banishing him from Kohayne as "a disturber of the peace," or simply assassinating him. Galen had rejected both ideas outright. *"Under no account,"* he had told Tesca, *"are we going to take any action that indicates His Grace is even remotely concerned with this affair. If anyone suspected that the Duke was harboring her, how long would it be before some of those freebooters tried to sneak onto the estate and have a look around? The castellan's having fits as it is, with the Ascension festivities so close."* And that had been that. Tesca felt that the only option left was laying a false trail, to make it appear that Kayrla had slipped on board a ship that had already left Kohayne.

But whatever ploy was tried, Tesca knew things couldn't go on like this much longer. At the best of times, Harborside could be a rough place for young women trying to make it on their own. Now it was perilous, especially at night. As part of the Quad's preparations for Ascension Day, the city watch had increased patrols, and was making sure all the street lamps in the city remained lit. These had made Harborside less dangerous, but Tesca was still hearing tales of women being accosted and sometimes even dragged off before their captors realized they weren't elves. Sometimes these women had been released, the stories said, and sometimes they hadn't.

Even if she perfects that new disguise spell, Tesca thought, *until that hunt's called off, she still might not be safe in Harborside.* He'd come to some basic understanding of how magic worked by watching Kayrla struggle through the spell she was working on, and it seemed to him that magic was a discipline, no different from swordplay. One could dabble in a discipline and develop a modicum of skill; enough to get by. But to become a master of a discipline took constant, concentrated effort. Kayrla, he judged, had been a dabbler with both sword and spell. She wasn't bad with a blade; in a tavern brawl or against almost any sailor she'd do just fine. But against one of these hunters, she'd be cut to ribbons in short order. Similarly, she had learned a few simple spells and was very clever in finding ways to use them. But for one reason or another, she had never learned any more magic than those few tricks. Now, she had to teach herself a new spell, one that required greater dedication than he suspected she'd ever applied to anything.

I hope she works it out, he thought. He enjoyed her company and knew how much she hated being cooped up in the manor, but unless she found a way to really change her appearance, she might be stuck there for a good deal longer. He wondered when her frustration might overcome her promise and drive her out into Harborside, where an ever-growing number of predators would be waiting for her.

He set his mug down, belched for effect, and leaned back in his chair, feigning a dreamy, contented smile. He called to Morwen, the innkeeper, for another mug of ale. "And who's paying for this one, you old sot?" Morwen called back from behind the bar, crossing her arms and glaring at him.

"Well, lass," Tesca replied in an easy, creaking drawl, "I hoped maybe I could play upon yer generosity. Or perhaps I could do you a... little service?" he said, grinning wolfishly at her.

"I doubt you've serviced any woman in over twenty years, Jargy Barluf!" Morwen snapped back, but there was laughter in her voice. Tesca had been coming in here as Jargy for some time now, and he and the innkeeper had formed an odd relationship. As barflies went, Jargy was less noisome than others and he generally found someone to pay off his bar tab. Sometimes, it was Morwen herself. The tavern-keep found him amusing, and also made use of him as a gossip source. Right now, however, his tab was higher than she was willing to cancel.

"It's been only twelve years and three months since my last tumble," he corrected her, his head lolling to one side as he continued to grin. "I'd still be making the ladies happy, though...if I didn't find ale generally preferable. Ale doesn't need you to tell it that it looks pretty once you've finished with it."

Morwen rolled her eyes as the nearby patrons at the bar burst out laughing. "Be that as it may, Jargy Barluf, your tab is getting fatter than you are. I'm not standing you another drink until it shrinks down, at least a little."

Tesca frowned. "Well, then," he said with a plaintive look at the other patrons around him, "is there anyone here who'd buy an old man a drink for a bit of news?"

"I'll pay for that honor," called Jolly Red from his corner. He'd stood up from the table to get a better look into the main room. "Give that old man a mug of ale and send him this way."

Tesca was surprised by this. Though he'd been in here almost every day since Jolly had declared the bounty on Kayrla, the captain hadn't so much as glanced at him before. It was risky getting within weapon's reach of him, Tesca knew. The booth was a cramped space; if Jolly recognized him, Tesca wasn't sure he'd be able to fight his way out. But he hadn't learned much by just watching the captain day after day. So with a cackling grin, he scooped up the new drink and ambled over to the other side of the tavern.

One of Red's men stopped him. "Got any weapons on you, old man?"

Tesca looked nervous. "Well, got a knife in my belt, but that's all." He raised both of his arms, took a sip of the ale with one hand, and drew out the knife by his fingertips with the other. The man took the blade from him, then looked him over for a few moments and stepped aside. Tesca slid into the booth on the opposite side from Jolly Red. "So, asking ol' Jargy for the news?"

Jolly Red adjusted his large frame behind the table, wincing as he sat down. Tesca took some satisfaction in the fact that the sword wound he'd dealt Jolly still pained him. "The longer I stay in this city, friend," Jolly rumbled, "the more I hear that you're someone I should talk to if I want to find someone in Harborside."

"That may be," Tesca rasped. He played up a nervous air, tapping his fingers on the table and glancing nervously at Jolly's guards. "I'll share what I hear with anyone who buys me a round." He laughed. "But there's those who know it's best to find me before too many have bought me drinks. I don't make up things, sirrah, but my memory does get a bit fuzzy later in the evening."

Jolly Red laughed with him. "And how many drinks have you earned today?"

"Yours is the first," Tesca replied proudly. "I'm as sharp as a pen, sirrah."

"Very well, Jargy," Red replied, his deep voice lowering to a near-whisper. "By now, you know who I'm looking for."

Tesca nodded. "Aye, sirrah. Everyone knows who you're looking for. The word of coin on the wind brings sharks faster than blood in the water. The streets of Harborside are churning like I've not seen before."

"But you haven't seen her, have you?"

Tesca cackled. "I'd have been to see you first thing with my palm outstretched if I had."

"Fair enough," said Jolly, chuckling. "What have you heard?"

Tesca sighed and took a fake pull from his mug. "Heard that somebody saw a girl with green hair sail out of Kohayne two days past, on the *Phaedra*, bound for Narlos."

"The *Phaedra*..." Jolly Red muttered. "No, the captain let my boys search her before she sailed. I offered the captain the entire bounty if we found her there. I make that offer to every ship that leaves Kohayne, you know, and most of them take it." He shook his head, chuckling with malice. "No, she's still here somewhere, Jargy. And she's not so stupid as to let her real hair color be seen. I know her."

Tesca shrugged, hiding his frustration. He knew when Galen learned of this, he would tell Tesca that he'd expected it all along. "Well, sirrah, that's a smart move, I'd say. But, well, that's what I'd heard."

The bulky man frowned and opened his mouth to speak when he stopped, glancing towards the front door of the tavern. Tesca turned his head to look, and was surprised to see the old Sabrian he'd almost dueled a few weeks ago enter the tavern, look around and then walk towards them.

Jolly's two guards stepped up to intercept the man, who stopped before them but did not waste a glance upon them. He was dressed in comfortable Sabrian silks, loose, billowing and brightly colored, though Tesca thought they looked a bit threadbare in some places. The Argument and the Retort, the long and short blades worn by the Sabrian elite, hung at his hips. "I understand," the man said to Jolly Red in his thick, sing-song accent, "that you are looking for someone."

Chapter Twelve

"I understand," said the Sabrian, "that you are looking for someone."

Jolly Red studied the Sabrian for a moment, then nodded. "That I am. Give my men your weapons, and you may join me at table." He gestured to the open space on the bench next to Tesca.

The man glanced at the two guards and the faintest expression of scorn crossed his face. "These swords part with me at death only," he said. "I will speak from here." His tone remained calm, but Tesca could read Sabrian body language, and the man's posture had shifted at Jolly Red's words. He was mortally offended at the idea of surrendering his weapons to men he considered to be barbarians.

Jolly scowled at the man. He'd clearly had his own share of Sabrian pride in his time and had no taste for more. "Speak, then."

"I saw the one you are seeking," the man said, "on the night she escaped you. There was a man with her."

"Yes," Jolly replied, "her partner."

"I can tell you about this man," the Sabrian said, "for a price." Tesca felt a chill run through him.

"The bounty is not on the man," objected Jolly Red, "it's on the elf."

"But I assure you that she is still with him," the Sabrian replied. "Find him and you find her."

Jolly considered the man carefully, chewing his moustache. Kayrla said the captain always did that when he couldn't make up his mind about something. Finally he spoke. "All right. Five marks for what you know."

"Ten of those gold coins is the lowest I will accept."

"Ten?!?" barked Jolly Red. "Are you mad? Ten marks for news that I might already know?"

"You do not know it," the Sabrian replied in that same calm, confident tone he'd used since he arrived. "And I will not settle for less than ten."

Jolly Red chewed on his moustache for a few more seconds. Then he grumbled and took the money from his purse. "If your news is worthless, I'll be having those back," he added, handing the coins to one of his men, who passed it to the Sabrian. The Sabrian accepted them and tucked them into a belt pouch. He made no response to Jolly's threat. Tesca thought perhaps the man hadn't recognized the statement as such.

"You have men in great numbers searching the streets of Harborside for this…being," he said, his lip curling slightly in distaste. "Her description is well-known to all by now. I heard this description and realized at once who you were searching for."

"You knew she was an elf when you saw her?"

The Sabrian paused in reflection. "No. But there was something not…correct about her. Her face, her manner of walking. These were not," he paused again, "proper. She had a purse at her waist, containing a pendant, with a red jewel."

Jolly Red went very still. "Does she still have it?"

The Sabrian shrugged. "She did when she left my sight." The lines at the corners of his eyes deepened for a moment, and Tesca realized the Sabrian, like him, had taken note of Jolly's intense interest in the pendant.

"Very well," Jolly snapped. "Get on with your tale."

"As you wish," said the Sabrian. "I have been paid. And I deliver you that which I promised. You speak to any and all of the elf that has escaped you, but you make no mention of the man that was with her."

"So you said before, Sabrian," Jolly snapped. "I said get on with it!"

"This man, he fought with two swords, did he not?"

Jolly hesitated, then nodded. "He did."

"Two swords much like mine, yes?"

Jolly leaned to one side to see past his guards. "Yes, like yours."

The Sabrian made a satisfied nod. "This is the same man I saw, then. Very well, I tell you that you are looking in the wrong place for her, and now I am certain. This man, he is in the service of another."

Jolly peered closely at him. "Who?"

"I do not know who the master of this man is," admitted the Sabrian, "but he will be someone of wealth. And power. Perhaps even this one who gives himself the self-important title of Duke." The Sabrian did not hide the scorn in his voice at that. "Men such as the one you should be seeking are valuable…" he paused, apparently trying to find the right word, "commodities. Only the richest can afford their services. If your elf was with this man, he was bringing her to his master, and there she will be found."

"But you don't know who the man is yourself, or who he works for?" Jolly replied, still angry. "I pay you ten marks so I can start a second manhunt?"

The Sabrian shrugged again. "Yes, if you wish to complete the first. Those who seek her have only done so in Harborside, I think. They have not looked to the slopes and manor houses above them. That is why they have not found her."

"I'm not about to start sending men into the homes of every single noble and rich merchant on this island," Jolly said. "Like as not I'd be dancing the jerk-neck jangle from the Eisenteeth before the day was out."

"Did I tell you to do that?" the Sabrian said. "I said you should find the man who fled with the elf. If you learn whom he serves, you will know where she is. I have told you what I know; I have been paid. I will go now." He stepped back crisply, turned on his heel and strode from the tavern. Jolly, his men and Tesca all stared at the ebon-skinned man as he left.

"Well, that's something I haven't seen before," wheezed Tesca, trying to break the ice. "That black fellow must be mad."

Jolly Red stared at the open doorway where the Sabrian had left, chewing on his moustache. "Maybe," he mused, "but he was right about the man with her." He looked at Tesca. "Have you seen a man like that, Jargy? Younger than me, dark hair. Wears two blades, Sabrian style, and knows how to use 'em."

Tesca shook his head. "Men with two blades I've seen aplenty, sirrah. But one such as that? No, that I've not seen, not wearing the Sabrian pair."

Jolly nodded as if that was the answer he'd been expecting. He glanced up, towards the tavern's wall, as if he could see through it towards the richer homes and estates rising up above Harborside. "Rich and powerful…" he muttered, shaking his head. "This is getting out of hand…"

"How's that, sirrah?" Tesca asked, but Jolly gave a start, alarmed that he'd spoken out loud before one of Harborside's most notorious gossips.

"Never you mind, old man," the captain snapped. "Finish your ale and leave me in peace." Tesca nodded, trying to appear scared. As he rose from the table, Jolly dropped his large, meaty hand over Tesca's own. "And another thing, Jargy." His voice dropped to a whisper. "If I hear any whispers about town concerning this Sabrian and what he told me, it's you that'll be doing the jerk-neck jangle, understand?"

"Well enough, sirrah," Tesca said, slipping his hand out from under Jolly's before the captain noticed the makeup. He stepped away from the table, retrieved his knife from one of the guards, and shambled to the door.

Once outside, he was tempted to track down the Sabrian. The black-skinned bastard had just pointed Jolly Red in the right direction to find Kayrla, and for only ten gold marks. But he didn't dare go after him immediately; Galen had to be told of this new development first. And in any case, he didn't want to start shadowing the Sabrian dressed as Jargy Barluf. The Sabrian had keen eyes and quick wit; he would surely spot the same old drunkard who'd been sitting with Jolly Red only a short time before.

He ambled past the docks, then crossed the Duke's Bridge into the northern half of Harborside. He took his time, moving at the speed Jargy Barluf always took to get anywhere, moving up one small alley to relieve himself, then over two blocks to beg a small, freshly baked slice of bread from a baker who didn't chase him away at first sight. He continued along this meandering course for some time, doubling back often enough to ensure that he wasn't being followed. Then, ducking into another alley, he jotted down a quick message to Galen in the Duke's private code language. After that, he resumed his amiable wandering, finally reaching a glassblower's shop, the front awning festooned with numerous examples of the shop's wares. Small bottles, flasks and wind chimes made from flat, round ovals of colored glass hung everywhere, clinking together in a pleasant, quiet sound that Tesca could hear long before he came in sight of the place.

A smile on his face, he lurched into the shop with a wide grin. "Amio!" he wheezed at the shopkeeper, "how nice to see you!"

The shopkeeper was a solid, aged man with wispy gray hair floating around his temples. He looked up, aghast, as Tesca entered. He had been speaking to two customers, a well-to-do matron and a young woman with her, probably her daughter. Their faces were already twisted in disgust as they turned to look at him. Tesca noticed that many people did that; he decided it was either because he'd successfully cultivated Jargy's reputation so that most people were repulsed by him on sight, or that the atrocious odor he also cultivated had gotten here ahead of him.

"Oh, Triad's Mercy," Amio muttered. Then his voice snapped out, powerful and clear. "Off with you, scum!"

"Amio, Amio," said Tesca, shaking his head, "is that any way to treat with an old friend?"

"Old friend, my arse!" Amio retorted, stepping forward to interpose himself between Tesca and his customers. Over his shoulder, he said to them, "I've never seen this fellow before, I swear it." The matron looked as if she might faint. Amio's expression became fierce as he moved towards Tesca. "Get out!" he yelled. "Get out of here now!" His arms were like pistons, alternating shoves as he pushed Tesca out the door. In the struggle, Tesca had plenty of opportunity to drop the message for Galen into Amio's pocket.

"Hey now, hey now!" Tesca said, sounding affronted, as Amio tossed him back into the street. Glaring down at him, the shopkeeper plunged a hand into the pocket Tesca had dropped the note. He sighed, drawing out a moneypurse.

"Thought you'd get this in your clutches, didn't you?" Amio snapped, waving the bag at him. "Now clear off before I call the watch!"

Muttering a curse, Tesca sneered at Amio and shuffled off. The message for Galen would be in his hands before long. He shambled back into the twisted alleys of Harborside. Once it was dark, he'd put Jargy Barluf to bed and reclaim his blades. Then, he thought, he would pay that Sabrian a visit.

Chapter Thirteen

Kayrla was excited. The new direction Ella had suggested for her spell-work was feeling more and more like the right one. Maintaining two spells at once would require a bit more concentration, but she thought she'd be able to handle it with practice. The real problem was the lack of mana; she still wasn't sure there was enough of it this far south to fuel two spells at once, even ones as small as these. *That's a second sea to sail,* she thought, staring at her altered appearance in the mirror. *Let's cross the one we're on first.*

There was a knock at the door. "Who is it?" she called.

"The castellan," came the gruff reply.

"Just a minute," she replied, letting her spells fade and resuming her normal appearance. "Come in."

The door opened and the castellan entered. Kayrla guessed that he was somewhere around Ella's age, but his stern, inflexible manner made him seem older. She wasn't sure if the man liked her or not; there had been an occasional tightening of his jaw muscles as he looked at her, as if he considered her a threat to the Duke. *He might not be wrong,* she admitted to herself.

"The Right Hand has sent for you," the castellan said formally. This was not an unexpected situation for Kayrla. Since she'd been here, Galen had called for her on several occasions. The first sessions had been full of questions about elves and the Elflands. When it became clear to Galen that she probably knew less about the Elflands than he did himself, he changed topics. He was curious about magic, but he also asked her about what she knew regarding various ships that sailed the Frees, when she'd seen them last and if she knew, where they were bound.

"Of course," she replied, stepping away from the mirror. "Let me put on the right colors first, if that's all right."

The castellan grunted in response and Kayrla began to cast her old disguise spell. With all the work she'd been doing, this spell was almost child's play now; as easy as putting on a favorite jacket. This gave her confidence that her new spell, once she'd finished with it, would become as easy to cast one day.

The castellan's face was unreadable as he watched the dark colors flow over her skin. "I've never seen magic before," he said after she finished.

"You've seen me with these colors before," she said, wrapping the bandanna around her head and tucking the tips of her ears beneath it.

"But I've never seen you actually do magic," the castellan replied. "Easy enough to imagine you pulling out a big jar of paint and daubing yourself up all brown. But to see you just wave your hands and…" he trailed off.

"It's not as easy as it looks," she said to him, buckling her belt around her waist. "And it doesn't do me much good outside the estate."

The castellan nodded. "True. It's good to keep up appearances while you're here, though. My men are loyal and can be trusted, but it's best not to give men too many opportunities to betray that trust. They've all heard about your old captain's bounty, and there's no point letting them see a blue-skinned girl about the place. Even the thickest of my men could make that connection." He shrugged. "Let's not keep the Hand waiting any longer, shall we?"

Kayrla nodded and followed him into the hall. She knew the way to the library by heart now; Galen had never received her anywhere else. They periodically passed guards who saluted the castellan. Kayrla noted that there were more guards in the halls than when she had first come here. The castellan had increased security with Ascension

Day fast approaching. Kayrla had spent a good deal of time watching what she could see of the bustling activity from her window. Workers were constructing a set of stands for guests to watch the performances, the groundskeepers were engaged in full-scale war with the undergrowth that constantly encroached upon the covered walkways and fresh foodstuffs were being loaded into the storerooms from sunup to sundown.

When they reached the library door, the castellan knocked twice, then entered. Kayrla followed him inside. Galen, as always, was reading a book that was lying open on the large table in the center of the room. He had glanced up as the door had opened, nodded in recognition, then bent down over the book again. "Thank you, castellan," he said as Kayrla approached. "You may go."

The castellan glanced at Kayrla, then nodded and left. Kayrla stayed where she was, waiting for Galen to speak. Sometimes this took several minutes, but she'd learned that Galen did things at his own pace and did not appreciate having his thoughts interrupted by her speaking out of turn. She didn't mind. *He's kept me safe this long,* she thought, *silence is simple enough to return.*

Galen did not keep her waiting long this time, however. Only a few seconds after the castellan had left, he gestured for her to have a seat on the couch. As he settled into a chair next to her, Kayrla could see the book he brought with him was a collection of illustrations of fine jewelry. The drawings were very finely done; she thought they might be works of art by themselves.

"I've had word from Tesca," the older man said, taking a folded note from a pouch on his belt.

"Is he still in Harborside?"

"He is," Galen said, "but he's in the middle of something and couldn't bring this news to me in person. It's rather interesting news, though."

Kayrla was intrigued. "Good news or bad news?"

Galen frowned. "All news has value. The worst news in the world is still better than ignorance."

"All right," Kayrla replied, more to humor the spymaster than to agree with him. "What's the news? I assume it's about me. You wouldn't have sent for me otherwise."

"It is," Galen began. "I have some more questions for you, though."

"Of course."

"When you took your share of Jolly Red's, ah…inventory," Galen said delicately, "you didn't only take coins, did you?"

Kayrla blinked, hesitating. "No, there was a pendant among the swag," she admitted. "I didn't want to get weighed down with a lot of coin, so I took something I thought I could sell later." She shrugged. "It's pretty enough, but didn't look that valuable, so I thought it was a fair portion of what was owed me."

"The pendant was tossed in among the loose coin?" Galen asked.

She bit her lip, then grinned impishly at him. "Well, no. There was a small coffer in with the coin. It was locked, so I…" she wiggled her fingers in front of her, "…rusted the lock out and took a look inside. The pendant was in there."

"Could I see it?"

Kayrla looked curiously at him, but did as she was asked. Opening the pouch at her belt, she drew out the pendant and put it in his hand.

Galen studied the jewelry for a long time, turning the chain over and over in his hands, then holding the gem in the center up to the light and peering through it. Finally, he spoke, his face still puzzled. "Where did Jolly Red get this?"

"I don't know," she said. "I'd never seen it until I took it out of the box."

"Did the box look like it belonged with the pendant?" the Hand asked. "Were they a set?"

"No," said Kayrla. "Just a small wooden box with an iron lock. If the box and pendant had matched, I probably would have left it there. I didn't want to take more than I was owed," she insisted. "The chain's not gold, and the gem is glass. It's pretty, but not valuable."

"Perhaps," Galen said. "It's the design that interests me, though."

"Why?"

Galen smiled at her. "Before I entered into His Grace's service, I, ah, made my way through the world on my own wits. I was quite fond of appropriating jewelry to make ends meet. Like you, I realized how much easier it is to carry a few gems or wear a ring rather than have a heavy purse loaded with coin."

He looked back at the pendant, smiling fondly at old memories. "I've had a good deal of precious baubles pass through my hands, my dear, even these days. I don't need to steal them anymore, but I still like to look at them, to figure out where they came from and, of course, estimate how much they're worth." He gathered up the pendant's chain in his fist and let the jewel dangle in front of him. "And I have to tell you, this piece has me at a loss."

Kayrla raised an eyebrow. "You don't know how much this pendant is worth?" she asked.

"I couldn't even tell you where it was made," Galen admitted. "Look here. The chain is double linked. That's common enough, but these are small links and each one has a twisted curve so they fit together smoothly. The craftsmanship is exquisite." He shook his head. "That level of skill is expensive. If the chain isn't gold as you say, why spend the money on the artisan but not the materials?"

"Do you think it's gold?" Kayrla asked, beginning to wonder if she should have only taken the pendant. *Or,* she thought, *maybe I should have left the damn thing behind in the hold and just filled my pockets with coins.*

"I'm not sure what it's made of," Galen said with a frown. "You say the chain's not gold. I agree; there's too much red in it. But it's not copper or bronze either. It's not any sort of alloy I've ever seen before. And this," he said, pointing to the gem in the centerpiece. "I thought it was glass too, but after I noticed the oddness of the chain, I took another look at the gem."

"And you don't recognize the gem either, do you?"

Galen shook his head. "Some sort of precious stone; one that's been deliberately shaped. It's as close to a perfect hemisphere as I've seen, without getting measuring tools to be sure. Smooth surface, which made me think it was glass as well, but there's an odd refractory effect when you hold it up to the light. It's like the gem has facets, but on the inside."

"So who could make something like this?" Kayrla said, taking the pendant from Galen's hand and holding the gem up to the light to see for herself. This was the first time she'd really looked at the pendant since she'd taken it from Jolly's hold, and back then she'd only had a candle for light.

At first glance, it still looked like a cheap, thin metal chain and a single piece of red glass in a simple setting, but in the full light of day, she understood why Galen was so puzzled. The chain was neither thin nor cheap; it was delicate and intricately linked. And the jewel wasn't glass either; as she held it up to the sun and looked through it she was momentarily dazzled by the sparkle of light that blazed through it. The light was split into every shade of red she could imagine, and the afterimage floated in front of her eyes after she'd lowered her hand. She felt light-headed; her fingers trembled slightly. More to stop herself from dropping the pendant than any other reason, she slipped the chain over her head, then clasped her hands in front of her. The dizziness and trembling passed in a few moments, and Galen didn't appear to have noticed. The spymaster was flipping through the book on jewelry, lost in thought.

"This book doesn't offer any clues," he said after a minute. "I don't know anyone who could make something like this, and I've stolen the best, in my day." He looked curiously at her. "Maybe you made it."

"Me?"

"Your people, in any case." Galen rubbed his chin in thought. "You mentioned your father before; did he ever wear any jewelry that looked like this?"

"My fath–no, we didn't have two coppers to rub together, much less a shiny bauble like this!" she exclaimed. "This can't be from the Elflands! How would Jolly Red have gotten hold of it?"

"Probably the same way you did," Galen observed. "But it would explain why he wants it back so badly."

"He what?"

"He wants it back," Galen said. "That's why he put the bounty on you, Kayrla. He let that slip within Tesca's hearing earlier today. You and I may not know what this pendant is worth, but it's clear to me that your former captain does."

Kayrla slumped against the back of the couch, stunned. "Everything that's happened is because of this stupid thing?" she muttered, looking down at the pendant hanging from her neck. She had a sudden urge to rip the chain off, open the window and hurl the pendant out into the grounds, or stomp it into junk, but she resisted it. Galen's musing that this might have been elf-made had struck a chord within her. She didn't know if he was right, but the possibility thrilled her.

"There's more," Galen said quietly, interrupting her reverie. "Tesca also reported that Jolly Red may now suspect you're being hidden here."

Her eyes flashed wide as she stared at him. "How?"

"I'll explain," Galen assured her. "But first, I have just a few questions."

"You and your damn questions…" she sighed.

He smiled at her. "My lord asks many questions of me, Kayrla. I ask you questions so I can give him answers. Now," he said, getting up from the couch and starting to pace in front of it, "I want you tell me everything you can remember about a particular Sabrian gentleman you encountered on the night you met Tesca…"

Chapter Fourteen

Tesca took a long breath, gauging the space before him. Then he started running. A quick ten steps, and then he leapt out, over the alley, landing on the opposite roof. He froze, listening hard for any noise of alarm, but all he could hear were the night sounds of Harborside, coming up to him from the street.

He moved along the roof to the crudely patched hole he and Kayrla had made weeks before. It was a simple matter to pull the wood panel off and slip through into the inn's bathing suite, which didn't look like it had been used since the last time he'd been here. Tesca crossed the room and after listening at the door, stepped out onto the balcony.

There were sounds of quiet conversation and movement on the main floor down below; Tesca could see two people walking in from the front door, heading for the stairs. He waited until they had climbed two flights and walked into one of the rooms on the floor below him before he started moving. Quickly he descended to the second floor and walked along the balcony to the Sabrian's room. With one hand on the hilt of his sword, he opened the door and stepped quickly inside.

He was surprised to find the room empty, and there was no sign that anyone was living there. *This is the right room,* Tesca thought. *He was staying here. Where did he go?*

Frowning, he returned to the balcony and descended to the main floor. The innkeeper glanced up from behind his desk as Tesca approached, then did a double-take when he saw who it was. "Hey! You're the one who wrecked my roof!"

"And I see you spent all the money I gave you on excellent repairs," Tesca said with a thin smile. "That thin board you nailed over the hole came off in about five seconds. The next storm that comes through here would have ripped it off even faster."

The innkeeper stared at him. "You broke in here again? I'm calling the Watch this time!"

"Don't waste your time with the Watch," Tesca warned him. "When they get here, the first thing they'll do is ask me what their orders are." The innkeeper blinked in surprise. "I've got some questions for you," Tesca went on. "What happened to the old Sabrian that was here?" He pointed up behind him towards the room he'd just entered. "He was here when I passed through before. Where is he now?"

The innkeeper licked his lower lip, uncertain. He appeared to still be thinking about Tesca's claim that the Watch would follow his orders, and after a moment of this, decided it wasn't worth calling Tesca's bluff. "He left. A few hours back, before dark."

"He left?" Tesca snapped. "Where?"

"As if I cared," said the innkeeper. "That black bastard, demanding food be brought to his room and trying to lord it over me and mine. And he didn't pay me a copper until he left neither. I was starting to think he wasn't good for it; would've chucked him out on the street days back, I would."

Except you didn't have the stones to get him angry, Tesca thought. The Sabrians' reputation throughout the Frees was not particularly good; the entire race was known as arrogant and easily offended, ready to draw steel over the merest slight. But the Empire was not called the Sabre Empire for nothing. It had a long tradition of mandatory military service; every citizen, male or female, was required to serve for a minimum of two years, which meant any Sabrians encountered most likely had at least passing experience with the weapon their people took as their namesake. And this Sabrian had had the calm, capable attitude of a veteran soldier.

"But he paid you in full today and left?"

The innkeeper nodded. "Paid in full; in gold, no less."

"Gold?" Tesca asked. "How long had he been staying here?"

"A few weeks before you crashed through my roof," the innkeeper said, looking up at the high ceiling and scratching his unshaved chin. "He was here a while; kept promising me I'd have my money when he left; got a funny look in his eye when I told him I'd like some portion of his bill paid."

"Not surprising," Tesca replied. "For someone like him, just staying in a rat-nest like this would have been shameful enough." The innkeeper shifted uncomfortably, but did not reply. "You've no idea where the old man went, eh?"

The innkeeper smirked. "I might recall something, sirrah…but I'm not sure…"

Tesca scowled and leaned in close. "You just got paid in gold, and probably overcharged that old man so much that he would have killed you if he wasn't in a hurry. You've gotten enough coin out of this entire affair as it is. Also, I suspect that if I call the Watch here myself, they might start searching the place and find some things you'd rather they didn't. So perhaps it might be best to just tell me where he went."

With a scowl to match Tesca's, the innkeeper gave in. "He went out this morning, came back about an hour or so later. He tells me he's leaving and that he'd settle up with me. So he goes upstairs to start packing, and about an hour later in comes this boy with a letter for him."

"Who was the message from?"

"No idea. Letter had a wax seal, red, but I never got my hands on it to see the mark. The little snot wouldn't let me touch it; said he had to hand it to the Sabrian personally, or take the letter back."

"Go on," Tesca asked.

"Well, I take the brat upstairs, figuring I've waited this long for my gold, an extra minute to read some stupid letter won't be a problem. The Sabrian reads the letter, gets all…I dunno, fidgety. Then he tells the boy to wait outside, writes another letter in response and the boy's off in a flash." The innkeeper scowled. "Little while later, the Sabrian's bags are packed and he's waiting up in his room, pacing back and forth. Kept sticking his head out the door to look down here anytime anyone came in. He was all..."

"Fidgety?" offered Tesca. "Like a bride on her wedding night?"

"More like the groom, I was thinking," the man replied with a grin. "Like he couldn't wait to get her dress off and get to the good part."

Tesca was unimpressed with the man's wit. "What happened next?"

"Not too long after he sends off the letter, a man walks in and heads right up to the Sabrian's room. A few minutes pass and they both come down, the pair of them carrying the Sabrian's bags. The Sabrian pays me what I'm owed, and they head out the door."

Tesca considered that. "How much did you charge him?"

"Eight marks," said the innkeeper.

"He must have been in a hurry if he didn't argue with you over that price," Tesca said with a scowl.

The innkeeper shrugged. "His purse was fat enough. There must have been over 20 marks in there while he was counting them out."

Jolly only paid him ten, Tesca thought. *He must have gotten the rest from the other man.* "The other man who came to visit him. Any idea who he was?"

"Never seen him before. Nice clothes, but not fancy. Yellow hair, mustache, cutlass at his hip."

That description was too broad to be of much use; it reminded Tesca of several men he knew in Kohayne. "How about the boy who delivered the message?"

"No, there's a few lads living 'round here who run messages. The Sabrian hired them for the first week he was here. Had them taking two or three letters a day. Then he was done with them."

"Did they bring any messages back for him?"

The innkeeper shook his head. "He didn't get any letters until today."

Tesca nodded as he took a silver coin from his purse and put it on the table. "Thanks for the tale, friend. Where can I find any of these messenger boys?"

The silver coin disappeared into the innkeeper's pocket with one sweep of his spotted hand. "There's a bell hanging outside the door, sirrah. Two pulls and if there's any messengers in earshot, they'll come running."

It took almost no time for two boys to respond to the ringing bell, and a third lad pelted up the street a few seconds later. All three clamored for Tesca's attention and shoved each other to stand closest to him.

"Settle down, lads," Tesca said, "I've coin for all three of you if you answer my questions." At once the boys stopped shoving and stood still, leaning towards him, curious. "There was a Sabrian who lived here," Tesca said with a gesture over his shoulder to the inn, "who had some messages delivered a few weeks back. Did any of you deliver some of those messages?"

"I did!" said the tallest one quickly.

"Me too!" chirped the shortest. The third boy frowned, disappointed, but he brightened up as Tesca put a copper coin in his hand.

"Thanks for your time, lad," Tesca told him. "Now," he said to the others, "where did you take his letters?"

"Ships at the dock," said the taller boy. "I was to find ships heading for Narlos and Hisvet in particular, and pay the captains to see that these letters got sent on from there."

"I had three letters to send," the other boy cut in. "Each one on a different day. One was meant to go all the way to Al-Kef, if you can believe it. Another went down to Nauticus."

"And the third?"

"Took it to a tavern on Southside; the Corsair's Eye." Tesca knew the place; he'd gotten himself thrown out of there a few times while posing as Jargy Barluf. It was a relatively high-end establishment, "a bit above the waterline," as they said in Kohayne. It was a popular meeting place for the more well-to-do merchants; the Eye boasted several small dining rooms, allowing rivals to meet on neutral ground in comfort and privacy. "I gave the letter to the barman," the boy continued.

"Who was the letter addressed to?"

"Can't read, sirrah," the boy apologized. "Barman knew the name right off, though. Took the letter and sent me back."

Tesca scowled. "You boys see everything that goes on around here, don't you?" All three boys nodded vigorously. "Did you see the Sabrian leave today?"

"I did," said the third boy, who hadn't delivered any of the Sabrian's messages. "I offered to carry his bags."

"And did you carry them?"

The boy scowled. "No, sirrah. The fellow that was with him, a right bastard he was. Pushed me down and told me to piss off; said he had a carriage waiting by the docks."

Tesca raised an eyebrow. "A carriage, eh?"

"Aye, sirrah. A nice one it was too; two horses."

"Two horses," Tesca muttered, thinking. There were a fair number of carriages in Kohayne, but two-horse carriages were generally only used by the most powerful families. This had started as more of a requirement than an exclusive privilege, though: a single horse sometimes had trouble hauling a carriage up to the highest parts of the city. "Did the carriage have any seal or coat-of-arms on it?"

"No, sirrah," the boy replied.

"Anything else you can remember about the carriage, or the man the Sabrian was with?"

The boy's face furrowed into a tight grimace as he concentrated, then suddenly brightened. "He had a gold tooth! I saw it plain as day when he shouted at me!"

Tesca tensed. A blond man with a mustache was one thing, but to also have a gold tooth was something else. "Which tooth was he missing? Was it this one?" he asked, tapping his upper right canine.

"That's the one!" the boy said eagerly. "How'd you know that, sirrah?"

"Because I was the one who knocked it out," Tesca replied with satisfaction. "You lads have done me good service," he said as he put a copper coin each into the hands of the two boys who'd delivered the Sabrian's messages. Then he gave each of them a silver coin as well. "I'd like you to keep your eyes and ears open. If you see that Sabrian, or the man he was with, I'll pay to know it."

Squealing with glee, the boys scampered off after making passionate promises to be on the watch. Tesca watched them go with a smile, then sighed once more as he turned to begin the long climb towards the Duke's estate. *Galen is* not *going to like this.*

Chapter Fifteen

"You still think that Sabrian was a retired officer?" Kayrla called, idly flipping through the pages of the book on jewelry Galen had been reading, one hand toying with the pendant about her neck. They'd been in the library for several hours now. After Galen had debriefed her about the Sabrian she'd seen, he had allowed her to stay and read any books she liked. For the rest of the afternoon she'd curled up in a large armchair next to the window overlooking the harbor, a half-dozen books piled around her, while Galen continued with his own tasks. Several people had come to visit Galen in the library during this period. Most of them were messengers, either delivering or receiving letters that Galen took from his own jacket pocket, but with two of them Galen had stepped into a side room to have a private conversation. Through it all, Kayrla remained in her chair by the window, absorbed in her reading. When Galen wasn't busy, he would come over to see how she was doing and talk to her about whatever she was reading. His company was a welcome change from being cooped up in her room day after day.

Now the sun had set, and the lights of Kohayne harbor were shining up at them with a warm orange glow. Galen came over to the window after hearing her question.

"That's what Tesca thinks, and I'm inclined to agree with him," he admitted. "Tesca knows the Sabrians well, better than I do in many aspects. I pay more attention to the bigger picture; what their Empire is doing and how they're going to move into the Frees. Tesca knows their people; their customs, their songs. I just wanted to hear what you remembered about him; there might have been something Tesca didn't notice."

Kayrla nodded. "You think the Empire will come north?"

"Oh, yes," said Galen, "I'm sure of it. It's only a matter of when and how."

"Invasion?" Kayrla suggested. "The way they took Valmor?"

"That trick won't work a second time," Galen replied. "No, my guess is that they're working on some way to get two or three of the Frees to go to war with each other, then bring their fleet north under the pretense of having to protect their own merchants." He chuckled. "I don't think the Sabrians have completely figured out how we operate. None of the islands are large enough to fight a war on their own; our battles are done with daggers and coin, not cannon."

"If that's true, why not just send the fleet in anyway?"

"They'd have to take each island by force and establish a large garrison on each one to maintain order. That's expensive; the amount of money the Empire makes trading with the Frees wouldn't be enough to pay for it. And the northern powers, Malachi, Terendor and Al-Kef, wouldn't want to share a border with the Empire either. All three of them prefer the Frees remaining independent. That way, they can safely play their intrigues with each other." He sighed. "At some point, hopefully, the Sabrians will share that viewpoint, and the Frees will continue as they are. But they're not there yet."

Kayrla grinned. "You know of a Sabrian fleet heading this way?"

"No, it just arrived, actually," Galen said, pointing down to the harbor. He grinned back at her as Kayrla blanched. "Just one ship, though. The Governor of Nauticus has sent an envoy to represent the Empire at His Grace's Ascension Day festivities."

She gaped at him. "Are you serious? A Sabrian warship? Here?"

"See for yourself."

Kayrla leaned towards the window and looked down into the harbor. It didn't take her long to spot the cutter passing under the Eisenteeth, its mast so high that the bridge had been raised to let it pass. There was no mistaking a Sabrian vessel. They were generally longer and narrower than other ships of their class, with an almost haughty elegance as they slid through the water. Every time she saw one, she imagined herself in the crow's nest while the ship was at full sail. "By the Deeps, but those black bastards make pretty ships," she muttered. "I count some 40 guns on her. A real warship, not just an envoy's transport."

Galen nodded. "And there's probably a detachment of marines on board as well. If they come this far north, they come prepared. Besides, the Empire rarely lets an opportunity to display its power pass by, especially such a notable one as this."

"Notable?"

"They're here for the Duke's fete. His Grace's Ascension Day is an annual holiday here in the Quad, of course, but every five years he has a formal celebration. That's what all the preparations around the estate have been for. All the other powers in the Frees, and the nations outside it, send representatives to pay their respects. With that many notables and luminaries in one place, there's a great deal of political haggling and other intrigues going on at the same time." He chuckled. "I imagine that's one reason the fete is so well attended. But the Sabrians always make sure to get their official envoy here first. Do you know why?"

Kayrla pursed her lips in thought. "I would have guessed they'd always make sure to come last, almost as an afterthought. To remind the Duke they don't think he matters very much." For a few moments, she remained silent, then her face brightened as it came to her. "It's a message, but not so much to the Duke as all the other guests. By getting here first, they make sure the first thing everyone else sees as they sail into the harbor is that man o' war sitting there."

"Not too subtle, our distant southern neighbors, are they?" asked Galen.

"No," Kayrla said with a sigh. "I imagine I'll be cloistered away somewhere safe and secure while all these important guests are on the estate."

"That is the plan," Galen confirmed. "How is that new spell of yours coming along, by the way?"

She turned away from the window. "Well, it's really two spells. The spell to change my skin color is one; the illusion to make my features look human is the other. I'm just…having trouble keeping both spells up at the same time."

Galen nodded. "Well, maybe we can replace one of the spells with something more mundane. We humans don't have magic, but we do have paint for your skin and dye for your hair."

"I've tried that before," Kayrla said. "They always look odd on me; my own coloring comes through and I look like I have jaundice, or some other illness no one's ever heard of. Either way, that hasn't been terribly effective."

"Perhaps," said Galen. "But I've been disguising myself and others for decades; perhaps if you make your features look human, I might find some combination of dyes and paint that will work for your skin. We'd probably have to make you as dark as a Sabrian, though."

She smiled ruefully. "A Sabrian girl walking through Kohayne? That'll draw more attention than someone with jaundice."

"Better a Sabrian girl than an elven one," Galen said. "I can't imagine you're enjoying being cooped up here on the estate. It's time to start trying some new solutions to the problem."

"Fair enough."

"Try your illusion spell now," said Galen. "Then we'll test some paints and see if anything can keep your skin color concealed."

Kayrla sighed. "All right." She released her coloring spell and in a few moments, her skin and hair were their natural blue and green once more. Then, closing her eyes, she began to weave her new illusion spell.

At first, the casting felt the same as it always had; she had begun to reach out for the mana about her and draw it into the patterns that would form the illusion. But something was different. Instead of sensing faint trickles of mana around her that she had to pull together, the mana was strong; a wellspring of power around her that she instinctively tapped into. Mana flowed swiftly into the accustomed pattern.

As her eyes snapped open in surprise, Galen was grinning at her.

"That took a lot less time than it used to," he said, impressed. "You just closed your eyes and..." he snapped his fingers. "You've really improved."

"No," she said, confused. "It wasn't me, it was..." she trailed off. "There's mana here. It's strong; stronger than I've ever felt in the Frees before."

Galen's eyes narrowed in astonishment. "That can't be," he said.

"No, the spell should have taken me a lot longer to cast, but I reached for the mana and it was just there! Maybe something about this room," she wondered, looking around.

"You've cast spells in this room before and this didn't happen," said Galen, shaking his head. "What's different between that time and this?"

Kayrla stared at the floor, thinking. She reached out for the mana again, not to cast a spell, but simply to feel that wellspring of power. It was there again, strong and ready to be tapped. But she did not tap into it; instead she studied it, and began to sense something she hadn't noticed before.

When she'd been further north, where mana was stronger, she could feel it all around her, as if she was standing in a strong breeze. But the power she was sensing now wasn't all around her; it was coming from a single spot, somewhere close...

Her hand moved to the pendant around her neck, and she knew with a touch of her fingers that she was right. "It's the gem," she whispered. "The gem is...full of mana!"

Galen stared at her pendant around her neck. "It MUST be from the Elflands," he said in satisfaction.

"But why haven't I noticed it before?" Kayrla asked, her voice becoming frantic. "I've had it with me for weeks; I've been casting spells around it since I got here!"

"Have you ever worn it before?"

The question was like a dash of water in her face. "No," she admitted. "This is the first time I put it on."

"Take it off and see if you can still feel its power."

She did so. As soon as the pendant left her neck, she could no longer sense the wellspring around her. The room, and the level of mana, were exactly as they'd always been.

She handed the pendant to Galen. "You try it on."

"Me? I can't perform magic. You said it yourself; no human can."

"Maybe there just wasn't enough mana around to try. Just try it on; see if you can feel anything."

He nodded, almost indulgently, and slipped the pendant around his neck. For several seconds, he stood still, waiting. Then he sighed and took the pendant off, handing it back to her. "I didn't feel anything different, my dear. By the way…your illusion is still intact, even without wearing the pendant."

She looked at herself in the mirror. Her features looked human, but her skin and hair were still blue and green. Ella had been right; it was a lot easier to do the illusion spell by itself without trying to merge the coloring spell with it. On a hunch, she put the pendant back into her pocket, and closing her eyes, started to cast her coloring spell. This time the spell took the normal amount of time she expected it to, and she had to draw upon the weak trickle of mana around her to fuel it. But she did not have to deal with the strain of maintaining the illusion spell still on her. The power within the gem had created the one; she only had to create the other.

When she was done, she looked at herself in the mirror again, and gasped in surprise, though she had known what she would see. A human girl with pale, freckled skin and strawberry blonde hair, was staring back at her, her mouth an open "O" of astonishment. She whirled back to Galen with a laugh. "How do I look?"

The Right Hand's silent, dumbfounded expression was the icing on the cake. Then he smiled broadly. "You look completely unimportant. Indistinguishable. Congratulations." He glanced at a grandfather clock against the wall and extended his arm to her. "I believe it will soon be time for dinner in the great hall. Would you like to join me?"

Chapter Sixteen

"Welcome back, sir," the guard said to Tesca as he approached the gate.

"Thank you," Tesca replied. "Where can I find the castellan?" When he needed to speak to Galen right away, he'd learned it was generally faster to find the castellan first, who always knew where the Right Hand could be found. Galen was usually in the library, but if he wasn't, there were a number of places into which he might have squirreled himself away, and Tesca rarely had the time to search them all out.

"The evening meal's coming to a close, sir," said the guard as the gates swung open. "The castellan should still be there."

Tesca nodded in thanks and moved through the gate before it had finished opening. He was across the courtyard and trotting up the first set of covered stairs before the gate had been closed again.

The groundskeepers had begun an all-out assault on the jungle growth in the estate now that the Fete was drawing near. Their efforts had not been in vain, Tesca noted. The porticoes were clear of any vines and were being diligently cleaned. *But the jungle will be back soon enough,* he thought, leaving the stairs and heading towards one of the larger buildings on this level of the estate. The sound of music and the dull roar of many men talking at once flowed out of the open doors. Tesca's stomach rumbled as he smelled the food inside.

He nodded to the guards, who saluted him as he passed, and he took in the room quickly. The Duke's chair was empty; either His Grace had finished dining and departed already, or he'd dined privately in his solar. To Tesca's surprise, Galen was seated in his customary place to the right of the Duke's chair, an empty plate in front of him. He was talking with a young woman Tesca did not recognize. She was blond, wearing a blue gown, and was laughing at something the old spy had just told her. Tesca wondered who she was.

Galen glanced up as he entered the hall, and as his eyes met Tesca's, Tesca smoothed his hair back with his left hand, a signal to Galen that there was news he needed to hear, though it was not an emergency. Galen nodded to him as if in greeting and motioned Tesca closer.

Unlike Galen, Tesca's title of "Left Hand" was not a formal one. On the rare occasions he was present for evening meal in the Great Hall, he did not actually sit at the Duke's left hand, but at one of the side tables reserved for officers of the guard and other lesser members of the Duke's court. He stepped up to the front of the high table, nodded to the empty chair in deference to His Grace, then approached Galen.

"You're getting back late," the older man said over the noise in the hall.

"There were things that needed doing," Tesca replied, glancing at Galen's dinner companion. The young woman seemed in her late teens, and smiled brightly at him. "And this is?" Tesca asked.

"I'll introduce you later," Galen said, a smile to match the girl's on his own face. "Let's get out of the noise. Are you hungry?"

Starved, Tesca thought, but he shook his head. "I'll get something later."

"All right," said Galen, rising and walking towards a door behind the table. As Tesca came around the table to join him, the girl finished her cup of wine and followed Galen as well.

Once the door was shut behind them, the noise of the hall diminished to a dull rumble. They were in a comfortable antechamber, used by the Duke before and after Formal Court. The room was richly furnished in carpets and several exotic wooden sculptures. Galen sat down in one of the cushioned armchairs and Tesca was perplexed to see the blond girl take another chair herself. "Who–" he began to say, but the girl burst out laughing.

"It was flawless!" she said, almost crying with glee. "Even Tesca's fooled!"

"I agree," said Galen, a wide smile on his face. "But I think it's time we let him in on it, don't you?"

"Oh, very well," said the girl. "I think it would have been more fun to string him along for a bit more, though."

Tesca was just beginning to understand what was going on when the girl's appearance flickered, shifted. Freckled skin turned blue and her blond hair darkened to green. But the girl's face was changing too. The cheekbones drew upward, turning the eyes on an angle. And her ears were growing as well. In a moment, Kayrla was sitting in the chair, the same wide grin on her face.

Tesca raised an eyebrow. "I see Ella managed to get you into a dress after all."

That turned her grin into a scowl. "I didn't want to, but Galen insisted."

"A girl dressed as a boy always attracts attention, whether her hair is blond or green," said Galen. "But as you can see, Kayrla has managed to solve her disguise problem."

"I even fooled you!"

"You were sitting down for the most part," Tesca evaded. "I might have figured it out if I'd had more of a chance to see you walk. Elves move a little differently than humans do."

She snorted in derision. "Just admit you were fooled, Tesca. It's not the end of world to admit that even you can be fooled from time to time."

Tesca sighed. "Fair enough. But I am glad you've worked out the problem. We have more than enough problems on our plate as it is."

Galen frowned. "What have you learned, lad?"

"The Sabrian. I went to find him this evening, but he'd moved out of the inn that day."

"Where's he gone?"

"That's the problem," Tesca said. "I think he's now a guest of the Feynes."

"Witchblood!" snapped Galen. "Are you sure?"

Tesca nodded. "The description of the man he left with matches Anbros Feyne, right down to the gold tooth."

Kayrla was puzzled at the long silence following that statement. "Feyne… Feyne…I've heard that name somewhere before."

Galen nodded slowly. "In your previous profession, I'm not surprised. They're a merchant family native to the Quad; they ship goods all over the Frees."

"So what's the problem?"

"They're scheming bastards who plot to overthrow the Duke," Tesca snapped.

Galen glared at him, shaking his head. "You have to put aside your grudges, Tesca. They leave you vulnerable."

"They tried to kill me last year!"

"Yes, and whose fault was that? If you insist on putting yourself in the path of a blade, don't start crying when it cuts you."

Tesca closed his eyes, getting himself under control. Galen watched him for a few seconds before nodding and turning back to Kayrla. "The Feynes are one of the wealthiest families in Kohayne. You've seen their estate every time you looked out across the city."

Kayrla remembered seeing the large estates on the opposite cliff and wondering who lived there. "They look down on the city from the same height as the Duke does," she said.

Galen nodded. "That viewpoint, equal and opposite, does create certain…tensions between the Duke and the Feynes. They are not a noble family; they started 'at the waterline', to use the common expression, and many of the family are quick to take offense if they are reminded of it."

"They have wealth, power and prestige, but no title," Tesca put in. "They're jealous, ambitious, treacherous and ruthless."

"So are all great lords from time to time if they wish to remain great lords," Galen said. He looked at Kayrla again. "Are you familiar with the history of the Quad, my dear?"

"I was reading something on that this afternoon in the library," she said. "The Quad was founded by an exiled duke from Terendor, correct?"

Galen beamed at her. "Correct. Mandran Kohaya, the twelfth Duke of Kevrensbury, renounced his lands and came here, with his family and entourage. There was a small settlement and port here already, using the lagoon as a natural harbor, but the arrival of the Kohayas and their wealth quickly turned this port into a small city. Mandran gave up his lands on the continent, but chose to retain his title, establishing himself as Duke Mandran the First, sovereign ruler of the 'Kohaya Quad,' as it became known." He looked up at Tesca. "The description you gave of the Feynes fits Mandran Kohaya as well. There were individuals who had power and authority in the small port before he arrived, but he pushed them aside and seized power for himself and his heirs."

Tesca shrugged. "I'm not denying that, Galen. But the Feynes consider themselves rivals to the Duke, not subjects."

"For the most part," Galen admitted, "but they know better than to admit it openly." He looked back at Kayrla, resuming his tale. "Once the Kohayas formally established themselves, the Quad began to prosper. The Kohayas, as a noble house, did not sully themselves with actually running merchant operations. Instead, they chose to make Kohayne a center of commerce in the Frees by making improvements to the harbor and building settlements for a growing native population to service the ships and crews that would come here. They kept the taxes relatively low to further encourage this city to become a center of trade. Naturally, some local citizens also became wealthy as trade increased. The Feynes were one of these merchant families."

"How did they become rivals? How did they find themselves on the opposite side of the lagoon?" Kayrla asked.

"Several generations of smart, ruthless businessmen increased the Feyne's wealth and social standing. They did not always make their money honestly, however. At least one or two of the Feynes were famous pirates in their day, and from the earliest days, the Feynes have been behind a great deal of the smuggling that goes on here. But they became true rivals to the Kohayas during the rule of His Grace's grandsire."

"Marcus the Third," Tesca put in.

Galen nodded. "Marcus was…well, I'll be blunt. He was not a good ruler. He spent far more money than the throne was bringing in. He threw large and frequent parties for himself and his courtiers, and he started to fancy himself a 'king of the sea'. He sought to build a navy and use it to conquer the rest of the Frees." Galen shook his head. "The throne couldn't cover his costs; so it had to take out loans."

"From the Feynes," Kayrla finished. "The Kohayas were now in debt to them."

"Among others, but the greatest debts were owed to the Feynes," Galen said. "Fortunately, Marcus didn't live long enough to give away everything to them, and his son, Andran the Second, was much more capable than his father. He came to the throne as a young man, and spent the better part of twenty years prying the Feynes' fingers off his throne. He repaid debts where he had to, and when the Feynes tried to squeeze him, he cracked down on smuggling operations to squeeze them right back." Galen smiled. "I became the Left Hand near the end of Andran's reign, when tensions between the Feynes and His Grace were at their height. Busy times, and dangerous. But by the end of his reign, Andran did manage to pass a debt-free, albeit poorer, realm to his son, who rules us now. The Feynes, however, have not forgotten that at one time they had the Quad in their grasp."

"And now the Sabrian is their guest?" Kayrla asked. "What does that mean?"

"I have no idea," admitted Galen. "Not yet, anyway. Tesca, tell me everything you found out today."

As Tesca repeated his tale, the older man remained seated, gazing at the floor, his brow furrowed and his hands clasped in his lap. When Tesca was finished, he remained silent for another minute before speaking. "I believe we are dealing with more than one intrigue at a time."

Tesca nodded. "That's what I think, too. The Sabrian was sitting in that hotel, waiting for...something. But he was running low on money. When he heard about Jolly Red's bounty and realized he'd seen us, he went to the tavern to sell that information. When he came back with a purse full of gold, there was a response to whatever he'd been waiting for."

"Just as you say," Galen replied. "This matter between the Sabrian and the Feynes intrigues me, though. A former member of the Imperial Navy in league with smugglers? That can't be ignored." He sighed, looking weary. "But before we can look into it, there's something else we have to do."

"What?" Kayrla asked.

The spymaster turned to her. "This business with Jolly Red has gone on long enough. The Sabrian gave Jolly enough clues to point him in this direction, and while your former captain may not have recognized Tesca from the description the Sabrian gave, there are many in Kohayne who will, especially the Feynes. Before long, anyone who is seeking you will be looking up towards the manor. This has now become a direct threat to His Grace." He glanced at Tesca, who grimly nodded, then he turned back to Kayrla, his face somber. "For the safety of the throne, you have to die."

Chapter Seventeen

Jolly Red pushed his empty breakfast plate away from him. "Clegg," he said with a chuckle, "I'm getting fond of the food they serve here. No chance of you taking a leaf from their book when next we sail?"

The *Cutlass's* cook frowned, annoyed at the oblique reference to his cooking. "The food here doesn't travel so well captain, though I'll grant you their biscuits don't have weevils in them."

"Aye," Jolly said, tearing apart a fresh biscuit with relish. "It's getting so I don't even look for the little buggers anymore. That'll be a sad moment when we're back at sea and I crunch a few of them between my teeth." He chuckled and tossed one half of the biscuit down his throat.

Clegg watched his captain eat, the frown still on his face. "Getting to the whole 'back at sea' business, Captain," he offered, "the lads were wondering when that might be."

"When that little thief is dead and our swag is back in our hands," Jolly replied as he lifted a mug of ale to his lips.

"No offense, Captain, but that's what you've been saying for three weeks now," said Clegg. "The lads have spent what they had on spirits and strumpets, and they're getting restless. There's no quicker route to trouble than a pack of sailors in Kohayne with no coin in their pockets."

"I know, Clegg, I know," the captain replied, his posture stiffening. "But the lads want justice, don't they?"

"They want to be paid, Captain. Can't eat justice, assuming the girl even is guilty."

"Now you hold your tongue, Master Clegg," Jolly Red snapped. "We've not forgotten you were found with the elf as she tried to escape. You bound my leg after that whoreson partner of hers sliced me up, and like as not I'd have died from that if not for you. That's earned you a place back with the crew, but don't start talking about whether the elf is innocent, you hear? Elsewise I'm like to forget that past kindness."

Clegg's eyes narrowed, but he nodded. "All the same, Captain, the lads are still getting restless. Four days to Ascension; the town's starting the celebrations already. As I see it, either we put to sea before things get really festive, or the lads need some more coin to share in it. Otherwise, if I may speak frankly..."

Jolly Red set his tankard on the table with a loud bang. "I'm warning you, Clegg."

The cook pressed on. "I can't keep silent on this, Cap'n. You're looking at desertion or mutiny if we stay on the course we're on. I've been in the hold; I saw how much she took. Two fistfuls of coin, it seems to me. It's not like getting that back will pay for the time wasted tied up at dock."

Jolly Red's eyes flashed wide in rage and he loomed over the table. "This is not open for discussion, Clegg!" he boomed as Clegg scrambled out of his chair and his captain's reach. "We're staying until she's found! I'll not have another word on this!"

Clegg stared at the captain, his expression wary, but not cowed. "As you say. Sir." He gave Jolly Red a nod and left the tavern.

With a grunt of frustration, Jolly Red sank back into his chair. He considered telling his guards to haul Clegg back, but a glance at their surly expressions made him suspect that if he gave such an order, it might not be obeyed. He drummed his fingers on the table, chewing his mustache. *One more day,* he thought, *one more day. If she's not found today, or tomorrow, I'll have to raise sail and get back to sea.* He considered opening the hold and dividing it amongst the crew. The contracted time for divvying up the swag was still a ways off, but Clegg was right, things were getting ugly on board the *Cutlass. A bit more coin in their pockets will give me more time,* he thought. *It's less coin than it was, paying these damn harbor fees for so long, but it's still enough to keep the lads happy. One more day. Maybe today I'll get some news.*

He nodded to himself, satisfied with his decision, and his thoughts turned to the Sabrian who'd been in to see him a few days before. *She's with someone rich. Someone powerful. Someone who can hide her.* He nodded. *The old black bastard might be right on that after all. So where do I turn to for something like that?*

A single word came to him: *Feyne.* But it was not a word he liked. If Kayrla was hiding behind a rich protector, the Feynes were as likely a suspect as anyone else. And if they weren't, the price they would offer for their help was not something Jolly wanted to pay. *"Once a Feyne shares your bed,"* went the old smugglers' warning, *"he owns it."*

One more day, he thought. *It's still four days to the Ascension fete; I'll get the necklace back in time.* He shivered for a moment, remembering a promise made. *My luck's got to change. Get the necklace back, get enough to pay the lads proper and still set myself up right. Just have to get it back. One more day.*

A sudden movement at the tavern entrance startled him out of his reverie, but it was only the old drunk, Jargy Barluf, stumbling inside. He blinked several times as his eyes began to adjust from the bright sunlight outside to the dark interior of the tavern. "Cap'n!" he called out, turning, half-blind.

"Over here, Jargy," Jolly called. "What do you want?"

"We've found her, cap'n!" croaked the old man with pleasure. "Me and one of my mates found where she's been hiding!"

Jolly Red stared at him, too shocked to move. *By the Triad, at last...* "Are you sure, man?!" he shouted.

"Aye, cap'n!" Barluf said, squinting up at him with a grin. "But if you want her, we'd best move smartly. Looked like she was packin' a bag; maybe to try slippin' out with the tide." He started heading for the door. "C'mon!"

Panic coursed through Jolly Red at the thought of Kayrla escaping him. "You're with me," he said to his guards as he lumbered after the old man, his injured leg twinging slightly each time he put weight on it. Even with his limp, the captain was a large man who took long strides and in short order, he had caught up with Jargy, who tottered and skittered a few steps ahead of him, constantly turning back to make sure Jolly was still following him.

"I started asking questions, cap'n…like you wanted. I put my nose in everywhere that I could, even in places I've been banned from!" He skipped and dodged a few passerby in front of him, bouncing in front of Jolly like a small dog begging for treats. *Which isn't far from the truth,* Jolly thought. "Anyways, one of my mates told me about this one kitchen, South Harborside, that'll make food and deliver it to a man's home for an extra price, and I get myself to thinking: 'well, Jargy…if you was all green and blue and afraid to go out on the street lest ye get killed, how are you going to eat?' And so I tells myself: 'I'd find someone to bring me food, as I've got lots of money here what that I've stolen from my old captain.' Then, I'd say–" he broke off as he bumped into someone and rolled away from them. Jolly was sorely tempted to tell one of his guards to just pick up the old man and carry him along before he hurt himself.

"Have you seen her?!" he yelled ahead, getting his question in before the old man started on another breathless chapter of his tale.

"Yes, cap'n, I have!" Jargy called back, once more bobbing and weaving through the crowd, though he was now taking more care to look where he was going. They were now along the docks themselves, heading west towards the Duke's Bridge. "I starts following these food deliveries and taking note of where they go," Jargy went on. "After a few days, I notice that there's one place getting more food than the others," he said, slipping on a wet paving stone for a moment, then catching his balance. "so I start to watch that place in particular. But I can't see who's inside. The delivery man goes in with food, he comes out empty-handed. So I ask myself: 'How are you going to get inside to see if it's her?' And I tells myself, I says: 'I'm going to start delivering the food myself, and she'll let me in herself!' That was smart, wasn't it?"

It was, thought Jolly in surprise as he puffed along in Jargy's wake. The old man was keeping a swifter pace than Jolly would have expected. *All men will run a race if there's gold at the finish,* he reminded himself. *And if he's right, he'll get paid.*

"And you…you saw her?" he panted.

"Just an hour ago, cap'n!" Jargy replied. "I had to deliver for a few days before I got that job, but simple and easy, once I got it, I walked up to the door, knocked and it opened right up." They were at the foot of the Duke's Bridge, and Jargy paused in his mad dash. Wheezing, he mopped lightly at his brow, and leaned in close to Jolly Red. "Just… gotta catch my breath, cap'n. Not as young as once I was."

"Take your time," said Jolly, trying to sound like he wasn't exhausted himself. "It was her in there?"

"Young lass, brown skin, black hair, wearing man's clothes. Saber at her belt. But she had a funny shape to her eyes, and her hair was all bound up in a big kerchief across her brow. Don't that fit the description you were giving out?"

Jolly's wide mouth split in a grin. "It certainly does, Jargy. It certainly does. You said she was packing a bag?"

Jargy nodded, his breath back to normal. "Aye, cap'n. A small bag on the bed it was, half full, with a pile of clothes next to it. And she told me, as she took the food and gave me some coins, that I could tell the tavernkeep she wouldn't need food delivered here anymore; she was leaving." Jargy smiled. "I've got a mate watching her place; he'll warn me if she leaves. But if we move sharp, we can catch her before that!" He grinned up at Jolly and started trotting across the bridge. Jolly Red, feeling better than he had in days, followed.

The Duke's Bridge was over a hundred yards long and wide enough for four wagons abreast to cross it. As the main thoroughfare from one side of Kohayne to the other, it was always choked with people, carriages and wagons flowing slowly from one bank to the other. Jargy dodged his way through the throng, keeping close to the western side of the bridge. He glanced behind him once more to make sure Jolly

Red was still following him, and promptly collided with someone coming in the opposite direction. Jargy went down and Jolly saw with astonishment that the other person was Kayrla, in the same disguise Jargy had described, a small bag slung over her shoulder. She looked like she was in a hurry and was about to step over Jargy and continue on when she saw Jolly and his two guards some ten feet ahead of her, and her mouth fell open in an "O" of surprise.

Time seemed to slow for Jolly Red. He pointed at her, shouting incoherently for his guards to grab her; Jargy was on his knees in front of her, fumbling at her leg to keep her from running away; and Kayrla was kicking out at him, slipping free.

"My mate, my mate, cap'n!" Jargy was yelling. "He'll be behind her; she's caught for sure!" And Jolly Red could see over the crowd, could see another man moving swiftly towards them heading for Kayrla. Kayrla saw him coming too; she glanced back at Jolly, a look of fear crossing her face as she realized she was trapped.

And then she sprang, a swift fluid motion up to the bridge railing. Jolly's guards were shoving through the crowd towards her, but Jargy's partner was closer. One hand grabbed for her ankle, but too late. She flung herself off the bridge. Jolly roared with frustration as he rushed to the rail, saw a low barge on the water beneath them. Kayrla landed on the barge, rolled and sprang to her feet.

"After her, after her!" Jargy yelled, staring down at her through the bars of the railing. The other man, Jargy's partner, leapt down from the bridge onto the barge in pursuit. Kayrla backed away from him. She reached into a pouch and pulled out… Jolly's heart skipped a beat as he saw the glint of a metal chain, the flash of red light off the large gem. It looked like she was trying to put it around her neck in case she had to swim for it.

"Kill her if you have to!" Jargy shouted. "Half the bounty's still a fortune!" and sunlight flashed off of a drawn knife in the man's hand. He sprang forward and Kayrla, still trying to get the pendant around her neck, couldn't avoid it.

Time seemed to resume normal speed as Jolly heard Kayrla's deep grunt from the knife's impact. She sagged into the man who'd stabbed her, one hand falling away. Jolly watched the red glint from the gem as the pendant fell from her limp fingers into the water.

"NO!!" he bellowed as the man pushed Kayrla's limp form away from him. She fell over the side of the barge and sank beneath the water. "Forget her! The pendant! Get the pendant!" Jolly roared down to the man.

"Get it!" Jargy echoed, and the man glanced up at them, nodded, and dove into the harbor.

Jolly Red pounded his fists against the railing. "No…no no nonononono!" he snarled through gritted teeth. It was a long minute before the man came spluttering up to the surface. He shook his head at Jargy.

"He'll keep looking!" Jargy said frantically to Jolly, who was now looming over him, his face purple with rage.

"He'd better," the captain said, his voice becoming glacial with malice. "If you want to get paid-no! If you want to live," he promised, "he'll find that pendant! You've got one day to get it to me, you hear? One day!"

Chapter Eighteen

As Kayrla hit the water, she let herself sink down a few feet, and waited until the barge had drifted over her before swimming back up. When she reached the barge's underside, she moved along it towards the stern, finding the opening Galen had told her would be there. She swam through it and her head broke the surface inside a dark enclosed space. The barge had been built with a secret compartment; an extension of the stern with an opening in the bottom, below the waterline.

Wondering what other bits of skullduggery Galen and Tesca had used this barge for over the years, she pulled herself out of the water onto the small bench above her and knocked softly twice on the roof. A moment later came a repeat of the same signal from above. One of Galen's men was piloting the barge, and now he would begin moving it towards a rendezvous point. She would wait here until after dark before leaving.

The other man Galen had brought into this ploy, the one who had appeared to stab her, would remain in the water for several minutes, keeping everyone's attention on him, diving and surfacing over and over in a vain attempt to find the fake pendant Galen had given her to drop in the water. "It doesn't look like the real one," she had objected.

"When you're this close, no," Galen had agreed. "But from the Duke's Bridge, I assure you it will."

I can't believe this worked, she thought to herself. *At least up to this point.* She brushed her hair back from her face. *Lost my bandanna when I hit the water. But if the rest of this plan goes well, I won't need one ever again.*

For her the first part of the plan had been easy. She'd waited near the southern foot of the Duke's Bridge in an upstairs room of a tavern, hidden from public view. The man who was going to stab her, Vilio, was watching for Tesca and Jolly Red's approach through a spyglass. When he saw them stop at the north foot of the bridge, he told Kayrla and she started off, heading down the stairs, out the tavern door and across the bridge. Vilio was about ten paces behind her.

Stepping out in public, with only the coloring spell for a disguise, had been the hardest part for her. There was still a price on her head, and the city was full of would-be bounty hunters. If she crossed paths with one at just the wrong time…well, that was another reason Vilio had been behind her.

Timing was the key to the operation, Galen had said. Jolly Red had to see her with his own eyes before she went off the bridge, to remove any doubt that it was really her. He also had to see the pendant in her hand, but only after she'd gotten far enough away that he couldn't just grab for it himself. *"If you think of this as a bit of theatre,"* Galen had told her during their preparations, *"Jolly Red is a member of the audience, not an actor. The same goes for any citizens standing on that bridge. Give them a show, but do not let them participate."*

And it went off just as Galen had planned. She'd been nervous, almost in a panic crossing the bridge, more afraid of being suddenly attacked by a bounty hunter than anything else. So she hadn't been looking when Tesca walked straight into her. Stumbling back, she'd looked up to see Jolly Red staring at her, dumbfounded.

He had been both more and less terrifying than she'd expected. It had been three weeks since she'd seen him, but she'd thought about him and the bounty he'd put on her every single day. There had still been some part of her that found it hard to imagine he'd done that. As he stood there, shocked and silent, he looked like just a blustery, burly man with red hair and beard. He seemed smaller than Kayrla remembered him. This was who she'd been in fear of for weeks? This was the man who had hired people to kill her? But as recognition dawned on his face, his glare of hatred paralyzed her. He seemed to grow in size as his face reddened, and she knew that he all he wanted at that moment was to get his hands on her, to hurt her, to break her, for stealing from him.

Her knees went weak in the face of his rage, but then Tesca was there, scrabbling at her legs, yelling in that ridiculous old-man's voice. He brought her back to the task at hand, and suddenly, it was as if she really was in a play. She forgot about her fear of Jolly Red, but kept the expression of fear on her face as she backed away from him, then wheeled and saw Vilio, forcing his way through the crowd toward her.

In one bound, she'd leapt to the bridge railing. Out of the corner of her eye, she could see the wide bow of the barge edging out from under the bridge below them, and in that moment, she knew exactly how this would turn out. She took an instant to pause, as if scared, then flung herself out into space just as Vilio reached for her.

It was a longer fall than she would have liked, but shorter than some she'd had, and she was ready for it. She landed, rolled and bounced back up onto her feet, looking back at the bridge as Vilio leapt down in pursuit. From here, she could see Tesca scrambling to the railing to look at her, getting in the way of Jolly's guards, preventing them from following Vilio.

Backing away from Vilio, she drew out the fake pendant, as if she was going to put it on before trying to swim for safety, and Vilio moved cautiously, giving her the time to display the pendant before striking. When he did, though, he was so fast that for a moment Kayrla thought he really was going to kill her. He put his back directly to those watching from the bridge, blocking their view as he thrust the knife through the narrow gap between her arm and chest. She grunted with the impact as his shoulder slammed into her. Then she led the pendant's chain dangle on her fingers and she closed her eyes, listening to the plop as it fell into the water, and the anguished yell of Jolly Red that followed immediately after. She went limp, sagging into Vilio, letting him shove her off the barge.

And now here I am, she thought, crouched down on a shelf in the dark, above the water. *Now I wait.*

Exploring the shelf with her fingers, she found a full flagon which proved to contain fresh water, and a small box filled with fruit. She lost all track of time, but occasionally she could hear the creak of the rudder above her as the pilot made adjustments to his course through the harbor, or the scrape of boots on the deck. Occasionally she could hear the sound of some Harborside noise, but it was muffled and directionless. The only constant sound was the lap of the water against the hull.

It was becoming hot in the compartment with the late morning sun beating on the deck. For a moment, she thought she might fall asleep, then she heard new sounds, a scurrying thunder of footsteps. As a sailor; she recognized the pattern of activity. *They're tying off the barge; we've reached a dock.* After that came more sounds she recognized; men were coming on and off, unloading the supplies. She heard the sound in her compartment change as the boat became lighter and the water line dropped away from her.

Then, silence, save for the lapping of the water. She sighed. *So far, so good.* The heat started to become oppressive, but it was a simple thing to slip down into the cool water below her and immerse herself periodically. She tried to measure time by keeping track of these brief swims, but she lost count around eight. In between these, she sat on the shelf above the water, ate one of the fruits and drank from the flagon. Otherwise, she dozed lightly, letting time pass.

She awoke, slightly chilled. Her coloring spell had worn off; she'd become so comfortable with casting it that now she could instantly tell when it was in effect. That told her it had been at least eight hours since she'd leapt off the bridge. The compartment was definitely cooler now; the sun must have set. She could also hear a faint patter of light rain falling on the deck above. But it was the sound of footsteps on the deck that had awakened her. A scraping sound from the hatch above told her something heavy was being moved off of it. Then, a triple knock. She responded with the same knock, holding her breath as the hatch was lifted up.

The sun had indeed set. A few drops of rain struck her face. But she could see far better in the dark than any human, and she recognized Vilio at once.

"All well?" she asked, shivering in the night air that blew in through the open hatch.

"All well," he said, offering her a hand and pulling her up to the deck. He wrapped a cloak around her, taking care to pull the hood over her head. "He's waiting for you in the coach," he said, pointing up the gangplank, past the dock, to a two-horse carriage on the harbor road. They were tied up on South Harborside, very close to the Eisenteeth Bridge. A small, fast cutter was easing past the barge into the harbor. She recognized the flag of Hisvet on its mast. *Another envoy for the fete,* she noted.

"Best be getting back under cover, miss," said Vilio, gently steering her towards the gangplank. "All's well so far. Let's keep it that way."

"Of course," she apologized. "Thanks for the help."

"Always ready to serve," he said with a quick salute of two fingers to the temple. "You did very well, miss. A real natural."

She grinned at him and started up the gangplank. The cloak was too large for her, so she shuffled her feet to keep from tripping. Ahead of her, the carriage door opened and it was Tesca, looking like himself, who helped her inside. Then he shut the door and thumped the roof of the carriage. Kayrla drew back her hood as the carriage began to move forward.

"Did it work?" she asked, accepting a cup of wine from him.

"We think so," he replied. "Jolly Red was nearly blind with rage when Vilio finally gave up searching for the pendant. I half expected him to throw me into the harbor to help look, or jump over the rail to look for himself."

"Where is he now?"

"He finally went back to the *Cutlass*, promising to skin me alive if I didn't bring him that pendant by tomorrow. We've got someone watching the ship; we'll know what he does next." He reached inside his jacket, drew out the real pendant and handed it to her.

She accepted it gratefully and put it over her head at once. Once the pendant settled into place, she could feel the mana within it. "I should pick a new appearance," she said, looking at her blue skin. "Something that I haven't used before."

"Nothing too unique, please," urged Tesca.

She laughed. "No, I imagine we can't fake my death twice in one week." She thought about it for a minute. "All right, let's try this." She closed her eyes and drew upon the gem once more, concentrating on some specific details that she'd be able to repeat. When her two spells were complete, she opened her eyes. "How do I look?"

Tesca appraised her. "Red hair, not too bright. Not native to Kohayne, but common enough. Were you thinking of Jolly Red at the time?"

She blinked, surprised. "Maybe I was," she chuckled. "How about the freckles? Do they look right?"

He nodded. "Better than the last time you added them in. Just don't claim to be some illegitimate daughter of Jolly Red's."

She laughed once more, and felt several weeks of tension start to loosen within her. "I promise." With a sigh, she leaned back into the seat and sipped her wine. "Where are we going now?"

"Back to the manor," Tesca said. "We'll talk to Galen to make sure everything went according to plan."

"And then?"

"And then, you have an audience with His Grace."

Chapter Nineteen

Kayrla shifted her feet nervously under the dress she was wearing. She hadn't wanted to wear the clumsy thing, but Galen and Tesca had insisted, so she had let Ella joyfully tease her hair into a tumbling mass of curls and tried on a dozen different outfits. This took a bit of time; she expected that the Duke, like nearly everyone she'd met so far on the estate, would want to see her natural appearance, so she wanted a dress that would compliment her real hair and skin color.

Once the dress was chosen and her hair was styled, she cast her spells once again to look human, choosing pale skin and dark brown hair for herself, then she had Ella open the door of her suite and she stepped outside, where Galen and Tesca were waiting. Tesca was looking quite handsome, wearing new clothes of black linen with a leather vest and boots. Galen was wearing his customary grey and black clothes, but this evening they were made of silk.

"Gentlemen," she said with a smile, "you both look positively presentable. For a change."

"And the same to you," said Galen, "for once, I daresay."

She gave him a fake scowl as Tesca sighed and asked "Shall we?" He gestured down the hall and Kayrla started that way, the men on either side of her.

"What will I be asked to do?" Kayrla asked Galen.

"Just talk to him," the older man replied. "He's heard a great deal about you from both Tesca and myself, of course, but he wants to meet you himself and take his own measure."

"And then?"

"And then we'll see."

"Is there anything I shouldn't bring up?" she asked. "Any forbidden subjects? I know he was married, once." She glanced up at her companions to see their reaction. Both men looked uncomfortable. "I'm sorry, Ella told me, but please don't be angry with her about it."

After a moment, Galen spoke. "That particular subject would be best avoided, yes."

"Maybe I'll just let him direct the conversation," Kayrla said in a quiet voice. "I don't want to embarrass myself."

"His Grace appreciates you've no experience with higher etiquette," said Tesca. "He's not going to be angry if you don't hold your curtsy for the correct span of time."

I have to curtsy? thought Kayrla, who wasn't sure if she ever had before. "What is the correct span of time?"

Galen smiled. "If we were on the mainland, the correct span of time would be to rise only after His Grace bids you do so. That custom is not held so strictly here in the Frees, and as Tesca said, His Grace is not expecting you to be the paragon of high society. Be polite, answer his questions and just…talk to him."

They reached the bottom of a long spiraling staircase, with two of the Duke's soldiers standing guard. As Kayrla started up the steps, her foot caught on the dress and she stumbled for a moment. "Why…" she snarled, hiking her dress up a little to keep her feet clear, "…do I have to wear this?"

Tesca sighed. "Because it's part of being polite."

Kayrla fumed as they made their way up the staircase, but she did not complain further. *Tesca was right,* she admitted to herself. *I've been living under his roof, eating his food, for weeks now. One night of wearing a dress and being polite to my host is a small price.*

She wondered, for a moment, if that was the only price she was expected to pay, and remembered why she'd left the *Cutlass*, and some other ships before that. *But no,* she decided, *Tesca wouldn't go through all this for me just to make me the Duke's whore. I've trusted him, and now Galen, this far, and they've played me fair. Let's meet this man they give their loyalty to, and I'll take my measure of him.*

At the top of the stairs they stepped into another hallway, not as long as the one below them. Halfway down the hall was a set of double doors, with two more guards standing at attention. They saluted to Galen and Tesca as they approached, and one of them opened the door for them.

Kayrla's first impression when she walked in was that they'd mistakenly entered an unused room in the manor. Thick curtains were pulled across the windows, and the air felt stuffy and thick. The only light in here was a dim, warm glow coming from a pair of small oil lamps on both sides of a large canopied bed on the far side of the room. A man was seated in a chair next to the bed, quietly talking with the bed's occupant, whose face was hidden by the draperies hanging from the canopy. The man rose as the three approached and Kayrla recognized the black robes of a physician. He bowed to the figure in the bed, and departed the room with a polite nod to Galen as he passed them.

"Good evening, Your Grace," Galen said as they approached, coming around the side of the bed. May I present to you Mistress Kayrla é sa-Kyrloun."

Kayrla walked alongside Galen and Tesca until both men came to a halt and bowed, whereupon she bent into a curtsy, trying to mimic the few times she'd seen it done. She heard Galen and Tesca straighten up, but she maintained her pose, with her head down and her gaze on the floor.

It was another few seconds before she heard a deep, hollow chuckle coming from the bed. "And you said she had no understanding of etiquette, Galen," came a voice that sounded like it had once been deep and commanding, but was a hollow shell of its former self. "Rise, child. We are pleased by your greeting."

"Mistress," said Galen as Kayrla rose, "this is His Grace Stephen III, Duke of Kohaya." Galen's master was propped up against a towering pile of pillows, a blanket drawn up to his waist. He looked like he had once been a large man with a thick frame, but who had now lost most of that weight in a very short time. The skin on his face hung loose; the wrinkles forming deep shadows under his eyes and cheekbones. His hair was thinning on the top in a sharp widow's peak, but it flowed past his shoulders in a gray and white torrent. There was still some black hair in the tips of his mustache and goatee, however. His eyes were a brilliant ice blue, gleaming out of his face with a piercing intensity. She saw in an instant that although the Duke's body might have become weak, his mind remained strong.

"Your Grace," she said cautiously, "I, um, want to thank you for your hospitality."

The wrinkles on the Duke's face deepened as he smiled, his blue eyes looking upon her with interest. "I would hazard a guess, child, that you are currently under the disguise which Galen has told me you can create."

"Yes, milord. I shall remove it if you wish."

"I do," said Duke Stephen, not unkindly. "I understand the need when you travel the streets of my city and the halls of my estate, of course, but I would have these old eyes look upon your true shape."

She curtsied again, more smoothly than the first time, then closed her eyes for a moment and released both spells. When she opened them again, the Duke was gazing at her with frank astonishment, his mouth hanging slightly open.

"Remarkable..." the Duke whispered. His gaze roamed up and down, taking in all the details of her appearance, lingering most on her face. After a moment, he nodded in satisfaction. "Yes, quite remarkable." He looked down past her face, to the pendant at her neck. "And that, I take it, is the talisman I've heard so much of?"

"It is, milord."

The Duke chuckled. "An elf who can wield magic south of the mainland..." he said, half to himself. "When I took the throne over twenty years past, that phrase would have meant the same as the Hells freezing over, or the oceans running dry." He smiled. "I wonder what other impossibilities are in store for us." Kayrla opened her mouth to reply, but she didn't know what to say. The Duke chuckled again, but his laugh turned into a slight cough, which worsened, a loud, hacking sound that echoed through the room. Galen stepped forward, but the Duke waved him off with a raised hand. The coughing fit subsided a few moments later, and the Duke sighed, sinking further back into his cushions.

"I hope you will pardon me, child," said the Duke, his voice thinner than before. "I am not feeling particularly well today."

"Is-is there anything I can do?" she asked without thinking.

"Can you use your magic to heal the sick?" the Duke replied with a casual tone.

"No, milord. I'm sorry." *Maybe I could have,* she thought, *if there'd been time for Father to teach me.* She pushed those thoughts out of her mind.

"A shame," said the Duke with one final, weak cough. "Now tell me, my dear, what are your intentions?"

"Milord?"

"You have been my guest, albeit unexpectedly, for over three weeks. My two Hands here tell me you've been very patient, but this confinement has been hard for you. So, now that those who sought your life think you dead, what will you do now?"

Kayrla swallowed in a dry throat. "To be honest, milord, I hadn't been willing to think that far ahead. Now that I can, I..." she glanced up at Tesca, "...I don't know. When I left the *Cutlass*, it was just to get away from Jolly Red. I wasn't looking forward, because I was still looking back over my shoulder. But now, I..."

Duke Stephen nodded. "You still don't know where to go from here." A glance passed between the Duke and Galen. "Perhaps you will allow me to make a suggestion, then. Both of my Hands speak highly of you. You are clever, resourceful, physically fit and of course, you have your magic. Perhaps you might remain here, on the estate, in my service."

Kayrla nodded as she considered the idea. She wasn't surprised by it; it was no more than she'd expected, and she knew what the Duke was offering. She would become an agent, like Tesca; poking her nose into all manner of affairs throughout the Frees and reporting back to Galen. *Can the Duke have two Left Hands?* she wondered idly.

Her magical skills made her ideally suited to be a spy. *Or,* she realized, *an assassin.* She had never deluded herself about the sort of duties Tesca and Galen performed in the service of the Duke. But Tesca was the closest friend she'd ever had, even in the short time she'd known him. Somehow, during that chaotic battle and escape from Jolly Red, they'd come to trust each other. Galen was also her friend, but she knew that he'd cultivated their friendship at least partially in hopes of recruiting her. That did not lessen him in her eyes, though; he had a duty to the Duke and had remained true to it. He could have tried force or some form of trickery to recruit her, but instead he'd used kindness, and that she appreciated.

I could say no, she realized, looking into the Duke's eyes. *The two men next to me are my friends, and they've given this man their loyalty. If I say no, he'll be disappointed, but I really think he would let me leave.*

But, she admitted to herself, *where would I go? There's no bounty on my head any more, but it's not like I can sail to another island and reveal myself as an elf. If I join a new crew, eventually someone will find out, and I'll be right back where I started. Someone will always want to get their hands on me, for magic or pleasure or just to display me as some sort of living trophy.*

She bit her lip, continuing to look at the Duke's face. *Here, I have a roof over my head, and a full belly. I have friends who've risked a lot for me and requested nothing in return, even though they all want me to sign on with them. They've given me the choice to stay, or to leave.* A smile spread across her face. *And besides, I still haven't found out about Tesca's past.*

"My lord," she said, performing another curtsey, and this time she really thought she'd gotten the hang of it, "I accept. Had I a sword, I would offer it to you in token of my service."

"Milord," said Tesca with pride, "perhaps my sword shall suffice?" And he drew his rapier and offered it to Kayrla, who took it and laid it on the bed at the Duke's side.

The Duke smiled broadly. "Your service is accepted, Kayrla é sa-Kyrloun. I place you under the charge of my Right Hand, who shall determine the best way to make use of your…talents." His chest heaved and he began to cough again. "Damnation," he muttered, catching his breath. "You two had best be off," he said, his voice catching as his chest continued to spasm. "Send Dr. Felton back in as you go. Galen, please remain."

Galen nodded. "As you wish, milord. Kayrla, see to your appearance."

Kayrla nodded. Not wanting to waste time, she drew upon the pendant for both of her spells. The Duke, his eyes half-closed, watched her appearance change. "Quite… remarkable," he said with a weary chuckle as they headed for the door.

A few minutes later, they were back in Kayrla's suite. They had traveled in silence, both of them lost in their own thoughts.

"What's wrong with him?" she asked once the door was closed. "He's not…dying, is he?"

Tesca smiled. "No. He's better than he was, though you may not believe it to see him. He took sick during the storm season last year, and his physician thinks that he never really recovered from that. Some months ago, we thought he was on his deathbed. But he's gotten some strength back, although he tires easily."

"Well, that's encouraging," she said. "I'd like a chance to get to know the man I've pledged my service too."

Tesca looked at her, his face serious. "You don't regret it, do you?" he asked her. "You don't feel like you were forced into this?"

She smiled up at him. "Everyone has their own agenda, Tesca. You and Galen have always wanted me to enter the Duke's service. I realized that soon after I came here. But you didn't force me into it; you gave me the choice. And I made it. No regrets." She sighed and stretched her arms up towards the ceiling. "No Jolly Red hunting after me, no bounty hanging over my head. I've got a room of my own, a job that–" she broke off, frowning. "It is a paying job, isn't it?"

He nodded, grinning. "It pays very well, though you'll have precious little time to spend it."

"Oh, I never need much time to spend money," she promised, laughing. "So, what's my first mission?"

"How about a walk through Kohayne?" Tesca offered. "You've entered into His Grace's service; you need to become acquainted with his city. You and I will take a tour."

"I get to leave the estate!" she squeaked with delight. "I don't really feel like today counted; most of the time I was stuck in a box."

"I thought you might like that idea," her friend replied. "But it's not just a chance to stretch your legs. Your training begins tomorrow; so I'd suggest you get some rest."

After Tesca bid her good night and left, Kayrla feared she would be too excited and curious about tomorrow to sleep, but she was unconscious only seconds after her head hit the pillow, and her sleep was deeper and more restful than it had been in weeks.

Chapter Twenty

The night was cooler than it had been for weeks in Kohayne. A gentle rain was falling on the city, but it had not stopped the revelry in Harborside. The unofficial festivities for the Duke's Ascension were in full swing, and the rain outside simply drove more of the residents indoors, packing the taverns, brothels and gambling dens tight and adding a humid energy to the celebrations.

There was little activity on the docks themselves, though small bands of celebrants could be seen staggering back to their ships from time to time, laughing and singing off-key in a myriad of tongues. The ships themselves were nearly deserted. No captain who wanted to keep his crew happy would keep them onboard during the Ascension festivals. Only the Sabrian warship, the largest ship in the harbor, showed a full crew and armed marines standing guard at the gangplank. The sound of their exotic music could be heard coming from within the ship, however, indicating that although the Sabrians might not deign to join the celebrations in Kohayne itself, they were keeping themselves entertained in their own fashion.

On board the *Cutlass*, a skeleton crew sullenly kept watch. These few unfortunates had won, or lost, depending on who was asked, the lottery Jolly Red had devised for deciding who would remain on board tonight. The captain had divvyed up the swag as a way of appeasing the crew and let them loose on Kohayne, but someone had to stay and keep watch on the ship, so he'd drawn random names from a hat.

The fact these guards got some extra coin as compensation did not lift their spirits; the captain had made it clear that they sailed with the tide next morning. So they sat huddled on deck in the rain, listening to the sounds of revelry all around them and feeling sorry for themselves.

Below deck, Jolly Red sat alone in his cabin, drinking and sulking. There was a knock on his door.

"Come," he spat out. As Clegg entered, he scowled at him. "I wanted to be left alone, Clegg."

"I'll not bother you again tonight, cap'n," said the cook. "Just wanted you to know all the food is stowed below. We're ready to sail once the crew gets back."

"Very well," Jolly replied, his voice dull with rum. His head lolled back to look out the window. Through the thick glass, he could see distorted shapes and lights moving along the main street, revelers traveling from one party to the next. "It's a shame, isn't it."

"Sir?" Clegg said, turning from the door. He'd been about to leave, and was surprised to hear the captain speak.

"The girl. The elf girl. Shame about her."

Clegg watched his captain closely. "Aye, cap'n. It is a shame."

"She was such a pretty little thing. So tiny. I could wrap her waist in both my hands and still have some room to spare." Clegg shifted his feet and looked uncomfortable, but Jolly didn't notice. "And her hair. I even got used to that green hair of hers. It was…it was beautiful. Like seaweed, it was. Bright and shiny."

"Yes, it was, cap'n," said Clegg. "If you won't be needing–"

"And those eyes," Red went on, oblivious, "like emeralds, they were. Why'd…why'd she steal from me, Clegg? Why'd she have to go and do that?" He took another pull from his bottle. "I fancied her; I admit it. I would have made her my mistress; given her jewels, silks, anything she wanted."

Clegg glared at Jolly and opened his mouth to tell him what it was that Kayrla had really wanted, but he paused, seeing the captain's condition. "Aye, cap'n. It is a shame about her." He plowed on, raising his voice a little before Jolly could start rambling again. "I'll be going ashore for the night. There are a few lads on deck if you need anything. Good night, cap'n."

Jolly didn't respond, so the cook opened the door and left. "Clegg?" Jolly asked, looking up at the sound of the door closing. "Fine. Who needs the bastard?" he muttered, turning to stare blearily out the window once more.

The door opened and closed again and Jolly turned back. "Back again, damn y–"

There was a figure standing in front of him, but it was not the ship's cook. Dressed in a long dark cloak with the deep hood pulled up, the figure had no shape, no face. "Captain," came a voice from inside the hood. The voice was delicate, precise and had a musical quality to it. "I understand that you are planning to leave tomorrow? I cannot imagine you would leave without first concluding our arrangement."

Jolly Red stared at the figure, recognition slowing dawning on his face. "How...how did you get on board?" he stammered.

"A blind man wearing bells could have done it without your so-called watchmen taking the slightest notice," the figure replied disdainfully. "We have business to conclude. You have an item; I am here to pay you for that item. Let us do this and be done."

Jolly scowled. "Keep your money, man...or woman, whoever you are. The pendant's gone."

The figure cocked its head to one side. "You have lost it?"

"Lost it? Not as such. I know where it lies. I just can't get to it," Jolly said, shrugging. "It was stolen from me by one of my former crew."

"Ah," the figure said, the voice becoming sharper, "this would be the infamous Kayrla, the...girl you set the bounty on? I have only arrived here tonight, but I heard of this bounty before I set out for the Quad." The voice quickened, betraying anger. "This matter was meant to be conducted privately, with discretion, as I told you before. All the Frees know her name and that she robbed you. Is this what you call discretion?"

Jolly shrugged again. "The little bitch robbed me. She had to pay for that. I offered her a place at my side and she stabs me in the back. Ungrateful–"

"Be silent," the figure commanded, the voice nearly a hiss now. "She stole this item from you, but you know where it is? Does she still have it?"

"Took it to a watery grave, she did," Jolly replied. "She died today, trying to take a ship out of here. I saw the pendant in her hand, and both of them fell into the harbor and were lost."

"Tell me exactly how and where this happened," the figure said, "from the beginning."

With stumbling words, Jolly explained. The figure interrupted him frequently, clarifying a particular point or asking Jolly to repeat a certain part of his story. When Jolly got to the part about the elf's partner, the swordsman who'd helped her escape on that first night, the figure insisted Jolly repeat his description of the man.

"There was a Sabrian who came in a few days ago wanting to sell me information on that man," said Jolly. "He said he'd be in the service of someone rich and powerful."

"He is," said the figure. "I know who that man with the twin blades is, and whom he serves."

"So there you are," Jolly replied with a belch. "Now, seeing as I don't have what you want, our business is concluded. Why don't you just shove off?"

"You incompetent fool," snapped the figure. "A simple transaction! One pendant for more gold than your entire ship is worth. A deal quietly done, with no one the wiser. Instead the thief, and the pendant, slip out of your hands!" The voice was trembling with rage now.

"The pendant's at the bottom of the harbor," Jolly snarled, lumbering to his feet. "Maybe I'll have my lads throw you overboard so you can find it."

"You are as stupid as you are fat," the figure replied. "You saw only what they wanted you to see. She is alive and in the custody of the Duke. That means the Duke also has the pendant. You've hopelessly complicated matters, you drunken sot!"

"Mind your tongue or I'll have it out!" snapped Jolly, his drunken gaze falling on his saber hanging on a hook near his bed. "No one insults me on my own ship."

"I told you to be silent," the figure spat, waving a slender, gloved hand at Jolly Red. The captain opened his mouth to yell, but no words came out. The big man froze, puzzled, his mouth moving as he tried to yell, but nothing he did made the slightest noise. Enraged, he pounded his fist on the table in front of him, but although the table shook with the force of his blow, nothing could be heard.

The only sound in the room was a sharp metallic ringing as the figure drew a rapier. Then the figure was dashing forward, leaping up onto the table, the cloak rustling. But as the figure drew close to Jolly Red, all sounds abruptly stopped. Like a pantomime performance, the figure thrust out expertly, stabbing Jolly in the chest, then a second time as the man sagged back in his chair like a deflating balloon. Jolly's mouth opened wide in a yell of pain and alarm, but still no noise came from his mouth. The figure leapt off the table, landing behind Jolly's chair. A second gloved hand came out from under the cloak and pulled Jolly's head back. The rapier flashed once more, slicing a thin red line across his neck. Blood exploded from the wound and Jolly clamped a hand to his throat, but it was only a vague, fumbling gesture.

The figure remained standing behind Jolly Red as the big man's movements slowed, wrapping a slender arm around Jolly's chest to keep him from slumping to the floor. Suddenly, a pale, sickly green light enveloped the pair of them. The light pulsed brighter in time with the dwindling spurts of blood from Jolly Red's slashed throat. Jolly stared at the ceiling, his face blank with shock, but after a few moments his expression twisted to one of fear, as if he saw something approaching he could not escape. His struggles became more urgent, but no less clumsy as the figure held him in place. As his movement stilled, the pulses of green light faded.

The figure let Jolly slide out of the chair onto the floor, wiped the rapier clean on Jolly's own shirt, then moved around the table, stepping lightly around the spreading pool of blood. When the figure was some ten feet from Jolly's body, the cloak began to rustle with noise and the figure's steps were audible once more. The figure looked around the room, then snarled in a brief burst of frustration before opening the door and slipping out into the dark hallway.

Chapter Twenty-one

"Don't turn around," Tesca said to Kayrla as they sat down. They were in a tavern called the Crone's Tooth, a South Harborside dive with few windows and deep shadows. The place was crowded and noisy for late afternoon; the Ascension revels were no longer confined to after sundown. Tesca was wearing a different disguise than his "Old Jargy" appearance, looking nondescript and scruffy, a sailor on his own in Harborside. "You had a chance to look the room over as we walked in. How many bearded men are in here?"

Kayrla was wearing her red hair and freckles disguise today. She bit her lip and thought quickly. "Six," she replied. "The bartender, three men by the door at one table, and two others. One's sitting alone and the other is with a woman."

"How many of them are armed?" Tesca asked, his eyes looking into hers.

"All of them, I think," she said after a moment. "Two of the trio have pistols and cutlasses and the third has a knife at his belt. The other two customers have sabers. The bartender doesn't have a blade at his hip, but I've never seen a bartender in the Frees who didn't have something near to hand to help him keep the peace. It's probably a pistol."

Why a pistol?" her friend asked.

"He's neither a large man nor a young one," said Kayrla. "If he's got a pistol, he doesn't have to come from behind the bar to use it." She held her breath, waiting.

He smiled at her. "Not bad. You're right about the pistol behind the bar; it's a Sabrian flintlock, double-barreled and very expensive. How an old seadog like Mazerin got his hands on it, I've no idea, but he's quite good with it. There's a seventh bearded man, though, passed out in the far corner, behind a table. You're shorter than most, so it's harder to see everything in a crowded room. Remember that."

She nodded. Her first day out of the estate as one of the Duke's agents had been much harder work than she'd expected. Tesca had taken her through most of the lower sections of the city, giving her a short briefing on how the Duke kept an eye on affairs in Kohayne, and showing her some of the basic code signs. One of them was in a particular second-story window along the docks in South Harborside. There was a lamp in the window with a red shade.

"If the lampshade is red, then that indicates there's no immediate danger to the Duke or to the city," Tesca had told her as they walked under the window. "Every time you're in Harborside, especially if you've been on assignment here for a few days, or you're sailing in after being away for a while, check that window."

"Do different colors mean different things?" she had asked.

Tesca had nodded. "Yes, but you don't have to learn their meanings yet. For now, all you have to know is that if you don't see a red lampshade in that window, return to the estate as quick as you can and report to Galen."

While they had been walking through the streets, Tesca had constantly tested her powers of observation by asking questions about her surroundings, and wouldn't let her take a second look before answering. Her brain was whirling with all the things she had to pay attention to. But he didn't scold her when she missed something, and gave her suggestions on how to improve.

As the day had progressed, she'd started to get the knack of it, to the point that Tesca had complimented her on being "a quick study," and had suggested stopping in the Tooth for a late lunch before heading back up to the estate.

"I'm not looking forward to that climb back up," she said quietly after the waitress had taken their orders.

"You get used to it," Tesca said.

She gave a snort of derision. "You were wheezing like a bellows after that climb the night I met you."

He scowled at her. "I'd been in Narlos for three months; the whole city's flat," he said defensively. "If you're here, you'll be going up and down that slope a few times a week, sometimes more than once a day. And it'll be a little while before you get an assignment that takes you out of the Quad, so you'll have plenty of time to get used to that climb."

"What sort of assignment will I get?" she asked.

He shrugged, glancing around. "It's not really something to discuss here, you know, although the Crone's Tooth is a good place to have a quiet conversation. It's too noisy to eavesdrop." He leaned over the table towards her. "In any case, you're only in training, which we'll have to postpone after today until the Ascension's passed. The fete's tomorrow night and with all the dignitaries, diplomats and their own spies in the city now, there's too much going on and too many eyes about to risk more than this afternoon jaunt."

She nodded, holding her response as the waitress set their drinks on the table. After Tesca paid her and she left, Kayrla waited until Tesca was taking a pull from his mug, then asked with a grin, "Galen must be busier than a bitch with eight pups and four teats, eh?"

Tesca coughed out his laugh, spattering the table with ale. "And twice as grouchy," he admitted with a grudging smile, wiping his chin. "He needs me close, but I insisted you get one day out of the estate before the fete. You've been cooped up in there long enough. Once the Ascension's over, we'll start your training proper."

She smiled at him, grateful for the chance to stretch her legs. "I'm ready," she said. "I won't let you down."

"I'm sure you–" he began to say, then broke off, glancing over her shoulder towards the front door.

Kayrla fought the urge to turn her head and look. Instead she stayed exactly where she was and said without changing her pleasant expression, "Someone you know?"

Tesca kept the smile on his face as well. "Actually, it's someone you know. That older man from the *Cutlass*. You said he was the cook, yes?"

"Clegg?" Kayrla asked, the urge to turn her head stronger than ever. "He wasn't much of a cook, but he was a good friend."

"He's not looking this way," Tesca said. "Slide your chair around the table and sit next to me." She did so and looking out at the room, she spotted her former crewmate quickly enough. He was with a second man, thickly built and balding, who led Clegg to a table where a third man was sitting, a slender man with a mane of long brown hair, nicely dressed. "Odd," Tesca said, leaning in towards her. "I recognize both of those other men. The bald one's a member of the City Watch, but the fellow with the long hair works for the Harbor Authority. He's an assessor."

"What is that?" Kayrla asked.

"He judges the value of goods that come into the Quad, so the proper tax can be levied upon them."

"A tax collector," she said with all the scorn a sailor and citizen of the Frees could muster.

"In a way," Tesca said, chuckling at her tone. "But you should be more kindly towards him. He collects your salary now, remember?"

She flushed. "So, um, what's Clegg doing with them?" she asked, changing the subject as quickly as she could.

Tesca's mouth twisted into a puzzled scowl. "I don't know. Usually the Harbor Authority does its business on the ships themselves, not a bar like The Crone's Tooth."

"And if it was something to do with the *Cutlass*, wouldn't they be talking to Jolly Red?" she asked. "Maybe he's late on the harbor fees."

Tesca nodded. "I don't know how far in advance Jolly paid the fees, but even if they were due again, I don't see why these two would be talking to Clegg instead." He glanced at Kayrla. "Is Clegg an officer on the ship? The first mate, perhaps?"

Kayrla shook her head. "That was Parkin. I…I killed him the night we met. After him, would have been Wharven, but …" she trailed off, remembering. "No, actually that's not true. Not anymore. Wharven's dead too."

"How?"

She shrugged uncomfortably at him. "Well…you killed him."

"Me?"

Kayrla nodded. "He was also in the group with Jolly Red when we first met. When they charged us, he was the first one you cut down."

Tesca blinked. He seemed surprised at the news, but not alarmed. "Wharven," he said simply. "Wharven. He was the drunkest of them and the easiest target. There were too many of them. I had to even the odds."

"There's no need to apologize," Kayrla started to say, but Tesca shook his head.

"I'm not apologizing. I did what I had to do and I'll have to do the same sort of thing again before long, I expect. It's the life I've chosen. The life we've chosen."

She nodded. "You're not telling me something I hadn't expected, and accepted."

His lip curled into a faint, bitter smile. "Well, here's something you may not have known beforehand. Consider this part of your training. In our line of work, it's a rare thing to learn the names of the men who must be moved from your path. Most of the time, fights will be like that one where we met; an unexpected encounter, the flash of drawn steel and suddenly it's kill or be killed. There's no time to find out who you're fighting, and there'll be no chance to go back and learn the names of the dead." He nodded, more to himself than to her. "Wharven. When you learn the name of someone you've killed, remember it. It's a rare thing."

She stared at him. "Tesca, are you all right?"

"Fine," he replied. "I'm just taking a moment to remember Wharven, that's all." He continued to watch the conversation Clegg was having with the two city officials, then sighed. "I'd like to know what they're talking about, but it's time we were heading back up."

"Can't we get closer?" Kayrla asked, burning with curiosity. "Clegg won't recognize us."

"I'm not taking that chance," Tesca replied, shaking his head. "You look human, but you don't exactly move like one, and if anyone might recognize that, it would be an old friend of yours." He chuckled at her stubborn pout. "Galen can send down an inquiry to the Harbor Authority and we'll get the whole story by tomorrow."

"Not as much fun," Kayrla said.

"No," Tesca said, and he looked disappointed as well. "But we can poke around all sorts of places in Kohayne once the chaos of the Ascension is passed." They got up from the table and made their way outside through the press of customers.

Kayrla stretched and yawned as they stepped out into the street. "I am glad we were able to get out. At least for one day."

"Happy to oblige," Tesca said. "All right, now we'll cross the Duke's Bridge, make a left at–" he broke off as he noticed she was looking at something on the docks. "What is it?"

"Over there," said Kayrla. "The *Cutlass.* There's members of the Watch standing guard over her."

Tesca turned and saw she was right. Two uniformed members of the City Watch were on station at the gangplank, and two more were walking the *Cutlass's* deck. There was no sign of any of the *Cutlass's* crew. "Now that is interesting," he said. "Come on, let's take a look."

"I thought you said we had to get back," Kayrla said, catching up to him as he started walking towards the guards.

"We do, but curious passerby won't be out of place," said Tesca. "You want to ask them, or shall I?"

"Oh no, I'll do it," said Kayrla, trotting a few steps ahead of him. Presently they came up to the two guards. Kayrla looked curiously at them and at the other two on deck. "What's going on?" she asked.

The watchman shrugged. "The captain's dead, that's all I know."

"Jolly Red?" she squeaked. "Jolly Red is…"

"You knew him?" the watchman asked, suddenly suspicious.

Out of the corner of her eye, Kayrla saw Tesca shift his feet. "Knew him? Of course not!" she scoffed. "But who hasn't heard of Jolly Red, captain of the *Cutlass*?"

"I hadn't," said the first watchman.

"Nor I," said the second. "Hey now, wasn't he the fat one who was promising gold to the man who brought him some elf ears?"

The first watchman nodded. "Aye, I think you're right." He chuckled, a snorting wheeze. "Seems there's someone who didn't take kindly to that, eh?"

"You mean he was mur–" she sputtered, but Tesca swept by her, tugging her along with him.

"Thanks for the news," he said quickly, shoving Kayrla in front of him and steering her away.

Kayrla didn't resist. Her feet didn't seem to want to move properly. "What happened?" was all she could say.

"No idea," Tesca replied, his face grim. "We'll find out faster by returning to the estate. Galen will know more than we do. He's probably waiting for us."

Chapter Twenty-two

"When you said I'd get to attend the fete," Kayrla said to Galen, "this isn't what I had in mind." She glanced down with disappointment at her uniform, the livery of a serving maid.

"My dear," said the Right Hand, brushing a bit of dust off the sleeve of his uniform, a snug black jacket and trousers with gold piping and a small golden hand pinned to his right collar, "despite the fact that the purported reason for this gala event is for everyone to celebrate and have a good time, I assure you that everyone here, from the Duke himself, to his guests, to the visiting emissaries, down unto the serving staff, everyone, is working tonight. Everyone is here to watch everyone else; to share and steal information from each other. No one is here to simply have a good time."

"There's going to be music," protested Kayrla, "and dancing."

"To be sure," Galen replied. "A great deal of both. And no little consumption of wine and spirits either."

Kayrla was confused. "But if everyone is here to watch everyone else, surely they won't want to muddy their eyes with drink?"

"It can't be avoided for two reasons," Galen said. "First, it's an old, old custom. Abstaining from drinking tonight is considered an insult to the Duke's hospitality."

"Why?'

"The fete formally begins with His Grace having the first cask of wine broached in front of his guests, filling his cup and drinking it to their health in welcome. This is the wine all the guests share. By the Duke drinking first, he is demonstrating that he does not intend to poison them; that they are safe within his walls and they may be at ease. During the night, refusing to drink when the Duke offers a toast implies the Duke is not to be trusted." Galen sighed. "In times past, such an insult resulted in imprisonment, or a duel if the offender's standing was high enough to avoid being put in chains."

Kayrla nodded. "So what's the second reason?"

"Abstinence at an event such as this draws undue attention. We are here for a party, after all. We want to put each other at ease, to relax and possibly let some tidbit of information slip. You're more likely to let your guard down around a person who also has a drink in his hand."

"This is a lot more complicated than a good old rum-and-punch in some Harborside tavern," said Kayrla. "I thought it just was a big party."

Galen chuckled. "It is, but there's a lot more going on as well."

"What do you mean? I'm just trying to figure out what I'm supposed to be doing."

Galen seemed to recognize her growing anxiety. "All right. Let me try to explain," he offered. For a moment, he looked at her, thinking. "As a sailor, you know that what you see on the surface of the ocean is not necessarily an indicator of what lies below?" She nodded and he continued. "Think of this affair as a body of water, then. What you see on the surface is a party; a grand celebration of the Duke's reign and the prosperity he's brought to his people." He raised a finger to her in warning. "But there are things below the surface as well. Things you cannot see from the deck of a ship; deep currents, shallows and sandbars to catch the unwary. And of course, there are predators."

Kayrla's eyes went wide in a flash of comprehension. She remembered a moment over two years ago, watching a pod of seals racing past the *Cutlass*. She had marveled at their sleek forms darting by, but gasped in surprise as a great shape suddenly burst from below them, breaking the surface of the water and scattering the pod. The shark fell back into the water, a seal trapped in its jaws, leaving only a few bubbles on the surface to tell that anything had been there. She felt a flutter of excitement pass through her. "And to see the dangers below the surface, you have to take a deep breath and dive," she said. "You have to swim among them."

"Exactly," said Galen, pleased that she understood him so quickly. "Think of tonight as your first swimming lesson. I won't ask you to dive into the deeps. Not yet. But I do want you to at least put your head under the water and look around." He gestured toward the open door and she followed him into the hallway, heading towards the Duke's private quarters.

"You said there would be predators," she reminded him as they walked. "Who are the biggest ones that'll be here tonight? Who should I be watching out for?"

"That's too broad a category," the Right Hand replied. "What some might consider to be the most dangerous predator, others wouldn't take any great notice of. Take Tesca, for example."

"Tesca?" she asked. "He's a predator?" She smirked. "He doesn't look like a shark to me."

"A shark," mused Galen. "Yes, I would say that he is a shark, though not yet a large one. He was not the Left Hand during His Grace's last fete five years before. So, some of the more distant visitors will not know who he is, or they may have heard his name, but nothing he's done has impacted upon them. Now the Sabrian Ambassador, on the other hand, will be carefully observed by everyone here, more for whom she represents rather than who she is personally."

"She?" Kayrla asked.

"Yes, this year they've sent a woman," Galen replied. "Fleet Captain Livia Maritius. Most of their naval officers are male, but there's no formal law prohibiting women from serving in the fleet beyond the mandatory term. As Tesca tells it, nearly as many women have ruled the Empire as men. But returning to Tesca for a moment," he went on, "guests who are esteemed citizens of Kohayne have a very different opinion of him. They know of his skill at swordplay, his reputation for ruthlessness, and his skill at discovering secrets they would rather keep hidden. They will want to know where he is and whom he is talking to at all times." He smiled. "From where you'll be standing, you should be able to see the attention he draws. I'll point out the local guests to you; tell me later if there are any foreign guests who also seem to keep their eye on him. That may mean he's developing a greater reputation than we thought."

Kayrla nodded, somewhat surprised to hear this about Tesca. "And who do you think will be the most dangerous predator here tonight?"

Galen's smile faded. "The one I don't know is coming. The unknown enemy." He stopped and turned to look down at Kayrla. "Tonight is a celebration and should be a peaceful affair, but make no mistake: There are many in the Frees who would be pleased if the Kohaya line was ended. It would be a brazen move to attempt to strike down His Grace here, in his own home, but we cannot ever rule out the possibility of someone deciding the reward is worth the risk. What I fear is the unexpected, Kayrla. Stay alert."

"Yes, Galen," she replied. He nodded, his expression softening. Patting her shoulder, he resumed walking and she followed him.

His Grace, Duke Stephen Kohaya, was waiting for them in his dressing room, wearing a festive outfit of dark red and gold, the Kohaya colors. He was frowning at his physician, Dr. Felton, who had the air of one who had just lost an argument.

"If you insist on this course of action, milord, then so be it," said Felton. "But I give my consent grudgingly," he warned. "You are recovering, not recovered."

"All I need do is reach my chair," the Duke said, his voice still hoarse, but stronger than it had been the first day Kayrla met him. "Then I stay off my feet and let everyone come to me." He looked at Galen and Kayrla as they approached, nodded in acknowledgement as they bowed before him. "Galen, this man would have me walk out with a cane or on the arm of a guard."

Galen gave Felton a polite nod. "And he has a point, milord. While it would be good for your people and your guests to see you walk out unaccompanied, it would be worse if they saw you stumble or fall."

"I'll be the judge of my own strength in this," the Duke grumbled. Kayrla sympathized with His Grace; the man suddenly reminded her of a large dog that had been confined indoors for too long and now strained to bound through an open door and run about on the grass. It was much the same way she had felt during her own recent confinement to the estate. The realization that she and the Duke were alike in that way made her smile. "I will take the risk," the Duke insisted. "Gentlemen, I am aware of your concerns, but trust that I am not being ruled by impatience. The matter is closed."

"As you wish, milord," Galen said with a nod. Felton sighed, then nodded as well.

"Very well," said the Duke. "Now, physician, will you excuse us? My Right Hand has some matters to share." The man bowed and left the room. The Duke sighed, his shoulders drooping in weariness. "Tired already," he muttered. "I'll sleep for a week after this night is past."

"It's rather grandiose," Galen offered, "but we could have you carried in upon your throne."

The Duke shook his head. "That's the sort of entrance my grandfather would have had. It's far too pompous to sit well in the stomachs of anyone from the Frees, even such jackals as most of my guests." He straightened. "I've been sick; they've all heard the rumors of that by now. If I come in with a cane or on the shoulders of other men, they won't see a Duke, they'll see an invalid. No, I must walk out on my own power." He looked at Kayrla. "Besides, what's the point of looking healthy if I don't act like it? Are you ready?"

"Yes, milord," she replied. The Duke sat in a chair before her, but then she heard footsteps outside the door and turned to see Tesca enter. He was wearing a uniform identical to Galen's but with red piping instead of gold, and a silver hand on his left collar.

"The first guests are arriving," he said after bowing to the Duke. "The contingent from Narlos and some of the local merchants."

Galen looked at the clock. "Half an hour before the fete is formally begun. I think it's time." He nodded to Kayrla. "Cast your spell."

Kayrla nodded back to him and turned to the Duke. She studied his lined face, making note of the shadows under his eyes and the hollowed cheeks. Then, drawing upon the pendant hidden under her uniform, she began to form her illusion.

It had been the Duke himself who'd come up with the idea of her casting an illusion on him, to help convince his guests that rumors of his poor health were groundless. She had practiced casting this spell on him for over three hours yesterday after coming back from Harborside. The spell was relatively minor because it was only a few cosmetic changes, but Galen and the Duke had been meticulous in examining every detail of the illusion and requiring her to cast it again and again until it satisfied them both. She was not trying to make the Duke look like someone else, or even look like a younger man. He had to look like himself, but healthier and more vigorous, which was a much more subtle piece of spellcraft than she'd ever tried before. Too much color to his cheeks and he looked like he'd been caked with makeup. Conceal the shadows under his eyes and cheekbones too clumsily and his face looked like it was made of wax.

She'd never tried to cast an illusion on another person before, but to her surprise, she found it easier than casting one upon herself. She didn't need a mirror to examine her work, she could just walk around him and correct minor details. The Duke, for his part, had been fascinated by the process. Holding a mirror before him, he'd been amazed to watch his features change as Kayrla made adjustments to the illusion and asked numerous questions about illusions and magic in general. Kayrla had answered them as best she could.

Kayrla stepped back and let Galen examine her work. The older man studied the Duke's appearance for a full minute before nodding in satisfaction. "Well done, I think."

"Good," said the Duke, standing back up. He did it slowly, but without any grunt of effort, and Kayrla was surprised at how well the disguise worked, even though she could see her own illusion as a transparent mask over the Duke's face. To anyone else, the Duke's slow, careful movements would be attributed to age, not illness. "I am ready."

As Galen brought the Duke his cane, which he planned to put aside just before he entered the Great Hall, Kayrla crossed to Tesca. "Have you heard anything more about Jolly Red?"

"The Harbor Authority sent a report up here." Tesca told her. He paused, as if he wasn't sure he should tell her. "Jolly was murdered in his own cabin. He'd been stabbed in the chest and had his throat cut. Looks like he never had the chance to get out of his chair." He paused again. "There was something odd; the report says Jolly had a look on his face as if he'd been scared to death."

"Scared?" she asked. "Jolly would stand on deck during a storm and laugh at the waves. He had a lot of faults, but cowardice wasn't one of them."

Tesca shrugged. "That's what the report said. I watched him myself for the past few weeks and I'd agree that he wasn't a man ruled by fear. There was something bothering him, though. Something more than just avenging a theft. He said once, 'this is getting out of hand.' But I never found out more than that."

She rubbed her brow, disbelief etched across her features. "I don't understand how this could have happened. You told me that we had people watching the ship!"

"They were only watching to see if Jolly left," Tesca admitted. "And he never did. Most of the crew was on shore leave by that point; only a skeleton crew was left on board, and they say they didn't see or hear anything out of the ordinary until that fellow you know, Clegg, found him dead the next morning." He shrugged. "It's likely one of the crew did it and the others are trying to cover for him."

Kayrla shook her head. "That doesn't make any sense. If one of the crew did it, they would have hid the body, or at least tried to." She was feeling torn between sorrow and relief. Jolly had been her captain and compatriot before becoming her enemy, and though she was glad to be away from him, she hadn't wanted him dead, at least not like this. She was more worried for Clegg. "What's going to happen to the crew now?"

"The Harbor Authority is rounding them up for questioning," said

Tesca, "though I doubt they'll get much more out of them. As for the ship, it seems that Jolly Red owned the *Cutlass* outright, and no papers have been found designating a new owner after him, so legally the ship becomes the property of the Duke."

"What will happen to her?" Kayrla asked.

"That'll be decided later," Galen said as he and the Duke approached them. "The ship may be auctioned off, or brought into His Grace's fleet."

The Duke chuckled. "Which would swell my armada to the grand total of six. This is a matter for another day. We've puzzles enough awaiting us in the Great Hall; let's be about it." Kayrla and Tesca bowed as the Duke walked past them, and followed him out.

Chapter Twenty-three

"Presenting Master Kebben Navir, envoy of Count Valyon of Mypor and his wife, Mistress Mayira Navir!" the herald called out. Tesca watched heads turn towards the pair coming through the large double doors at the far end of the Great Hall. The doors stood at the top of a wide descending stair, allowing the assembled guests plenty of time to observe the newcomers. As he'd expected, the susurrus of conversation ebbed at the herald's announcement, but resumed again a few moments after the Mypor delegation had begun to descend the staircase.

Diving in with the sharks, Kayrla had called it just before she'd gone out into the room herself, though in her maid's uniform she drew little notice herself. Tesca was glad for that. Her metaphor was quite apt, and he needed to stay focused tonight.

He had not wanted to attend this function as himself; he'd argued briefly with Galen about it, saying that his rank of Left Hand was unofficial anyway and he'd be of more use disguised as Kayrla was, eavesdropping on conversations. But Galen had been firm about it. *"This is not one of His Grace's private parties, lad,"* the older man had said. *"It is a state function; an opportunity for the Duke to display his wealth and power. The locals will expect to see you there. They will become uneasy if they don't; like as not they'll suspect His Grace ordered you to sneak into their homes while they're away. Tonight, for once, your job is to be visible. And enjoy yourself. That's an order,"* he had added with a smile, enjoying his lieutenant's discomfiture.

Fingering the silver hand badge on his left collar, Tesca felt uneasy. The item had been presented to him by the Duke himself this morning, something no other Left Hand had ever received, not even Galen. *Is he going to formally acknowledge my position?* he wondered, not happy about the further loss of his anonymity. *"It erodes my efficiency if everyone knows who I am,"* he had told Galen, trying one last time to get out of this function. *"They already do, lad,"* Galen had told him. He took a long sip from his cup of watered-down wine and moved through the crowd of celebrants, noting not for the first time that night that several conversations died away as he approached, then resumed once he'd passed. *Are they actually afraid of me?* he wondered. It was an odd sensation, but he thought there might be ways to take advantage of that in the future.

To his right, the orchestra blew a short fanfare, letting all the guests know the Duke was taking a drink. All the guests turned towards the dais where the Duke was sitting and raised their own glasses in unison, then drank as well. Conversations began again as the moment passed. On his right, he saw a circle of people talking. Among them he recognized Amio the glassblower, who'd thrown Tesca out of his shop during their last encounter. Amio did not give Tesca a single glance, though of course the two men knew each other. As one of the most successful craftsmen in the city, Amio had a reputation to maintain, and while no one would take notice of him throwing a beggar like Jargy Barluf out of his shop, it would be quickly noticed and commented on if Amio showed any familiarity with the Duke's Left Hand.

Tesca was about to turn away when another man in the group called to him, "I say there, my fine fellow, I don't recognize your badge of rank." Before Tesca could respond, the man had stepped out of the group, leaving a gap, and genially drew him into the circle of conversation. "I've asked these others here, but they've all gone and lost their voices," the man said, swaying slightly on his feet. He was a short, thickly built man, his burliness turning to flab. For a moment, Tesca thought he was being addressed by a miniature version of Jolly Red, for there was something in the man's posture that reminded him of

Kayrla's former captain. But this man's hair and beard were yellow, not red, and the accent to his Freespeak suggested he was from Kreigstat, one of the northernmost of the Frees, only a day's sail from the coast of Terendor. It was still early in the party, but the man appeared to already be well into his cups.

"I am Tesca Secarius, sir," Tesca said to him, shaking his hand in greeting. "And you are?"

"Zakaras fen Brunnenfeld," the man replied with a toothy smile. "Envoy from Kreigstat. I am here to present the best wishes of my lord, the Meisterherran."

"Envoy?" Tesca asked sharply. "I did not hear your name announced by the herald."

"Ah," Brunnenfeld said, stifling a belch, "I was one of the first guests to arrive. The herald announced me but only the orchestra and servants were there to hear it. Not even the Duke had arrived yet." He shrugged, then laughed in surprise. "Goodness, but I have forgotten to present myself to him!"

"Yes, I daresay you have," Tesca chided him. "I would suggest you clear that oversight without delay."

"Of course, of course," Brunnenfeld said quickly. "Are you in the employ of His Grace?"

"I am," Tesca replied with a nod. "The badge you were curious about identifies me as His Grace's Left Hand."

Brunnenfeld seemed puzzled by the title at first, but then Tesca's words appeared to have at last penetrated his drunken thoughts. "Ah, but of course! I had heard that some rulers appoint two hands." He smiled. "It is not done so further north, not in Kreigstat."

"Indeed?"

The envoy paused. "Ah, well…" he said, trailing off. "You will, I hope, accept my apology in this. We are very close to Al-Kef, yes? The Al-Keffi, they would not respect such a title as yours."

"Really?" Tesca asked. "Why is that?"

Brunnenfeld looked amused. "They…have strict rules for eating. They use neither fork nor knife, only the right hand." He paused again, fighting to keep a smile from his lips. "The left hand, they say, is only good for other, ah…functions."

Tesca's eyes narrowed as several onlookers gasped. He allowed himself a thin smile, feigning suppressed outrage. "I see. Well, perhaps the Al-Keffi have the right of it. I find it is often my job to clean up messes. Speaking of which, sir, I expect you to present yourself to His Grace without delay."

Brunnenfeld did not miss the inference any more than Tesca had. Scowling and swaying slightly, he gave a polite nod and moved into the crowd, heading towards the Duke's dais at the other end of the Great Hall.

Tesca watched him depart. "If you ladies and gentlemen will excuse me," he snapped, "I find my cup is getting low." He raised his cup to them and drained it before turning and striding away. As he expected, the group was silent for a few moments before conversation resumed in hissing whispers, barely audible over the orchestra.

He was not nearly as angry as he let himself appear to be. In fact, he was somewhat amused by the exchange. It was not the first time he'd heard his rank compared with Al-Keffi dining practices. Galen had shared this curious fact with him the night he'd agreed to become the Duke's Left Hand. *"If the only way they can find to insult you is to draw upon the little-known customs of another culture,"* the older man had told him, *"it means you've given them nothing else to work with. I should take that as the highest compliment."*

His mind was churning with curiosity over Brunnenfeld. He was certain, for example, the Kreigan's little jibe was not an accidental slip of the tongue. *Most like he's pretending to be drunk to try putting others off their guard,* he decided. *Was he trying to test my temper? Did he hope to belittle me in front of the Kohayne citizenry?* There was something about the man that put his instincts on alert, but he couldn't narrow down what it was.

Annoyed, he waved to a servant to bring him a fresh cup of wine, accepting the one offered. The servants had been instructed to always have at least one cup of watered-down wine on their trays, so that the

Duke's agents in the crowd could drink freely without becoming as intoxicated as the guests.

Sipping the wine and tasting mostly water, he scanned the crowd for a sign of Galen, wishing to share his thoughts with him about Brunnenfeld. But surrounded by people, it was hard to see all the way across the Great Hall. A glance showed him that Galen was not up on the dais with His Grace. Only the Duke was seated there, talking with the two recent arrivals from Mypor, one guard standing on each corner of the dais. Behind him to one side stood Kayrla, a decanter of wine and a single cup on a table beside her.

The official opening of the fete had gone as planned. The Duke had strolled, albeit slowly, to his chair, and raising his glass to the assembled guests, he drained his cup. Tesca had relaxed after that. The first hurdle was past. *Now we just have to hope nothing unexpected happens,* he thought, taking another drink.

"Presenting the esteemed Alezandra Feyne and her guest, Captain Caius Grivus!" came the herald's call. Tesca turned to look, feigning a casual manner, but he was so surprised at what he saw that he barely noted the sudden hush that came over the entire hall.

In the entrance stood two figures that he recognized, but it had never occurred to him that he might see them standing next to each other. The first, Alezandra, was a tall slender young woman with long brown hair that cascaded over her left shoulder, as was her habit. Tesca knew she did it to conceal an old dueling scar. She was not beautiful in the classic sense of the word; her nose was too long and her green eyes had a predatory look to them, but she moved with an animal grace, wearing a gown of dark red that clung to her waist and flowed loosely about her ankles. In her left hand was a small fan made of exotic red-orange feathers. As she fluttered it lazily at her throat, it looked to Tesca as if her hand blazed with fire.

But it was the other figure who truly surprised him. Taking her right arm in his left, standing as escort, was the older Sabrian who'd sold news about Kayrla and Tesca to Jolly Red. His head was freshly shaved and gleamed like an obsidian sphere. He was wearing dress clothes of sea green, with dark red cuffs and collar. The outfit's resemblance to a Sabrian officer's dress uniform was deliberate, but it was not simply a copy. The jacket had no sideboards, epaulets or sash and Grivus wore no badge of rank or decoration except for a single golden pin fashioned in the shape of a sabre.

Trust Allie to start trouble tonight, Tesca thought. Grivus' choice of garment was surely her doing. *The Sabrian Ambassador will have a fit when she sees him.* There was a subtle and deliberate insult in what Grivus was wearing, though Tesca suspected no one at the fete, with the exception of himself, Grivus and possibly Allie, would realize how serious it was. The insult here was not to the Duke, but to the Empire itself. Grivus was clearly a retired officer; he would not claim the rank of Captain otherwise, not at an event where a senior Sabrian official would be present and would be like to recognize an imposter at once. He could not wear a proper dress uniform to the fete and come as Allie's guest, for by wearing the uniform he became a representative of the Empire, and the Empire was not to be seen as an escort to a mere commoner, however rich her family might be. However, by wearing an outfit that resembled a uniform, Grivus was both obeying his people's custom and deliberately ignoring it.

Tesca was more interested in who Grivus was than ever before; doing something like this suggested that Grivus bore a deep, furious resentment towards the Empire. He could not possibly wear something like that without knowing the ramifications of it. But he was also the man who had tried to challenge Tesca to an impromptu duel for wearing the Argument and the Retort, which spoke of a strong pride and fierce devotion to Sabrian ideals. The contradiction intrigued him.

Allie must be happy, he thought, noting that the conversations in the hall had still not resumed, that everyone was still staring abjectly at Alezandra and her guest as they were descending the stairs. Alezandra's eyes were bright with amused triumph. *The Feynes are always happiest when more people are looking at them than they are at the Duke,* Tesca reflected.

He moved through the crowd towards them, but to his surprise Alezandra turned in his direction once they'd descended the stairs. She looked at him and smiled as conversations renewed about him, a loud mosquito buzzing in his ears. *Dammit,* he thought, *she's one step ahead of me again. She knew exactly where I was before she walked in.*

"Tesca, darling," she said to him, neatly disengaging herself from Grivus to embrace him briefly and lightly brush her lips against his cheek. She stepped back and examined his uniform. "You clean up well. I always said you would." Her hand moved up to his collar and for an instant, her eyes tightened in irritation as she saw the silver hand badge there. But then it was past and she tugged at his collar, her lips pursed in a moue. "But you leave the collar buttoned up. So formal. Opening it would be far more dashing."

"Hello, Allie," Tesca replied. "It is a uniform, you know. One should tread carefully when making changes to a uniform."

She grinned at him, a wide smile that always seemed to him to show too many teeth. "You noticed," she said sweetly. "I knew that out of everyone here tonight, darling, only you would get the joke."

"The joke?" Tesca asked her. "Allie, do you know what the Ambassador will do when she sees hi–"

"Oh, yes. May I present my guest?" she interrupted him, gesturing towards Grivus, who stepped forward, studying Tesca. "I suppose formal introductions are in order, although from what I hear, you two have already met." She watched Tesca's face for some reaction, but Tesca was quickly remembering how to dance with Allie Feyne. He kept his face calm and politely took Grivus' hand when it was offered.

"Tesca Secarius, may I present Captain Caius Grivus, retired from Imperial service. Captain Grivus, this is Tesca Secarius, Left Hand to His Grace, Duke Stephen Kohaya."

"A fine evening to you," Grivus said, a knowing smile coming to his face. "I have been wondering whom you served since we first met. Mistress Feyne was quick to recognize your description. And now, here we are."

"Yes, indeed." Tesca and Grivus stood silent, looking at each other.

Allie looked back and forth between them, until finally she sighed.

"This must be some sort of Sabrian custom: To stare at one another until someone blinks. Come now, boys...neither of you are paying attention to me. We can't have that."

Both men smiled and turned to her at the same time. "That's more like it," she said, grinning. "Now Tesca, darling. You're not here alone, are you?"

"I'm on duty," Tesca said.

She frowned at him. "Oh, that's such a shame." She glanced down at the floor as if she was looking for something small. Her hand brushed some hairs away from the top of her ear as she said, "I was hoping to meet your...little friend."

Tesca frowned in a convincing display of confusion. "Allie, I have no idea what you're talking about."

The herald's announcement cut across any response she might have made. "Presenting the envoy from His Imperial Majesty Vorius VI, Fleet Captain Livia Maritius, and escort!"

Allie's face broke into an eager smile. "Oh, this should be interesting, don't you think?" she asked Tesca, winking at him before turning to see the new arrivals.

Chapter Twenty-four

"Presenting Master Kebben Navir, envoy of Count Valyon of Mypor and his wife, Mistress Mayira Navir!" the herald called out. Kayrla studied the two new arrivals at the opposite end of the hall.

"You wouldn't need the herald to tell you who those two are, "the Duke muttered to her, squinting. "It's those sashes they wear. Even these old eyes can pick them out. I must remember to tell Galen to have those sashes checked before they leave. I expect some of my silverware will have fallen into the folds."

She fought to keep a smirk off her face. She had expected waiting on the Duke to be a somber affair where she had to stay perfectly still, refill the Duke's cup and not spill a single drop. Instead His Grace appeared to be doing his best to make her burst out laughing, saying the most outrageous things under his breath about all of the guests who came to do him honors:

"Look at that one coming this way, the Esteemed Master Cartonne and that great cow of a wife. Look at the way he's got to steer her past the buffet table. 'No, dear…we have to bow before the Duke first,' he's saying to her. 'Come now, he holds this every five years, most like he'll not live to see the next one.' Little squab. Rumor has it he was conceived on the night of one of my father's fetes some forty years ago. Not sure her husband was the father, though; might have been one of my father's guards. The last Madam Cartonne had a thing for men in uniform; she'd hike her skirts at the first sight of brass buttons."

She didn't think it was proper for her to join in on the catty remarks, so she simply nodded and kept her giggles as quiet as possible. Her suppressed mirth seemed to greatly amuse the Duke.

"Would you care for a refill, milord?" she asked him.

He shook his head. "The only vice I intend to indulge in tonight is insulting my guests out of earshot. They're all doing the same to me, I assure you. 'Doesn't he look tired?' 'By the Triad, he looks so much older than he did at the last fete. My, what five years has done to him.'" He started to chuckle, which became a cough.

"Milord?" she asked.

The Duke's cough continued for another few seconds, then subsided. "Perhaps a touch more wine," he said hoarsely, "just to clear the throat." She poured a small amount of wine and the Duke lifted the cup to his lips. To his left, the orchestra blew a short fanfare, and the guests turned to look at the Duke, raised their glasses and drank as well. "That's one reason not to drink much at these things," the Duke said in a clearer voice, handing the cup back to her. "Every sip is a damned ceremony." He looked back at the crowd, his eyes narrowing. The delegation from Mypor was making its way through the crowd towards the dais. "How are we on the envoys?"

Kayrla thought back. The herald had been very busy over the last hour, but she'd been instructed how to tell his introductions apart. Guests who were native to Kohayne were announced as "esteemed." Foreign dignitaries representing their nation were called "envoys." She recalled the number of times she'd heard that word used. "Galen said there were two envoys who arrived before you entered, milord. The envoys from Narlos and Kreigstat. You know, I don't think the Kreigan envoy has presented himself yet."

"He hasn't," the Duke replied, amused. "When Galen finds out, that Kreigan will wish he'd stayed home."

Kayrla smiled. "There are still two envoys who haven't arrived yet, milord. Hisvet and the Empire."

"Hisvet," the Duke growled, his smile fading. "I didn't think I'd heard them announced. They're probably stalling, hoping to upstage the Sabrians by arriving last." He sighed. "I'd best enjoy this while I can. Seeing anyone from Hisvet in my hall turns my stomach."

Kayrla nodded, not surprised at the vehemence in the Duke's tone. While all of the various realms within the Frees competed fiercely with one another for trade and secrets, the rivalry between the Kohaya Quad and the Barony of Hisvet had become more akin to a feud. Clegg had told her once of a time he'd crewed on a ship that flew the flag of Hisvet, and in the three years he'd served on it, it had been boarded six times by patrol ships flying the Kohaya colors. They always gave the excuse of "searching for contraband," and on the last occasion seized the ship and divested it of over half its cargo. She knew that Hisvet practiced similar persecutions of Kohayan vessels. "Milord," she asked, "I know there's no love lost between the Quad and Hisvet, but what started it all?"

The Duke shrugged. "There's been some trouble with Hisvet as far back as both realms were settled. Principally, it's due to geography; the trade winds take our ships more or less right past Hisvet; raiders there need do little else than sit and wait for their prizes to sail by. Over the years, the various Barons have repeatedly pledged to crack down on piracy in their waters, but it's always a token gesture. Those bravos plundering our ships are really privateers, operating as the Baron's tax collectors." He shook his head. "We can thank my grandfather for adding his own amount of trouble into the situation."

"What did he do, milord?'

The Duke chuckled, then took a slow breath to make sure he didn't start coughing again. "No one's certain, but the popular story is that he deflowered one of the Baron's daughters. And it might be true; I know he was fond of being 'the first through the door,' if you'll pardon the expression." He smiled as Kayrla suppressed another giggle. Then he looked thoughtful. "If we ever make a list of the problems that old fool left for my father and me to fix, that's one more." His face took on a stern, regal bearing as the Mypor entourage reached the dais and he gently gestured a dismissal to Kayrla.

Kayrla bowed and stepped back two paces from him. The Myporeans stopped at the foot of the dais, between the two guards armed with pikes, and bowed low to the Duke. He accepted their greeting with a courteous nod.

"My lord Duke," said Master Navir, "please accept the best wishes and greeting of my sovereign, Count Valyon. He regrets that he could not attend your fete, but hopes for your health and prosperity so that he may perchance attend your next celebration."

"We accept your lord's greeting and best wishes," the Duke replied, his voice strong. "Please convey to him my deepest thanks and respect. Enjoy yourselves tonight under the ancient laws of hearth and home, bringing us together in peace and friendship. You are most welcome to Kohayne."

The Myporeans bowed to him once more, then backed away three paces before turning and merging into the crowd. The Duke signaled for Kayrla to stand beside him once more. "A dash more of wine, my dear," he said, "just to wet the throat."

Kayrla dutifully poured a small amount into the Duke's cup, but before she handed it to him, the herald's voice boomed out once more. "Presenting the Esteemed Alezandra Feyne and her guest, Captain Caius Grivus!" *Feyne?* she wondered, glancing up at the entranceway. Her keen eyes picked out the new arrivals immediately, and her mouth dropped halfway open in surprise before she caught herself. "Milord," she said to the Duke as she handed him his cup, "I recognize the Sabrian man who came as her guest. He was the one who challenged Tesca to a duel the night I met him!"

The Duke peered across the room, squinting. "Are you sure?" he asked, accepting the cup from her.

"Yes, milord. I'm certain of it."

The Duke appeared amused and glanced at Galen who had emerged from the crowd and was stepping up to the dais. "Well, Galen," said the Duke. "Little Allie's made quite an entrance, eh?"

"She always does," Galen said. "What is she up to this time?" He looked at Kayrla. "Is Grivus the Sabrian you met before?"

"Yes," Kayrla said, continuing to study the newcomers as they descended the stairs. As the guests began to move and talk once more, a chance break in the crowd revealed Tesca near the foot of the stairs before the gap closed again. "Oh, I see Tesca. She's stopped to talk to him."

Galen sighed. "Like a moth to a flame."

The Duke chuckled. "Which is which?" Galen simply shrugged and gave a thin, humorless smile in response.

Kayrla didn't think she liked the sound of that. As she was trying to think of a way to get Galen to explain further, she saw a short, fat man with yellow hair and beard make his way through the crowd, heading for the dais. She was struck by how his walk reminded her of Jolly Red. Before he reached the dais, however, suddenly the pendant around her neck began to feel hot. She gasped as the heat intensified, almost burning her. She saw the blond man check his step, wincing as if he was feeling a sudden pain as well. Then, with a deftness she would not have expected for a man who looked so clumsy, he turned on his heel and disappeared back into the crowd.

"What is it?" the Duke asked, noticing her discomfort.

"I…I don't know," she said, putting a hand to her chest to feel the pendant through her clothes. The sudden heat was gone. "There was a man, he was–"

"Presenting the envoy from His Imperial Majesty Vorius VI, Fleet Captain Livia Maritius, and escort!" called the herald.

"And here we go," said Galen, who was standing on the other side of the Duke's chair. He'd been watching the crowd, lost in his own thoughts, and hadn't heard Kayrla's gasp. "I don't think Allie Feyne's arrival right before them was a coincidence."

Despite her confusion and a lingering pain, Kayrla looked across the hall to the entranceway once more. There were five Sabrian officers descending the stairs, all in full dress uniform, sea-green cloth with red collars. Their jackets were festooned with colorful medals and ribbons. Sabrians were a tall people, as a general rule, and two of them were so tall Kayrla could still see their shaven heads above the crowd once they'd reached the main floor.

Almost at once she heard noises and commotion coming from the far side, and the majority of the guests went silent to listen. The two guards standing at the entranceway began to move down the steps after the Sabrians. Like a shot, Galen was off the dais and plunging through the crowd as raised voices, shouting in Sabrian, could now be heard clearly through the hall. Kayrla's understanding of that southern tongue was far from perfect, but there was one word repeated often enough for her to catch: *traitor*.

"Best fill my cup all the way, child," said the Duke calmly, handing the cup back to her. "I expect before all this is sorted out, I'll be needing it."

Chapter Twenty-five

"Traitor!" Fleet Captain Maritius was shouting in her native tongue, pointing down the stairs at Grivus. "This insult cannot be borne!" Two of her escort, tall male Sabrians so alike in appearance they might have been brothers, leapt forward to stand guard before her, glaring with anger.

Tesca spared one glance at Allie Feyne before he pushed his way past her. She was watching the entire spectacle with a thrilled expression, but Tesca could see that she was also taken aback at the fury of the Sabrian response.

Captain Grivus stood quietly, gazing up the stairs at his countrymen, bearing the Fleet Captain's tirade with dignity. He looked neither angry nor ashamed, as if her words meant nothing to him. This seemed to further enrage the Fleet Captain. "How dare you stand here, in my sight!" she demanded.

"He is a guest, your dignity," Tesca called out as he stepped up to Grivus, replying in Sabrian and using the Imperial honorific to address her as a superior. "As are you."

Maritius' dark eyes flicked from Grivus to Tesca, her anger blunted momentarily by surprise at being politely and correctly addressed in her own language. "And who are you?"

"Tesca Secarius, your dignity. I serve His Grace." He bowed before her, but kept his head raised to meet her eyes and clasped his forearms in front of him. In Imperial etiquette, this posture sent Maritius a specific message: *my eyes are ever watchful, and my hands are never far from their blades.* It was the traditional method of identifying oneself as an *agentis*. Maritius looked even more surprised, frowning in suspicion at him as the members of her escort looked with disbelief at each other. Tesca seized the silence and pressed on. "Is there some trouble you are having with another of His Grace's guests?"

Mauritius pressed her lips together. "That one," she said, pointing once again at Grivus. "He mocks my nation and my sovereign with his…costume."

Grivus bristled at this. "Your hypocrisy offends me," he spat. "How is it, Livia, that you should take offense over a garment but found it easy to ignore the greater insult suffered by me?" He sighed. "How far our people have fallen."

"Our people!" Maritius shouted. "How dare you claim to share a people with me, when we no longer share a nation!"

"We were a people before we were an empire," Grivus replied. "As to this," he said, gesturing to his own clothes, "these were traditional colors for our people long before they became a uniform. If your studies of history had encompassed more than the wars we have fought, you would know that." He gestured dismissively at Maritius' uniform and her numerous medals and badges. "You hide your colors under the gilded medals and badges, as jewels given to a favored concubine."

Tesca knew that the listening crowd could probably understand only a tenth of what they were shouting at each other, but no one needed to be fluent in Sabrian to know that Grivus had just crossed a line. The Sabrians on the stairs froze in an outraged hush, their eyes widening in shock. Then Maritius' two male escorts each took a step down the stairs toward Grivus.

Tesca stepped in front of Grivus, his hands outstretched. "Enough!" he yelled as the crowd around him writhed in excitement, an explosion of noise coming from every throat. The chatter around them died away in anticipation as all eyes turned back up the stairs to Maritius. Her face was cool with anger as she drew one of her gloves from her belt and tossed it down the stairs to land at Grivus' feet.

With slow dignity, Grivus bent down to pick up the glove, but Tesca was quicker. "Your dignity," he said to her, holding the glove in his hand, "you offer dishonor to His Grace by demanding satisfaction of a fellow guest while under my master's roof."

"You understand our speech well enough to know what he said to me," Maritius said. "Is this how your master treats his guests, allowing them to be insulted from the moment they enter his hall? Did all these guests have to run such a gauntlet upon their entrance? I think not." She sneered down at him. "And why should I recognize your attempts to present yourself as mediator? I would take offense at your bow to me if greater insults had not come before it. You have not the right to claim yourself as an *agentis*."

"No offense was intended, dignity," Tesca replied. "It was no claim, but rather a courtesy to you. I identified myself to you and yours to avoid a future misunderstanding." His voice held a tone of such calm, assured competence that Maritius paused, studying him afresh.

Tesca used the delay to review everything that had just happened. Grivus and Maritius had some sort of history together. By the way he spoke to her, Tesca guessed that Grivus had either been her superior officer or her instructor at the Academy, or both. Clearly they knew each other well enough for him to address her by name, and even though she may have called him a traitor, she would not have challenged him to a duel unless she considered him of roughly equal social standing.

There were numerous subtle factors of Sabrian etiquette at play here, which Tesca was quickly trying to sort out. It seemed likely that Grivus was not a convicted criminal, but had instead committed some sort of gross social impropriety sufficient to permanently disgrace him. Sabrian etiquette had a place for these social outcasts: to preserve what little dignity they had left, they were expected to avoid the company of other Sabrians and remain mute when forced to be in their presence. But Grivus had not "taken the silent road," as it was known in the Empire. To Tesca, that meant he'd gone into exile unwillingly. *Perhaps he thinks he's innocent,* Tesca thought, *or he feels that whatever he did should not be considered a crime. But why make such an obvious public spectacle here?*

As if in answer, Grivus turned to him, looking curiously amused. "You take up the glove thrown at my feet, sir," he said. "And you step between me and those who would challenge me." He nodded thoughtfully. "I accept your suit to stand as my champion."

Tesca felt like he had been punched in the stomach, as the twisting coils of Sabrian etiquette curled around him and held him fast. He'd been too long apart from Imperial society to see this coming. By doing his duty as a servant of the Duke and preventing Grivus from taking up the glove, he'd inserted himself into the opening phase of a formal Sabrian duel, volunteering to stand in Grivus' s stead if Grivus so chose.

And he also realized, as he looked at the calculating, satisfied smile on Grivus' face, that he had badly underestimated the man. He had deliberately goaded Maritius into challenging him, knowing that Tesca would not let a duel take place.

So I have begun, so I must proceed, he thought, hoping that by going along with this, he would be able to keep this from boiling into an international incident. He racked his brain for any other details of the Sabrian dueling customs he could recall, and plunged ahead. "So be it," he said to Grivus. "But as I am not a member of your entourage or company, sir, I lay before you the Champion's Price, to be paid to His Grace, for it is on his behalf that I stepped forward."

Grivus, curiously, seemed pleased at Tesca's words. "I accept that price."

"And I will champion my Captain!" shouted one of the two male Sabrians escorting Maritius. He turned to look up the stairs at her. "Sir!" he called, addressing her without regard for her gender, as was the Sabrian custom, "do not sully yourself with this false *agentis*! Let me defend your honor!"

Maritius frowned, but she did not seem angry at her subordinate. Tesca, reading her body language, suspected that she, like him, was feeling that somehow she'd been maneuvered into this confrontation and could not find a satisfactory way out. After a moment, she nodded in assent.

"Challenge given, challenge accepted, champions presented," replied Grivus, using the formal words that began a duel in the Empire. He abruptly switched back into Freespeak and turned to Tesca. "We shall arrange your price after the duel."

The other guests had become used to hearing the entire scene spoken in Sabrian, and as such had been making their own speculations on the matter of the argument based on their own skills at gossip and their varied fluency. Now, suddenly hearing Freespeak once more, the full import of Grivus' words was slow to sink in.

"Wait…what?" said Allie Feyne, confused, as the crowd began to buzz with conversation. "Duel? What are you talking about?"

"That's what I'd like to know," Galen said, pushing through the crowd to join Tesca and Grivus at the foot of the stairs, two of the Duke's guards flanking him. "I would like this explained to me, in Freespeak if you please. The Right Hand is not so fluent in Sabrian as the Left."

"Two of our guests have come to a disagreement," Tesca said to Galen, loud enough for Maritius to hear. The crowd, also eager to get a full account, went silent. "By their own customs, they have agreed to a duel of honor to settle the matter between them. This man," he said, pointing to Grivus, "has no entourage with him, so I have volunteered to stand for him in the duel. By Kohayan custom, His Grace defends his guests, yes?"

"Yes," said Galen thoughtfully, glancing up at Fleet Captain Maritius. "But is she not a guest of His Grace as well? His Grace cannot defend one guest against another."

"True," Tesca admitted. Maritius was watching him closely, waiting to see how this would be handled. In his mind's eye, he could see a fleet of Sabrian warships blockading Kohayne in response to tonight's incident. But then, as he recalled more and more of Sabrian customs, a solution came to him. "But…" he began slowly, organizing his thoughts, "in this instance, His Grace may defend Captain Grivus alone, for it is

Captain Maritius who offered the challenge, making her the aggressor." Out of the corner of his eye, he saw Grivus give an almost imperceptible nod, confirming his tactic. He pressed on, feeling more confident. "Sabrian custom allows for duels between guests if their host permits it, and the host, while not obliged to offer defense to the challenged, suffers no disgrace to do so. Indeed," he continued, "it is considered a mark of honor to defend a guest against a superior adversary."

Galen looked up at the young soldier who stood as Maritius' champion, who was obviously taller and more powerful than Grivus. In fact, he was at least half a foot taller than Tesca as well, with wider shoulders to boot. "Superior adversary…" he muttered, glancing at Tesca.

Tesca shrugged and feigning a nervous gesture, rubbed his jaw line, which was a code sign to Galen that Tesca knew what he was doing and that Galen should play along. Galen, frowning at Grivus, cleared his throat, which meant that he had noted Tesca's signal and was in agreement.

"So be it," Galen said. "This meeting of Kohayan and Sabrian customs will stand. We shall arrange a space for this duel to take place presently, and all involved parties shall attend."

"Including me!" snapped Allie Feyne, pushing her way next to Tesca. "Grivus is my guest!"

"Does that mean you'd be willing to take Tesca's place in the duel, Mistress Feyne?" Galen snapped at her. He smiled grimly as she glared at him. "I thought as not. All the same, you are permitted to attend." In short order, Galen had dispatched a servant to make one of the outdoor pavilions ready for the contest, and while Allie was quietly interrogating Grivus about what had just happened, drew Tesca aside to confer with him.

"What are you doing, lad?" he asked, concern etched into his face. "Surely you could have found some other way to handle this."

"Not without sending the Sabrian envoy off in a rage," Tesca replied. "That might have led to a trade embargo, or worse. You know the Empire would twist any excuse, any affront, to gain more power in this region."

"I know, I know," Galen replied, "but a duel?"

"It's the best way to deal with them," Tesca countered. "Their sense of honor and etiquette can be very complicated, but if you honor their customs, you gain a measure of respect with them, whether you win or lose. Besides," he said, tilting his head in Grivus' direction, "there's more going on here than just some ruffled feathers. I'll warrant Grivus came here tonight with the intention of forcing this duel to take place."

"Are you sure?" Galen asked. Tesca nodded. "Why would he do that?"

Tesca shook his head. "I have no idea. But I don't think he would go to all this trouble to drag me into a duel if he expected me to lose."

Galen looked back at Grivus. The man had apparently chosen to "take the silent road" with regards to Allie Feyne, who still berated him to no effect. "Remember lad, Grivus is the man who drew a pistol on you for wearing weapons he felt you had no right to bear. Perhaps he thinks this is a more fitting way of punishing you. Would a Sabrian's sense of honor drive him to such a complicated scheme?"

Tesca did not reply, recalling that half of the classic works in Sabrian literature were based on tales involving schemes even more complicated than this, all set in motion for the sake of honor.

Chapter Twenty-six

"A duel?" the Duke asked Galen, frowning.

The Right Hand nodded, leaning in close to the Duke's chair to speak quietly. "I didn't have time to make sense of the details, milord, but Tesca believes that he knows what he's doing."

"I'm not convinced," the Duke replied. "That lad's not always thinking clearly when Allie Feyne is involved. You know that."

Galen sighed. "Well, as for her, I know this isn't what she intended. Make a big entrance, get some tongues wagging, that's what she was after. But I think this fellow Grivus played her for a fool. He wanted this duel to take place; Tesca is sure of it."

Kayrla, standing on the other side of the Duke, desperately wanted to ask how Tesca could possibly know that, but she knew that a serving maid wouldn't insert herself into a conversation between the Duke and his Right Hand. *Everyone's watching us now that Tesca and the Sabrians have left the hall,* she thought, looking out at the crowd, doing her best to maintain her pose as a serving maid. She could read a lot of different intentions in the gazes of the people looking her way. *Some are just curious gossips, but some of them look like they're gloating! Are they just eager for blood, or are they happy the Duke's having problems?* As she looked over those faces, she tried to spot the man who'd approached the dais just before the Sabrians arrived, the one whose approach had somehow caused her pendant to grow painfully hot. But she'd lost sight of him after that first moment, and now that things were settling down again in the Great Hall, he was nowhere to be seen.

"Tesca told me that in return for standing in for Grivus," Galen continued, "Grivus now owes you something called a 'champion's price,' milord. It's a debt of honor among the Sabrians. Tesca is also positive that Grivus wanted to owe you that debt, milord."

The Duke was taken aback. "Why in the Hells would he want to do that?"

"Tesca feels that the only way to know is to play this out, milord."

The Duke's frown deepened. "I don't like someone playing games on my board with my pieces," he growled. "I'm half tempted to drag the lot of them before me and hear the entire story myself rather than let my Left Hand get himself killed over some minor slight."

Galen nodded in agreement. "I made that very suggestion, milord. But Tesca feels that would only antagonize the Sabrians further. He says that they're going to be very unwilling to present themselves to you until this matter of honor is settled; 'like going to a formal dinner wearing soiled clothes,' as he put it. He believes that by choosing to honor their customs, they will accord you more respect, regardless of who wins the duel itself." He looked up at the milling crowd of celebrants before them. "And perhaps this affair has become more of a public spectacle than it warrants already," he added ruefully.

The Duke remained silent, tapping one finger on the arm of his chair. Kayrla knew how tired he was even before the Sabrians arrived. Now he was also angry, and beneath the illusion, Kayrla could see a flush had crept into his cheeks.

"Milord," Galen asked, "What are your orders?"

The Duke sighed, his anger ebbing away. "Tesca knows those black-skinned devils better than we do. We'll do this his way."

"Very well, milord," Galen nodded. "I'm having the western pavilion cleared now. They should be able to conclude this business with some privacy there."

"But you've got someone keeping an eye on the lad, of course. Just in case?"

"The castellan has sent Lieutenant Kelvo along with him, along with a few other trusted men," Galen assured him.

"Very well," the Duke replied. "Now we just have to put our trust in our lad's blades."

"It's not like we haven't done that befo–" Galen started to say, but then the herald's voice came from the entrance once more.

"Presenting Master Victor Laveau, *Main Droite* from Baron Malviere of Hisvet, and entourage!"

"And there's the icing for this cake," the Duke grumbled. Kayrla lifted her head, as did everyone else still in the Great Hall, to see the Hisvetian contingent coming down the steps. Master Laveau was an elderly, rail-thin man in a green and black outfit and an expression on his face sour enough to curdle milk. He walked with a cane shod in metal, which he drove down onto each step with enough force to make the ringing sound reach the far corners of the hall. Behind him walked two others, a middle-aged man and a young woman, who wore similar outfits to Laveau.

"Listen to that cane of his," the Duke growled, squinting as he watched the newcomers approach. "If he cracks my marble floor, he's paying for it." He gave a quiet cough, then a second.

"Another dash of wine, milord?" Kayrla asked, reaching for the decanter. The Duke's coughing, though slight, persisted. Her eyes met Galen's and she saw that, like her, the Right Hand was trying to hide his concern.

"Not right now," the Duke replied, waving her off with a gentle hand. He coughed twice more, with greater force, then relaxed, breathing deeply. "You two can stop hovering over me like birds over an egg. I get quite enough of that from Dr. Felton. But," he admitted, "I wouldn't mind a draught of that elixir he made for me; the one for this cough."

"At once, milord," Galen said, glancing at Kayrla. "You know where the physician is?"

Kayrla nodded. "The hallway behind us, in the alcove to the right."

"Very good. He'll have some of the elixir with him. Bring it back with you."

"And put it in a goblet," the Duke suggested. "If Laveau sees me taking a spoonful of medicine from a bottle, we might as well have had me walk in with a cane," he added with a dry chuckle.

Kayrla bowed briefly to the Duke, then retreated and walked up the stairs, fighting the urge to run. Stepping through the door, she found herself amid a rapid, but controlled, flurry of activity. Servants carrying trays of food and drink bustled past her in one direction and servants with empty trays were going in the other. There were guards posted at the door and in stations along the hallway. In the alcove to her right sat three more guards, quickly wolfing down some food before going back on duty. But she didn't see Felton.

"Where's the physician?" she asked, walking up to the guards. "Where's Dr. Felton?"

One of them looked around, puzzled. "He was just here a moment ago," he said, pointing to an empty chair. He turned to his fellows. "Did either of you see where Felton went?"

"He left," said one of the others. "Someone came by and said there was a problem; he went off at once."

"He left?" Kayrla asked. "He's supposed to be here! Who came for him?"

The man shook his head, taken aback. "I was eating," he apologized. "I saw a uniform out of the corner of my eye and didn't look up."

"I saw him," said the third guard. "It was Lieutenant Kelvo. He looked like he was in a big hurry. He only came by about a minute ago."

Kelvo? Kayrla wondered, remembering where she'd heard the name. *Tesca!* she thought, a bolt of fear shooting through her. *He's hurt!* Then she realized that the duel couldn't have started yet. *Something's wrong…*

"Which way did they go?" she asked. The guard thought for a moment, then gestured in one direction. Kayrla dashed back into the crowded hallway. With nimble steps, she darted between the servants, all the while calling out, "Dr. Felton! Dr. Felton! Has anyone seen Dr. Felton!"

"Kay!" called a voice to her. She whirled to see Ella standing in a doorway. "Child, you're supposed to be with His Grace!"

"I know," Kayrla replied, urging her friend back through the door and closing it behind them. They were in a smaller hallway off the main one, and alone. The bustle of the servants on the other side of the door was muffled and distant behind the thick wood. "I need to find Dr. Felton," she said in desperation, "his Grace has asked for his elixir."

"For his cough?" Ella asked. She was one of the Duke's personal servants and knew the true state of his recovery. She smiled. "I'm not surprised he's asking for it. Bless me, I'm only surprised he's waited this long."

"But where's Dr. Felton?" Kayrla interrupted. "He's supposed to be waiting in the alcove, but he was called away by Lieutenant Kelvo."

Ella turned serious. "Kelvo? That can't be right. Kelvo would never take Felton from his post."

"Well, he's not there now, and that's who they say came for him," Kayrla replied. "Now I've got to find him. His Grace needs that elixir!"

"Calm yourself, child," Ella replied. "There's more of that elixir about than what Felton carries in his pocket. Now, tell me: was his cough a quiet and steady sort of thing?"

"Yes."

"Was he wheezing and short of breath as well?"

"No, the coughing fit seemed to pass and he sounded all right afterward, but he looks tired."

Ella nodded with a smile. "It's not too bad then, yet. Trust me, girl. I've seen him much worse. You wouldn't know this, but there's always some of the elixir on his bedside table if he needs it; I'll go fetch it myself."

Kayrla sagged in relief. "Oh, that's good to hear. I was afraid..."

"You thought there wasn't a moment to lose," Ella assured her. "And so would I if I hadn't been taking care of him all these years. He'll be all right, child." She headed towards the door. "I'll be back in a trice."

"Oh, could you put it–" Kayrla began.

"In a goblet?" Ella finished for her with a laugh. "It's not the first time His Grace has had to trick his guests; I know what we're about." She opened the door, letting the noise of the activity swirl past her. "Now run along and let His Grace know Felton's missing." Then she pulled the door closed behind her and was gone.

Kayrla sighed, taking a moment to compose herself. She was embarrassed at panicking, and couldn't understand what was behind it. *I didn't panic when Jolly's men were chasing me and Tesca,* she thought. *I didn't panic when I had to jump off the bridge and fake my death. But one physician goes missing and I fall all to pieces.* She gave a nervous giggle. *It's going to be all right. Ella will bring the elixir; Tesca will win his duel. It'll be all right.*

A sound at the other end of the hallway startled her; an echo of an opening door. To her surprise, Dr. Felton came out and shut the door behind him, then started walking down the hall towards her.

"Hey!" she shouted, running towards him. "Where were you?" As Felton saw her, he stopped, a look of annoyance on his face. But instead of waiting for her to reach him, he turned back and went through the door he'd just come out of. Kayrla charged after him. When she reached the door, she flung it open and dashed through, almost falling down the long narrow staircase that yawned before her, its steps illuminated by torches. She saw the shape of Dr. Felton ahead of her, walking quickly down the stairs.

"Dr. Felton!" she called. "Where are you going? The Duke has need of you!" This stopped the man in his tracks and he turned to look up at Kayrla, who was quickly running down to meet him.

"What is his need?" Felton asked. There was something odd about his voice that Kayrla didn't recognize. It seemed higher-pitched than normal, almost musical.

"The elixir," she called down. "For his cough. I was sent to get it." Felton did not reply; he stood motionless, watching her approach. "You were gone. They said Lieutenant Kelvo came for you."

"Kelvo," Felton replied, pronouncing the name as if he'd never heard it before, "yes, yes."

"You left your post," Kayrla said, now angry. "You're not supposed to–aiii!" She staggered on the steps as the pendant suddenly became hot again, almost burning her. Grasping it through her uniform, she could feel the heat radiating through the fabric. She had been looking at Felton when it happened, and she was shocked to see that his face was likewise contorted with pain and he too clutched at something under his shirt. He took a faltering step down the stairs away from her, and abruptly the pain ceased.

She stared at him, dumbfounded, as his eyes took on a predatorial gleam. "I knew you would be here somewhere," he said in that high, musical voice, and she knew in an instant that this was not Dr. Felton. "I knew you had thrown yourself behind the Duke for protection, Kayrla. But posing as one of his maids…that was well done. I would not have guessed."

"Who-who are you?" she asked. "How do you know my name?"

"Once there is a price on your head, little one, everyone knows your name," said the false Felton, absently rubbing at the spot on his chest he'd been clutching. "You are Kayrla é sa-Kyrloun, recently on the run from your former captain, Jolly Red, for stealing from him. And believed by all to be dead." He smiled at her, but it was not a smile that Kayrla liked to see. "They are, obviously, wrong about you being dead. But they are not wrong about you being a thief." He pointed directly at the pendant under her blouse. "You have something that does not belong to you, little one. I am here to retrieve it."

Chapter Twenty-seven

"You have something that does not belong to you, little one," the man posing as Dr. Felton said, pointing directly to the pendant under Kayrla's blouse, "I am here to retrieve it."

Kayrla glared at him. "We both know that's not the only thing you're here for." The figure did not reply but simply watched her, a cold smile writhing on his lips. "There was a man earlier tonight, who approached the Duke. When he got close to us, suddenly he and I both experienced a flash of pain, just like now. That was you as well." It was not a question; she knew she was facing the same person as before.

The figure remained silent, studying her with amused curiosity. Kayrla was reminded of a cat watching a mouse, deciding whether or not to strike. He bore no obvious weapon, but cloaked as he was in the long black robe of the physician, Kayrla knew he could easily conceal any number of small blades in those folds, and she had nothing in her pockets but a corkscrew.

Get him to start talking, she thought, unnerved by his silent stare, by the way his lips twitched. "So...what do you want with this?" she asked, gesturing towards the pendant. "I expect you've already got one," she continued, pointing at his chest where he'd clutched it in pain.

"So observant," the figure replied in mocking admiration. With a languid gesture, he reached inside his robe and drew out a pendant on a chain. "Indeed I do. It is not, however, entirely identical to the one you wear." Kayrla could see this at once. The thin chain of the pendant, as well as the metal setting for the gem, appeared to be of the same delicate style as her own. But the gem in the setting was green and oval, not red and circular like hers. She thought at first that the lights she saw coming from it were reflections from the sparse lamps set into the wall, but then she realized that they were small pulses of green light emanating from the gem itself, in regular rhythm like a slow heartbeat. The pulses were faint, a sickly sort of fluttering that made her uncomfortable.

"Why does it emit light?" she asked, the skin on the back of her neck prickling.

The figure pursed his lips. "As I said, this pendant is not entirely identical to the one you wear. It operates on," he looked away and smiled, as if remembering something amusing, "a different set of principles. These principles conflict; the pendants do not operate properly if they are in close proximity to each other. However, though both pendants use different means, the end result is the same."

"What do you mean?"

The figure looked back at her. "Do not play the fool with me, Kayrla. You know the difficulties in casting spells this far south, where the mana is thin. You could not maintain this appearance," he gestured at her, "without relying on the pendant to do so. When I travel south," he said, absently toying with the pendant, "I make use of this pendant in a similar way."

"Then why need two of them, especially if they can't both be used at the same time?" She almost offered to trade the pendants as a joke, but stopped herself. There was something in back of her mind, a piece of a memory regarding that strange, sickly light emitting from the figure's gem. *It was something Father told me...* she thought as she tried to recall more, but she'd never been the most attentive pupil, and she'd been very young. Even though she couldn't remember exactly why, she knew that even if the figure had agreed to a trade, she could not have brought herself to go through with it, to let that green gem hang around her neck.

The figure's smile became bitter. "There are…advantages that one has over this," he replied. "I have made use of this one for some time, but always I have sought for one like the one you bear, offering great wealth for even news of such an item."

She blinked in surprise as something clicked into place in her mind. "Jolly Red was supposed to sell this to you. You were the buyer he was waiting for." The figure grew very still, the smile slipping off his face. "And when he didn't have it," she continued, "you killed him. Didn't you?" The figure's silence was all the answer she needed.

Silent seconds ticked between them. "You look like Felton now," she said. "The guards said someone got him to leave his post. Was that you as well?"

"You seem to know all the answers, Kayrla."

"Is Felton dead?"

"Does it matter?" It was the complete lack of concern in the figure's voice that truly terrified her.

"It matters to me," she said after a moment.

The figure sighed and shook his head. "You have been too long among these humans."

"'These humans'," she repeated. She had known the figure before her wasn't human; she'd recognized the graceful poise and fluid gestures in him that Tesca was teaching her to conceal. But to have him say it, to confirm it, was somehow very important to her. "You're an elf too."

"Elf," the figure spat in disgust, the first real display of emotion she'd seen in him. "I *hate* that word. A single sound, a cough. As if our people, our culture, could be distilled into a single syllable. That is not what we call ourselves, little one."

"What do we call ourselves?"

He looked surprised. "Your father did not…?" he trailed off, looking confused.

"My father?" she sputtered. "You knew my father?"

The figure studied her with a fresh interest, as if he was seeing her for the first time. "Yes, I did. He and I were colleagues, after a fashion.

This was before you were born, of course. Before we both came...here," he concluded, gesturing with both hands all around him.

"From the Elflands," she finished. Seeing the look of disgust on the figure's face, she started again. "I'm sorry, I don't know the proper name for our homeland! He wouldn't tell me anything about it. What...what do you call it?"

He smiled his cold smile at her again. "You wish to learn these things?"

"Of course. What do we call ourselves?"

The figure shook his head with a sad smile. "You ask me to summarize. This is the way of humans. To take a concept their short-lived minds cannot encompass and truncate it, abbreviate it. But by doing so, they distort the meaning, and they do not recognize the damage they have done." He sighed. "I cannot do as you ask without first telling you all, so you know the meaning of the terms and names I would share." He glanced around him, seeming to recall where he was standing. "And this is not the place to begin, is it?"

Kayrla studied him. There were a thousand questions racing through her mind; questions she'd been waiting to ask for years. "You'll teach me, but only if I come with you?'

"You must give me the pendant first, and then come with me. There is one task I must perform before we go, but it will not take long."

An icy chill clutched at her stomach. She knew what he had come here for. She'd known it the moment he'd first tried to approach the dais and been driven off.

"You're an assassin." It sounded so awkward to her, saying what both of them already knew, but she had to keep him talking. The silence only made her fear grow.

"Among other things," the figure replied. "They're only humans anyway." She glared at him, but he simply shook his head with that sad smile once more. "You actually care about what happens to them."

"Not all of them," she protested. "Most of them would have sold me to Jolly Red without hesitation, but some of them are my friends."

"The ones you label friends are, deep down, no different from the others," the figure replied in a lecturing tone. "Kayrla, what you must understand is that everyone on this island, every single one of these humans, will be dead and gone long before you have truly reached maturity. Why make friends with those who will be with you for such a short time? All you do is bring yourself needless grief."

"No," she said, shaking her head. "Being alone forever, constantly having to hide who I am…that's needless grief."

"But you are not alone any more," the figure replied, with a smile that just fell short of genuine compassion, "now that we have found each other, neither of us need be alone again."

She bit her lip. "Leave the estate with me now. Let the Duke live, and I'll come with you. I'll give you the pendant, but we have to leave now."

The figure shook his head once again. "I honor my promises, Kayrla, even the ones I make to humans. And I expect the same of those who make promises to me."

"Is that why you killed Jolly Red?" she snapped.

"He promised to deliver me the pendant; he failed," the figure replied with a shrug. "I believe, Kayrla, we are coming fast to an impasse. Give me the pendant, put aside the morality imposed on you by living among these humans for so long, and come away with me to embrace your true heritage."

"Or else?" Kayrla asked, stalling for time.

The figure sighed, the predatorial gleam returning to his eyes. With his left hand he gestured towards the top of the stairs and behind her Kayrla heard a bolt slide, locking the door. The light in the green gem flickered, then resumed its slow pulse. As his right hand drifted towards a pocket in his robe, he spoke in a detached tone. "I said before you seem to know all the answers, Kayr–"

Kayrla leapt down the steps towards him, knowing that there was never really a choice, not for her. No vague promises of instruction or allegedly true stories about her father were worth the life she was building for herself here. As she had guessed, her pendant blazed with heat as the two gems came into proximity with each other. But she was prepared for the burst of pain, and gritting her teeth, she dove past the assassin as he stumbled against the wall, groaning in agony.

The pain ceased as she hurtled down the dark stairs, and Kayrla heard the assassin stagger to his feet. Immediately he was charging after her, but she already had a good lead on him. As she blindly led him down into the depths of the estate, all Kayrla could hope for was that she wouldn't find another locked door ahead of her.

Chapter Twenty-eight

The sound of his boots against the stone bricks brought a faint smile to Tesca's face. The western pavilion of the Duke's estate was a wide platform, open to the air on all sides. Thick wooden pillars held up a high roof. Lieutenant Kelvo stood next to him, watching the servants setting up hurricane lamps along the edges of the platform. "We should be ready very soon, sir," he said, leaning in close to be heard over the wind as it whistled past the pillars.

"Thank you, Lieutenant," Tesca replied.

"It's a good choice," Kelvo went on, looking at the pavilion. "Set off from the manor like this, we shouldn't get too many onlookers to follow, and my men will keep those away."

Tesca nodded, watching the Sabrians climb the steps to enter the pavilion. He couldn't hear what they were saying to each other, but Captain Maritius appeared satisfied with this location for the duel.

"A good place to settle a matter of honor," Kelvo said. Tesca nodded and turned his heel on the stone once more, gauging the rough surface for its traction. "You'll remember, of course, that patch of stone in the northeast corner, sir," Kelvo went on. "A bit of repair work from last year; the stone's not a perfect match and it's smoother. Might be slippery there."

"Indeed," Tesca replied, shrugging his shoulders to loosen them up.

"And there's that spot in the center, sir, that one loose stone that's sunk a few inches. Someone could trip on that if they didn't know about it."

"I seem to remember someone tripping over that during a recent sparring session last month," Tesca replied. "Didn't his opponent lure him into stepping there?"

"Aye, sir," Kelvo replied with a grin, "but you didn't catch me on that move the next time you tried it."

Now Tesca smiled back at him. "No, you learned your lesson well."

Kelvo nodded and looked back at the Sabrians. "Think that lot would like this spot so well if they knew how many hours you've spent here in practice?"

Tesca chuckled. "The host may select whatever grounds he wishes for the duel. This place is isolated and provides more than enough room to maneuver, which I'm sure they find most satisfactory. But they can't take any real objection to the fact that the host's champion will be fighting on his own ground."

"Are you required to tell him about the loose stone, then?"

Tesca shook his head. "Oh, no. It's his responsibility to examine the ground and find out those sort of things for himself. If he doesn't find them before the duel, that's his mistake."

Kelvo chuckled, then turned his attention to Tesca's opponent. "Any advantage would be helpful against that fellow. By the Deeps, he's a tall one. And he's got the longest arms I've ever seen; you'll have a devil of a time getting inside his guard."

Tesca nodded, looking towards the steps where Allie Feyne and Captain Grivus were coming onto the platform. He took some amusement from the look of bewildered frustration on Allie's face. *At least I know I'm not the only one Grivus played for a fool,* he thought as she stormed up to him.

"Tesca," she demanded, "what in the Deeps is going on?"

"You were there," he evaded, drawing on a set of leather gloves and flexing his fingers.

"No," she snapped, "that ship won't sail with me, Tesca Secarius! You can fool the rest of the city with your silent, brooding swordsman pose, but not me!" Kelvo coughed, muttered something unintelligible in the wind and stepped politely away from them. Allie seized their new privacy and stepped in close, putting herself directly in front of him. "Was this something you planned with Grivus beforehand? To embarrass me?" She searched his face and looked surprised. "No…no, it wasn't, was it?"

"Allie," Tesca said, looking at her. In her high-heeled shoes, she was almost at eye level with him. "Regardless of what you may believe, I don't spend every waking moment plotting ways to bring about your social downfall."

She scowled at him, but there was a smirk in her expression as well. "So why are you going through with it?"

He shrugged. "Grivus has done such a fine job of arranging matters so far, I must admit I'm curious to find out why."

"But what do you hope to gain?" she asked.

He smiled at her. "Unlike you and your family, Allie, I don't consider every action in my life either a profit or a loss."

Now her scowl was genuine. "Fine. Satisfy your curiosity. See if it's worth getting skewered on that Sabrian's blade." Her voice wavered at the last. "Tesca…be careful." Then she turned away, and walking back to the edge of the platform, she leaned against one of the pillars, watching.

Tesca looked after her for a moment, then saw Grivus studying him. He beckoned the older man to join him, which Grivus did, strolling over with a casual gait. "Any advice for me in this duel, since it's for your benefit?" Tesca asked him in Sabrian.

The Sabrian studied his countrymen across the platform. "Even among my people, Mantey is a tall man. He relies on this and his greater reach to keep his opponents at a distance. But he relies too much on this, and as such, he is slower than he should be."

"You know him?" Tesca asked, although he was not surprised. He had underestimated Grivus too often already.

Grivus smiled. "Oh, yes. He is the second son of Captain Maritius, and has always been hot-tempered. I suspected he would demand the right to champion his mother."

"His mother," Tesca repeated, frowning. That added another twist to the situation, one that he did not like. "I was under the impression that fleet officers did not usually have immediate relations as members of their staff."

"Normally, you are correct," Grivus said. "I too was surprised to see members of her family with her."

"There is more than one of her family here?"

Grivus glanced towards the Sabrians to check. "Yes, another son; her eldest. Also, I think, the daughter of her eldest brother. Very unusual. But perhaps Livia arranged this so as to give some of her family a bit of diplomatic experience." He smiled. "Livia may be seeing this area as a place of future importance for the Empire, and is making sure her family is well-positioned to take advantage of it."

Tesca nodded, digesting this new information. "I compliment you," he said after a few moments, "on your skill at arranging this duel."

The old man shrugged. "It was luck as much as anything. If the Imperial envoy had been anyone other than Livia, I doubt I could have brought matters to a boil nearly so quickly."

"But you still would have done it," Tesca commented.

"Oh, yes," Grivus replied with a slight smile. "Pride and honor are strings upon which any Sabrian can be played."

"Even yourself?"

The smile faded. "Indeed, my young champion," Grivus admitted after a moment. "Though I only learned this about myself after my disgrace." He studied Tesca once more. "But now, the matter is balanced upon the tips of your blades. If you are truly an *agentis*, as you claim to be, then you will be victorious here and you may claim your debt from me."

"I thought you believed my claim after we first met," Tesca pointed out. "You had a pistol aimed at me, but you withdrew your challenge."

"You know I would only have fired if you had tried to attack me. If honor is to be satisfied, then the blades must be used. Instead you spoke to me without fear. That was what sparked my suspicion that you might indeed be what you claimed. Also, when we met, your clothes were stained afresh with the blood of other men. I was not willing to test my old bones against your young and hale ones. But you puzzled me. A white man, speaking our tongue so fluently, following the customs of our people." He shrugged. "In short, you behaved so much like an *agentis* that I had to accept the possibility that you were telling the truth. It was only after I made the acquaintance of the Feynes and learned who you were that I put this plan into motion. But it has been a very great gamble."

"How so?"

"I have had to put a great deal of trust in you, based only on what I have heard about you from the Feynes. And the charming young lady aside, they do not like you very much."

Tesca frowned. "I don't think you have to exclude Allie from that category."

"As you wish," Grivus replied with a chuckle. "But what I heard from them about you was encouraging. I began to think that if I could bring matters to a boil here tonight, you were the one person who had both experience with our customs and sufficient skill at argument," he added, gesturing at Tesca's blades, "to help me. I will admit, I was also curious to see just how skilled at arms you were, and whether I was right to withdraw my challenge the night we first met. That question has sat upon my mind for some time now."

"Well, so far everything has gone as you hoped," Tesca told him. "And if I win the duel, you'll tell His Grace why you need his help?"

"His Grace?"

Tesca frowned. "I will admit that I, too, am curious about you, and that I have played along to see what game you're about. But make no mistake, Captain. A victory here is a victory for his Grace. He is your host, and your champion, not I. I am merely his hand. If I win the duel, the champion's debt is owed to him."

To his surprise, Grivus smiled broadly at him. "That, my young friend, is an answer worthy of an *agentis*. Putting the cares and needs of his master over his own."

Tesca sighed. "You still aren't convinced of my claim?"

"I am convinced that you honor the principles and follow the discipline of that noble profession. But I must also see your skill at argument," Grivus said, gesturing toward the Sabrian delegation. "Can you defend your principles with your blades?"

"You're about to find out," Tesca said, bowing to Grivus. Grivus returned the bow and retreated to the edge of the platform. Allie Feyne stepped up to him and began talking angrily in a low voice, but the older man politely rebuffed her questions and gestured her to silence.

Tesca twisted his boots against the stone once more as Kelvo came up to him. "I think we're ready, sir. The lamps are all lit, my men are in place."

"Then let's get started," Tesca replied.

"Very well, sir. I'm not familiar with Sabrian dueling customs, but I'm prepared to stand as your second."

Tesca was touched by the offer. "Thank you, Lieutenant, but that won't be necessary. Sabrian duels don't require seconds. The only thing you have to watch for is one of us giving the signal of submission. If you hear either of us call the word '*pacem*,' the duel is over."

"As you wish, sir." Kelvo saluted him. "Good luck."

Tesca returned the salute, and walked out into the middle of the pavilion.

Chapter Twenty-nine

Every door Kayrla came to was locked, so she kept running. She passed intersections, choosing directions on pure instinct, knowing that there was no chance to go back if she guessed wrong. There were lamps set into the walls, but no one had been down here for some time; most of them were dark, and the few remaining gave only feeble flickers of light, reminding her of the pulsing green light coming from the gem in the assassin's pendant.

When she'd begun this mad dash she'd leapt over a body at the foot of the stairs, recognizing Dr. Felton, stripped of his physician's robe. She was running so fast she was some fifty feet down the hall before she realized that Felton's dead face had been twisted into a look of horrified agony. *Just like Jolly Red,* she thought, the understanding giving her no comfort. Panic welled up, threatening to overwhelm her, but she could not let that happen. She had to get away, to raise the alarm.

Tesca. As she ran, she tried to hold his face in her mind. What would he do in this situation? Her friend always seemed to know what to do next. There had been a few practice sessions with him during her stay at the estate, where he'd tried to help her improve her swordplay. *He never stopped talking…always giving me advice. By the Abyss, how I wanted him to just shut up!* A door on her left suddenly loomed ahead out of the darkness. She tugged at the handle, found it locked and kept going, barely breaking step.

Tesca couldn't help me down here, she thought, a shiver of despair coursing through her. *It's too dark for human eyes.* If the assassin were human, she'd have lost him easily down here. *But he's got the same advantage down here that I do. Oh, Hells, is he gaining on me?* she thought, the panic surging up again.

And then suddenly she remembered something Tesca had told her during a practice, and if she had any breath to spare, she would have laughed. *"An enemy's strength can become his weakness." We have the same strength, but the same weakness too!*

She had long ago learned that her eyesight was sharper than a human's, especially at night, but there was a drawback to this as well: her night vision was far more vulnerable to sudden flashes of light. One more than one occasion, she'd been looking in the direction of a muzzle flash when a pistol was fired in the dark and had been blinded for several minutes. A plan came to her. *I've got to try it,* she thought. *I'm going to hit a dead end eventually.*

She saw a wall appear ahead of her and for an instant, feared she'd reached that dreaded dead end already. But then she realized she was approaching a T-intersection, not a blank wall, and knew that this was her chance. She deliberately slowed her pace, as if she wasn't sure which way to go, and heard the assassin's footsteps close behind. *He* has *been gaining on me!* she thought for a moment, but she kept the panic down as she ran underneath another darkened lamp.

As she passed by the lamp, she threw one hand up towards it, flinging a spell at the dead wick. It was the simple ignition spell she'd demonstrated to Galen when she'd first met him. But this time, she drew upon the power within her pendant, pouring far more mana into the spell than was required. The lamp burst apart in a shower of fire and glass, but Kayrla was already past, feeling the heat on her back. The assassin yelled in pain, his steps faltering as he stumbled into the wall. The light had not been as bright as a pistol flash, and already the hallway was nearly pitch dark again, but Kayrla hoped it would be enough as she veered to the right and stopped. Pressing against the wall and crouching low, she took the corkscrew out of her pocket and hurled it down the hallway in the opposite direction. Muttering a quiet curse in his native tongue and keeping one hand on the wall, the assassin reached the intersection and turned left, following the sound of the clattering tool.

Quiet as a cat, Kayrla slipped around the corner and began cautiously heading back the way she had come. She was tempted to break into a run, but she knew that she'd never be able to retrace her steps, and the assassin would be sure to hear her if she started running. Before long she reached the door she'd passed earlier. As she knew from before, it was locked, but that didn't daunt her. Pressing her fingertips to the keyhole, she murmured her entropy spell, infecting the lock with rust and decay. There was a faint creak as the mechanism within came apart. Kayrla tugged the door open.

To her horror, the door groaned on old hinges as it swung open. *Oh, please don't let him hear that,* she thought, slipping inside. She only got a momentary glimpse of the room's interior before pulling the door shut behind her, as slowly and quietly as she could, which plunged the room into total darkness. Now even she was blind.

The first impression she'd had of the room was that it was small and cramped, with tall, narrow shelves filling the space. There had been a few glimmers of light off of glass before she'd shut the door, and the air in here was stale and dusty, but there was a faint, sour odor that she recognized. *Wine,* she thought, sniffing the air again to confirm her guess. *I'm in a wine cellar. I don't think anyone's been in here for years, though.* She edged along the wall, keeping one hand in front of her. She touched the side of a wine rack and moved around it, now keeping one hand on the shelf next to her and the other reaching ahead. Before long her outstretched hand touched another rack in front of her, and she realized she'd reached a corner. In this careful manner, she continued to move around the edge of the room, getting further away from the door.

These wine racks seem mostly empty, she thought, noting the few times her fingers brushed over the butt of a dusty bottle sitting in a niche. *Pity. I can only imagine how good some of these would taste after being down here undisturbed for so lon–*

Her fingers now brushed against a door, and for a moment she thought she'd come full circle. *No, I've only hit one corner. This is another door.* She tried the handle and to her delight, discovered that it was unlocked. But before she could open it, the other door groaned open and she dropped to the floor. Glancing through the empty wine racks standing in the middle of the room, she saw the silhouette of the assassin before he moved inside and shut the door behind him, returning the room to darkness.

"I know you are in here, Kayrla," came his voice. "That was a very clever trick, with the lamp. But I heard you opening this door." She heard him moving along the wall, in the opposite direction she had taken. "There is a trick I know," he went on, "that would have helped you. A simple spell, a sphere of silence. I showed that trick both to your former captain and to the doctor. It is very useful to keep your activities…uninterrupted."

Kayrla remained frozen in place, holding her breath for fear of being heard. *That little scuffling noise; was that him? Is he on the opposite wall now? Or is that a trick? He can make himself silent, can't he? He might be just a few feet away now!* Her thoughts were going wild; she kept imagining him coming upon her; feeling hands in the darkness closing on her throat. Fear paralyzed her. Wide-eyed, trembling, she was locked in place, afraid to move and afraid to stay where she was.

And then she saw something. It wasn't utterly dark in here, not anymore. Ahead of her, somewhere, was a very faint, flickering green light. The assassin's pendant. She knew where he was now, and the knowledge of it dispelled her terror. She was still afraid, but she could move. And think.

She stared intently at the green glow, trying to gauge its true distance from her. It flickered as usual, but it also kept disappearing completely for a moment, then reappearing. She realized that the assassin was moving along the opposite wall from her, and the light was being blocked as he passed the wine racks.

Another idea came into her head, fully formed. Keeping her eyes on the light, she reached behind her for the door handle. A thorough examination of it with her fingertips confirmed something; the door was built the same way as most of the other doors in the estate. It had a keyhole on this side, and that meant there was a knob to turn the lock on the other.

The realization moved her to instant action. She stood up, putting her hands out until they touched the wine rack in front of her, and she pushed. The rack was heavy, but it was also nearly empty, and without the extra weight of the bottles, it was much less stable.

She heard the assassin's feet twist on the floor ahead of her and knew he'd heard her moving. That only made her push harder. The wine rack creaked, quivered under her hands, and began to tip over. It hit the next rack in line and that one began to fall as well, starting a cascade of ruin that swept across the small room towards the assassin.

The noise was deafening. She heard wood splintering, mixed in with the musical crash of the few abandoned wine bottles breaking as they hit the floor. But she was already pulling the door open, slipping through and shutting it behind her. As she'd expected, there was a knob for the lock on this side and she twisted it.

The sounds of crashing wood and breaking glass seemed to go on forever. Then there was silence. Kayrla waited, panting, listening for any sounds of motion. *Maybe I killed him…*

The jiggling of the door handle shattered that hope and she yelped, leaping away from the door. "Kayrla…" came the assassin's voice from the other side, a harsh whisper. The door handle rattled once more, then stopped. Kayrla breathed a sigh of relief, then suddenly remembered the spell she'd seen him cast just before she'd fled from him. In a flash, she dashed back to the door and frantically grabbed the knob of the lock just as it started to turn of its own accord. It moved under her fingers like a living thing, trying to twist up, unlocking the door, but she held on with both hands, gritting her teeth with the effort. And it was enough.

Her pendant was starting to get warm; she knew he was on the opposite side of the door. She could feel him there; a cold yet furious presence. She heard a movement on the other side of the door. *Is he going away?* she wondered, but she knew it wasn't that. Her pendant was still getting warmer, and she could feel his rage, only separated from her by a few inches of thick wood.

Something was happening to the lock. It wasn't moving, though; it was crumbling. *The entropy spell!* she instantly realized. And just as instantly, she knew what to do. Drawing upon the gem's power, she sent her repair spell into the lock, countering him. The metal stopped growing brittle, and in fact began to feel more intact under her fingertips. But then the decay poured forth again, stronger this time. Again, she countered, keeping the lock intact.

In the darkness, only able to feel the lock under her fingers, only able to feel his rage on the other side of the door, Kayrla began to feel like she was actually in a swordfight with him. She could see him in her mind as a faceless green wraith, whose blades were cold and poisonous. He shifted and slithered before her like some sort of writhing vermin, constantly on the verge of getting past her guard and cutting her down. What little she could see of herself was red, wielding two blades like Tesca's. She was as fast as the assassin, but moved with a fluid grace completely unlike his scuttling, darting motions.

She was drawing heavily on her pendant's power now, countering each of his assaults with a defense of her own. *If the lock breaks, I'm dead.* Thoughts of his hands about her throat came back into her mind, breaking her concentration, and it seemed that her red form stumbled for a moment. The assassin's form darted in and scored a hit. The lock began to crumble once more. *No!* she thought desperately, pouring more mana into her spell. *No, don't think of that. Think of....think of...* then she realized whose swords she'd instinctively imagined wielding. *Tesca.* Thoughts of her friend, of seeing him again, of not letting him down, coursed through her and she focused every last shred of her concentration into maintaining her spell. The lock became sturdy once more. The assassin poured more mana into his destruction spell, but she held on, drawing ever more on the pendant around her neck. She needed more power and let her two disguise spells dissolve, pouring that additional mana into the spell.

The assassin's effort increased, but also became erratic. It seemed as if his green form was pulsing, like a heartbeat. To use this much magic, down in the Frees, he had to be relying upon his pendant's power, but she could tell that for some reason, he was loathe to do this more than necessary. Encouraged, she doubled her efforts, drawing upon her own inner strength. Her knees wobbled and spots of light appeared before her eyes. The pendant was painfully hot against her chest.

The assassin tried to push against her defense one more time, but her spell was too powerful to overcome now. She sensed outrage, as she had before, but it was muted by pain. *And…fear?* she wondered. *What is he afraid of?*

The spell of decay ceased. Kayrla stopped her own spell, but kept both hands on the lock, ready to resume the struggle if need be. The pendant around her neck began to cool and she heard him moving away from the door. *Now what?* she wondered, waiting.

A faint orange glow appeared under the door, and she realized he must have lit a lamp. Then she heard some sounds of movement, followed by a loud slam against the door. At first she thought he was trying to break the door down, but then she heard other noises in the room outside. He was picking through the wreckage of the wine racks in the middle of the room. She also could hear his breathing, quick and ragged. The spell battle had exhausted her, but he sounded as if he was injured and in great pain. *He said his pendant operated on "a different set of principles,"* she wondered. *Could that have something to do with it?*

There was another slam against the door, followed by another, and she realized that he wasn't trying to knock the door down, he was piling the wine racks in front of it. "Oh, Hells…" she muttered, staring at the thin line of light coming from the outer room, which was getting fainter as more and more wreckage was piled up against the door.

After a few minutes of this, it stopped. She heard the assassin step close to the door again. "Kayrla," he said, his voice a strained hiss of pain, "you are most resourceful. A pity I cannot show you my appreciation as I should. But," he said with a weary chuckle, "as I said before,

I have a task to accomplish, and I honor my promises." She heard his feet shift on the floor as he walked away. "And I promise you this: after I have completed my task, I shall return here, and conclude this matter between us." She heard the outer door close, and the last glimmer of light was gone.

Chapter Thirty

"There is nothing more dangerous than entering into a duel with a man whom you refuse to kill," Tesca remembered his old instructor telling him time and time again. He kept trying to push that memory away as he composed his mind for the battle, putting aside all distractions, but the warning kept echoing back, sometimes as a whisper, sometimes as a shout. It had been the old gentleman's favorite advice, even repeated one last time on his deathbed.

He tried to shift his focus by recalling other advice he'd received. *"Always study the ground before you cross it." I've done that,* he thought. *This is my home ground. I know every square inch of this platform.* But he knew how his instructor would have responded to that. *"The ground you walk on is not the only ground, is it?"*

No, he admitted to himself. *Grivus played a clever game to get me here. I didn't study that ground before stepping onto it, did I?* But replaying the events in his mind did not present any other way he could have handled this.

The only way to go now is forward, he thought as he reached the center of the platform. His opponent, Mantey, was slowly whirling his long arms through the air, loosening his muscles. His mother, Captain Maritius, saw Tesca and quickly spoke to him. The tall Sabrian looked annoyed, but she repeated herself, her stance shifting to one of admonishment. With a frustrated shrug, Mantey whirled away from her and began to walk around the platform, making an examination of the ground.

Tesca kept his face calm, hiding his emotions as he watched Mantey. *She had to remind him to study the ground,* he thought. *And he's only making a cursory examination. He just wants to get started. Overconfident, eager. Letting his emotions cloud his judgment. Good.*

He reviewed his appraisal of Mantey, trying to make sure he was not letting overconfidence cloud his own judgment. And once again, there came that warning memory: *"There is nothing more dangerous than entering into a duel with a man whom you refuse to kill."*

Tesca knew he did not want to kill Mantey. There were several factors outside of the duel that he had to consider. He had been certain that the Sabrians would appreciate a duel arranged and conducted according to their rules, and in future dealings between the Empire and the Quad, whatever the duel's outcome, they would grudgingly give the Duke more respect than they previously had. But the news that the Sabrian emissary was Mantey's mother changed all that.

Within the Empire, ambitious individuals could seek any number of political appointments or promotions that might further their career. Being named emissary to a diplomatic function in a backwater frontier region was not one of them. Tesca knew that in the past, such emissaries to the Frees had been selected from naval officers stationed at the closest port who had nothing else to do. They might have been officers injured in the line of duty and needed time to recover before returning to active duty; they might have been paying back a debt of honor or accepted this assignment as punishment for a transgression. But no one ever wanted the job; no one sought it out.

Livia Maritius, it appeared, did want the job. To Tesca, the fact that she brought members of her family with her confirmed this. For the Sabrians, the status of one's family, and doing one's part to maintain or improve that status, was extremely important. If Maritius had been dishonored in some way and sent here as punishment, she would never have brought members of her family along with her to share in that shame. In fact, she would have encouraged them to get as far from her as possible.

She's up to something, Tesca decided. *She sought out this posting, and she's brought her family with her; this is a permanent move. She's not just an emissary; she's a neighbor. And a neighbor with enough power to start making things difficult for His Grace if her son dies while visiting Kohayne.* Tesca did not think a mother could ever truly forgive and forget the death of one of her children, even if, as a Fleet Captain, she was honor-bound to abide by the terms of the duel. He spared a glance at Mantey to look at Captain Maritius.

She was looking back at him, studying him the way he had been studying Mantey. No, he decided, that was not a woman His Grace would relish having as an enemy. No, he did not want to kill that woman's son. But not wanting to kill Mantey was not the same as refusing to kill him. He was not fighting in this duel for Captain Maritius, or to preserve the honor of the distant Sabre Empire. He was fighting this duel for his master, and that duty superseded all other concerns. He met Captain Maritius' gaze, gave her a formal nod, then resumed his study of Mantey, his old instructor's voice silent at last.

The tall Sabrian had finished his circuit of the floor and had returned to his mother. Maritius motioned him to bend down so she could whisper in his ear. He dutifully obeyed, then straightened up and formally bowed before her. Tesca could see that whatever advice she had tried to impart upon him had been politely ignored. Duty struggled with a mother's love in her face, but duty won out. She offered him a formal benediction, pressing only a formal kiss to both sides of his face. When Mantey turned and started walking towards Tesca, her resolve cracked for a moment, and she stepped back to the edge of the platform, sinking into a chair that had been brought out for her.

Mantey strode out to meet Tesca, overconfidence radiating from him like heat from an oven. Tesca calmly stood waiting for him, his face unreadable. "Is the challenger ready?" he called out in Sabrian.

Mantey stopped some ten feet from Tesca. He drew out the Argument and the Retort. "He is," he responded in the same tongue, flicking his wrists, torchlight reflecting off the steel blades. "Is the challenged ready?"

Tesca gave a single nod, drawing his own weapons. "Perhaps my esteemed opponent is aware of the parable regarding the sea snake and the shark?"

Mantey blinked, his face drawing into a scowl. Tesca had chosen to begin his Argument with words instead of swords. "I am not here to debate with you, like two old men too weak to lift their blades!" the Sabrian spat out.

"Yet you took up your mother's challenge against an old man," Tesca countered, watching Mantey react to the word "mother." *He didn't think I knew that. Of course he should realize that Grivus must have told me, but now he'll start to wonder what else I know about him.*

"I took up the challenge against you, white man!" Mantey snarled.

"No," Tesca replied, "I am only championing Captain Grivus. The challenge is against him. Though we two are the ones who fight, we are but instruments in this affair. Weapons to be wielded. We are ourselves, in essence, the Argument and the Retort. Is it not so?"

Mantey looked furious, and Tesca could hear the Sabrians urgently whispering to each other. By concluding his words with that specific phrase, "is it not so," Tesca was now on the attack. He had presented an opinion; if Mantey could not present a satisfactory counterargument, Tesca could claim the verbal equivalent of a hit. It would not be enough to claim victory; the Sabrians did not judge a single clever metaphor to be equal in value to a sword wound. But it would be a start.

Groping for words, forced by custom to duel in the manner Tesca had chosen, at least for now, Mantey sputtered: "No…no it is not so! We…we are…the ones who fight. We are not mere blades to be brandished; we shed blood!" he cried, looking relieved that he had come up with something. "Is it not so!"

"I disagree, esteemed opponent," Tesca countered instantly. "During a duel, the blades are damaged. Nicks and dents appear along their lengths. Surely this damage is to a blade as the loss of blood is to us, fatal without repair. We remain as the Argument and Retort in their hands. Is it not so?"

Mantey's eyes shifted back and forth as he tried to think of another counter. Tesca took note of this, but his attention was focused on the blades Mantey held. They shivered in his trembling grip. "I…it is…" Mantey stammered.

"I remind my opponent of the time," Tesca said, adding a touch of mockery to his tone. "Does he concede the point?"

Mantey ground his teeth in frustration. "It is…it is not…"

Tesca allowed himself a patronizing look. "Then I claim the point," he sighed. "The challenger may now present an Argument." All the time he spoke, he kept watching Mantey's blades. *I've scored first, and with words instead of blades. Worse, his peers and his own mother have seen it. Now is when he's the most dangerous.*

"No more words," Mantey snapped, lowering into a crouch and bringing his blades up.

Tesca smiled. "So now we dent each other, as blades are wont to do?"

"No more words!" Mantey yelled, surging forward.

Tesca brought up his own blades, countering Mantey's attack and letting him go by on Tesca's left. Tesca flicked his rapier out in a quick counterattack as they passed but he was too far away to hit Mantey. Mantey whirled, and began to circle around Tesca, preparing for another charge.

Tesca was comparing his initial estimation of Mantey with what Grivus had told him. The man did make good use of his long reach; keeping his arms extended and crouching low. He wasn't as fast as some Tesca had fought, but the extra distance Tesca would have to cover just to reach him compensated for that. Kelvo had been right; Tesca would have a devil of a time getting inside his guard.

Unless I can get him to open his guard for me, Tesca thought. He didn't usually talk during combat, feeling that it usually gave away too much information to his opponents, but words seemed to do well against Mantey. He began to circle Mantey as well, the pair of them now slowly spinning about the center of the platform.

Tesca chuckled openly, as if something funny had occurred to him.

"Why do you laugh?" Mantey demanded.

"The way you're bent over double, with your arms outstretched," Tesca said. "You look like an armorback."

"An armorback?" Mantey said. "What is that?"

"Oh, yes…your people don't know armorbacks. You're afraid to sail that far north, aren't you?"

"Afraid?!!?" Mantey choked out.

"Armorbacks are like giant lobsters," Tesca went on as if he hadn't heard Mantey speak. "They can leap onto a ship from the waterline. And when they attack, they look like you…all bent up with their claws far out in front of them." He nodded towards Mantey's feet. "You scuttle along the floor sideways, just like they do." He chuckled again. "But they're slow and stupid; quite easy to kill, actually."

"Be quiet!" Mantey roared, launching a fresh attack. Tesca turned it aside to the right, but this time he stepped in towards Mantey as they passed instead of away from him. He feinted with the rapier and Mantey flinched from it, leaving his side exposed for a instant. Tesca jabbed in with his dagger, slicing along the edge of Mantey's ribcage. Mantey gave a sharp hiss of pain and stepped back, sparing a glance at the wound.

"It's not fatal, just a scratch," Tesca called to him in a casual tone, as if that was what he'd intended to do all along. "I claim first blood. Do you yield?"

Mantey glared at him. He was in a towering rage; his pride had been pricked too often tonight. But Tesca could see fear in his eyes as well; a desperate understanding that he was outmatched. *Let the fear grow,* Tesca thought. *Let it take hold of him. He'll be more frantic; more dangerous, but he'll leave more gaps in his guard.*

"This is your last chance," he said to Mantey, choosing his words carefully. "I will not ask you to yield again." And he saw those words strike as deeply as any sword thrust. He spoke as someone who knew he was going to win, and Mantey, shamed and fearful, believed him.

But that did not make him yield. He clung to his pride as if it was the mast of a sinking ship, the only thing still above the water. With a yell of desperation, he charged forward once more. He came straight on this time, his two blades a whirlwind around him. Mantey's fear had given his strikes more speed, but he was swinging wildly. Tesca fell back, holding him off, waiting for an opening. And he found one.

Mantey spread his arms open a fraction too wide, and Tesca darted forward, inside Mantey's guard, his long arms above and on either side of him. Tesca kept moving, passing by Mantey on the right, dragging his dagger along the length of Mantey's right thigh.

Blood flashed from the wound, splashing on the stones. There was a burst of noise from the spectators as Tesca stepped clear of Mantey and the tall Sabrian tumbled to the ground, his leg giving way under him. He struggled to rise for a moment, but collapsed again, dropping his rapier to the ground with a clatter.

"Captain!" Tesca called to Maritius, who had risen from her chair, her face stricken. "Your champion is down! I now offer you the chance to yield. Choose swiftly; he is bleeding out."

She stared at him for only a moment before she found her voice. *"P-pacem! Pacem!"* As she spoke, four of her entourage, including Mantey's brother and cousin, dashed out towards their fallen champion, carrying medical supplies. Tesca gave way before them as they set to work on Mantey's leg. The Sabrians were well-versed in dueling, and because of this, well-versed in dealing with its aftermath. If anyone could save Mantey's life, it would be his own people.

Tesca walked back to Lieutenant Kelvo, who offered him a towel to clean his bloody dagger. "Well done, sir," Kelvo said in awe. "You've been holding back in our practices, I see."

Tesca gave a weary chuckle. "I don't think so, Lieutenant. Mantey did half of the work himself."

"Indeed," said Grivus, who had come up to join them. He spoke in the Freespeak. "They may save him, but I do not know if his leg will ever completely heal. You cut him very deeply."

Tesca looked sharply at him. "Are you chiding me?" he snapped in Sabrian. "I only danced to the tune you called, Captain. Would you rather I had killed him? Does that not fit in with your plans?"

Grivus was taken aback. "No, I was not chiding you," he apologized, responding in his native tongue. "You showed mercy on that final blow. His entire body was open to you; you could have just as easily opened his belly, or his throat. Instead you passed the right to yield to his mother." He looked at Tesca with admiration. "He may always need a cane to walk, but Livia still has her son. Well-played, *agentis.*" Tesca smiled, catching Grivus' term of address, as the Sabrian spoke again. "My only criticism is that it was a good thing Mantey did not see the flaw in your first Argument."

Tesca was irked. "And that was?"

"Your claim that two champions are no more than blades in the claimants' hands. That may have been an ingenious opening argument when you were learning your craft; but it has been used quite often since. The correct Retort to your first Argument is that the champions are more than blades, for they have free will; they choose to be champions in the duel. Blades have no choice when they are drawn. If Mantey was a scholar of past duels; he would have countered your point easily."

Tesca sighed. He switched back to Freespeak. "Well, I'll keep that in mind the next time I try to make headway against the riptide of Sabrian etiquette." He turned to Kelvo. "Lieutenant, please ask Captain Maritius if they require anything from His Grace to see to her Champion's comfort. Like as not they'll politely refuse and just take him back to their ship as soon as they can, so also offer one of His Grace's carriages to make Mantey's trip as smooth as possible. That, they're like to accept."

"Of course, sir." Kelvo saluted and headed off.

Now Allie Feyne came up to him. "There's...not a mark on you," she said, breathless.

Grivus glanced at Tesca, chuckled and drifted several feet away to watch his former countrymen tending to Mantey. Tesca waited until he'd moved off before responding. "You did tell me to be careful, didn't you?"

She gave a weak laugh, a flush coming to her cheeks. "I did, didn't I? Oh, Tesca...that was...it's been a long time since I've seen you fight.

I'd forgotten…" she trailed off.

Tesca started to feel uncomfortable. *Always study the ground before you cross it,* he reminded himself. "Allie…" he began.

"I mean I just didn't know whether you were going to fight at all, at first," she suddenly went. "You two just talked in Sabrian for a while… something about blades, and I thought, well, typical men, they always have to compare their swords, and then he just came right at you!"

"Allie…"

"And he was so tall, and his arms were so long, he could have put his hand on your head and you couldn't have reached him, and–"

"Allie!" he said quickly, cutting her off.

"What?"

He smiled at her. "Thank you." He paused, not sure where to go from here.

She noticed his hesitation and smiled, a slight curl twisting one side of her mouth. "Yes?"

"Maybe…maybe we can have a dance, back at the ballroom."

"A dance?" she asked, the old challenging, calculating look returning to her eyes. "I think I could find time for a dance with you, Tesca Secarius."

He smirked. "Well, it couldn't be more dangerous than the one I just had."

Her smile widened to a grin. "Are you sure? You might be sur–" she broke off as Tesca suddenly looked past her, over her shoulder. "What is it?" she asked, turning.

Another lieutenant had come into the pavilion, flanked by two more guards. They moved at a brisk walk, coming straight for Tesca.

"Duty calls," he said as an apology, stepping around her. "You'd best get back to the ballroom."

"All right," she called after him. "But I won't wait forever for that dance, Tesca."

Tesca chuckled one last time, then put all distractions out of his mind as the lieutenant stopped in front of him and saluted. "Sir, you must return at once." The officer looked around the platform, his gaze resting on Lieutenant Kelvo. He looked puzzled. "Sir, has Kelvo been here all this time?"

"Yes, he has," Tesca replied, a chill running down his spine. "Why?"

"I have orders to bring him before the Right Hand as well, unarmed," he added, looking uncomfortable.

"What's happened?" Tesca quietly demanded.

"I don't know, sir, but the Right Hand sent me to bring you back at once, even if I had to interrupt the duel." He handed Tesca a folded note with Galen's seal upon it. "The duel is over, isn't it?"

"Yes, it's over," Tesca replied absently, breaking the seal and reading the coded message: *Dr. Felton and Kayrla have disappeared.*

Chapter Thirty-one

Kayrla tentatively explored the dark space she'd been imprisoned in, keeping her hands outstretched in front of her. She kept her eyes open for two reasons. First, she was hoping to notice even the faintest glimmer of light from somewhere. Second, if she closed her eyes, she started to sag, exhaustion tugging her down towards the floor.

You can't sleep, she told herself, though her body screamed in protest. She'd never been so tired before, never tapped so much of her own body's energy to cast magic. Her body trembled and ached as if she'd run from the Duke's estate down to Harborside and back up. Sweat beaded on her skin, giving her chills in the cool air. Only fear for His Grace's safety kept her conscious. *Figure out where you are, then make a plan.*

Her shins contributed as much to the exploration of the room as her hands did; she walked into several items that felt, to her questing fingers, to be pieces of furniture. She found a chair, a small table, and then to her surprise, a bed. It creaked with age as she pressed down on it. Another urge to sleep rolled over her as she felt the mattress. *Soft. Sleep. Just for a minute. Wait, what's a bed doing down here?* she wondered, snapping out of her reverie. Curiosity held back sleep as she pressed on the mattress again. *A feather bed? And a big one.* She coughed in the darkness, smelling the erupting dust around her, and continued her exploration.

Moving past the bed, she came across another table, larger than the first one. As her fingers passed over its surface, she gave a small cry of relief as she found a candlestick with a short nub left in it. Holding the candlestick in both hands, she reached for the mana from her pendant once more to light the wick. But she felt nothing. Frantically, she reached up to her throat, fearing the pendant had somehow fallen off, and sighed when she found it still hanging about her neck. But there was no feeling of power within it. It was empty. Dead.

I used it up, she thought, a sob escaping her throat. *No more than an empty bottle now.* Despair rolled over her like a wave as she realized that she'd lost her new disguise spell, and with it, her freedom. *I swore to serve the Duke, but what good is that trapped on the estate?* She thought of Tesca and Galen, and the looks of sympathetic pity they would have on their faces when they learned of her loss.

"Stop it!" she suddenly barked out, shattering the silence. *Stop it,* she thought. *Stop feeling sorry for yourself. You were doing fine for years without that stupid pendant; it's a crutch. But you're not crippled; you're just tired. You swore an oath to the Duke, and you can save him, if you can get out of this room.* Furious with herself, she brushed the tears away, and reaching for the faint trickle of mana around her, cast her light spell.

Even this simplest of spells took more concentration than normal, and she barely completed it. The wick flared and popped into flame, and she winced at the sudden light after being in the dark for so long.

As her vision cleared, she saw that she was in a small square room with mortared stone walls. The table where she'd found the candlestick turned out to be a writing desk. There was an inkpot and a quill pen next to it. Cobwebs clung to the feather's edges and the ink inside the pot had dried to a hard, crumbling layer. Turning around, she looked at the bed. Kayrla could see at once that it was far too large for a room this small. It was set into one corner out of necessity; if it had been put against the middle of any one wall, there would barely be room for the other furniture, to say nothing of any people being able to move around in here. The small table she'd come across earlier was a nightstand with nothing on it. On the far side of the room from the bed, attached to the wall, was a small cabinet with a few plates and two large goblets in it.

Taking the candle with her, she did another exploration of the room, looking under the bed and even lifting up the mattress to see what was under it. She heard something metal clink to the floor as the mattress moved, and bending down to retrieve it, she found it was a woman's earring, a gold letter "F" set against a field of amethyst chips. *Pretty,* she thought as she sat in the chair. Although she knew a woman must have slept in this bed, she still had no idea what the purpose of this room was, or rather, had been. *The only thing I'm sure of is that no one's been in here for years.*

Her eyes itched from all the dust she'd stirred up and as she was putting the candle on the floor to rub them, she saw something glitter out of the corner of her eye. It turned out to be the door handle, reflecting the flickering candlelight. She got up and as she approached the door, she was startled to see how brightly the metal gleamed. She'd cast her repair spell many times into it, and now she could see that this had produced an unexpected effect.

The brass on the latch and handle was so clean and bright that she could see her own reflection in it. *It shines like new. By the Deeps, did I do that? Is it essentially brand new again?* She held the candlestick close to the door and with surprise, she saw that this effect wasn't limited to the metal. There was a rough circle of wood about a handspan's width around the handle that also looked clean and new. The door must have been polished once, for now that circle of wood had a sheen of fresh varnish on it that also gleamed in the light.

She shivered in the cool air once more, amazed at the results of her magic. *Well, even if I can't leave the estate, I suppose I could earn my keep just repairing things,* she thought with a laugh. She shivered again. *Is it getting colder in here?*

Heading back to the chair, she felt the chill lessen. Puzzled, she returned to the door and stood before it. Once again, she felt a chill, but only on the left side of her face. *There's a draft in here,* she realized. *And it's not coming from under the door!* Holding the candle in front of her, she moved to the left of the door, which put her up against one corner of the room. She watched the candle flame, waiting. A few moments later, it flickered, the tip of the flame moving away from the wall, into the room.

She licked the tip of one finger and began to feel for where the breeze was coming from. *Somewhere in this corner.* She bent in close to examine the wall, and to her surprise, realized that while the two walls came up against each other, there was no mortar set into the corner between them. There was a faint but steady stream of air coming through the thin space, from floor to ceiling.

There's a door here, she realized, getting excited. *Somehow this other wall moves back, or in, or…something like that.*

An idea came to her. She looked back at the bed. It was in the opposite corner of the room from this hidden door, and something clicked in her mind. *A secret entrance, more cups and plates than one person needs, a really big bed, and a private wine cellar next door.* She grinned. *A love nest!*

She turned back to the secret door. *Well, there must be a way to open this.* Setting down the candlestick, she braced herself against the door and pushed with all her might, but the door maintained its disguise as an immovable wall. Frowning, she picked up the candlestick and began looking for the other edge of the door.

Now that she knew what she was looking for, she found it with little difficulty. The door was not very wide, only about two feet. The other edge was right up against the side of the wooden cabinet holding the plates and dishes. Kayrla looked at the placement of the cabinet and nodded. *That's not a coincidence. Maybe a switch, hidden behind the plates?*

After a careful search inside the cabinet and around it, the switch turned out to be a stone in the wall beneath the cabinet that did not look imbedded in the mortar as the other stones were. The stone moved in a few inches when Kayrla pushed hard against it. She heard a loud clank and rattle on the other side of the wall, and the portion of the wall she had identified as a door moved away from her with a shower of dust and a grinding noise. She tasted the dust on her tongue as her breathing sped up. Cautiously, she peered into the new opening. A narrow passageway led into the darkness.

Taking a deep breath, she entered the passage, spending a few moments examining the door from this side to see how it worked. Pulling a lever next to the door pushed the door back in place, and she saw that there was an iron bar that could be set across it, locking it behind her. For a moment, she debated setting the bar in place, deciding at last that it would be safest to do so. *That's one more barrier between me and...him.*

Once the door was sealed off behind her, she headed down the passage. It was narrow, and bent slightly, but generally ran straight, and Kayrla noticed that it had a stone floor and solid oak beams supporting the ceiling. *Someone put a good deal of effort into making this tunnel,* she observed. *I'd love to know who.*

After thirty feet, the tunnel stopped at the base of a stone spiral staircase, going up. *Up is better than down,* she hoped as she began to ascend. There was a central pillar to this staircase, so she could only see the bending passage ahead of her as she climbed.

Before long, she lost track of time or how much distance she'd traveled. The constant turning made her lose any sense of direction she had as well. There was only the steady curve to the left going up. *This has to end somewhere,* she thought. *I only hope I can get back out into the estate to raise the alarm. But who can I tell?* Her legs were blazing with pain at each step now. *There's only five people on the estate who will recognize me on sight. Galen, Ella and the Duke should be in the great hall; there's no way I'd make it there before a guard spots me. I don't even know where to start looking for the Castellan, and Tesca's got to be fighting his duel by now. Galen mentioned the western pavilion. That's where Tesca took me for sword practice.*

One step was a little higher than the others and she didn't lift her leg enough to clear it. As she stumbled, the candlestick fell out of her fingers. Desperately, she flung out one hand and caught the base again before it hit the ground, a few drops of hot wax splashing her hand. *I don't know what I'd do if I lost the light,* she thought. The idea of trying to climb these steps in the dark was not something she wanted to consider. She sat on the step for a minute to catch her breath. *Just… have to keep going. Get to the end of this staircase, then get outside. I can find the pavilion if I get outside. Stay under the trees, stay under cover. Just get outside.*

Struggling to her feet, she resumed her climb up the steps, taking time to be more careful. *I must be higher than the great hall by now. Where in the Deeps is this going?*

As if in answer, the staircase ended in a wall. From this side of it, however, she could see another door mechanism similar to the one far below at the other end of the passage. She studied the door, thinking. *This one's barred. Whoever was the last to use this passage must have come in this way and sealed the door behind them.* This door was a different shape than the other; it was wider, but only about three feet high.

Trying to convince herself it was caution more than her aching legs that prompted her to sit down on the step and listen at the door, Kayrla spent a few moments with her ear pressed to it, listening for any voices or sounds of movement. She didn't hear anything at all, and deciding the coast was clear, she lifted the bar and turned the handle that released the door. There was a creak of gears and a similar shower of dust as the door rolled back on old machinery. The warm glow of lamplight beckoned. Squinting against the new light, she bent low and went through the open door, straightened up, and looked around.

Her mouth fell open in surprise. *I'm…I'm in the library!* She looked back at the secret door she had come through. *The fireplace!* She gave a small laugh, still astonished. *Does Galen know about this? I can't imagine so.*

The library was her favorite room in the manor, and just finding herself back in it restored a great deal of her confidence. Moreover, she knew how to get to the western pavilion from here. *There's a window with a big tree outside just down the hall,* she recalled. *I jump to that tree, then I'm on the grounds. Stay under the cover of the trees, get to the pavilion. Tesca will know what do to next,* she thought, crossing the room and opening the door to the hallway.

It was hard to say which of them was the more surprised, Kayrla or the young guard posted at the door. Both of them yelped and leapt away from each other as Kayrla came out into the hallway, but after that awkward moment, the guard lowered his pike at her.

"H-Halt!" he cried. Then he stared at her. "Hey...you're that elf I heard about!" His suspicious face brightened. "Isn't someone offering a lot of money for you?"

Chapter Thirty-two

"I don't understand, sir," Kelvo protested as he handed his weapons over to Tesca. They had moved off the pavilion to keep the Sabrians from seeing one of their host's officers being arrested.

"Neither do I," Tesca told him. "But we have our orders. Whatever's going on, we'll sort it out."

"Yes, sir," Kelvo replied, looking nervous but not panicked.

Tesca turned to the lieutenant who had brought him the summons from Galen. "Where is the Right Hand now?"

"His Grace's antechamber, off the ballroom, sir."

"And His Grace?"

"He's still at the ball, sir. The castellan is with him."

"All right, I'll take Kelvo with me to the Right Hand. I want you to take Kelvo's place and stay with the Sabrians. They have a wounded man and should receive whatever courtesies we can provide."

"They accepted the offer of a carriage back to the Harbor, sir," Kelvo put in. "They're making sure he's ready to travel now."

Tesca nodded. "Very good. Stay with them until they leave the manor, then return to the Right Hand and inform him they departed safely."

The lieutenant snapped off a salute. "Aye, sir."

"Kelvo, we'll take the path through the gardens." It was a longer route back to the great hall, but Allie Feyne would be on the main path now and Tesca did not want her seeing him run past with an unarmed officer in tow.

"I understand, sir," Kelvo said, with a look on his face that said he did, and started up the narrower path at a trot. Tesca followed him, appreciating Kelvo's unspoken understanding that he would go in front, where Tesca could keep an eye on him.

Kelvo's a good man, he thought as they jogged up the steps and around a small fountain. *Whatever reason Galen has for arresting him, it's got to be a mistake.* But that would not stop him from doing his duty, whatever that might entail. *I've been blindsided often enough recently; if Kelvo's really up to something, I won't be tricked again.*

Before long they reached the great hall. The two guards at this side entrance snapped to attention as they approached, and eyed Kelvo suspiciously.

"He's in my custody," Tesca told them, holding up Kelvo's weapons for them to see. The guards saluted and let them pass.

"They all have orders to arrest me," Kelvo said over his shoulder to Tesca as they walked down the hall. "I saw it in their eyes; what does the Right Hand think I've done?" Now Tesca could hear fear in the man's voice.

"I don't know," Tesca told him, wishing he could give him more reassurance. "Best not to say anything more until we get there, all right?"

"Yes, sir," Kelvo said, squaring his shoulders and continuing forward.

By taking less-traveled corridors, they stayed out of the sight of any guests, some of whom would be taking the opportunity to stroll through the wider hallways for a breath of fresh air or a chance for more private conversations. They passed several guards, all of whom kept their eyes on Kelvo.

When they reached the antechamber door, one of the guards held up a hand. "Sir, this man may not approach the Right Hand with any weapons."

"I have his weapons," Tesca said, holding them up.

"I am sorry, sir, but I must search him for concealed weapons," the guard said with genuine regret. "The Right Hand's order."

Concealed weapons, Tesca thought as the guard began to search Kelvo's person. *Galen's worried about an assassin. But it couldn't be Kelvo.*

"Thank you, sir," the guard said to Tesca as he finished his inspection. He opened the door for them. "You may proceed."

Galen was sitting behind a desk, talking with another guard. The look on his face shifted from relief at seeing Tesca unhurt to grim caution at seeing Kelvo with him. "I'm surprised you're the one who found him, Tesca. The duel took less time than I thought, eh?"

"He's been with me the entire time," Tesca replied, puzzled. "Since we first went down to the pavilion."

Now Galen looked puzzled. "Are you sure?"

"During the duel, I had other concerns than his whereabouts," Tesca admitted, "but the other guards who came with us can confirm Kelvo was there the entire time." He studied Galen; the man seemed genuinely surprised by this news. "What's happened?"

Galen turned to the guard next to him. "Tell the Left Hand and his…charge what you told me."

The guard nodded, looking uncomfortable. "Well, sir, I was grabbing a quick bite to eat in the hallway behind the Duke's Door. Felton was there with us, at his post, as he was supposed to be." He glanced at Kelvo and gave the barest shrug as an apology. "Then Lieutenant Kelvo comes along and tells Felton that he's needed."

"Needed?" Tesca put in. "For what?"

"Didn't say, sir. He just looked like it was urgent. Felton got up and went with him."

"That's a lie!" Kelvo shouted, his composure cracking at last. "I was with the Left Hand the entire time!"

"It's not a lie!" the guard shouted back, his own temper rising. "I saw what I saw!"

"Where is Felton now?" Tesca cut in before things got worse, addressing Galen.

"We can't find him," the Right Hand replied. "And we can't find… her. She was the one who first noticed Felton was missing."

"Yes, the serving maid," the guard said. "The one serving His Grace tonight. She came by looking for Felton, then took off when she saw he wasn't there."

"The maid," Tesca repeated, a chill running through him. "Why was she looking for Felton?"

"His Grace was in need of his elixir," Galen replied. He raised a hand as Tesca's eyes went wide. "No need to worry about that for the moment. Ella brought him some; she's with him now, along with the castellan."

Tesca, relieved, focused once more on the issue of Kelvo. "He's been seen in two places at once. We have an imposter." He looked at Galen, who nodded in agreement.

The guard looked confused. "Beggin' your pardon, sir, but if it was someone in a disguise, sir, it's the best I've seen. He walked right past me and I looked him in the face. I'd swear on my mother's grave it was Kelvo."

"I would say the same thing about the man who was with me," Tesca countered. "But if we can't tell them apart by looks, then we have to go by their actions. The one with me was following the orders he'd been given, but the one you saw drew Dr. Felton away from his post. That's not something he should have done. The real Kelvo would never have violated that order."

The guard thought about that for a moment, then nodded. "Yes, sir. I understand."

Kelvo made a noise somewhere between a sigh of relief and a snarl of rage. "So I'm free to go?"

Galen shook his head. "By now every guard has orders to place you under arrest, and there's still someone out there posing as you, so we'll leave things as they are for now. You will stay with me until this matter is cleared up."

Kelvo ground his teeth in frustration. "He's out there on the grounds right now!"

Galen glared at him. "Lieutenant," he snapped, his voice cracking like a whip, "you must remain in the sight of either myself or the Left Hand at all times, or we will have to treat you as the imposter! That is all."

Kelvo got himself under control. "Yes, sir. My apologies."

Galen nodded in grim satisfaction. "Tesca, you may return his weapons to him." He turned to the guard. "You will tell no one of this, do you understand? For the time being, Kelvo is still to be immediately placed under arrest if he, or whoever is posing as him, is seen. Only an order from His Grace, myself or the Castellan countermands this."

The guard saluted. "Aye, sir."

"Return to your post." The guard saluted once more, nodded to Kelvo as a means of apology, and left.

Kelvo finished buckling his weapons around his waist. "Sirs, I hope you'll give me the satisfaction of being the one to pull that imposter's disguise off." He loosened his rapier in its scabbard. "If he's wearing a wig or a false nose, I'll feed it to him."

Tesca and Galen shared a look. The guard's comment about the best disguise he'd ever seen had struck a chord with both of them. Tesca glanced at Kelvo, then looked back at Galen. *If we want to discuss this further,* he thought, *he'll have to be told.*

Galen nodded reluctantly, coming to the same conclusion. "Lieutenant, it's possible that this disguise wasn't done in the…normal way. Have a seat. We have some things to tell you. Pray do not interrupt until we are done."

A few minutes later, Kelvo let out a long whistle. "So, this elf everyone was tearing up Harborside for, she's been here the whole time?"

"Yes," Tesca confirmed.

"And she can disguise herself with magic?" Tesca nodded. Kelvo shook his head, still taking it all in. He looked at Galen. "Forgive me for being blunt, sir, but I have to ask. Could she be the imposter?"

"No," Tesca and Galen said at the same time. There was an awkward moment as the two men looked at each other in surprise, then Galen chuckled. "No, Lieutenant. If I had thought there was the slightest chance she was a threat to His Grace, I would never have put her at his side tonight, serving him wine."

Kelvo blinked in surprise. "She was the serving maid? Well, her disguise worked, I can tell you that. I was wondering who the new girl was. Thought she was a pretty one. I was going to try to look her up tomorrow."

Galen looked exasperated. "Lieutenant, all the chaos in Harborside that recently occurred was set off by her former captain making unwanted advances toward her. I'll not have a repeat of that inside the walls of this estate, is that clear?"

Kelvo was abashed. "Yes, sir…I meant no offense. It's just, well…her disguise was good enough to make me more interested in her."

Galen paused, then chuckled ruefully. "The prettiest girl in the room attracts the most attention, regardless of her species. I should have encouraged her to make her disguises more plain."

"You can do that after we find her," Tesca urged, mindful of the time passing.

"Indeed," Galen replied. "Lieutenant, the Left Hand and myself both vouch for the girl's loyalty to His Grace. Triad willing, you will get a chance to meet her and see why. Tesca," he said, looking at him, "there's only one reason why His Grace's physician would be targeted: we have an assassin on our hands, who is a master of disguise." He paused. "We have no way of knowing how he was able to look like Kelvo so convincingly, so we must consider the idea that he, like Kayrla, can magically alter his appearance. Thus, he could look like anyone."

"I agree," said Tesca. "Now that we know magic works this far south, there are a lot more security issues for the future. Right now, I suggest we start using code words to identify each other. If we don't hear the code word, we have to assume the other is the assassin, and act accordingly."

Galen nodded. "We'll use some nonsense phrase. Let's see…pickles and pears," he offered.

"Apples and…chairs?" Tesca replied.

"That should work," the Right Hand agreed. "Share those phrases with the Castellan, Ella and His Grace."

Tesca nodded and headed for the door. He stopped before opening it. "Should I suggest to His Grace that he retire for the evening?"

"As strongly as you can," Galen said. "Brief the Castellan on what we've discussed here, he'll know best how to arrange His Grace's safety. Then, start the hunt."

Chapter Thirty-three

"Isn't someone offering a lot of money for you?" the guard asked Kayrla, a greedy look coming over him.

"Not any more," she replied. "He's dead."

The guard frowned at her, then glanced at the door to the library. "Where'd you come from? That room was empty."

"It's a long story," she said. "I need to talk to the Left Hand…or the Right Hand…or the Castellan…anybody!"

"Oh, you'll be talking to them," the guard said. "They'll want to know how you got in here." He paused, looking her over once more. "And you're wearing a maid's uniform! How'd you get your hands on one?"

"It's not like I wanted to wear the stupid thing," she said, getting frustrated. "Listen to me! There's an assassin, in disguise, here for the Duke! You have to let me talk to someone in charge; I've got to warn them!"

"An assassin in disguise," the guard repeated, looking dubious. "You answer my questions first, elf. How did you get past me into that room?"

"I didn't!" Kayrla said, nearly shouting now. "There's a secret door in the fireplace; I was down in the cellars and I just found my way up here."

"Don't give me that cock-and-bull story," the guard sneered. "Secret door in the fireplace…rubbish! Like as not you stole that maid's uniform, hoping to sneak around and nick something else."

Kayrla stared at him in disbelief. "If I was doing that," she said, trying to keep herself under control, "then why would I have green hair and blue skin? It's not like the maid's uniform hides that fact, now is it?"

The guard's face furrowed, but then it brightened again. "Wait a moment, I heard you can change your appearance!"

"Then why wouldn't I have done it before coming out of the library?" Kayrla asked. She wished she could have done just that, but without the pendant to draw upon, it would have taken several minutes to cast the spell, and there wasn't time. The assassin was still out there; she needed to raise the alarm.

"Please, just listen to me," she begged, imploring him. "You can arrest me, you can throw me in a cell, I don't care...but let me talk to someone in authority. The Left Hand, Right Hand, the Castellan... any one of them will want to hear what I have to say."

She saw with relief that her words had some effect on him. "All right, I'll arrest you for trespassing, then. However, I'm not allowed to leave my post." He gestured with his pike toward a door. "I'll lock you in that closet until my relief comes along; sit tight for a few hours and then we'll be off."

"No!" she shouted. "I have to talk to someone now!"

"Not another word out of you," the guard warned. "Now get your skinny blue arse in there before I–hey!"

As Kayrla fled down the hall, the guard in furious pursuit, Kayrla hoped that this would all be sorted out before she got herself impaled on a pike. The guard was yelling for assistance, and far ahead of her she heard footsteps scrambling in response. But she reached the window before any more guards arrived. As she'd hoped, it was open, letting the night breeze in to cool the manor's interior. And just outside was the tree she'd seen every time she'd walked to the library.

When there had been a price on her head, she had kept her promise to Galen and Tesca not to leave the estate, but that had never stopped her from thinking about it, from planning what she would do if things suddenly went bad. This tree was always the start of those various half-formed plans.

The guard behind her was not prepared for her sudden left turn, and he skidded past her on the polished floor as she sprang to the window sill and leapt out towards the tree. She heard her uniform rip as one sharp branch stabbed into her side, but she didn't even think about the pain. The guard appeared at the window and glared at her as she scrambled deeper into the branches, then down the trunk. There was no danger of him coming after her; the branches had barely supported her weight and in any case, with his breastplate and weapons weighing him down, there was no way he'd be able to leap that distance.

She dashed away from the building into the dark gardens ahead. Behind her, she heard more voices and realized that another guard had joined the first at the window. *Well, the anthill's been kicked,* she thought. *Maybe raising the alarm will make it harder for the assassin to reach the Duke. But they'll be looking for me, and he can look like anyone.*

Her keen night vision allowed her to move easily through the darkest parts of the grounds, and by staying away from the lit paths that wound around the small gardens and linked the terraces of the sloping estate, she was able to avoid other guards and the occasional strolling guests.

After several minutes darting through the shadows, she crouched behind a hedge next to a small fountain to catch her breath. The wound in her side ached, but the cut was not deep, more a scrape than anything else. Her uniform by now was nearly in tatters, and she was tempted to use a repair spell on it. But she decided against it; she knew how tired she was, and miscasting even that simple spell might send her into unconsciousness. It was hard enough staying awake as it was; even the grass under her feet felt as comfortable as the feather bed in her suite right now.

Have to keep moving. Have to get to the Western Pavilion and find Tesca. She tried to figure out exactly where she was in relation to it. The straightest route there, she calculated, would take her across at least one or two well-lit areas, which she knew were sure to have guards. *It's a roundabout way then,* she decided without enthusiasm. *And what am I going to do when I reach the pavilion? I should just shout for Tesca as soon as I get there, but what if he's fighting? That might distract him at the wrong moment.*

Oh, you're thinking too far ahead, girl! she finally told herself. *Just get to the pavilion first.* She was about to get to her feet when she heard people approaching, and she froze.

It was the ringing sound of a metal-shod cane that identified one of them immediately. "Insufferable," rasped Victor Laveau.

"I agree, Father," said a second man. "The Duke interrupts you in the midst of your sentence to drink the wine brought him by that serving wench! And then you had to wait for that presumptuous fanfare to finish before you could continue!"

"A set piece, an ostentatious reminder of his power," Victor muttered. "The Kohayas have always been so. Unfettered arrogance, trying to lord it over the rest of the us with their stolen title. In the Frees, a Baron sits as high as a Duke!"

"Higher," the other man assured him. There was a pause. "Where is Yvette?"

"I sent her to circulate through the party and learn more details of this Sabrian incident that occurred before our entrance," Victor explained. "Sabrians..." His chuckle was more akin to a wheezing cackle. "They claim to be so cultured, treating us as barbarians...we do not start brawls under a host's roof, do we?"

"Indeed not," came the other voice, gloating. "We handle our enemies in other wa–"

"If you speak another word, Bernare, you will find the voyage home a most painful one," Victor snapped, cutting him off. "You were told not to say a word on that subject while we are here."

"I am sorry, Father," Bernare replied, real fear in his voice.

"Apologies are for lesser men. Let us return inside and see what your niece has learned. She, at least, knows how important it is to listen."

Kayrla listened to the clanking sound of Laveau's cane diminish as the two moved off. She tried to recall everything they had said. Galen, she was sure, would find all of it very interesting. *Like as not he'll understand more of it than I do,* she thought.

She was going to start moving off again when she heard more footsteps approaching the fountain. It sounded like one person was walking at a normal pace, while the other was further away, walking faster to catch up. "Wait…wait there!" came a woman's voice. The first person stopped.

"I want to know what sort of game you're playing," came the woman's voice, young and angry. "Your stunt made me look like a fool, not to mention almost getting Tesca killed!"

"I apologize," said the other. *A Sabrian,* Kayrla realized with surprise.

There was a long silence. Finally the woman spoke again. "Well?"

"Well…what?"

"What are you up to?" the woman demanded.

"I am not 'up to' anything," the Sabrian replied. *I know that voice,* Kayrla realized. *It has to be Captain Grivus.* "It seems that the Imperial envoy took offense at the clothes you selected for me to wear tonight," Grivus continued. "You know that my people are easily slighted and are quick to demand satisfaction."

"Oh, no…that ship won't sail with me!" snapped the woman. "You deliberately goaded that other captain into making that challenge! I didn't have to speak Sabrian fluently to hear that!"

"Livia and I have some…previous acquaintance," Grivus admitted. "I was not willing to ask for her pardon."

There was another pause. *If the man is Grivus,* Kayrla thought, *then I think I know who the woman must be.* "I'm still not convinced," the woman said at last. "And now that I think about it, you were very reluctant to come to this party until you heard that a Sabrian envoy would be there! And…" she went on, remembering something else, "…I may have purchased the clothes you're wearing, but it was you who told me that you were nostalgic for wearing the green and red of your homeland! The Triad knows why she'd object to you wearing those colors…but you knew she would, didn't you?"

"I have been away from my people for some time," Grivus said, "and I underestimated her reaction. Once again, I apologize."

Kayrla wished she could see the woman's face as there came another long pause. "Very well, Grivus. You're lucky Tesca came out of that duel without a scratch. If he'd been hurt..." she trailed off. Kayrla closed her eyes in relief at hearing that Tesca was all right. After a moment, the woman continued, her voice level once more. "You can play dodge-the-hook as long as you like with me, but my father doesn't play games. When we go back home, you'll have to come up with better answers for him. You just think about that for the rest of the night." Kayrla heard the woman turn and stride away. Grivus remained where he was for a moment, then Kayrla heard him give a quiet chuckle and stroll away in the opposite direction.

Kayrla remained in her hiding place, reviewing what she'd overheard. *I've still got to tell Tesca about the assassin. If he's finished the duel, where would he go next? Back to the Great Hall?* Her heart sank at the thought of trying to get in there unseen with the guards on alert. Suddenly an idea came to her. *Wait...I don't have to see him myself to warn him...there's someone who can take a message for me...someone who owes the Duke a debt of honor.*

She stood up, her weary body aching in protest, and started running in the direction Grivus had taken. She stayed off the path, moving through the underbrush, in case she ran into anyone else, but it wasn't long before she caught up with him.

He was waiting for her. In her haste, she hadn't been very quiet, and she saw that he was facing her direction, squinting into the darkness, trying to see what was coming his way. She took a deep breath, trusting her hunch, and stepped out onto the path before him, letting the light of a nearby lamp fall on her.

The older man's jaw clenched in surprise as he saw her. She saw his eyes move over her like Tesca's, taking in every detail, lingering neither on her eyes nor her ears as most humans did, but on the tattered maid's uniform, and the bloodstain on her side.

"Captain Grivus," she said, "I need your help."

Chapter Thirty-four

"I believe that this is the second time we have met, yes?" Grivus asked Kayrla with a wry expression.

Kayrla nodded. "The first time was when you met the Left Hand."

Grivus smiled. "Yes, I did take note of you. Your skin, your hair, they were common enough, but there was something about how you stood, how you moved, that set you apart." He studied her again. "You are dressed as a servant. Are you a slave to this Duke?"

"No," Kayrla replied in a calm voice. She suspecting that he was trying to get a reaction out of her, to learn more about her, but she did not want to make it that easy for him. "I serve His Grace, as do you."

"Serve him?" Grivus countered. "No…child."

"I am not a child," she replied sharply. She reminded herself to keep talking in the same formal manner as Grivus did; it would help her seem older. The man was testing her, seeing what he could get away with, but he had no knowledge of elves or magic. "You are unfamiliar with my people, as I am unfamiliar with yours. I am, in fact, older than the Left Hand."

"Ah," Grivus replied, nodding in apology. "I say child for that is how you appear to me. I shall not repeat it."

"My thanks. But I think I am correct, in a way, that you do serve his Grace. You owe the Champion's Price to him, yes?"

Grivus looked taken aback. "I…do. But as you say, you are unfamiliar with my people. I owe him a debt. There is a difference between that and service."

She nodded, thinking fast, trying to recall exactly what Grivus and Allie Feyne had said to each other. "Very well. But as one who owes his life to His Grace, I would ask that you help me save His Grace's life."

Grivus looked amused. "Are you claiming the Champion's Price now, on your master's behalf?"

"No," Kayrla countered, "I do not have that right. But I believe it is in your best interests to help me save his life."

"And why is that?"

Kayrla smiled. "Because if he dies, you would be obliged to return to the Feynes, and that is something you are clearly trying to avoid."

She watched the wrinkles around his eyes deepen for an instant at that, but otherwise he remained impassive. "Let us, for the moment, follow the course you are charting," Grivus offered. "What help do you need from me?"

"There is an assassin on the grounds, here to kill His Grace," Kayrla told him. "I need someone to warn the Left Hand."

"Why can you not go yourself?" Grivus asked, but then he took another look at Kayrla's tattered appearance. His eyes seemed to brighten with understanding. "Not all of the guards know about you, do they?"

"No, they don't," said Kayrla. "I don't have the time to put my magical disguise back on; and the guards would never let me inside the manor looking as I do."

"Why trust me to do this?" Grivus asked her.

"You've known for weeks that I was in the company of Tesca; you told Jolly Red that I was with him and even suggested that I might be up here."

"How do you know that I met with your former captain?" Grivus asked, surprised.

She shrugged. "Tesca is an *agentis*, isn't he?" She smiled, letting Grivus's imagination answer the question for her. "In any case, Captain, I realized that of all the people here tonight, you might be the least surprised to see an elf suddenly step out of the darkness and ask for your help."

Grivus looked impressed. "Very well. I will deliver this message to the Left Hand for you, but you will owe me a debt."

Kayrla sagged visibly. "Oh, please…can't you just–"

"No," Grivus said, shaking his head. "There was a time when I did not require debts in return for actions taken, but that generosity cost me too dearly. No, a price must be set." He smiled. "It need not be a great debt."

"You mean…a favor?" Kayrla asked.

"Favor," Grivus repeated, rolling the word around in his mouth. "Yes, I know that word. Yes, a favor. That is all. Do you agree?"

"Yes," Kayrla replied, her legs starting to tremble from exhaustion. "Yes, yes…I'll owe you a favor."

"What is the message?"

"There's an assassin on the grounds," Kayrla said, trying not to rush over her words in her haste to get the man moving. "Another elf. He uses illusions to change his appearance; I don't know what he really looks like. He murdered Dr. Felton and took his place to get close to the Duke. He might still look like Felton, but I don't know for sure. Do you have all that?"

"Assassin, elf, illusions, Felton," Grivus repeated. "I will deliver the message." Kayrla nodded. "Thank you, Captain." She glanced around. "I'll wait by that tree for your return, all right?"

"Of course," Grivus said. He turned and jogged up the path towards the manor. Kayrla was glad to see him running; while the man seemed to enjoy using two syllables when one would do, he wasn't wasting time now.

She sighed. *I only hope he can find Tesca faster than I could. He seems pretty resourceful.* Slumping against the tree, she let her eyes close for a moment, then jerked herself awake again. *Can't relax, not even for a second. I'm dead on my feet, but I can't give up now. Must find something to do, to keep myself awake.*

Stepping a few feet away, she started to cast her old illusion spell, very slowly. *I've got the time now,* she thought, moving her arms and hands through the well-practiced routine. *It's not a perfect disguise, but it's better than blue skin and green hair. And it keeps me focused on something.*

She reached for the mana around her, gently drawing the faint threads of power into her spell. There was no spell she knew so well as this one; but she wouldn't let herself rush through it. The pendant had no mana left to offer, and she was so tired that if she got the spell wrong, the mana would be drawn directly out of her own body. At best, that would send her into unconsciousness. At worst…

Don't think about that. Don't think about anything, she told herself. And so she lost herself in the spell, a lone elf slowly dancing in the dark, with only an occasional moonbeam slipping between the leaves to illuminate her.

She could almost see the mana around her now, obeying her commands, weaving into the pattern she desired. She was doing it so slowly, so carefully, that she realized she was actually drawing more mana than she would need for the spell itself. Curious, she continued the slow casting, but she held the extra mana in reserve, wondering if this overflow might be of use.

The spelldance went on, her hands and arms shifting postures as she smoothly rotated in place, drawing the mana from all directions equally. It was the most efficient way to cast a spell, her father had told her, but it took so long that it was rarely practical.

She truly had no idea how long she'd been there, and some part of her was alarmed at that. She had hidden herself behind the tree, in a dark portion of the grounds, but a guardsman deliberately searching for her would find her quickly enough. She checked on the progress of the spell, and noted with some relief that she was almost done. Then she examined the overflow of mana she had been hoarding. It was a tiny amount of energy, not enough to fuel the second half of her new magical disguise. *But it might be useful for something,* she thought.

She could feel the illusion become complete, and chose the red hair and freckled skin combination. She had not seen many of tonight's guests with that complexion, and it was one that she hoped Tesca might recognize on sight.

As she ended the dance, she wondered what do so with the extra mana she'd collected. *I could just let it disperse again; it's not enough for a new spell.* But instead, on impulse, she drew the mana into her own body. *I used some of my own body's power casting spells tonight. Maybe it works the other way.*

The change was immediate. She felt a tingling sensation all over, which turned into a warm, comfortable feeling in the very center of her chest. It reminded her of a time when Jolly Red had acquired a bottle of expensive Terendan *oskay*. She had managed to wheedle one drink of the potent liquor out of her captain. The feeling of the mana being absorbed by her body was very similar to when she'd downed the drink, but without the intoxicating fuzziness. She stopped the spelldance, and found herself invigorated. She still felt ragged around the edges, but she was no longer dead on her feet. *Second wind,* she thought. *Let's hope it's enough.*

Chapter Thirty-five

"Apples and chairs," the Duke said with a chuckle. "Damn silly password if you ask me."

"The silly ones are harder to guess, milord," Tesca reminded him.

"True, true," agreed the castellan, looking over the crowd. "Milord, I must insist that with this new threat upon us, you should return to your chambers."

The Duke looked frustrated. "I don't want this lot to see me carted off by my guards. It'll undo all the work we've done tonight, with Kayrla's disguise and all." He sighed. "But I would rather be thought of as a helpless invalid than a healthy-looking corpse."

"Perhaps Your Grace could retire for the evening?" Ella asked. She had taken up Kayrla's position on the dais, standing to the Duke's left. "You've been out here long enough for everyone to see that you don't have one foot in the grave, if you'll pardon my saying so."

"Not a bad idea," said the castellan. "I'll need a few minutes to make sure the route to your suite is secure, milord. Dragging you out of here into a trap wouldn't do at all."

"I would think not," said the Duke drily.

As the castellan briefed the Duke on his planned escort route through the manor, Tesca took up watching the party. The night was beginning to wind down; a number of guests had either left, or more likely, were out on the estate grounds, enjoying the splendor of His Grace's gardens to engage in gossip or...other pursuits. It was said that a notable percentage of Kohayne's leading citizens had coincidentally been born roughly nine months after one of the Duke's Ascension fetes. It was also said, more quietly, that the true parentage of these citizens was often in question. Tesca chuckled. While he was certain the rumors were greatly exaggerated, the night was warm, the wine was plentiful, and he had observed that among some of Kohayne's elite, intrigue and scheming could be powerful aphrodisiacs.

With fewer guests in the ballroom, it was easier to pick out individuals. Amio the glassblower was still there, sitting on a small couch against one wall next to his wife and some other Kohayans, as the local citizens called themselves. Elsewhere in the Frees, the more commonly used, and less polite term, was "Quaddite."

On a hunch, Tesca started looking for the foreign guests, recalling his conversation with the Kreigan envoy, Brunnenfeld. There had been something about the man that had made Tesca suspicious. He arrived early, even before the Duke. *Kreigstat is a small realm and far off; there aren't many here who might spot someone pretending to be from there. And he didn't bring an entourage or an escort, as all the other envoys had.*

He reminded himself that he had to find out where the Kreigan envoy was staying. Either he was on the ship that had brought him here, or he'd rented a room somewhere in Kohayne. He was sure that Galen would have that information among his many files, and gladly send Tesca to take a look.

A lieutenant approached the dais and saluted the castellan, who stepped down to speak with him. A moment later, he beckoned Tesca to join him. "All right, lad. Tell the Left Hand what you just told me," he ordered the lieutenant.

The younger officer nodded. "Sir, word's just reached us that an intruder broke into the library. The guard there said…well, sir…he said it was an elf, that one everyone's been looking for in Harborside."

"An elf?" Tesca said. "You have a description?"

"Yes, sir," said the man. He hesitated, as if he didn't think his report would be believed. "Um, the guard said she had blue skin, green hair and was…was wearing a maid's uniform."

That's Kayrla all right, Tesca thought. *What happened to her magical disguise? Why was she trying to get into the library?* "Where is she now?"

"Sir, I'm sorry to report that she escaped when the guard tried to arrest her. She got outside, onto the grounds, and we lost her."

"Damnation," muttered Tesca. "We have to find her."

The castellan frowned. Tesca knew the man didn't trust Kayrla entirely. "My lads will find her before long."

"But they'll spit her on a pike unless you order them not to," Tesca objected.

"If she's not guilty, why did she run?" the castellan asked.

Tesca wanted to argue the point, but the Duke had long ago laid down a directive that his senior staff, however much they might disagree with each other in private, did not do so in public. *"Nothing erodes morale faster than the perception that your leaders don't know what they're doing,"* he had said time and time again.

He tried a different approach. "We agree she needs to be found... surely a live prisoner is easier to question than a dead one?"

The castellan shrugged, but appeared to take Tesca's point. He looked over Tesca's shoulder, suspicious, and Tesca turned to see Captain Grivus emerging from the crowd. The man looked like he was in a hurry.

"*Agentis,*" he said with a nod of greeting. He sounded slightly out of breath.

"Captain," Tesca replied, "this is not a good time."

The Sabrian shook his head. "I am afraid it cannot wait. Likely, it bears a connection to whatever it is you and these officers are looking so concerned about."

Tesca frowned. "I'll be right back," he said, leading Grivus a few feet away.

"Don't be long," the castellan replied, still looking suspicious.

"I have a message for you," Grivus said in his mother tongue. "I encountered your...little friend in the gardens, and she asked me to warn you."

"Warn me?" Tesca asked, replying in Sabrian. "About what?"

"There is...an assassin," Grivus said in a low voice. "Understand, this is her account; I have not seen any such thing myself. According to her, he is an elf, like her...but he can change his appearance."

"Go on," Tesca asked.

Grivus seemed a little surprised that Tesca took the news without a trace of disbelief. "She says he murdered a doctor... Dr. Felton. He took this Felton's place, trying to get close to the Duke. He might still look like this doctor, but she is not sure. She does not know what he really looks like."

Tesca nodded. "Where is my friend now?"

"In the garden where I left her. She awaits my return." He hesitated. "She was not hiding behind any illusion, *agentis*; her skin was blue and her hair was green; most unusual. Also, she was injured."

"Injured?"

"A wound to her side...her uniform was in shreds and stained with blood. At least, I think it was blood. It seemed to glitter?"

"Yes, yes, her blood does that," Tesca confirmed. "How badly was she hurt?"

Grivus shrugged. "I am no student of elven anatomy; but if I thought she was dying, I would not have left her alone. She is more weary than wounded, I think."

She wouldn't walk around without her disguise unless she couldn't put it back on, Tesca thought. "All right," he told Grivus, "I want you to get back to her. Find a place to for her to rest; somewhere out of the way where she won't be seen." He took his silver hand pin from his lapel and handed it to Grivus, who looked at it curiously. "If any guards question you, show them this. I don't have authority to command the guards, but that should be enough for them to at least hear you out. When this is over, I'll come find you."

"Of course." Grivus nodded and turned to go.

Tesca caught his arm. "Wait...why are you bringing me this message?"

Grivus smiled. "She drives a hard bargain." And then he was off, moving back through the crowd towards the exit.

Tesca returned to the foot of the dais. "There's more you need to hear," he said to the castellan, tilting his head back up towards the Duke.

The castellan's sour expression deepened. "Wait here," the castellan told the lieutenant.

"I've had word from Kayrla," Tesca said when he and the castellan had reached the top of the dais. "She says it's as bad as we feared; the assassin is another elf. He killed Felton and," he paused as Ella gasped in shock, "took his place, trying to get close to the Duke."

"He couldn't have gotten much closer," the Duke commented. "Is she all right?"

"She's hurt, apparently," Tesca confirmed, "but it's not serious. She's going to lie low until this is over."

"If that's really her intention," the castellan put in. "Milord, I've just had word about her myself. She was caught trying to break into the library, but escaped onto the grounds. Perhaps this is all part of her plan?"

"What are you suggesting?" Tesca demanded.

"This whole business of an assassin may be false," the castellan said. "We've only heard word of an assassin from her...and even that she didn't tell us herself. A Sabrian exile you just fought a duel over comes up and tells you this out of the blue?" The castellan shook his head. "Master Secarius, I respect you, but I think you've developed a blind eye around her. Milord, I submit that perhaps this entire affair was a ploy by her to keep us running in circles while she steals what valuables she can? She did come to us running from a theft gone bad, after all."

"What a horrible thing to say!" Ella scolded him.

"Don't get me wrong," the castellan said. "I don't dislike the girl; I just don't trust her completely. Everything we've heard has come from her. Ella, you never saw anyone lead Felton off, did you? We only learned he was missing after she told you, yes?"

Ella looked uncertain. "Well, yes..."

"If I'm wrong, I'll apologize to her personally," the castellan went on. "There's no malice here, I'm just doing my job."

"That you are, Castellan," said the Duke, "and I thank you for it. But you have forgotten something. It is true that the first we heard of Felton's absence was from Kayrla, but we also have a guard who witnessed Kelvo lure Felton away from his post. Kayrla was standing next to me at that time, while the real Kelvo was with the Left Hand at the western pavilion."

The castellan looked uncomfortable as he realized his error, and he gave the Duke a short bow. "Milord, my apologies."

"It's all right," the Duke told him. "Your suspicions are what make you so good at your job, Turvin." The castellan blinked; the Duke did not usually address him by name. "I think once you get to know her, she'll turn you around eventually. Now, we should proceed with the plan to get me out of here."

"Of course, milord," the castellan said, returning to his stern and efficient demeanor. "I'll just be a few minutes, checking the route. I'll pass the word that if the girl's found, she's to be escorted to the Right Hand, unharmed."

"Thank you," Tesca told him. "I'll stay here until you get back."

"Very well," the castellan agreed. "You're with me," he said to one of the guards flanking the Duke. "You other three, until I get back, take your orders from the Left Hand." Tesca was one of the Duke's closest advisors, and while the guards on the estate generally deferred to his requests, it was more out of respect than duty. He could not actually order them to do anything unless the Duke, Galen or the castellan granted him that temporary authority. As Galen had once remarked, *"The Left Hand has other things to concern himself with than directing troops."* The guards glanced at Tesca, then nodded to their commander. The castellan saluted the Duke and left the dais.

"Some more wine, milord?" Ella asked the Duke.

"Save it for later," the Duke said. He chuckled. "With this elf around, that's the only bottle I know hasn't been poisoned. If I make it back to my bedchamber alive, then I'll have another drink."

Ella sighed. "Such maudlin talk, milord," she said, her voice in mock reproof.

The Duke shrugged. "My father used to tell me, 'Son, if you've managed to get someone to send assassins after you, it means you're doing your job right.'"

As the castellan and the guard approached the doorway leading out of the Great Hall, a wine steward, coming the other way, stepped aside to let them pass, bowing low. No one noticed a brief pulse of green light shine out from a gap in his shirt as he straightened up. A moment later, he had turned back through the door, following the castellan into the hallway.

Chapter Thirty-six

Grivus returned to the fountain only a few minutes after Kayrla had finished her spelldance. He did not dash over to the tree where she'd said she would be waiting. Instead he eased himself down onto a stone bench with a satisfied groan, glancing around himself as if he was merely taking his ease after a long evening. Kayrla could see his eyes dart over to the tree periodically, and knew he was being cautious. However, she'd heard no one but him approaching, so she stepped out from behind the tree and joined him at the bench.

The old Sabrian studied her in the moonlight. "You look…different. Your hair and eyes, they are not the same color now."

She nodded. "That's right. While you were gone I had the chance to use one of my spells. It's not perfect, but maybe it'll help."

"Quite remarkable," Grivus replied, still gazing at her hair in polite interest. "I was able to find the Left Hand and give him your message."

She sighed. "That's a relief. What does he want me to do now?"

"He wants you to find a quiet place to stay out of the way and get some rest. He also gave me this to help convince any guard we might meet to hear us out." He held out the silver hand pin for her to see.

Kayrla scowled. "That might be useful, but he wants me to just hide somewhere? He thinks I can't handle myself? I've been doing all right so far tonight."

"That is what he told me," Grivus said with a shrug. "I told him you were hurt, and looked exhausted."

"Just a scratch," Kayrla said with a dismissive wave. "Poked myself on a branch while jumping into a tree. And I managed to get a little rest while you were gone. We've got to find a way to help."

"We?"

"Do I have to owe you another favor?"

"That depends on what you wish to do," Grivus countered.

She looked down at the ground, thinking. Her gaze fell on the dusty tatters of her maid's uniform. "I have to get back to my room and change my clothes, before I do anything else."

Grivus nodded in agreement. "Perhaps we can find you some sort of hat, or a cloth to wrap around your head as you did the first night we met? The tips of your ears protrude from your hair."

"Trust me, I know what I need to hide my ears," she said, getting to her feet. "There's one entrance to the manor that's close to my room; let's go."

Grivus rose and followed her without making any mention of requiring further payment. She led him down the path, then cut across a small enclosed garden, heading for an opening in the hedge that led to a set of steps rising to a higher terrace.

"Your night vision must be very sharp," Grivus observed.

"Sorry," she apologized. "I just didn't think it would be wise to stay on the main paths, in case we meet any guards."

"A prudent choice," the Sabrian replied. "Please warn me if we approach any low branches, however. And do not move too far ahead; I can barely see you as it is."

Kayrla led Grivus to the opening in the hedge. "I think once we get up to this terrace, we can circle around the manor to the entrance I'm looking for."

"You don't know for certain?"

She sighed. "Tonight's the first time I've had a chance to explore the grounds at all. This place is like a maze."

"A maze that goes up and down as well," Grivus muttered. "These old knees keep reminding me of that."

"Well, these steps should be the last ones, for a while, anyway."

"How delightful."

Kayrla patted his arm, then started up the steps. They came up onto a surprisingly clear space, a lawn with hedges and trees only around the edges.

"More moonlight up here," Grivus said as he looked around. "A gaming yard, I think."

"Gaming yard?"

"A clear space for any sort of sporting event to be played," he explained. "I am unfamiliar with the games played in the Frees, but this would be a good space for *volay*."

"I don't know that game," Kayrla replied.

"I am certain your Left Hand does," Grivus said. "An *agentis* would have at least learned the rules, even if he has no time to play."

"What is an *agentis*, anyway?" Kayrla asked, as she decided which way to go next. "Tesca's never gotten around to explaining it to me."

"An *agentis*..." Grivus trailed off. "An *agentis* is...an *agentis*. He serves a master, and does whatever that master requires of him."

"You could describe a butler that way," Kayrla objected. "Tesca doesn't bring wine for His Grace or make sure his clothes are cleaned."

"A butler would not necessarily kill on his master's behalf," corrected Grivus, "nor would he be expected to be capable of it. An *agentis* is trained for such matters."

"So...an assassin?"

"If required. He watches his master's enemies, steals their secrets, and, if necessary, ends their lives." Grivus shrugged. "However, if an *agentis* were solely used to kill his master's enemies, it would be wasteful of his training. In the Empire, a master who does such a thing attracts more attention than may be...healthy for him."

Kayrla was struck by a curious thought. "You only refer to the *agentis* as a male. Can a woman become one?"

"Yes, but to my knowledge, there are no female *agentii* at this time," Grivus said. "It is rare for a woman with the capability to become an *agentis* to follow that path."

"Why?"

Grivus smiled slyly at her. "Because women that capable often have an ambition to match, and an *agentis* is forever a servant, never a master." He looked about the yard. "Do you know which way to go from here?"

She nodded, gesturing to the left, and started moving across the yard. Grivus followed her.

She heard a rustling in some bushes off to one side and froze. For a moment she was afraid the assassin would rise from the shrubbery and charge them, but then she recognized the sounds of two people enjoying each other's company. Grivus held still as well, but after a moment, he chuckled. "I believe those two are too preoccupied to bother us," he said in a low voice.

She rolled her eyes and started to move forward again. "Ella told me that there'd be a lot of that going on later in the evening; I didn't think I'd come across it myself."

"Yes, the woman who brought me here said much the same thing," Grivus replied. "Although it sounded as if she might have been looking forward to the possibility."

She frowned. "With Tesca, I'll bet. There was something in her voice when she said his name."

"Ah, you were listening to us behind the hedge, then?" Grivus asked, but there was amusement in his tone. "Yes, I heard that too, and something of a similar nature in the Left Hand's voice when he spoke to her."

Kayrla stopped and turned to him. "Did you?"

Grivus looked even more amused. "Does that bother you?"

"No!" she snapped, stepping back from him. "Well, no…not the way you're thinking! He's…he can do better, that's all."

"I see," was all Grivus said in reply. She scowled and started across the lawn again.

They traveled in silence for several minutes, Kayrla guiding them through the grounds. They stayed off the wider, well-lit paths as much as possible. There were some guards on patrol, but there were also a number of guests strolling about now or sitting on benches, talking loudly and laughing or whispering in private conversations. Kayrla wished she had the time to listen in on some of those; with her keen hearing, she was hearing snippets of all sorts of interesting things. *When this is over, I'll tell Galen about it. Maybe at the next party he'll pick out a few folks that he wants me to spy on. It would be more interesting than standing next to the Duke pouring him wine.* Then she remembered that the fete was only held every five years. *The Duke has to throw more parties than this one, doesn't he? Maybe a smaller one, I'll can get some practice and–*

Suddenly a woman's scream broke through the night, not far off. Grivus tried to grab Kayrla's arm but Kayrla was already dashing forward. She came upon the scene in a moment: two guests, partially dressed, scrambling out of the underbrush, the woman sobbing hysterically. They stumbled down the path past Kayrla, not even noticing her.

Kayrla moved into the brush where they had come from. In a dark space under a tree, she saw a male body partially concealed under a pile of leaves. There was a pair of women's shoes and a man's belt on the ground nearby, presumably left behind by the couple in their haste to get away from the body. As Kayrla dragged the body out from under the leaves, she saw that he was naked except for his underclothes. She knew what to expect as she turned the man over to see who he was, but despite that she still gasped in dismay as she saw his face, frozen in an expression of utter terror.

Grivus came up behind her. "You…should not run ahead," he panted. "There are too many reefs below the waterline." He squinted through the darkness at the body before him. "Who is that?"

"I don't know," Kayrla said, "but that look on his face; other people the assassin killed looked just like that."

Grivus squatted down next to the body, his knees creaking. "You said the assassin can change his appearance; is that why this man has no clothes?"

"That must be it," Kayrla replied. "He's posing as someone else now. Perhaps one of the envoys?"

Grivus looked doubtful. "A difficult role to play, with so many here that may know the real person."

Kayrla turned on her heel, looking for any other clues, and something crunched under her foot. Looking down, she saw that she'd stepped on a slender length of glass, snapping it in two. *A broken wine stem.* Then she was rummaging through the pile of leaves, gingerly picking through them. There were more glass shards here, the remains of at least four or five wineglasses.

"He's posing as a wine steward now," she said, holding a few pieces of glass out for Grivus to see. "He must have lured the man here and killed him."

"No wine tray?" Grivus asked, glancing around.

Kayrla thought about that. "No, he'd keep the tray. Full or empty, having the tray completes the disguise. You see the tray, you know who he is without ever looking him in the face." She thought of Galen at that moment; it sounded like something he might have said. *He must be rubbing off on me.*

Grivus looked impressed. "That is most clever. But we should be away from here; that scream will attract others."

"Yes," she said, heading back towards the path. Then she froze. "Someone's coming now!" She could hear the clink of a metal breastplate. "Damn, it's a guard!"

Grivus got to his feet. "We have to run. I do not think even the Left Hand's insignia will help if he finds an elf and a Sabrian next to a dead man."

"There's no time!" Kayrla whispered. "What do we do?" Grivus took off his jacket and began to quickly unbutton his shirt. "What are you doing?!" she hissed at him.

Grivus grinned at her, kicking the woman's shoes and man's belt further into the darkness. "Pretend you are the one who screamed for help," he said, his voice completely calm and unruffled. "We can pose as the ones who found the body." He started to pull off his boots.

Kayrla stared at him for a moment before she understood what he meant. "Oh, Triad's Mercy..." she muttered, unfastening the top three hooks on her uniform, then taking Grivus' jacket from him and wrapping it over her shoulders like a cloak.

"Now start crying," Grivus said, tugging his shirt loose from his belt so it looked like he'd just thrown it on in haste, "and make it convincing. Grab your head in your hands, to hide your ears." He put his arm around her in a comforting gesture and led her out towards the path. Kayrla huddled under his embrace. She tried to cry, but couldn't get any tears started. *I wonder if Galen can teach me how to do that,* she thought to herself, going for gulping sobs and holding her head in her hands.

The guard she'd heard coming skidded to a halt before them, his pike at the ready. His eyes flashed angrily at Grivus. "What's going on here, Sabrian?" he snapped.

"A body," Grivus said, his voice quavering as if in fear. "There is a body back there."

"What?" the guard repeated, incredulous.

"It…was h-horrible!" Kayrla sobbed. She let Grivus' jacket slip down for a moment, revealing a bare shoulder. "He…he's under the leaves…"

Grivus guided her into a tighter embrace, tugging the jacket back into place. He murmured comforting words to her in his native language, and she clung to him, letting silent sobs wrack her body.

The guard stared at the pair of them, then glanced at the dark area beneath the tree. "Stay here," he growled, plunging off the path.

Kayrla heard people approaching from both directions now. She felt Grivus suddenly tense and turned her head to see what he was looking at.

Allie Feyne was standing by herself on the path, staring at the two of them. Her slender, sharp features were bent into a furious scowl. At first, she was glaring at Grivus, but then her gaze fell on Kayrla, and her expression became more scornful. "Caius, really…" she scolded him, "…the help?"

Letting another fake sob wrack her body, Kayrla turned back into Grivus's embrace. *Tesca can do a* lot *better than her.*

Chapter Thirty-seven

"Caius, really…" Allie Feyne scolded Grivus, looking suspiciously at Kayrla, "…the help?"

"Mistress Feyne," Grivus called to her, "this is not a safe place. There has been a murder."

"A murder?" Allie scoffed. "That's ridiculous." Grivus remained silent. Kayrla, still huddled in Grivus' arms, trying to display hysteria at the dead body not far away, heard Allie come closer. "You wasted no time between evading my questions and chasing this little minnow, Caius. And her crying act is just an act. Trust me, girl…I've seen better performances from a one-legged pirate dancing the hornpipe." She bent in close to Kayrla, speaking low. "What is Caius paying you to carry on this way? I'm sure my family has more money to loosen your tongue than he has to keep it still."

The guard came back out of the bushes. "By the Deeps," he grumbled, "he's dead all right."

"What?" Allie said in confusion. "He's telling the truth?"

"Aye, Mistress Feyne," the guard replied, recognizing her. "A single stab to the back, and a look on his face that I'd not like to see again."

"I am unarmed," Grivus said, still holding Kayrla in a comforting embrace. "We found the body when we retreated there for…a bit of privacy."

"Oh, Caius," Allie cut in, sounding very disappointed, "if you were looking for a bit of pleasure, I could have found ladies far more skilled and pretty to entertain you."

Kayrla began to twist in Grivus' grip, trying to turn towards Allie, but Grivus held her firm. "Sir," he said to the guard, "I will admit I convinced this young one to join me."

"For the last coin in his purse, I'll warrant," Allie interrupted again. "Girl, you've sold yourself short, spreading your legs that fast."

"But…" Grivus went on, his voice rising over hers, "…we are guiltless in the man's death. In fact," he went on, "we would gladly submit to questioning before your…" he paused.

"…castellan…" Kayrla said between sobs.

"Yes, your castellan," Grivus finished. "We would welcome a chance to prove our innocence at once."

There were more sounds around them, as more people came to see the source of the noise. Kayrla could hear the clink of armor, indicating another of them was a guard. "Wick," said the first one, relief in his voice, "good to see you."

"What's going on?" came the second guard's voice.

The first guard paused; Kayrla took a peek at him and saw that the man was glancing at the growing crowd with unease. He waved the second guard close and drew him into a quiet conversation. Kayrla's keen hearing could pick up every word.

"There's a dead body back there, Wick. Murder."

"No! Was it the Sabrian?"

"Might be…might be that elf we were warned about not too long back."

"I got new word from up top about her," Wick replied. "If we find her, we take her to the Right Hand, straight off. Alive and unharmed, mind you."

"Too many odd things happening tonight," the first guard muttered. "First that business with Kelvo, then some elf tries to break into the library. Then we're told to arrest Dr. Felton?"

"Things have been odd for weeks around here," Wick agreed. "Castellan's been on eggshells; and it's more than just getting ready for the fete."

"I agree," said the first guard. "But I'm not getting dragged into all that. There's a body back there, sure as sunrise, so I'll just focus on that."

"I like that plan," Wick said, "how do you want to handle this?"

"I'll stay here; keep the gawkers back. You take the Sabrian and the girl back to the manor and send some more of us down here to secure the area. The Sabrian says he took the maid back in there for a bit of fun and found the body. Whoever the stiff is, he was stabbed, and it looks fresh. If the Sabrian did it, the weapon can't be far."

"Probably find it in daylight, I'll wager. So, just put the two of them somewhere till morning, then?" Wick asked.

The first guard chuckled. "Aye. Maybe he can get her back 'in the mood'." They both laughed, then Wick walked over to Grivus and Kayrla. "All right, you two, up to the manor."

"The rest of you," the first guard addressed the crowd as Kayrla and Grivus started up the path, "I'll have to ask you to move along. Nothing more to see here."

Kayrla extricated herself from Grivus' embrace as they trudged up the path, a plan forming in her mind. "Give me Tesca's pin," she whispered.

"Why?"

"Trust me," Kayrla urged him. Grivus put his hand into hers for a moment, transferring the pin to her. When she judged that they'd walked far enough away from the murder scene, she turned back to face the guard.

"Keep moving," the guard said, looking suspicious.

Kayrla took a deep breath before proceeding. She brushed her hair away from her face, revealing her ears in the moonlight. "I'm the elf you've been looking for," she said. Grivus stared at her in surprise, but then he hadn't overheard the guards' conversation. "I need to see the Right Hand immediately."

"I knew it!" shouted a triumphant voice, as Allie Feyne ran up to them. Kayrla was forced to reassess her impression of her. *She certainly can be quiet when she wants; I never heard her coming.* Allie pointed her finger at Kayrla. "You're Tesca's little friend," she said with condescending pleasure. "I knew you were around here somewhere!"

Kayrla looked at her as she opened her palm, showing the silver hand pin to the guard. "And as a friend of the Left Hand, I have his complete trust."

The guard looked at the pin as Allie goggled at it. Kayrla had gambled that Wick, already too confused by the goings-on tonight, would prefer to let someone else sort it all out. It paid off. "How can I help you, miss?" Wick said at last, moving into a more formal stance.

"The man who died back there is a victim of an assassin seeking His Grace's life," Kayrla said. "I need to report to the Right Hand with this news. Immediately."

"I've orders to bring you before the Right Hand, miss," he said. "Let's be on our way then."

"One more thing," Kayrla said, turning to point at Allie Feyne. "She's coming with us."

"What?" said Wick, Allie and Grivus at the same time.

"She's heard too much," Kayrla replied, enjoying the stricken look on Allie's face. "The Right Hand will have to decide what's to be done with her."

"As you say, miss," said Wick, turning to Allie. "If you'll be good enough to give me no trouble, Mistress Feyne, this will go more smoothly."

"What?" Allie said, shocked. "How dare you? When my father hears of this–"

"Come on, Allie," Kayrla said, using the same condescending tone that Allie had used, "you're too curious to stay out of it now, aren't you?"

Allie glared at her, but she did not object. "This way, then," said Wick, gesturing up the path.

Castellan Turvin knew he was dying. He'd never felt this way before, but he'd inflicted this same wound on many men in the past, and all of them had died soon after. He cursed himself for failing His Grace. It had been so sudden; he and the guard were checking the Duke's route back to his residence, and had entered a small corridor off the main hallway. He'd heard someone else come through the door behind them, and as it had closed, he had turned to see a wine steward walking towards them. As he started to tell the man to find another route, the first thing that surprised him was that although he could feel himself speaking, no sound came out of his mouth. The second thing that surprised him was the speed at which the steward had produced a knife from somewhere and had slit the guard's throat. Then, as the castellan drew his own blade, the steward had drawn the dying guard's own weapon and launched an attack.

The castellan had been caught off guard at first, but he was a veteran of many battles and had cut his way out of more than one ambush. As they battled in the narrow corridor, he realized that he wasn't the only thing to go mute: he couldn't hear the sound of either the clashing blades or their feet scuffling along the floor. For a moment, the castellan thought he must have gone deaf, but he knew that hadn't happened. The steward had done something, had made everything silent in the corridor.

Magic, thought the castellan, doing his best to keep the assassin at bay. In their first pass, he drew a long cut along the steward's arm, and the other drew back, grimacing in pain. For a moment, Turvin thought he could take the man, and then suddenly there came a dim pulse of green light from something under the steward's shirt. When the steward attacked again, he moved with incredible speed, and now the castellan was falling back. In a moment, it was over. Idly the castellan wondered, as his enemy slipped past his guard and drove the rapier into his abdomen, if even the Left Hand, the deadliest blade he'd ever faced until now, would be able to stand against this foe.

Maybe with his two blades to this fellow's one, he'll have a chance, the castellan thought as he slumped against the wall, sliding to the floor. He stared up at the assassin, who seemed to be quietly studying him as his life ebbed away. Then, after the castellan could not feel anything in his feet or hands, the assassin stepped in close and bent down over him.

Abruptly, the castellan could hear again. He heard his own weak breaths and the assassin's quick, urgent ones. "Now, my friend," said the assassin in an odd, musical voice, "before you go, I need to know if there are any security measures or passwords in place that limit access to your Duke."

"Drown you," the castellan whispered. He wished he could draw enough breath to yell for help, to sound the alarm, but a whisper was all he could manage. There was such a weight on his chest. "Go…to the Hells."

"Perhaps," the assassin replied with an odd giggle. "This affair has cost me a great deal already. But I still need you to answer my question."

"I…won't…tell you…"

"Oh, I rather think you will," the assassin said, moving in closer. The castellan could see an odd green glow coming from something hanging around the assassin's neck. The green glow pulsed in time with the castellan's own fading heartbeat. As his heart weakened, the glow strengthened until he could see nothing but green light. There was something drawing him deeper into that light, and some instinct knew he did not want to go there. There was something waiting at the heart of it, something hungry. He tried to struggle against the pull, the undertow that drew him closer to the heart of the light with each pulse, but he could not. *My Duke…forgive me!*

The assassin rose from the castellan's body, smiling. "Pickles and pears…apples and chairs."

Chapter Thirty-eight

Tesca decided he could not wait any longer. "Your Grace, I think we should begin our withdrawal now."

The Duke frowned. "The castellan's not back yet," he objected.

"He's been gone long enough," Tesca countered. "He wouldn't want you out here, exposed, any longer than this, whether he was here or not." Tesca was sure something was wrong; the absence of the Duke's master of security only made his unease worse. "Milord, I must insist."

The Duke studied his Left Hand for a moment. "If I disagree, you'd most likely carry me out of here, wouldn't you?" he asked wryly.

"No, milord," Tesca said. "I would never do that." He waited a moment, then: "I'd have one of the guards do it." He shrugged as the Duke chuckled. "I need both my hands free."

The Duke continued to chuckle for a few moments, only coughing slightly. "Very well, Tesca. I'd rather avoid that outcome. What's the plan?"

"We exit the hall in the normal manner, then get you to the secondary residence. You'll be safer there than your regular chambers."

His Grace nodded. "The bed's less comfortable, but as tired as I am, I daresay I could fall asleep on the floor." He gestured to Ella. "My dear, signal the orchestra to play the exit fanfare."

As Ella motioned to the conductor, Tesca spoke to the seniormost of the three guards on the dais around the Duke. "When His Grace retires, we'll escort him to the secondary residence."

The guard nodded. "Are we taking the planned route, sir? It's the shortest."

Tesca thought about that. "No," he said, "not with the castellan still absent. He left to make sure that route was secure. We'll take the alternate route, the one through the gardens. We'll stay under the porticos to avoid anyone perched in a tree with a rifle or crossbow."

The guard frowned, glancing at the Duke. "Sir, besides the extra distance that will entail, it also means His Grace will have to take the Long Stair." As the orchestra blew a fanfare, bringing all dancing and conversation in the hall to a close, the guard continued in a low voice. "I'm not sure he's up to it."

"I know, but we can't trust the primary route with the castellan missing. We'll carry him if we have to," Tesca said, watching his master carefully get to his feet. The Duke was still trying to maintain the illusion of health, even now, but this close, Tesca could see his legs tremble slightly as he put weight on them. *That damn illusion's fooled us too,* he thought. *He's exhausted. We should have gotten him out of here long before.*

"My friends, my guests," said the Duke, gesturing broadly to the celebrants, "I bid you good night, and thank you for attending this festival. Please continue to enjoy the hospitality of my estate until dawn is upon us." He took the wine cup from Ella and raised it to his lips in a final toast, though Tesca knew the cup was empty.

The guests applauded His Grace as he turned and strode off the dais. Tesca signaled the guards to take up station around him, moving to the Duke's left side. Ella walked on his right.

As they left the Great Hall and the doors were shut behind them, the Duke paused, sagging. "I left my cane out here; I wouldn't refuse it now," he grudgingly admitted. Ella saw the cane resting in a corner and brought it to him.

"Right. Let's start moving," Tesca ordered, sending one of the guards ahead to keep the hallway clear. "Are you ready, milord?"

"Yes," the Duke sighed. "Let's be about it."

Duke Stephen and his entourage headed down the hallway towards an open doorway onto the estate grounds. Tesca felt their progress was agonizingly slow, but the Duke was doing his best, and using his cane, they were moving at about the speed of a casual stroll.

Once they were in the gardens, they encountered no small number of guests already outside. All bowed before the Duke as he passed, and some attempted to engage him in some conversation.

"Milord, if I could beg a moment…"

"By your leave, Your Grace, there is a tariff dispute with the Harbormaster that perhaps you could look into…"

All of these requests the Duke politely declined with dignity and aplomb, never stopping to explain further. Unfortunately, once His Grace had seen the first group of guests, he had handed the cane back to Ella and walked without it. *Still keeping up appearances,* thought Tesca. *At least he knows better than to stop and actually talk to any of them. We might get there after all, if he doesn't pass out first.*

They maneuvered through the gardens under the covered walkways, until at last they reached the foot of the Long Stair. The longest unbroken staircase on the estate, it linked the top three terraces. There were no guests on the staircase ahead of them, so Ella gave the Duke back his cane, then slipped the Duke's other arm over her shoulder and helped him make the climb. The Duke did not object, breathing through clenched teeth and staring down at each step before him as though it was an enemy. His pace slowed as they continued up, but it did not falter, and at last they reached the top.

A circular platform, the nearby foliage cut low so as not to block the spectacular view, awaited them. There were benches set around the edges of the platform, a further reward to anyone who had made the climb.

The Duke slumped onto the closest bench. "I don't care if someone's here to kill me," he wheezed. "If I don't take a rest, that bastard will be out of a job."

"Very well, milord," Tesca assured him. "No more stairs tonight. Gather your strength for a few moments, then we'll press on."

His Grace nodded, keeping his breath steady and even, trying to keep a coughing fit from coming on. Ella sat next to him, watching him closely.

"You're doing marvelously, Your Grace," she assured him. "Just a month back, you could never have made that climb."

"No," the Duke admitted with a weary smile. "If I'm not dead by dawn, I just might have a few more years left in me."

"Many more years, milord."

Tesca kept his eyes open for any movement in the darkness around them. The portico continued on towards the manor. He could see a few guests on the grounds ahead of them, but not nearly as many as there had been below. They were in the highest reaches of the estate now, and guests were not permitted inside this portion of the manor, so the only way to enjoy the view from here meant that guests had to climb the Long Stair. Most of the guests had decided the view was just fine from the lower levels.

He saw someone come out from the manor, watched the guards at the door snap a salute and breathed a sigh of relief when he recognized the bobbing feather in the castellan's cap. The guards around the Duke relaxed as well as they saw him approaching. He looked like he was in a hurry, and Tesca thought the man was walking oddly. There was something about his posture that wasn't right. Suspicion began to writhe in the back of his mind, and he stepped forward to intercept him.

As the castellan came close and was illuminated in the lamps set around the viewing platform, Tesca realized the man was wounded. There was blood on his white shirt and his jacket sleeve had a dark, shiny stain on it. Tesca held himself back from dashing forward to see how the man was doing. Instead he waited, following protocol.

The castellan came up to Tesca, his breath coming in quick hisses of pain. He looked into Tesca's eyes, waiting.

"Pickles and pears," Tesca said, keeping his arms crossed in front of him, his hands resting on the grips of his blades.

"Apples…and chairs," the castellan panted.

Tesca relaxed. "What happened?"

"Bastard…ambushed us," the castellan grunted. "Killed the one with me; stuck me in the gut, but someone heard us fighting and he took off before more of my lads arrived. He's still out there."

"Are you all right?" Tesca asked.

The castellan shrugged. "I've had worse. Cut's not deep. Needed to make sure His Grace was all right before I find a surgeon."

"I didn't want to start off without you, but when you didn't come back…"

"You did the right thing, Master Secarius," the castellan said, clapping Tesca on the shoulder and starting to move past him. "Now let's get our man to safety."

Tesca didn't let him go by. The castellan looked at him, surprised, and the two men stared into each other's eyes. "Master Secarius…" the castellan warned, "…let me pass."

Tesca glanced down at the stone around the castellan's feet for a moment, then without warning he shoved the man back, away from the Duke. "It's him!" he yelled, his blades flashing free of their scabbards. Behind him, he heard the guards shifting on their feet, confused.

The castellan looked shocked, but an instant later his mouth twisted into a thin, predatory smile Tesca had never seen on Turvin's face. "How did you know?"

Tesca smiled back at him. "Turvin would never have referred to His Grace as 'our man,' even if ordered to do so. And," he gestured with his dagger towards the ground, never taking his eyes off the assassin, "I've seen elf blood before."

The assassin's eyes flicked down to the ground where Tesca was pointing, and saw the glittering orange drops where he'd been standing. He drew the castellan's sword with a flourish, saluting Tesca. Then there was a burst of green light about him, and he surged forward.

Tesca had never seen anyone move so fast. The assassin dropped underneath his attack, rolling along the floor and springing back to his feet, heading straight for the Duke. The three guards were among the most experienced and trusted of the Duke's troops, and while they were startled by the abrupt turn of events, they reacted instinctively to anyone charging their master with a bare blade. They flung themselves into the assassin's path, pikes thrusting forward.

The assassin evaded them all, darting to the left, rolling under the stabbing pikes. Then he was on his feet again, with only Ella between him and his target. Ella, her eyes wide, stood her ground, holding up something she'd drawn from her pocket, but it was neither the Duke's elixir nor his wine. The assassin's eyes widened as he saw the small pistol in her hand, stopping short as if he'd run into a wall, then scrambling back as Ella pulled the trigger.

Only the assassin's unearthly speed saved him. He fell into a backward somersault, the shot passing over his head and striking one of the pillars. But that gave the guards enough time to shift position, putting themselves once more between the assassin and the Duke. Tesca hurled himself toward the assassin, who parried Tesca's attack, again sliding past him with unbelievable speed, leaping clear and trying to get around to the other side of the guards. The closest guard moved forward while the other two stepped in behind, guarding his flanks.

The assassin sidestepped the jabbing pike, then moved closer, stabbing the guard in the throat. As the man fell, his pike clattering to the stones, Tesca charged in again. He tried to get past the assassin's guard, but his enemy's lone blade was a match to his two, countering every attack. Abruptly Tesca was reminded of his duel with Mantey, but now he was the one fighting the smaller and faster opponent.

The similarity ends there, Tesca thought. *He's faster, but it's only magic giving him that speed.* The assassin had a natural grace that Tesca suspected most elves possessed, but his fighting style had none of the subtle elegance that a master swordsman would have developed from years of constant practice. *He's all about the ambush, the quick kill. He's already bleeding, the castellan must have wounded him. So work with that; grind him down.* He adjusted his tactics. Every time Tesca had attacked him directly, the assassin had been able to slip away and get closer to the Duke. Now Tesca fought defensively, keeping the assassin from getting around him. Instead of striking at the assassin himself, he struck out at the enemy's blade, forcing him to parry the blows instead of dodging them, wasting the elf's strength; tiring him out. Tesca still couldn't get past that lightning-fast guard, but now he wasn't really trying to.

Behind him, Tesca could hear the guards moving the Duke behind the bench as an added obstacle between him and the assassin. He heard Ella reloading her pistol. His lips drawn back in a silent snarl, the assassin spared a glance over his shoulder. There was movement back at the manor; drawn by the sound of the gunshot. More guards were spilling out of the door, heading towards the platform.

Tesca watched an expression of fury writhe over the assassin's face, the stolen face of Turvin twisting into a grimace. His attacks started to lose some of their blinding speed, and Tesca realized that the magical boost the assassin had given himself was wearing off. He couldn't keep a cold smile off his face. "You've lost your chance," he taunted the assassin.

"There…will be other chances," his opponent replied, flashing a smile to match Tesca's. Moving slower than he had, but still faster than a normal man, the assassin abruptly leapt backwards, away from Tesca. With a quick flourish of his blade, the assassin saluted the Left Hand, then ran for the Long Stair. "Get the Duke inside!" Tesca yelled at the guards before hurtling down the steps in pursuit.

Chapter Thirty-nine

Allie Feyne had finally stopped complaining. At first, Kayrla had enjoyed the silence, but when she took a sidelong glance at Allie, the Feyne woman was looking back at her. She didn't look away either, continuing to study Kayrla without any hint of discomfort. It was Kayrla who at last broke eye contact, and she could still feel Allie's eyes upon her.

They made their way through the gardens in this awkward silence for some time, with Kayrla in front, Grivus and Allie next to each other and Wick bringing up the rear. Then, abruptly, Kayrla found that Allie had moved up next to her.

"So how did you meet him?" Allie asked in a low voice.

"What?" Kayrla said, glancing up at the taller woman.

"Tesca doesn't make friends easily," Allie went on, her tone as friendly and conversational as if they'd known each other for years, "so I imagine whatever brought the two of you together must have been something really interesting."

"As if I'd tell you," Kayrla scoffed. "It's none of your business."

"Oh, I understand," Allie replied in that same friendly manner, "my apologies." Their procession passed a pair of guests strolling in the garden. "Look, she's an elf," Allie Feyne suddenly said in a casual tone, pointing at Kayrla.

The male member of the pair looked at Allie, more surprised at being addressed than really hearing what she had said. "I'm sorry?" he asked, recognition dawning on his face. "Mistress Feyne?"

"The girl here," Allie said matter-of-factly, pointing to Kayrla again. "She's an elf."

The man reflexively followed Allie's gesture and looked at Kayrla, who was staring open-mouthed at Allie.

"Look at her ears," Allie said. "She's an elf. The Duke's pet elf."

Wick quickly stepped forward. "Come along now, Mistress," he said, putting his hand on her elbow.

"Oh, dear...I've said too much," Allie replied, completely unruffled. "The Duke doesn't want anyone knowing he's got a pet elf, does he? It's the dungeons for me." She let Wick draw her along the path, away from the couple, who were now watching them leave, but their eyes lingered most on Kayrla.

"Stop that!" Kayrla hissed when they were some distance further on.

"Or what?" Allie asked, leaning down, bringing her face close to Kayrla's. "You think you can actually have me arrested? You think he," she added, pointing at Wick, "can drag me inside the manor before I draw a crowd, screaming my head off about elves and assassins?" She smiled sweetly at Kayrla. "Answer my questions, and I'll come along gentle as a lamb."

Kayrla locked eyes with her for a few moments. "Fine," she said.

Allie straightened up with an air of amused triumph. She turned to Wick. In her heels, she was actually an inch taller than him. "And if you lay a hand on me again," she said in that same friendly voice, "you'd best get comfortable living on this estate, for your life won't be worth a copper outside it."

"Don't threaten him!" Kayrla snapped as Wick blanched and took a step back from her.

"Feynes don't make threats; we make promises," Allie said, looking back at Kayrla. "You're clearly new to the Quad, else you'd know that. His Grace is not the only power in Kohayne." She nodded her head towards Wick. "Even his guards know it." She started walking down the path towards the manor.

Fuming, Kayrla caught up with her. *Just get her inside,* she thought. *Let Galen handle it.*

"So," Allie asked again, "how did you two meet?"

It was a few moments before Kayrla replied. "I met him when I was trying to leave my old ship," she grumbled.

"The *Cutlass*," Allie finished. "Captained by the late, unlamented Jolly Red." She glanced down at Kayrla, who looked surprised. "My little friend," Allie said with a laugh, "all of Kohayne knows your story. Second question: can you really cast spells in the Frees?"

"Yes," Kayrla admitted.

"What kind of spells? Everyone is saying you can change your appearance." Allie chuckled. "I must say, you're not impressing me at the moment. I mean, your ears reach up nearly to the top of your head!"

Just get her inside, Kayrla thought, longing to drive her fist into that wide, smiling mouth.

"Let's try another question, then," Allie continued, "how did you fake your death? Dozens of people saw you get stabbed and fall into the harbor."

"I'm a good swimmer."

"Don't try to take all the credit," Allie replied. "I'll bet fifty marks it was one of Galen's little productions." She rolled her eyes. "That old spider can't resist the big spectacle, keeping everyone's eyes where he wants them."

"Don't talk that way about Galen," Kayrla snapped.

Allie glanced sharply at Kayrla, her smile widening. "Oh, really! So old Galen's got another devotee?" She shook her head in pity. "Little one, you're just a pawn on his chessboard. One day you'll be of more use to him dead than alive." She looked amused at Kayrla's silent fury. "Let me guess," she went on, "he lured you into staying here with a little fair treatment, clean sheets and three square meals. That's his siren song. And you sailed right in."

"Is that how he got Tesca to leave you?" Kayrla quickly asked, acting on a hunch.

Allie was taken aback. "What?"

Kayrla was sure now that she'd struck the mark. She started counting on her fingers. "You won't stop asking about Tesca, and I know the two of you had some sort of past. He wasn't the Left Hand here for the Duke's last fete, so whatever happened between you two wasn't that long ago. You don't like Galen, and when you mentioned that I'm another of his devotees, that means you think he already has one." She paused, looking up at Allie. "And that look on your face tells me I'm right."

"And two more things, Mistress Feyne," Kayrla continued before Allie could reply. "One, I'm older than you, so that's the last time I'll be hearing 'little one' from your mouth. And two, I don't make threats either. If you cause any more trouble for me, Tesca, Galen or His Grace tonight, I…will hex you."

"Hex me?" Allie asked, confused.

"You wanted to know what I could do," Kayrla said, "what sort of spells I can cast. I can hex you. I could make warts appear on your face or turn your pretty hair white."

"You wouldn't dare…" Allie said, glaring at her. But Kayrla could see a glimmer of doubt in the woman's eyes.

"All right, then. I could sour the wine on your father's estate instead," Kayrla went on, "or rot the hulls of his ships and leave the sails in tatters. You tell someone I'm an elf again tonight, and one of his ships will be at the bottom of the harbor by morning."

Allie stopped walking and turned to face her. "I think you're bluffing," she said after a long silence.

"Then call my bluff," Kayrla said. "It's up to you if it's worth risking your father's property, or his temper." She hoped she sounded more confident than she felt. Sinking a ship in one night really was beyond her, especially now that she'd drained the pendant of its extra mana. Her threat had been made in the heat of the moment, but now, she realized, that with careful uses of the entropy spell directed at key points of the hull over several days, she probably could sink a ship, or at least leave it vulnerable to sinking in rough seas. She smiled at Allie. *Whether a ship sinks tonight or in a week doesn't really matter, does it?* she thought. *It'll still be sitting on the harbor floor.*

Allie frowned at Kayrla's smile. She shrugged. "I'm not in a mood to gamble with my father's property tonight, elf."

"My name is Kayrla. Remember it."

"Oh, I will. That…is a promise," Allie replied, coldly smiling back at her.

Kayrla didn't have time to savor her victory as they heard, from a higher level of the estate, the sound of a gunshot. Silence, save for the echoes of the shot, seemed to descend upon the estate's gardens as all the guests outside froze and turned in that direction.

Wick was already moving forward. "That came from the personal residence!"

Too late! Kayrla thought, panic flashing over her as she took off after him. "How do we get up there?"

"The Long Stair," Wick replied, trotting along in his armor. He gestured towards a dark shape some distance ahead of them. "Never…wanted to take that…at a run," he panted, "but…there's nothing else…for it!"

Behind them, Kayrla heard Grivus running after them in pursuit and Allie Feyne, after kicking off her heels, coming after them as well. *What an odd procession we must make,* she thought distantly. She wanted to run faster, to pull ahead of the lumbering Wick, but she was too tired, nearly tripping on a marble bench as she jumped over it.

Ahead of them loomed the Long Stair. They were approaching it from the right-hand side, so she could see one long line of lamps extending up into the darkness, towards the highest portion of the estate. At first, she thought her eyes were playing tricks on her, her weariness and the way the glowing lamps seemed to float in space making her vision swim, but as they got closer she recognized what she was seeing: two figures racing, almost falling, down the staircase.

"Wick," she called out, "someone's…coming down! Two people!" The pillars supporting the roof of the Long Stair kept her from seeing them clearly; she only got brief flashes, but she saw light glinting off drawn steel. One was chasing the other, she was sure.

Wick gritted his teeth and picked up the pace. They were close enough now that he could see them too, and he was trying to get to the foot of the stairs before they did. Kayrla tried to keep up, but the surge of energy she'd gotten from her spelldance was gone at last. Her legs trembled with each step, and she began to fall behind.

Grivus caught up to her and pulled her along with him as Wick reached the foot of the Long Stair. He had just enough time to plant his feet, set his pike before him and yell "Halt!" as the two runners leapt off the steps, one to each side of him. Then, as he realized the two men were the Castellan and the Left Hand, he froze, confused.

"This man has killed the Duke!" the Castellan yelled, pointing his blade at Tesca. "Kill him!" Wick looked horror-struck and whirled to face Tesca, grief and rage twisting his features.

"No, damn you!" Tesca yelled in response. "His Grace lives! This man is an impos–" but then Wick was driving forward, pike extended.

Kayrla felt numb, wondering if she'd already lost consciousness and was dreaming. *Tesca a murderer? No! It can't be! But the castellan just said that...*

"That's not the castellan," she gasped to Grivus. "That's the assassin!" As Wick pressed his attack on Tesca, the castellan began to circle around the pair, trying to flank the Left Hand.

"If you are right, then he must have killed the castellan and taken his place," Grivus said. "But what can we do?"

"Even the odds," she panted, taking the pendant off her neck and running forward.

"You're making a mistake!" Tesca called to Wick. He was trying to stay clear of the guard's pike and keep the assassin from getting in behind him. He thought how strange it was that twice in one night, he was in a deadly struggle with someone he did not want to kill. But the guards would not disobey a direct order from the castellan, not for him. If he didn't kill this guard, the assassin would get behind him before long, and with or without his supernatural speed, that would be the end of it.

His duty took precedence. He waited for the guard to jab in once more, planning to duck past the pike, get inside the man's guard, end him quickly, and resume his battle with the assassin. But just before the guard stabbed out, suddenly Kayrla was there, shoving the guard hard to one side. She wasn't strong enough to knock him over, but he stumbled a few steps, giving Tesca enough room to get out from between his two assailants.

Kayrla waved the pendant at the assassin, and the gleam of recognition in his eyes confirmed his true identity. He looked utterly dumbfounded to see her here, or perhaps he was distracted by the pendant in her hand, so close. "You want this?!? Then take it!" she yelled, flinging the pendant at him.

The assassin started to instinctively reach for the pendant, but then he remembered what had always happened when the two pendants got too close to each other, and he flinched away. Tesca didn't hesitate, taking advantage of the distraction and plunging his rapier into the assassin's chest.

The assassin gave a sigh of pain and seemed to fold around the weapon like a cloak dropped over a chair. His sword clattered to the stones and he collapsed beside it as Tesca stepped away.

"Tesca," Kayrla called, "around his neck…he's got his own pendant! Get it off him!"

Tesca kicked the assassin's sword away first, then bent down to get the pendant. As he tugged out the delicate chain, there was a moment when his palm touched the green gem, and he suddenly suffered a wave of vertigo so intense he nearly fell over. He thought he heard a multitude of voices from far off, yelling, moaning and pleading. The voices overlapped each other, making their speech indecipherable. But there was something else…a hungry presence, watching him. But in the next instant he tossed the pendant aside and the sensation passed.

"Nooo…." moaned the assassin, fumbling up towards Tesca. "Nooo… don't…take it!" At that moment the gem in the assassin's pendant flashed, illuminating the entire area in green light. The assassin screamed, a thin, quavering note of pain, his body arcing backwards and stiffening into a contorted shape. As the green light faded, his body slumped to the ground and was still.

Then he began to change. The castellan's face shifted as the illusion melted away. Tesca had expected to see elven features under the illusion, and he was not disappointed, but he'd also expected to see hair and skin color similar to Kayrla's. This elf's skin was a reddish bronze, with glints and sparkles that reminded Tesca of the glittering motes he'd seen in elven blood. His hair was long, straggly and a uniform medium gray.

"How's the Duke?" Kayrla asked, stepping up to Tesca.

"He's fine," her friend assured her. "Didn't take a scratch."

She sagged with relief, leaning against his arm and looking down at the assassin. "Fire Clan."

"What?"

"The bronze skin; the grey hair," said Kayrla. "My father said those were hallmarks of the Fire Clan." She looked up at Tesca. "Think he's dead?"

"I'm not sure," Tesca admitted. "The number of odd things I've seen tonight; he might just be playacting, hoping for someone to get close."

"True," Kayrla said. She looked at Wick, who was staring at the assassin in open-mouthed astonishment. "Wick," she said, getting his attention. "Check him."

The guard nodded in grim satisfaction, raising his pike and jabbing it into the elf's chest. Nothing happened.

"Well, I think that answers your question," Tesca chuckled, approaching the body. Kayrla joined him. There were shouts of guards around them, coming down the Long Stair and approaching from elsewhere in the gardens. Tesca knelt down next to the assassin, studying the body. "He looks...old," he commented, noticing the elf's hollow cheeks and a fine network of wrinkles crossing his face. "Back at the top of the stairs, he did...something. There was a green glow around him; and then he was like lightning. I've never seen anyone move that fast."

"He was drawing on the pendant's power," Kayrla said, "a spell of some sort." She looked down at the body. "I'm not sure how old he really is, or was. I think the pendant might have something to do with his appearance."

"How do you know?"

She shook her head. "Just…a feeling."

"His pendant's not like yours, is it?" He was horrified to think that Kayrla could bear to put that pendant against her skin, if it was even close to what he'd felt touching the green gem.

"No," she said in a hollow tone, looking in the direction Tesca had tossed it. "It operates on a different set of-put that down!" she suddenly yelled. Tesca whipped his head up to see Allie Feyne looking back at them, rising from a crouch, the pendant hanging from her hand.

"What?" she asked, putting on a look of innocence that was almost convincing.

Chapter Forty

"Remarkable," said the Duke, opening the secret door in the library fireplace for the tenth time. It was early morning, and the ceiling glowed with the fuzzy reflection of sunlight coming from the harbor far below. "I've spent so much time in this room, and I never knew it was here…just feet away."

"I daresay your father never knew either, milord," Galen commented, "or I'm sure he would have shared the knowledge with you."

"I agree," the Duke said, pushing the concealed button that closed the door once more. He sighed. "Quite fascinating, but we'll look to that mystery later on. There's more immediate concerns."

"Just so, milord," Galen agreed. They turned away from the fireplace. "Tesca, has Kayrla finally followed my order and gone to bed?"

"She has," Tesca said with a smile. He was standing by the large table, sorting out the notes that Kayrla had frantically scribbled out before at last succumbing to sleep. "It looks like she overheard a few conversations in the garden while she was trying to get a message to us." He raised an eyebrow at one written word, turning the paper one way and then the other in an attempt to decipher it. "I hope her penmanship improves when she's fully awake."

The Duke shrugged. "We'll sit her down and have her translate those scrawls for us later on. She's earned a bit of rest."

"That she has," Galen agreed. "It's a pity her pendant's lost its power, but we do have that other one now."

Tesca frowned. "If it was up to me, I'd sail past the Eisenteeth and toss that other one into the Deeps." Galen looked at him. "It's not her pendant with a different gemstone," Tesca went on, "there's something about it that scares her. I don't know what; I couldn't make much sense of her explanation. But I think she's right to be afraid; when I was pulling it off the assassin, I touched that green gem and I felt…something." He started to shrug, but the motion turned into an involuntary shiver. "I don't think she'd put that pendant around her neck for anything other than a direct order from you, milord. And if you'll pardon my saying, she'd never forgive you for giving that order."

Several seconds ticked by in silence. "Well, then…" the Duke said, "we'd best find a way to use her talents without the benefit of any trinkets, eh?"

"Indeed, milord," Galen replied, still watching Tesca. "I've had the other pendant secured in the vault for the present. That should be safe enough."

"Next item of business, then," the Duke said, firmly changing the subject.

"Castellan Turvin's body has been found." Galen was somber. "Given that the assassin impersonated him, it was only a fool's hope that the man was still alive elsewhere on the grounds, but at least now, we know for certain." He sighed. "Recommendations for his successor?"

"Lieutenant Kelvo?" Tesca offered. "If there was a task to be done, the castellan usually put Kelvo in charge of it."

Galen smiled. "Turvin and I had discussed possible successors should anything happen to him. Kelvo was his choice."

"Done and done, then," the Duke said. "Kelvo's a good lad. Still young, but I daresay you two can bring him along quickly. Next?"

"We need to find you a new physician."

The Duke sighed. "Ah, Felton…I will miss him. Not the warmest bedside manner, but a genius of an apothecary. I do hope he wrote down that formula for his elixir?"

Galen nodded. "Yes, milord. He had an apprentice that became a doctor herself only last year…she's opened a practice in North Chanelside."

"She?"

"Yes, Dr.…Marren," Galen confirmed, reviewing his notes. "Felton spoke highly of her; said that a woman wanting to make a living as a doctor has to be twice as smart as a man and work three times as hard. He pursed his lips, thinking. "We'd have to investigate her carefully first, to make sure she's not in the pocket of anyone like the Feynes."

"But a woman…" the Duke muttered.

"She's very likely the best doctor in the entire Quad," Galen said. "Do you have a problem with a female doctor?"

The Duke studied his Right Hand, a wry smile on his face. "I'd rather not drop my pants for a woman unless I intend to bed them, that's all." Then he sighed. "Oh, never mind…it's been long enough since that happened anyway. If she meets with your approval, she'll be fine. Next?"

Galen turned to a new page in his notes. "Laveau and the Hisvetian contingent set sail shortly after dawn."

"Good riddance," the Duke muttered.

Galen smiled at that. "They might have left exactly at sunrise, milord, except my counterpart took the time to explain to me, in great detail, how he felt slighted and insulted at every turn. From disrespectful harbormasters to being held up at the front gate due to the 'Sabrian ruckus,' as he put it, he promised that the Baron would hear everything." Galen paused. "I told Laveau that if the Baron actually bothered to host his own fete from time to time, then his own Right Hand would have known that the best way for a guest to avoid delays is to arrive on time."

The Duke roared with laughter, only coughing once at the end of it. "Oh, I wish I could have seen the look on that sour old face!" He wiped a tear from his eye. "I expect the pirates around Hisvet will turn more aggressive after this; the Baron's way of repaying us."

"Likely so, milord…though I daresay Laveau would have found a reason to be offended even if we'd lavished him with every luxury."

"Very true. Warn our merchants to stay as far off Hisvet as possible while they sail past her for a while. It'll slow things down, but it's cheaper than losing some ships to the Baron's tax collectors."

"Indeed, milord." Galen took out a small black leather book, made a few notes in it, then put it back in his pocket. "As to other diplomatic matters, on Tesca's suggestion we boarded the ship of the Kreigan envoy. Our men found his body in his cabin, with the same look of horror we've seen on other victims from last night. As one might guess, the crew swears to a man that they saw the envoy leave the ship last night and take a carriage up here to the estate, and no one saw him return." He looked at Tesca. "You were right about how the assassin got in here."

Tesca nodded. "It seemed the most likely choice. Kreigstat's small and remote. Little chance their envoy would be known to anyone else here."

"I agree," said Galen. "I'll have a letter expressing your condolences ready for your signature by this afternoon, milord. The Kreigans can take that, along with the envoy's body, back to the Meisterherran."

"Very well. And what of the Sabrian envoy?" asked the Duke. "Will her son recover?"

"We've heard nothing on that matter, but they did send up a messenger, asking permission to remain in harbor an extra day. Captain Maritius has asked to present herself to you this evening."

"Tesca?" the Duke asked. "You're the Sabrian expert here. Is this normal behavior for them?"

"Let me check something before answering, milord," Tesca said as he stepped away from the other two men and went to the large window. There was a brass telescope off to one side and he aimed it down to the harbor, sighting the Sabrian warship through it. "They've not added any black flags to their rigging," he said to them. "If Mantey had died during the night, they would be flying mourning colors. If you wish to know more about her son, milord, the politest way to find out would be to ask if she cares to remain in port for several more days. If he's not ready for travel, she'll accept the offer." He left the window and returned to the table. "In any case, milord, it's a mark of respect, her asking to present herself to you. She didn't get a chance to do it last night, and like as not she's grateful you didn't demand it."

The Duke shrugged. "Well, we did have a few other things going on, didn't we?"

Tesca shook his head. "From the Imperial viewpoint, milord, the only important event that took place last night was the duel."

The Duke looked skeptical, but Galen nodded in agreement. "No, milord, he's right. In public, an Imperial envoy cannot find any foreign news more interesting or important than Imperial events. I think that when Maritius speaks with you, she'll not offer more than a polite inquiry as to whether the rest of the night went well for you." Tesca nodded in agreement. "Privately, however," Galen went on, "Maritius is sure to have received intelligence about the assassination attempt. The Empire has more than one set of eyes and ears in Kohayne, and at least one of them was a guest at the fete, I'm certain. She'll have heard rumors about the assassin impersonating people on the estate, but more than that, there were guests who witnessed the assassin's final moments." He looked frustrated. "Hells, anyone in Harborside who was looking up toward the estate would have seen that burst of green light; it was as bright as a bonfire." He sighed and made a weary shrug. "Milord, the cat is out of the bag. The magic from the mainland is spreading, even as far south as Kohayne. From what Tesca's said of Captain Maritius, she can't fail to appreciate the implications of that."

The Duke nodded, thinking. "Your suggestions on how to proceed, then?"

"We will have to get some assets into Nauticus and the organizations of those who trade with the Empire," Galen told him. "The Sabrians must be watched very, very closely now, to give us the earliest warning possible if they are preparing to invade."

"If?" the Duke asked. "You've always said when before, Galen."

"My best guess at the moment, milord, is that they still wish to invade the Frees, but I am no longer certain that they will. They appear reluctant, for the present, to expand any further than Nauticus. I believe this is because they have finally come to accept that their superior cannon become unreliable in areas where magic exists. I have recently heard that on the mainland, in the northern reaches, closest to the

Elflands, gunpowder is all but useless, and cannon are being melted down, and the metal is being turned to more useful items." He spread his hands. "Like as not the Sabrians have heard these rumors as well. Will this news of magic spreading south prompt them into a swift invasion, before they lose their advantage?"

"We can't know for certain, milord," Tesca chimed in. "The Frees is only one frontier for the Empire. There are other lands it borders on, far off, and we've precious little way of learning how matters fare in those distant lands. If the Empire is currently devoting resources to expansion elsewhere, then those who seek a swift invasion of the Frees will find little support. If the Empire is not busy elsewhere, then its eye will focus here."

"So…we watch," the Duke said.

"We watch," Galen said. "If they do decide to invade, like as not they'll try to spark some dispute between two of the Frees, then move in to 'protect their interests.'"

"I agree," the Duke replied. "But they won't be able to hide their preparations completely. More warships coming north, more restrictions imposed on merchants from the Frees trading with the Empire. If those things start to happen, we'll know. Will we be ready?"

Galen smiled. "I have…a few ideas regarding that, milord. We can discuss them whenever you wish."

The Duke smiled in turn. "Oh, I look forward to hearing those ideas, but I daresay it can wait until tomorrow." He paused, snapping his fingers. "Oh, yes…speaking of Sabrians, what of that Grivus fellow?"

"Captain Grivus is waiting outside, milord," Galen told him. "Allie Feyne wanted to come in with him, as he's her guest, but I thought you'd prefer to meet him privately."

"Oh, indeed," the Duke replied. "I always like to meet my most interesting guests. Tesca, bring him in."

Tesca collected Kayrla's notes from the table, handed them to Galen, then crossed to the door. He opened it and beckoned Grivus to come inside. The older man looked tired after last night's events, but he held himself with poise and dignity as he approached the Duke. Stopping ten paces away, Grivus bowed deeply. "Your Grace."

"Captain Grivus," the Duke said, "you are a most intriguing fellow. If I am not mistaken, not more than five minutes after you came under my roof, I was forced to risk my Left Hand to defend you, over what I am told comes down to, in essence, a disagreement with your taste in clothing." The Duke's voice lost some of its warmth. "I am sure there is a very interesting explanation for this, and I would very much like to hear it."

Grivus straightened up. "It would give me great pleasure to explain, Your Grace. I am most grateful for your defense of me last night. As such, I owe you the Champion's Price." He gestured towards Tesca. "Has your *agentis*, I mean, your Left Hand, explained this term to you?"

"He has," said the Duke, "albeit briefly. It is a debt of honor, yes?"

"It is a burden of honor that I now bear for you, yes," Grivus said. "Among my people, there are few burdens of greater weight."

"I see," the Duke said. "Then let us cut to the heart of the matter, as we are both old men who have had a very busy and sleepless night." He smiled at Grivus, who gave a small smile and nod of agreement in return. "As I am sure you know, last night an assassin came into my home and killed several of most trusted servants in an attempt to get to me. Perhaps it has occurred to you that if my Left Hand had not been drawn into a duel that you deliberately started, he might have been in a position to find this assassin and stop him before he did so much damage." The smile fell from Grivus's face. "I am not placing the blame for all that happened last night upon you, Captain," the Duke went on, "I do not breed scapegoats. I am aware that you assisted Kayrla while she was trying to warn us about the assassin, and that was good to hear. It appears to me that your intrigues complicated matters last night, but unintentionally."

"That is very true, Your Grace," Grivus replied. "I am most grieved to hear of the losses you have suffered, and consider my burden of honor to have increased due to those losses."

The Duke studied Grivus for a moment. "Piecing together all I have heard about you, it seems to me that there is something you desperately want. At first, you were hoping the Feynes could provide this for you, but rather than remain in their household and in their debt, you deliberately sparked a duel that puts you in greater debt to me. Why?"

Grivus took a moment before answering. "There is a quality my people value highly, which we call *vertu*. It…I cannot think of a word in your language that properly conveys the meaning. Are you familiar with this word, Your Grace?"

"Yes," the Duke replied, looking at Tesca. "Shortly after I first met him, my Left Hand told me that I possess some measure of this quality."

Grivus nodded. "A true *agentis* would not choose a master who lacks *vertu*. Mistress Feyne's father has none. I could see this about him the instant we met. When he speaks of men that owe him debts, he speaks as though he owns them. And it gives him great pleasure to talk this way. He speaks only of acquisition, of possessing things and then showing others that he possesses them. He is a baseborn thief, and his expensive clothes and home do not disguise it."

"I know Draxen Feyne quite well," the Duke commented. "He is a most esteemed citizen of Kohayne, and the Feynes have been one of the wealthiest and most influential families here for many years." He chuckled. "That's the public line; it doesn't mean what you say about the man is wrong, of course. So…he failed to make a good first impression on you, eh? And that was sufficient to try to get free of him before he closed his hand on you?"

"Yes, Your Grace. I could not bring myself to enter into a business arrangement with the man, realizing within a moment of meeting him that I would likely be killed the instant I ceased to be of value."

"And what makes you think I won't do the same?" the Duke asked. "I'm no more a Sabrian than Draxen Feyne is. We're all pale barbarians to you lot, aren't we?"

Grivus gave a knowing smile in response to the Duke's baiting question. "That is, as you said, Your Grace, the 'public line.' Privately, those of my people who cultivate wisdom know that all people are capable of possessing *vertu*, regardless of their color. To answer your first question, though, the fact that you have him in your employ," he continued, pointing at Tesca, "tells me that you would not simply kill me off at the first opportunity. An *agentis* always seeks to serve a master who is willing, at need, to strike without warning, without mercy, but most importantly, without malice."

The Duke smiled. "Both of us have trodden up and down the many steps of my estate long enough. Please, Captain, be seated." He eased himself into an armchair; Grivus did likewise. "Now, you said you were seeking a business arrangement. I do not normally engage in such matters; leaving that to the merchants of my city. What are you proposing?"

"I offer to you, in payment of my debt, an opportunity to fund an expedition, one that may bring you a great deal of wealth."

The Duke managed to convey skepticism and curiosity in a single expression. "An expedition? Where?"

Chapter Forty-one

"An expedition?" the Duke asked Captain Grivus. "Where?"

"Perhaps we can discover that together," Grivus said, taking a slim leather pouch out of his jacket. Opening the pouch, he withdrew a piece of parchment, then laid it down on the small table between the Duke's chair and his own. The Duke leaned forward to examine it as Galen and Tesca stepped closer.

"Part of a map," the Duke commented, noting the left side of the parchment ended in a torn edge. "It shows part of a landmass, extending out into the sea."

"It is, I believe, Your Grace, half of an island."

"Tesca, your eyes are better than mine or Galen's, and I'm too tired to translate Sabrian this morning. What does the writing say?"

Tesca leaned in close as the Duke settled back in his chair. He frowned, puzzled. "It's not written in Sabrian, milord. It looks like an Imperial navigational chart, even down to the standard practice of putting the legend and compass rose in the lower right corner." He looked at Grivus. "What language is it written in?"

"I do not know," Grivus admitted.

"Where did you find it?"

"It was given to me by a dying man on his deathbed. A Sabrian officer, he was a former lieutenant of mine during my first command. He swore to me with his dying breath that he retrieved this map from the cabin of the late pirate, Praeditorus Rex."

Galen and the Duke snapped their gazes up towards Grivus, shocked. "That's a name I've not heard in years," said the Duke.

"The King of Plunder," Galen said, "roughly translated from his native Sabrian."

Grivus nodded, an unhappy expression on his face. "It was not his original name, of course. That name we do not repeat, for it is dead, and a shame to his family if spoken aloud. He was an Imperial officer, one of our best. He received orders to command one of our exploration vessels, sailing north to chart the lands beyond the Empire's border. Our merchants, always the first to arrive anywhere, had begun to trade with the southernmost of the Frees some years before this, but his ship was the first to enter the Frees flying the Imperial banner."

"That was him…" the Duke said in a quiet voice, lost in a memory. "I remember one day, my father received news from a patrol, of a ship the like of which they'd never seen before. They could tell she was Sabrian; larger than any of our own ships, and faster. She never answered any hails; none of our ships could get near her. After a few days circling the Quad, the ship continued north under full sail."

"Yes," said Grivus. "That was him. It is our way when first entering an area already inhabited. Explore the region, take depth readings, do not make contact. He was filling in blank areas on a map, that was all. He would have made many maps on that voyage, much like this one," he tapped the parchment on the table.

"But those would have been written in Sabrian," Tesca objected. "You can't say that Praeditorus Rex wrote this map."

Grivus smiled. "I believe that in fact, he did."

The Duke shifted in his chair, now looking more skeptical than curious. "Let us cut to the heart of the matter, Captain. Praeditorus Rex is a legendary name among the pirates of the Frees. If even half the stories about him are to be believed, then there's no one more successful, or bloodthirsty, than he was. Most of those stories also add that although he plundered countless ships and collected enormous wealth, he didn't spend any of it. That means most folk believe his treasure trove is still out there somewhere, waiting to be found. While I admit the idea of a secret haven, filled to the ceiling with gold and jewels, fits itself rather comfortably into one's imagination, I am not someone who dashes after fantasies like a child chasing butterflies with a net. Are you going to try to convince us that this," he gestured towards the map, "could somehow lead to the fabled hoard of the greatest pirate to sail the Frees? If that's your goal, Captain, then I must tell you, you're sailing against the tide."

Grivus nodded, looking like someone who has heard such objections many times before. "I understand completely, Your Grace. It is a tale I would not easily believe either, were I in your place." He shrugged. "However, that is indeed my goal. I believe this map was written by that man, and that it may guide me to a secret haven where, if not gold, then a great many of his secrets may be found. Finding this place could at last answer a question that has haunted me for over half of my life: what caused this man to turn traitor?"

"Traitor?" the Duke asked, surprised at the word.

"Yes, traitor," answered Grivus. "There are very, very few of my people who turn to piracy. To us, it is treason; our greatest crime. The Empire is composed of many, many islands…most no larger than your own realm here. The greatest threat to the livelihood of its people is to attack the trade routes between these islands. They are truly the arteries of the Empire. For a Sabrian to actually become a pirate is to reject everything we value, to become anathema, outcast without hope of pardon. Of those few who turn to piracy, even fewer last long, for we hunt them relentlessly, showing no mercy to them or those who harbor them."

The Duke considered that. "All right. So he undertook an exploration of the Frees, and headed north after charting the Quad. What happened to him after that?"

"We do not know," Grivus said. "He never returned to us. Not as an Imperial officer, in any case. We believe that he sailed as far north as the mainland, and went ashore." Grivus looked uncomfortable. "The idea of land that stretches on and on, past the horizon, endless…it is not something many of us have seen before. I can only imagine that he was curious about it." He shrugged. "When he sailed south once more, returning to our waters, he now called himself Praeditorus Rex and his ship had been renamed the *Pistrix Cruentus.*"

"The *Bloodstained Shark*, milord," Tesca offered, translating.

"Yes," Grivus said. "He had become a reaver. He fell upon any and all ships that crossed his path, plundering their holds. To all the crews he defeated, he gave a choice: join him or die. Those ships he saw value in, he took, adding to his fleet. The rest he burned to the waterline. Of those who joined him, there was never a tale of mutiny or defiance. At least, we never heard news of it." He sighed, then continued. "Naturally, the navy pursued him, but his brilliance kept him one step ahead of us for some time. At length, when we brought enough ships into the hunt for him, he retreated north."

"Into the Frees," Galen said. "And you followed him."

"Yes," Grivus said. "I took command of my first ship not long after his predations had begun, and I was assigned to the taskforce committed to his destruction. He fled north, and we came after him. We quickly learned caution, for he knew these waters far better than we did. One more than one occasion he lured his pursuers onto sandbars, then destroyed them from afar with his cannon. But each trick he used worked only once, and we hounded him and his fleet, picking off his captured ships and blockading ports in the Frees that had given him harbor."

"Speaking of those blockades," Galen cut in, "they still rankle those that remember them. It's part of the reason why Praeditorus may be considered the worst pirate by your people, but the greatest to many of the Frees."

Grivus nodded. "I can say now that I understand this, but at the time, I was a young captain, pursuing the greatest criminal in living memory. We would have done anything to destroy him, and we cared nothing for the objections of these little realms and their small, slow ships." He sighed. "We have a saying: *'The only sight that improves with age is hindsight'.*"

"In the long term, the strategy has had some unfortunate consequences," Tesca commented, "but in the short term, it was effective. You did catch him."

"Yes," Grivus said. "My ship was one of the three that finally cornered him near Narlos." His eyes took on a distant look. "I have never been in a greater battle. When we finally boarded the *Pistrix Cruentus*, he set it afire, and would not be taken alive. I myself slew him, though he was the better swordsman."

"He let you kill him?" the Duke asked in wonder. "Why in the Hells would he do that?"

"An honorable death, milord," Tesca answered. "He knew the battle was lost, so he chose to die fighting a fellow captain."

Grivus nodded. "Those of his crew who had been with him from the first followed their captain's example, flinging themselves onto our blades rather than be captured." He broke off, a haunted expression crossing his features. "I have often thought of that battle, of that duel. I came on board expecting to find a raving monster, a madman guided by animal cunning, but instead he ended his life in a manner any Imperial officer would choose." He sighed. "Adding that new unanswered question to the others, I and my lieutenants raced to his cabin. The man was dead; if there were any answers to be found, they would be there, among his papers."

"But you did not find your answers, did you?" the Duke asked.

"No," Grivus said, his voice bitter. "His cabin had been struck by cannon more than once; debris was scattered everywhere and many of his possessions had already been blasted out into the sea. We grabbed every scrap of paper we could lay our hands on, and we dared not linger for a longer search, for we feared the fire would reach the powder magazine. It was not until two days later, after we had completed all emergency repairs and my ship was fit for travel once more, that I and my lieutenants had at last a chance to sit quietly for an evening and examine all that we had retrieved. His logbook was gone, but his personal journal, that we found. However, it was only the latest volume; he had filled no more than a quarter of the pages. If his writing in this volume was anything to measure by, he must have filled twenty volumes since he began his expedition north. I had not seen anything to indicate the other volumes had been in his cabin, so we had to conclude that he had left them onshore, somewhere he considered secure."

Grivus paused and looked up at three other men. "Yes, somewhere onshore. A secret haven. Now we return to the map. The night after the battle, one of my two lieutenants, Malius, found the map amidst the papers he had retrieved from the pirate's ship. He recognized it as being in the Imperial cartographic format, but written in a language he had never seen before. My other lieutenant, Benaeto, came upon Malius as he was trying to decipher the script." He gave a rueful smile as memories came to him. "Benaeto was the more clever of the two, the one I would send into town for procuring needed supplies that I did not have the funds to purchase. He was always willing to bend protocol in service to the ship or to his own ambition. A very useful asset, if carefully watched. After the battle, alas, I had no eyes to spare for him. Benaeto could not read the map any more than Malius could, but he persuaded Malius to hold it back, to keep it hidden from me, at least for a short time. He said that I would not become suspicious if Malius happened to find the map had fallen behind his bunk. And he was likely right; Malius was a good lad, if a bit easy to manipulate." He sighed. "They both knew they had likely participated in the greatest naval action they were likely to see in their careers, but as mere lieutenants, they would not receive the lion's share of the glory and rewards. I think both of them hoped this map would provide a chance for them to reap some glory for themselves in the future."

"In any case, after we had looked over the other papers and concluded that Praeditorus Rex had a secret haven somewhere, both lieutenants became convinced that this map would lead to it, if they could just decipher the script. Benaeto could not convince Malius to let him hold onto the map. Malius was naïve, but not a fool. Instead, Benaeto convinced Malius to split the map in half, so that neither could find the island themselves."

"How is that possible, when we don't know what the map says?" Galen asked.

"The map follows the format of all Imperial Cartography charts," Grivus explained. "The writing at the top of the chart would give the latitude and longitude. This line was halved when the map was torn. It is likely that one half has the latitude, but the other has the longitude. If you could read the script, you could make a guess as to the island's location, but without both halves, you would have a great deal of ocean to search."

"He's right," Tesca confirmed.

Grivus nodded to Tesca in thanks. "After the battle," he went on, "the three ships returned to our Fleet Captain and presented him with the trophies of our victory: Our enemy's banner, his blades and his head. I also turned over all the papers retrieved from his cabin." He smiled at an old memory. "My fortunes rose quickly after that. As the man who slew Praeditorus Rex, I received the *Tactus Aurus*."

Tesca made a low whistle, impressed. As the Duke and Galen looked at him, he explained. "The *Golden Touch*, milord. Literally, it means that the Emperor takes off his glove and cups your chin with his naked hand. There's no greater honor within the Empire." He paused, surprised. "As I recall, the recipient also receives a badge to commemorate the event; a golden hand."

"Yes," Grivus replied as Galen reflexively touched the golden hand pin on his own lapel. "It is an odd coincidence, is it not, that both our peoples put great esteem in such an adornment? In any case, I returned to my ship and some years later, became commander of another. I did good service for the Empire during that second tour as well, and when it was finished, I found myself in the enviable position of being able to choose my next posting myself. I chose to become an instructor at the Imperial Academy. Can you guess the reason?"

The Duke studied Grivus for some time, thinking. "You still did not know why Praeditorus Rex turned on the Empire. The papers you turned over to your Fleet Captain; they were archived at the Academy, weren't they?"

Grivus was impressed. "Yes, Your Grace. I would, at last, have the opportunity to study those papers in depth, to look for any clues as to what had happened to this man that turned him renegade. There had been an initial perusal of his papers by the archivists, but no real effort had been made to explore the deeper question that had gnawed at me since the battle. I enjoyed my time at the Academy; I was a good instructor. I had the opportunity to spend time with my wife and children; a rare thing for a career officer. I formed regular correspondence with many graduating cadets, advising them in their careers and enjoying some of the rewards and credit for their own successes; Livia Maritius was one of them." He sighed. "However, there were reefs ahead, and I was not looking forward. As my fortunes had risen, so did the number of those who envied me, notably the other two captains who had fought alongside me against Praeditorus Rex. They too, had received rewards for defeating him, but they had not killed the man themselves; they did not receive the *Tactus Aurus*."

Grivus shrugged. "I cannot blame them for their envy…if the winds had blown only a little differently, one of them would have boarded the *Pistrix Cruentus*, and received the *Golden Touch* in my place. They kept their jealousy secret, until they learned that I was studying the papers retrieved from the *Pistrix Cruentus*. Then, they began to speak quietly against me; questioning why I would spend so much time poring over the ramblings of a madman. You see, I learned soon after the pirate's death, that most of my people, especially my fellow officers, would not entertain the idea that Praeditorus Rex was anything but a madman. It was simply not possible to them that a decorated commander would turn into the most fearsome pirate the Empire had ever seen. They did not want to examine the cause of such a thing, and they distanced themselves from me. These are the ones whose ears were receptive to the new whispers against my character.

"These two fellow captains, Argillius and Verasus, became my political enemies, damaging my name within the fleet and at court. I returned the favor to them both twice over. I could do nothing else. To accept such slander without retaliation; this is not an admirable quality within the Empire. One's honor must be defended at all times." A disgusted look came over him. "What a waste."

"Then one day, some years after the feuding had begun; I received an urgent request to visit Malius, my former lieutenant. The man had gone on to captain a ship of his own for a brief time before he was injured in a battle. His wounds never truly healed and his health had become frail. I went to see him at once, for I had always held Malius in high esteem. He was dying, and wished to clear his conscience. He gave me the map, begging my forgiveness for hiding it from me."

"He never had a chance to go looking for it himself?" Galen asked.

Grivus shook his head. "Perhaps he would, if he had not been injured. But he was never able to decipher the script. I could not decipher it either, but I was able to compare it to the other papers we had taken from the pirate's cabin. Though the language is different, the penmanship is the same. Somehow, Praeditorus Rex learned to write in an unknown language."

"What about the other lieutenant," asked Tesca, "what about Benaeto?"

"Ah, Benaeto," Grivus mused, "he came to see me not long after Malius's death. Benaeto did not receive a command of his own; he was clever and sly, but not so clever as to conceal his slyness from those who had the power to promote him. He left the Navy after his first tour was concluded. He was not of noble birth, so he drifted into the merchant trade. Benaeto and I discussed old times, but I knew why he was there: He wanted the other half of the map, and he was trying to find out if Malius had told me about it before he died. I grew tired of him nosing around the subject like a dog sniffing for food to steal, and told him that Malius had both given me the map and confessed the entire story. He then had the unmitigated gall to ask me for the map, saying that Malius and he had agreed if one of them died, the other would get both halves. When I refused, he then invited me to work with him as a business partner, sharing all profits from the island equally. I told him that I did not sully myself with a member of the merchant class, least of all one I knew to have deliberately lied to me in the past."

Grivus's expression turned angry. "I thought that would be the last

I would hear of him, but I was wrong. Once Benaeto knew I had the other half of the map, he could only imagine that I was trying to find the island on my own, and he quickly decided that I must have found some means of deciphering the mysterious language; a means I would not share with him. But as I said, he was clever and sly, and it did not take him long to wrangle invitations to dine at the homes of Captains Argillius and Verasus.

"The whispers against me grew more toxic; it was now being bandied about that I had become enthralled by the legend of the man I had killed; that I was a..." he broke off, eyes flashing with anger, "...I cannot repeat the word, but the closest translation would be 'pirate-lover.' During this time, my wife died of a fever, and my enemies added whispers that I was being punished by the gods for my vile obsession with a dead madman."

Grivus gave a cold smile. "But they miscalculated. After my wife's death, I had nothing to lose, and I baited one of them, Argillius, into openly calling me a 'pirate-lover.' We settled the matter with the Argument and the Retort."

"Did you kill him?" Tesca asked.

"Yes," Grivus answered with a satisfied sigh. "But his friend Captain Verasus claimed that I ignored Argillius's cry of *pacem*, making his death a murder. He was lying; Argillius did not say a word during the duel. But by that point, my reputation was so tarnished that Argillius's claim was investigated." He shook his head. "The investigators found no proof of murder, but they did not proclaim me innocent either. My peers, my students, my fellow citizens, all were free to decide for themselves whether they thought me guilty." He looked at the Duke with a bitter smile. "You can guess which opinion most of them have, judging by the reaction of my countrymen to seeing me here last night."

"I am sorry for the direction life has blown you," the Duke said. "So you left the Empire. But, why have you come here?"

Grivus remained silent for some time. "Only two things remain to me: My blades, and my question; the question that has haunted me since I slew the pirate those many years ago. If it were not for that question, I would have put myself out on a raft and let the sea consume me, as some of our elders do." He looked at the Duke, and his pain was naked on his face. "But so long as I have strength in me, Your Grace, I cannot rest until I have that question answered. So I have come north, hoping to find clues in the Frees that could not be found in the Empire."

"With only half of the map?" Galen asked, looking skeptical.

Grivus shrugged. "Perhaps one of the local cartographers has drawn a map with an island that bears a similarity to the one drawn here. As to the other half of this map, Benaeto is also in the Frees, somewhere. When I came north, it did not take him long to follow. He caught up with me, and tried to take the map by force." His smile was almost feral. "He was not nearly as practiced in argument as he thought; I put a scar across his cheek before he escaped me. Likely he is doing what I am doing; seeking to find the island first." He spread his hands. "My tale is done, Your Grace. I believe that this map, if it can be deciphered, will lead to an island where the treasure and secrets of the most infamous pirate in either of our histories can be found. As payment of my debt to you, I offer you everything we find there, relinquishing all claims, save that I have the right to study and read any written materials or maps we find there, for as long as I wish. Are you interested?"

Chapter Forty-two

"A treasure map?" Kayrla asked, nearly jumping out of bed in excitement. She was wearing a voluminous nightshirt that was too large for her, making it look like she was wearing a white tent. The tattered remains of her maid's uniform were piled in front of her dresser.

"Half of a treasure map," Tesca corrected. He had pulled a chair up next to her bed and was helping himself to one of the oranges in her breakfast tray.

"And the Duke's going to help Grivus find the treasure?"

Tesca smiled at her excitement. "He's...considering it."

"Oh, he's just got to!" Kayrla said, eyes wide. "Oh, sails and spray! I've heard stories about Praeditorus Rex for years! They say he had he melted down all the gold he stole and made a throne for himself, since he was a king and all."

"How'd he pay his crew then?"

"With all the stolen silver, of course!"

Tesca shook his head. "Of course."

Kayrla laughed. "Oh, there's so many stories about him that contradict each other. You know that there's some who claim that he wasn't a Sabrian at all...but a man of the Frees who took a Sabrian name?" She grinned at him. "Remind you of anyone you know, Tesca Secarius?" Tesca shook his head, a puzzled expression on his face. Kayrla scowled at him, not sure whether he was joking or not. "Well, there's others that swear it wasn't one man," she went on, "but three, who all agreed to fly the same colors and hunt in different places, so it seemed like he was everywhere at once."

"Grivus's story is a new one to add to the others," he told her. "First one I've heard from the Sabrian side of things, though. What I'm suspicious of is this 'secret island.' Galen says the news of Praeditorus's death reached Kohayne not long after the Duke took the throne." He frowned. "That's over twenty years ago. In all that time, no one's come across this island he used for his haven? Even if we found it, it might already have been plundered."

"Oh, it's possible no one's found it yet," she assured him. "There's plenty of islands out there that no one's charted, especially as you head east, beyond the trade routes. There's no reason to head that way unless you want privacy, and unless you know where you're going, there's little chance you'll even see land. It's mostly open ocean."

"That's as good a guess as anyone else's," Tesca said. "What we could decipher from Grivus's map is a mark that shows some sort of cavern, or hidden entrance."

"See? Even if someone else landed there, they wouldn't be able to find the haven and all the treasure! It's got to still be there!" She grinned and started to peel her orange. "Anything else on the map?"

"There's some writing on the side of the page and a few notes with arrows pointing towards that cave," Tesca said. "If you use other Imperial maps as a model, those would be notes and warnings to anyone using the map, perhaps revealing the location of traps, or dangerous monsters to be alert for."

"Traps?" Kayrla was dubious. "Who makes a map showing where the traps are?"

"Grivus said if there were notes about traps, they'd be more like riddles. Think of it like this: if you've been away from the island for several years, you might not remember exactly where you put the traps or how to get around them. And the trap doesn't care who built it, it'll kill whoever sets it off. So you write down a little riddle or code for yourself to jog your memory; something only you would know."

"And the monsters?"

Tesca shook his head. "I've no idea. An armorback could be scary if you've never seen one before, but I can't imagine someone like Praeditorus Rex being so worried about armorbacks that he'd put it on a map."

Kayrla shrugged. "Well, the mana on the mainland's a lot stronger, and it's done odd things to some of the animals up there. There's some that might rightly be called monsters, especially to Sabrians who've no experience with magic at all. Have you ever heard of blinders?"

"Blinders..." Tesca murmured. "Yes, I think so...large rodents, aren't they?"

"Yes, but they make people go blind, then they attack!" Kayrla said, waving her hands towards Tesca's face. "I hear it's only temporary; your sight returns in an hour or so. All you have to do is survive being swarmed by a pack of giant rats."

"Have you ever seen one?"

"I don't think anyone's ever seen one! Get it?" She fell back on the bed, giggling, as Tesca rolled his eyes.

"You clearly need more sleep," he said, half-rising from his chair.

"No, no, stay!" she begged him. "I'm not sleepy."

"Really? I would think you'd be exhausted, after everything you did last night."

She nodded. "Well, my legs hurt something fierce; that spiral staircase in the secret passage was really long."

"I know. I've been through it."

She was crestfallen. "You knew about it?"

"No, no," he assured her, "you discovered it right enough. But Kelvo and I inspected it last night, while Galen was debriefing you."

"Any idea who built it?"

Tesca shrugged. "I'm no scholar or architect, but it looked to me as if it was part of the original construction of that portion of the estate. Galen suspects that it was meant as a secret exit for the Ducal family if they had to make an escape."

"Then why didn't the Duke know about it?"

He shrugged. "His Grace was wondering that himself. I can only guess that someone died before they could pass the secret on. That can't have happened too long ago, though. The furniture in that room–"

"The love nest," she corrected him.

"Yes, the love nest," he went on, rolling his eyes at her. "The furniture's been down there for a while, but it's not that old, probably less than fifty years. Most of it's solid, durable but nothing special. The bed, though…that's well-made, good craftsmanship, and expensive. And it's too big to have come through any of the doors, secret or otherwise. It must have been assembled inside that room."

"Someone wanted only the best for, well, what the room was being used for," she giggled, then her eyes went wide. "I think I know who it must have been! Marcus Kohaya, the Duke's grandfather!"

"Really?" Tesca said, looking interested. "Why do you think that?"

She paused, getting her thoughts in order. "First, Galen thinks the passage was meant as an escape route for the Ducal family, so let's assume that after a few generations, only each Duke, and maybe his immediate family, would know about it. And you said the bed's expensive, right?"

He nodded. "It could probably be considered a valuable antique."

"Right. And the bed needed to be assembled inside the room. Not a job for one person. So, it's someone with enough money to pay for a large bed and have it built there. And the adjoining room was used as a private wine cellar." She looked at him. "If someone went to all that trouble to try and keep it a secret, what would the Duke do to them if he found out?"

He smiled. "You're right…it would have to be a member of the ducal family."

"When was Marcus on the throne? Does it match the age of the furniture?"

Tesca counted back. "He died…forty-six years ago." He looked impressed. "The time is right."

"And from what I've heard about him," Kayrla started to say, then she giggled again. "Oh, you've no idea the stories I was hearing about him last night from His Grace!"

"His Grace?"

She gave him a sly grin. "His Grace was keeping himself entertained by trying to make me burst out laughing. He said some really funny things, and some of them were about his grandfather. It sounds to me that turning his family's old escape route into a secret love nest for himself is exactly the sort of thing he'd do. And if he's using it for his own pleasures, it's no longer something he's like to tell his son about. So, when he dies, so does the secret."

Tesca looked at her, impressed. "That's…as good an explanation as I'm like to hear. I'll tell Galen."

"Just don't take credit for it, Tesca," she said. "It was my…idea," she broke off, yawning.

"All right, now I'm going to let you sleep."

"No, I'm fine, really. I got a little sleep after Galen ordered me to."

"Only a little?"

She hesitated, looking uncomfortable. "Well, it was hard to sleep through that screaming fit Allie was having outside, yelling at you and Grivus."

"Ah…you heard that, did you?"

She pointed to the open window, where a warm breeze was slowly pushing the curtains. "You were on the same patio where the orchestra was practicing, remember? The sound comes right in." She popped an orange section into her mouth and chewed it for a moment, remembering. "I haven't seen someone that angry since Jolly Red caught me stealing."

Tesca grinned ruefully. "It's probably a good thing she wasn't armed. Allie has a horrible temper, especially when she thinks she's been cheated. What really upset her, though, was the fact that she was going to have to tell her father that Grivus is now a guest of His Grace."

She looked at the left side of Tesca's face. "Does it still hurt, where she slapped you?"

He looked embarrassed, a flush coming into his right cheek to match the left. "You saw that?"

"I came to the window to see what all the noise was about." She shook her head sadly at her friend. "You shouldn't have let her slap you."

He shrugged. "She really didn't put all her strength into it; she just needed to let off some steam."

She studied him, still slowing shaking her head. "What do you see in her?"

"Nothing," he replied, looking towards the window, watching the curtains drift in the breeze. "We made our choices."

"No regrets?"

He looked back at her, a curious smile. "Didn't I ask you much the same question after you entered the Duke's service?"

"Yes, and you're evading the answer."

"Regrets…not really." He paused. "I could never have stayed with her. If you're in bed with one Feyne, you're in bed with them all, if you take my meaning." She nodded, watching him. "An *agentis* is supposed to forsake romantic entanglements. If I'd taken up with her family, Allie would have made that…complicated." He chuckled softly. "But the truth of it is, I couldn't have put myself in her family's service. Galen understood that the first time he met me…and when he offered me a chance to meet His Grace and enter his service, it wasn't really a choice at all."

"I understand," she said. "I felt the same way when you brought me to meet him. He's just…he's a rock. A big rock, sticking up out of the water. And if the weather gets bad, you just hold onto that rock, knowing you'll be safe till the storm passes."

Tesca looked at her, raising an eyebrow. "I really think you need to get some sleep."

She stuck her tongue out at him. "You know what I mean!"

He laughed, nodding. "Well, what's done is done. Allie thinks I lured Grivus away from her family, that it was some sort of planned double-cross. She's too angry to believe anything else, and even if she did, her father never will. He's not a man who'll let that sort of thing pass, especially with as much wealth as he imagines is waiting on that island."

She looked serious. "So…what do we do now?"

"The Feynes will start watching Harborside like hawks for any indication that the Duke is putting together an expedition to find the island. You don't need a map if you can follow the man who has one. But we'd still want to find the other half of the map, and a way of translating it."

"That sounds like a job for the Left Hand, doesn't it?"

Tesca shrugged. "It all depends on whether the Duke decides to look for the island at all. If the Feynes are desperate enough, they'll expose some of their informants and spies in Kohayne while digging for information on the Duke's plans. Galen's more excited about that prospect than a large pile of gold added to the treasury."

Kayrla shook her head. "I'm sorry, I can't really get past the thought of that much money in one large pile. Oh, I'd just jump right into it and swim around!"

He chuckled. "Whatever happens, it won't be dull around here."

She sighed. "I wish I could help you with that." She looked at a jewelry box sitting on her dresser. "I put the pendant away," she said. "I just…I can't even look at it right now. I just get depressed, thinking that I'm stuck in here. So much of what's happened is because of that stupid pendant, and after all that, it doesn't even work anymore!"

She'd been long dreading the look of sympathetic pity that she knew he was about to give her, but instead he smiled. "Well, you'll need to be further north for there to be enough mana to create your full disguise, right?"

"Yes," she replied, still not looking at him.

"Well, that just means we'll need to send you on missions further north."

She was puzzled. "But…I thought I was supposed to stay here, in Kohayne, and train here for a while. How can I do that?"

His smile widened. "There's a silver lining to Allie leaving her in a bad temper. She's sure to tell everyone that you're here, in the Duke's service. Soon the whole city will know."

"How is that a good thing?"

"There's no point in hiding anymore, is there?"

She blinked in surprise as the meaning of his words sunk in. "I'll…I'll be able to walk around as myself?"

"Around the estate, yes. You're free to go anywhere you want inside the grounds, without any disguises. The guards need to know who you are; can't have them trying to arrest you again."

Kayrla's smile spread across her face. "And what about the city? Can I go down into the city?"

Tesca hesitated, drawing out the moment, until Kayrla reached over and smacked his arm. "Yes, yes!" he finally said. "But not in the same way. Galen has an idea. The first few times you go down into the city, you look just like yourself, with no disguise whatsoever. He thinks that before long, most people that might be looking for you will just keep an eye out for that green hair of yours. You should be able to start using your old disguise again after that."

She sighed, but ended it with a smile. "Well, I was hoping I wouldn't ever have to bind up my ears again, but it's better than being trapped inside the estate."

Tesca nodded. "Just remember, it's not a perfect solution. You'd have to be on guard at all times. You're still an elf that can wield magic in the Frees, and that's a precious rare thing. Rare enough that some would still like to get their hands on you, even without a price on your head. The old disguise won't fool them for long." He paused. "And of course the Feynes wouldn't mind getting rid of you either. You did tell Allie you could sink one of her father's ships single-handed."

She burst out laughing. "Oh, that! Well, I had to tell her something to shut her up, didn't I? Who told you I said that?"

"That guard who was with you. Wick. She threatened him too, remember? He liked the way you stood up for him."

"Oh, I should go find him and say hello, now that I can!" She hopped out of bed, her nightshirt trailing along the floor. "Out, out, out!" she ordered, flicking her hands at him.

"I thought you were going to try to get back to sleep," he objected, rising from his chair.

"It's almost noon! I can't sleep now! Besides, who could sleep, now that I get a chance to have a proper tour of this place during the day!" She flicked her hands at him again and he backed towards the door. "I'll get dressed, and then we can get started!"

"Ah, I guess I'm expected to give you that tour."

"Naturally," she laughed. "I'll be just a minute." With a mock bow, Tesca left the room, and Kayrla busied herself throwing on a set of clothes. After tugging her boots on, she spent a few moments watching herself in the mirror, realizing that it had been a very long time since she'd walked out into the world, looking exactly like herself.

About half an hour later, Ella came into the room to tidy up. She made the bed and collected up Kayrla's stray clothes. When she picked up the tattered remnants of the maid's uniform from last night, she clicked her tongue and shook her head. "There's no point trying to mend you, is there?" she murmured, turning it this way and that. As she did so, an earring fell out of one pocket, clinking against the floor. Ella picked it up, squinting at the gold letter "F" set against a field of amethyst chips. "Now where did Kay find you, I wonder?" she asked. "You certainly are a pretty little thing." She searched the uniform more thoroughly, looking for the matching piece, but found nothing. "Like as not she came across you in the gardens last night, eh?" She smiled. "I daresay there's a lady back in her home, just now realizing she left you behind after a tumble."

Neither getting nor expecting an answer, she cast about the room for a place to put the earring, and her gaze came to rest on the jewelry box. Lifting the lid, she looked down at the pendant all by itself. She smiled. "Kay will find a few more pretties to keep you company in there before long, of that I'm sure," she said to the pendant. "Here's a start," she added, putting the earring inside the box and closing the lid. In another moment, after a final sweep for anything else out of place, she slipped out of the room and closed the door behind her.

Epilogue

The black two-horse carriage swept through the gates of the Feyne estate. It did not stop as it entered the large courtyard. Instead, it rolled on towards a smaller gate, which was opened at once, and headed up a narrower track, winding its way through the rising estate in gentle switchbacks. The Feyne estate was not as large as the Duke's, but it had nearly as many buildings, pressed closely together with narrow cobblestone streets between them. It resembled nothing so much as Kohayne in miniature, albeit with the refuse, human or otherwise, removed. The buildings all gleamed with whitewash and used matching red clay shingles for their roofs.

As the carriage rolled through this network of roads, pedestrians moved quickly out of its way. They glanced at the two dark red plumes fluttering from the roof, recognizing which member of the Feyne family was inside it from the color, and bowed as it passed. It continued in this manner all the way to the highest terrace, stopping at last before the manor itself, a large and ornately decorated house built up against the rock wall. Rumors of how far the Feynes had delved into the rock at their backs, adding vast vaults to house their wealth, were a common subject in Harborside taverns.

"Welcome back, mistress," said the majordomo as he opened the door of the carriage and extended a hand to Alezandra Feyne. Allie took it and stepped down to the paved stones, then strode towards the house, looking neither right nor left. The majordomo turned to offer assistance to Allie's guest, but looked puzzled as he gazed into the empty carriage. "Mistress, did Captain Grivus not return with y–" He broke off as Allie plowed ahead. She swept through the double doors that were opened as she approached.

The entrance hall was a circular chamber with a high domed ceiling, the floor and columns set into the walls made of a rich golden marble. A long hall stretched ahead and twin staircases coiled down the walls from the second floor. She turned and took one of the staircases, hiking up her dress in one hand, not slowing down. On the floor below, several servants came out to wait upon her, but she ignored them, continuing up the stairs. They stood about in awkward confusion, looking at each other, until the majordomo came into the chamber and dismissed them with a few snaps of his fingers and silent gestures. He watched Allie finish her ascent and disappear into the second floor hallway.

Allie's personal maid started awake in her chair as Allie flung open the doors to her suite. She dashed up to her mistress as Allie shrugged out of her dress, letting it pool at her feet and stepping out of it. However, the maid was used to Allie's moods and manner, and she had the long, soft robe in Allie's outstretched hand even as Allie was putting her hand out.

"You're home late, mistress," the maid offered, turning back to shut the open doors as Allie slipped the robe on. "I can only assume the fete went well?" Allie crossed the room to a small dining table and lifted the lid on a large silver platter. "I'm afraid the juice isn't chilled any longer, mistress," the maid apologized, "I brought it up at the regular time, but as you weren't home yet, well..." she trailed off.

Allie did not seem to find any objection to the juice, pouring a generous amount from the carafe into a waiting goblet and gulping the contents down. She selected a pastry from the tray and turned away from the table. The maid quickly set the tray back over the platter, watching her mistress with an anxious expression.

Allie's eyes moved to the large bathtub set in front of the balcony doors. The maid bustled forward. "A bath, mistress? I can get that ready for you in a trice. I've had a low fire set on the water since this morning." The bathtub was one of Allie's most prized possessions. A wonder of Sabrian artifice, it was a large copper basin set into a wooden frame with four panels of carved wood, each showing a different scene from Sabrian myth. A faucet was mounted to the frame, attached to pipes that led to two large water tanks installed on the roof above her suite. A small fire could be lit beneath one tank, and by adjusting the flow of water coming from both with a set of knobs attached to the faucet, the water temperature could be controlled with ease.

As the maid began to fill the bathtub, adding various scents and powders to the water that produced an aromatic, bubbling froth, Allie turned away from the balcony and walked to her dressing table. Watching her own reflection in her mirror, she removed her jewelry with slow, deliberate movements, setting them on the table before her. Then she dabbed a cloth in a small dish of water and began to remove the makeup from her face.

From somewhere else in the house, there came a quiet noise. The noise grew louder, resolving into someone running down the hall, heels clattering on the marble floor. Allie turned her head slowly, without surprise, just as the doors burst open. "Where the scrump is Grivus?" her brother Anbros yelled into the room as he walked in, his head turning this way and that before he spotted her, watching him.

So Anbros heard the news first, she thought. *That means the majordomo answers to Anbros, and not to Father. I wonder what Father will think of that?* She filed the new piece of information away for later consideration.

"You," Anbros snapped to the maid, "out."

"Leave the bath running," Allie called to the terrified servant in mid-curtsy. The woman nodded to Allie and scampered out of the room.

"I asked you a question," Anbros said between clenched teeth as he advanced on her.

"No, you shouted a question," she replied, remaining calm. She'd had her tantrum an hour before, in front of Grivus and Tesca, and now her fury had ebbed to a simmering, quiet rage. "And rudely too."

The gold tooth in Anbros's snarl glinted, and as always, she was reminded of Tesca, of how he'd knocked out Anbros's real one when her brother, in one of his rages, had leapt at her lover with a knife in his hand. But this time the memory was not even a bittersweet reminder. Instead it fanned her own anger once more.

Calm, she told herself. Stay calm. *If you lose your temper, you lose the game.* It was her father's favorite advice to her, though it irritated her every time he said it. *As if Father never lost his temper, the old hypocrite.*

"Don't dance around with me, Allie!" Anbros fumed. "Where is Grivus?"

She sighed. "It appears the Duke found him interesting company, so Grivus accepted an invitation to remain there." It wasn't exactly true, but it was far politer than what Grivus had actually said to her, and it shifted the blame off of her shoulders and firmly onto someone else's.

The look of stupefied shock on her brother's face was just about all the comfort she could salvage from this disaster, she knew. She rose from her chair and walked past him towards the bathtub. "You...lost him?" he finally spluttered, turning towards her. "To the Duke?"

"I wasn't in a position to argue," she called over her shoulder, checking the water temperature and making a few adjustments. "We were at the ducal estate and the Duke said he enjoyed Grivus's company. He invited him to stay; I couldn't exactly refuse, could I? Don't make it sound like Grivus was a bracelet I left on a bench by accident."

"If you took a piece of jewelry to the party and didn't come home with it," Anbros snapped, "you'd be crying like an unpaid whore that you'd lost it." She glared at him, the word "whore" chipping away at her composed veneer. He sneered at her. "More like you'd be whining that someone stole it. It's always someone else's fault with you, isn't it?"

"Well, that's certainly true in this case. I didn't lose Grivus; the Duke stole him away from us."

Anbros pounded his fist against the wall in rage. "I knew we shouldn't have let you out of the house with him! You just had to parade him around, dressing him up as if he was one of your dolls; showing him off to that bastard Secarius." He watched her face for a reaction, but looked surprised when he didn't get one. "What? Finally put out that torch for him, eh?"

Allie didn't answer; she wasn't sure she could answer without losing her composure. Anbros shook his head, watching. "We have to…I can't believe…" He was sputtering, walking in circles and waving his arms. "Do…do you have any concept, even the slightest notion of what Father's going to do to you when he hears about this?"

"To me?" she snapped.

"You're the one who lost him."

"No, I told you…the Duke invited him to stay and he accepted, even after he made a deal with Father! Grivus double-crossed us! It's not my fault he stayed!"

"That ship won't sail with me, little sister!" Anbros threw back. "You should have gotten home sooner; your story would be more believable. I already heard that Grivus started some sort of trouble with the Sabrian emissary, but I didn't know he'd end up staying there!"

"How did you hear…?" she asked.

"Just because I wouldn't waste my time stepping onto the Kohaya estate doesn't mean I don't have eyes and ears there." He grinned at her. "Let's just say some of his servants have more than the Duke's coin in their pockets."

He's lying, she decided, studying his body language. *Father's never been able to get a spy past the Right Hand, damn him, and Anbros isn't half as smart as Father. No, someone's told him what happened with Grivus, but it must have been one of the other guests, currying favors. That could be anyone.* She shrugged, not bothering to either admit or deny her story. "Who cares how it happened? In the end, the Duke offered him a place to stay and he accepted."

"It wouldn't have happened at all if you'd just thought for one moment beyond your own fun! You begged Father to let Grivus go to the fete as your guest, when you knew we hadn't gotten the map from him yet!"

She glared at him from across the room, but kept her temper in check as she shut the water off. *So...we were going to betray him,* she thought, shaking her head sadly. "Anbros, he could have been of more use to us than just half of a map we can't read! A trained Sabrian officer, an instructor at the Imperial Academy! We could have put him in command of one of Father's ships, or hired him on as an instructor for our own captains. Father told him we were considering it, and he seemed interested. We would have had his loyalty." She put her hands to her head, exasperated. "It would have cost us almost nothing to show him a little respect and make him feel welcome!"

"It would have cost us even less to just get the map and look for the island ourselves," Anbros threw back. "He wanted a share of the treasure; a full third." He walked towards her, his voice relaxing. "Allie, do you have any idea how much wealth Praeditorus Rex accumulated? Father's gotten his hands on some of the account books from two Sabrian merchants who were plundered by him. You multiply what they lost just a few times over, and it's...it's amazing. You have no idea how vast a sum it is. And he didn't spend more than a fraction of it; just enough to keep his ships supplied. The rest..." he trailed off, a faraway look in his eyes. "It's there, Allie. All of it. Enough wealth that we could buy the entire Quad, own it outright." The smile on his face faded as he focused on her once more. "What's that compared to one old man that no one was going to look for?"

She opened her mouth to object, but he cut her off. "And don't pretend you cared about him, either. It was the right move and you know it. Just business. He had nowhere to go; barely a copper to his name. He was probably a day away from selling those precious swords of his before I found him." He shrugged. "Better investment to just get the map and be rid of him. And we would have, but you had to take him to the fete!"

"Grivus was poor and desperate, but he wasn't an idiot, Anbros," Allie threw back at him. "He read you and Father like a book; he could tell you were planning to kill him." She shook her head in rueful admiration, realizing then what Grivus had been up to last night. "It's funny," she said absently. "Tesca only had to fight one duel to save Grivus's life twice."

Anbros laughed at her. "Ah, you still carry a torch for that bastard! Don't deny it; I heard it in your voice!" He sneered at her. "I don't see why you bother, anyway. These days, I hear he prefers his women with green hair."

She came around the tub towards him, bringing her hand up to slap him, but he caught her wrist and twisted it. She gasped in pain, her knees buckling. "You know better than to lose your temper with me, sister. I hit back. Remember?" He twisted her arm again and she grimaced, her other hand scrabbling at the edge of the tub.

"Say it. Say it's your fault," he ordered her, twisting her wrist even further.

"You...you scared him away," she said between clenched teeth. "It's not my...ahhh!"

"Say it! Just once in your life, Allie, admit when something is your f–" he started to say, but paused, feeling a sharp pain pressing into his side. Looking down, he saw the gleam of the short dagger in her free hand, the point just under his ribs.

"Where did you get–" he asked, more surprised than scared.

"A girl can never be too careful taking a bath, Anbros," Allie said in her sweetest voice. "If you want to keep playing this game, I will bet you a hundred marks that my broken wrist will heal before your belly wound, if you don't die first."

"Father will lash the skin from your bones," he warned her.

"You let me worry about that, Anbros...you'll be dead and I can tell the story any way I like. Now," she commanded, "release me."

Anbros gave a quiet laugh, then looked in her eyes. He didn't appear to like what he saw. A moment later, he let go of her wrist and quickly stepped clear. He touched his side, wincing as he examined the small cut, while she shifted the knife to her right hand. "Now, brother," she told him, "let us understand each other. If there is a treasure to be found on that island, I do not relish the idea of the Duke finding it any more than you do. However," she said, gesturing with the dagger as he opened his mouth to speak, "I will not take the blame for something that is not my fault. I took Grivus to the party, yes, and he used that as an opportunity to escape, but that was only because he realized you and Father planned to kill him. Your unmasked greed has brought us to this, not my vanity."

She strolled around the tub, deliberately keeping the dagger pointed in his direction. "So the Duke knows about the island? So what? He's no closer to finding it than we are. Now that we know it exists, we don't need Grivus, or his piece of the map, to look for it."

Anbros's expression changed. He was still angry, but now he was listening to her, the wound in his side forgotten. "What are you suggesting?"

"There's another half of the map, isn't there? The Duke may rule here, but outside the Quad, we're the ones with the longer reach. We find that other half of the map, we're right back in the race. Make no mistake, brother, if the Duke ever finds that island, all I want him to see when he gets there is our banner on the beach, waving at him."

Anbros chuckled. "All right, little sister. It's a course worth sailing. Let me suggest that to Father; it might blunt his anger when he learns about Grivus." He gave her a half-bow and headed for the door.

"Just don't try to take the credit for the idea either," she called after him, following. "At least not all of it."

"No, I'd rather not get a second hole in my shirt," Anbros called back as he entered the hall. "Come down after your bath."

Allie watched him leave, then closed the doors of her suite. After a moment, she turned the lock on the doors, throwing the deadbolt for good measure. Then she walked back to her dressing table and settled herself in the chair. She opened her jewelry box.

The race is on, she thought, putting her necklace in a velvet-lined tray, straightening out the twists in the chain, then closing that drawer of the box. *If the Duke sends people out to find the island, he'll have to send Tesca. There's no one else he has that's so capable, no one else he can trust to do it. Tesca...and her.* A scowl crossed her face as she put away her bracelets, closing that drawer as well. *That little seaweed-head.* An image of them holding each other, after the assassin had been killed, flashed through her mind, and in the next instant, she'd flung the jewelry box off the table. The box was well-made; none of the closed compartments popped open. Only the last open tray spilled its contents, earrings falling onto the marble floor, bouncing away.

She fought back tears as she composed herself once more, then busied herself gathering up the scattered jewelry. There was one she came across that brought a smile to her face. It was the first piece of jewelry her father had ever given her, though it was only a single earring, missing its mate. *"This was your grandmother's, Alezandra,"* her father had said. *"But it's only one, Papa,"* she had objected, running her tiny finger over the gold "F" set against a field of amethyst chips. *"Yes, she lost the other one before I was born,"* her father replied. *"How did she lose it, Papa?"* She recalled that her father had laughed. *"Someday, little one, I will tell you." "You promise?" "I promise."*

Feynes keep their promises, Allie thought, turning the earring this way and that. She hadn't looked at this earring in years, and now she found that she quite liked the design. Still, amethysts weren't her favorite gemstone. *I think it's time for a new pair of earrings... maybe a necklace to match. But not amethysts,* she thought, smiling. *Rubies.*

About the author

In his secret identity, John Meagher is a voice actor and graphic designer who lives in Northern Virginia with his wife, daughter and two cats. Looking to give himself some practice narrating audiobooks, John began producing chapters of *Tales of the Left Hand* as a weekly podcast, and quickly discovered that the series had taken on a life of its own. Links to the audio version of the series can be found at www.talesofthelefthand.com.

For the latest news on *Tales of the Left Hand* (including how John is coming with the next novel in the series), please visit Tales of the Left Hand on Facebook.

Made in the USA
Middletown, DE
18 March 2023